The Hidden War series:
The Battle

By R.W. Allen

Copyright 2014 R.W. Allen
All rights reserved
ISBN-13: 978-0692237762
ISBN-10: 0692237763

Cover design by John Owens
Editing by Invisible Ink Editing

www.theAllenHub.com

To my Caleigh,
Thank you for being amazing.

To my family, spiritual and biological,
Thank you for all the love you have shown me.

Thank you Samantha Gordon, of Invisible Ink Editing, for making this novel readable.

Thank you John Owens for the sweet cover art.

Table of Contents

Prologue 5
Chapter 1: Omega and Alpha 10
Chapter 2: Our Word 23
Chapter 3: The Forest 48
Chapter 4: Eagle's Wings 72
Chapter 5: Training 82
Chapter 6: The Battlefield 100
Chapter 7: The Prisoner 118
Chapter 8: The Campground 133
Chapter 9: The Infirmary and the Door 149
Chapter 10: The Next Mission 171
Chapter 11: Into the Canyon 192
Chapter 12: A New Land 211
Chapter 13: Finding the Balance 229
Chapter 14: A General Imitation 251
Chapter 15: A Warrior Returns 275
Chapter 16: Time Apart 296
Chapter 17: The King's Drink 315
Chapter 18: Tremors 331

Prologue

They started out as incoherent mumblings heard off in the distance. They pierced their way through the rough metal bars, which enclosed the young boy, only to fall upon deaf ears. The words that were spoken were not having the desired effect that those on the outside intended. You see, Jon Smith was twelve years old at the time, and he was very comfortable with where he laid his head at night. He had made this place his home. This home was free from the effects of the harsh weather and violence that occurred just beyond its protective custody, but it was not free from the metal shards, which rained down on top of him from the routine bludgeoning happening outside. He just wanted to be left alone with the other caged men and women around him. He felt safe where he was.

Jon Smith had a common name, a common appearance, and generally a good attitude. Most nights involved him being curled up into a ball on the cage's floor, twiddling his thumbs in various ways, engaging in conversations with the caged people near to him, or making failed attempts at picking the crusted dirt from his toes. He would do this every day as he waited for the sun to go down, so he could get enough sleep to do it all again the next day. His routine was not all that different from everyone else's around him.

He specifically remembered an older man, almost twenty years his elder, continuously staring down at his hands and only looking up when his home was being threatened by the "enemy." The "good guys," as Jon referred to them in his mind, just left the caged people alone to do whatever they wanted. The good guys did not constantly try to yell inside and ruin their sleep, nor did they use any weapons to make annoying noises on their cages. The good guys sure looked weird, but a person cannot really argue with the free "food and water" they provided. Sure the water was slightly brown and the food a little molded, but it was either that or go hungry.

For years it was like this. The same routines continued on, and Jon was left undisturbed, until one day something peculiar happened. Jon was going about his usual, non-threatening business, and to his dissatisfaction one of the enemies gently approached his cage. Jon was quite used to them being outside, clamoring around with their fancy swords and shields, but this time it caught his attention. Jon could tell it was a male around his age, but he spoke with a unique accent for the region they were in. This enemy frequently approached with his sword tucked away and something always in his hands. Jon gave him the nickname Poland, since he could not remember the male's actual name.

What he brought in his hands was something resembling a sandwich. Jon only knew what they were called because the good guys would bring them by as well. However, the difference with these was that it did not have mold on it whatsoever. It seemed fresh and smelled edible, but Jon always declined the offers, since he was convinced it would have poison somewhere in it.

It was not until another enemy approached him that he started observing their movements and actions. This one was a female around his age, a little shorter than Poland but not by much. She was dressed in pink and white armor with long brunette hair trailing from the back of her helmet. She caught his attention because she was very pretty and was very friendly toward the other enemies. Jon was hesitant to talk to her, because she was often seen fighting off the good guys around his cage. Instead of getting angry with her, he decided to observe what she did.

It only took a little while of watching until Jon Smith noticed he was trying to imitate the enemy's movements with his hands. He had nothing better to do, other than the twiddling of his thumbs and playing in the dirt, so he committed to watching these strange creatures. "Why do they look like me if they are so bad?" was a frequent question he would ask himself while he sat there with his imaginary sword firmly gripped in his hands. After the female had introduced herself several times, Jon finally remembered her name was Cay. He would see her almost every morning in the autumn, winter, and spring months, and while she was around she would try her hand at bringing the same type of food that Poland had brought. However, Jon would still decline.

During the summer months she was not around anymore, but she would still manage to send letters now and then to check up on how he was faring inside his cage. Jon spent much of his time reading those letters and practicing his imaginary sword fighting skills when he was not writing the young enemy back. He had a good feel for his developing skills, so now and then he would include some form of advice for her in his replies. She expressed graciousness in her return letters, but kindly explained to him how the sword actually functioned on the outside. Jon was cramped inside his cage and could not feel the true weight of a sword to know how it actually moved and flowed through the air.

    It was not until the following autumn season Jon began acting very differently. He was handed a slender wooden branch through an opening in his cage by one of the older enemies who went by the name of Emet. This gave Jon a better feel of what a sword felt like, but he knew it still was not the same. He even began accepting morsels of food from a much larger bearded man, but still chose not to eat them. Instead, they were used as something for him to play with as he tried not to draw too much attention to himself. You see, he did not want the other caged men and women, or the good guys, to know of his newfound curiosity. He just wanted to indulge his curiosity.

    Something else happened to him during the following spring months. He began to realize how cramped he was in his home. He was quite aware of its small living arrangements, but he never really had anything to compare it to. That is, until he heard stories of a most peculiar man. They were stories of a war general that went by the name of Iam. He had many other names, but this is the one everyone seemed to call him. The stories he heard of this man were truly remarkable. At first Jon took them as folklore or an exaggerated remembrance of a man whom was friendly toward everyone, but then one night Jon got to see him.

    Everything he had heard was true, all the way down to the large scars on each of his palms. From that moment on Jon Smith became very aware of how free everyone was on the outside. He wanted what they had. So he started eating the food and drinking the water the enemies offered, instead of stashing it away to play with it later. To his astonishment, it far exceeded the nourishment the good guys offered. It was not laced with poison, seeing as how he did not roll over and die upon consuming it, and it actually helped him think more clearly due to what the enemy deemed as "vitamins and nutrients."

Jon Smith spent those nine months learning everything he could from the people who looked like him. He stopped considering them to be the enemies and observed all their actions instead of just focusing on their shortcomings. Much to the good guys' dismay, he asked to be brought along on their excursions, so he could learn more of their ways. Mind you, he never ceased testing everything they said with extreme caution. He just could no longer deny that he needed to get out of his cage. Its comfort had worn out, and he had grown too big for its borders. He wanted to be able to do what that general did instead of spending his days and nights playing around in dirt. The moment he had this realization, the night sky became even darker. Storm clouds had gathered overhead, and the door to his cage sprang open.

R.W. Allen

Chapter 1:
Omega and Alpha

"Jon? Are you ready to come out yet?" A calm-voiced man inquired.

A large, human-sized cage sat in the middle of a forest clearing. The door was open, and a tall and lanky, eighteen-year-old, Caucasian male was hunched over at its opening, staring down at the dirt between the steel bars that inhabited him. The inside of this cage was smooth and somewhat comfortable; however, the outside was laced with sharp, jagged, abusive metal that had been welded onto it. His knees trembled as they pressed against the inside of this metallic structure, leaving their indentions on his dirty flesh while his hands felt the ground beneath the cage's boundaries. His head hung, just teetering at the imaginary line this border had created in his mind for so long. He had pictured this moment, but he still had doubts. He must choose to leave the place in which he had spent so many nights in exchange for a life of uncertainty.

The sound of his own breathing filled the air around him. The vibrations of his heartbeat banged an unfamiliar tune on his eardrums. His fears had taken center stage, hungry for attention. He thought to himself, "Do I let them starve, or do I feed them?"

The Battle

A few recognizable people were standing around him, watching this scene unfold. All of whom told him this would happen. They told him that he would reach the point where the door was open and he would have to choose. They stood there in silence beneath an overcast night sky that also seemed to watch what was unfolding. Several gold locks lay scattered on the ground around their feet, discarded from the cage's door.

Jon knew he must make a decision, to feed the fears or to let them starve. He started listening to his heartbeat as it slowed down. His breathing steadied. He once more felt the ground between the metallic bars and knew what he must do. They must not eat, not today. Dismissing his fears from the banquet, Jon reached a hand out of the cage and seized the metallic-free dirt on the other side of the boundary line. The instant dirt climbed underneath his fingernails, a single drop of rain spilled down from the saturated clouds above and collided with his hand. The first move was made.

Dressed in a dirtied white shirt and pants, Jon continued his journey out of the place he once called home. He moved inch by inch over the mangled bars beneath until he felt dirt sticking to his knees. A few more inches passed, and he started to feel his feet dragging across uninterrupted dirt.

More rain spilled from the clouds above, unleashing a torrential downpour on the scene below. Jon was still on his hands and knees, but now completely out of the cage's bondage. His eyes remained transfixed on the ground while rain trickled through his short brown hair and down his clean-shaven face. He was finally out. He was finally free.

"He's out!" A raspy-voiced girl cried. "He's crawled out!"

The calm voice he heard first spoke again, "Let me help you up, Jon."

Jon reached up to grab hold of the man's hand, and in a swift motion he was up on his feet looking this man in the eyes. He stood a few inches shorter than Jon and had tan skin. His appearance was that of a Middle Eastern Jewish man, with blue eyes and curly brown hair. He had an average build, which was covered by the cleanest white robe Jon had ever seen. A gentle smile showed through his neatly trimmed beard as Jon inspected him and everything around.

He saw two other people standing nearby. Jon knew them both from when he was inside the locked cage. One was a short Caucasian girl with long brunette hair wearing pink and white armor. She was also eighteen years old. The other was a taller, older-looking man with short blond hair and a neatly trimmed beard that were both peppered with many silver strands. He had scars welded into his forearms and hands, and there were even a couple on his face. His armor was painted with gold and silver, almost matching his hair identically. Once he saw Jon getting his bearings, he slapped him on the shoulder and said, "It's about time you came out of that thing."

Aside from the three people standing around him, Jon noticed there was not much else to look at. He was in a forest, but none of the trees had leaves on them and there were no animals of any kind scurrying around. It was dark and gloomy. Noticing the disappointment on Jon's face, the first man broke the silence by saying, "I suppose introductions are in order." Jon's focus snapped back to the man talking, and he eagerly awaited the new information he was about to hear. "You know Emet and Cay already, and my name is Iam. There are more people we will meet when we arrive."

The Battle

Taken back by the last statement, Jon pried open his lips to ask, "When we arrive? Where are we going?"

All three politely laughed before Cay gently asked, "Don't you remember what we told you?"

"We are going to the castle!" Emet excitedly answered.

Remembering previous conversations and stories, Jon smiled toward Iam and exclaimed, "Let's go!"

Iam returned the smile and said, "Alright, but I do have to tell you the road there is difficult. Just follow me and you will be ok." Jon, unaware of what awaited him, nodded his head.

The rain steadily saturated Jon's skin and clothes as the four of them began walking toward the castle. They passed several dead trees and rotting logs along the way, as well as a few skeletons of long-deceased animals. The moonlight occasionally pierced the clouds to reveal various claw marks and deep gashes embedded in tree trunks and large fallen tree limbs in the distance. Everyone pressed on along the path that wound through this dead forest. This continued for what seemed to be hours.

The only noise Jon heard was the heavy rainfall, thunder rumbling overhead, footsteps, and trees swaying with the breeze until Iam said, "There is a clearing up ahead. We are going to split up there. Emet and Cay will meet us at the castle, and we will go a different way." Jon nodded again and followed Iam with Cay and Emet behind.

They walked until Jon could see a vast open space ahead. Iam turned around and said to Emet and Cay, "You two could go on up. Tell the King we will be there shortly." Then he turned to Jon and said, "Do not look back from here on out. Just keep looking forward and trust me." Although he greatly wanted to watch his friends leave, Jon agreed and walked with Iam.

In the distance Jon began to hear a new sound; it was the sound of rushing water. He turned to Iam and asked, "Is there a river near us?"

To this, Iam answered, "Yes there is. We will see it soon."

As they continued on, the sound of the river grew louder and louder, and with this Jon's eagerness to see it grew greater and greater. A few more minutes of walking proved to be all that separated Jon from having his eagerness fulfilled. Since it was so dark outside Jon could not see the entirety of the river, but it did not appear to have an end. It was incredibly wide, and the current was like a stampede of bison. It chiseled away at the embankment and rushed on by as though nothing happened. It flowed toward the southwest, from where Jon's journey originated. Iam and Jon continued their travels along the east side of the river, staying plenty distant from the river bank.

As they continued on Jon noticed hills appearing on either side of him, only allowing the moonlight to appear occasionally. The darkness of the valley they were in hardly allowed Jon to see anything up ahead. At this point Iam looked back and yelled over the stampeding current, "Put your hand on my shoulder and follow me! I know where to go!" Jon did as he was told, and they continued on into the valley.

A few minutes passed before Iam spoke up again, "We are passing under a bridge, if you are able to see it. We were not able to use it, because you do not have your armor yet. On the other side of these hills, to the right of us, is a part of the battlefield. This is why we had to travel a separate way. You will be able to use it later though."

Jon looked above and was vaguely able to see an enormously long rope bridge gently swaying in the breeze. It was suspended seventy-five feet in the air and looked extremely dangerous from where he stood. He shouted up to Iam, "Do many people try to cross it?"

"Nobody has tried for a while. They think it will break or they would fall, but they don't realize the King is the one that put it there. He made it himself. Sure you have to watch your step, but it is extremely stable," Iam replied.

The water's voice strove to be heard as they continued along. They kept walking for a couple hours, occasionally exchanging conversation, until they came to a spot where the water got incredibly loud. Iam turned to talk into Jon's ear and told him, "There is a rather large waterfall up ahead, which is also where this trail stops."

"How are we going to get to the castle then?" Jon asked.

"There is a cave behind the waterfall, more than halfway up. It has a series of tunnels that will bring us within the castle walls. It is a steep climb inside the mountain from there," Iam answered, "Are you sure you want to do this? It will be extremely difficult."

Before any doubt had time to creep into Jon's mind, he answered, "Yes."

"Alright then, I will show you how to get back there; just follow me." At this final statement, Iam turned to walk down the remaining stretch of path with Jon close behind. As they approached the waterfall, the noise of the water crashing down on the rocks below was too loud for anything else to be heard. There was no sound of trees swaying, no footsteps were heard, and the sound of the rainfall, ironically, was drowned out. Fortunately, Jon's eyes had developed keen night vision from being in the dark for so long. He was able to see the majestic waterfall in front of him, but he almost strained his neck in an attempt to see where it began. The next thing he saw when he looked back down was Iam diving headfirst into the pool that collected at the base of the waterfall.

After several minutes of searching for his guide, Jon ran over to the edge of the riverbank. He looked down river to see if Iam had washed down, but he could not find him. He scanned the glass-like face of the waterfall to see if Iam had indeed managed to climb up, and to his amazement he saw an arm waving and Iam's smiling face interrupting the water's flow. Iam then pointed down at the base, telling Jon it was his turn to dive in.

Trusting Iam's example, Jon instantly jumped headfirst into the same place Iam jumped before. The intensity of the water met him with force. It thrashed him around against the weathered rocks underneath the surface and turned him upside down several times, completely submerging him. He fought against the current and the increasing urge to just let the water flush him down river. His muscles were growing weak, and he was becoming increasingly disoriented. He just wanted to get air. He just wanted one breath, but the greedy water did everything it could to prevent him from getting even that.

After minutes of battling, Jon mustered enough strength to find the surface and paddle toward it. Gallons of water kept rushing down on his head, but he pressed on. Before passing out, he lunged one last time and felt a cool breeze hit his arm. He grabbed onto a nearby rock and swallowed as much air as his lungs would allow. He looked toward the waterfall and realized the hard part was still ahead. He had to ascend fifty feet to reach the spot from which he saw Iam peering out.

With one last huge breath, he turned back into the pool of water and swam toward the mountain that waited behind the glassy downpour. He did not get thrashed around this time. He did not get trapped underneath its relentless greed. He pushed. He fought. He swam until his hand touched the slimy, moss-covered wall of the mountain. He then started to climb. Ten feet passed. Then twenty-five feet. Soon he was within arm's length of the last hold. More water came rushing onto his face, almost causing him to let go and fall into the river, just as the rain had been falling onto his face all night, but he continued to fight. Both hands rested on the floor of the cave's entrance, and Jon hoisted the rest of his body into the waterless shelter.

He laid there exhausted and completely drenched, collecting his breath and strength while Iam sat down beside him and smiled. He helped Jon to his feet, and they both stood up in the cave with the waterfall behind them. They looked into the dark pathway ahead of them, and Jon said to Iam, "You lead. I'll follow." Iam nodded and started walking with Jon close behind.

They encountered many different paths while hiking up the mountain's steep entrails. Jon's sharp night vision allowed him to see the stalactites and stalagmites protruding all around. Various bats flew by, curious to see who was intruding in their home. Other than those obstacles and the steep, steady climb, the cool temperature made the trip relaxing for Jon and Iam. It also helped that there was no obnoxiously loud river rushing by, demanding travelers' to listen to it. A serene calmness filled the air as they hiked toward the summit.

After several minutes had passed, Iam's gait started to slow down. He turned back to Jon and said with a calm excitement, "We are almost there. The King is incredibly eager to see you."

This statement caused extreme nervousness to flow through Jon's body. He immediately became self-conscience of his face, his hair, and his clothes. He did not want to appear in front of the King with dirty clothes or mud still under his fingertips. Noticing the franticness of his demeanor, Iam gently said to Jon, "Do not worry about your appearance. The rain here is a little different. It has a tendency of washing your clothes and skin instead of making dirt stick. I assure you, you are spotless. When we step out of this tunnel you will see." Believing Iam's words, Jon relaxed and stopped eagerly dusting himself off. He did not understand how it was possible, but Iam had not lied to him on the entire trip.

They walked a few more yards before turning around a corner and seeing a light in the distance. The light sat at the top of a wide stone stairway and cascaded down the pathway. As they walked toward the stairs, Jon noticed indentions in the walls large enough to fit multiple people. He tapped curiously on Iam's shoulder and motioned to them, "What are those for?"

Iam smiled and explained, "We have built-in areas to post guards, so no unauthorized people or things can get inside the castle. This entire tunnel is one remarkably large maze, so I doubt anything would get this far anyway."

"So where are the guards?" Jon asked.

The Battle

"Well since I am here, there is not really any need for them to be in their posts. Also they are in the banquet hall waiting for us to arrive. The entire city is there actually," Iam replied.

Jon nervously laughed at the thought of how many people could be waiting. He knew Cay and Emet would be there, and Iam had said before that others were waiting as well. He did not realize this meant the entire city was gathering for this event. Overwhelmed by this new development, Jon slowed to a stop, catching the attention of Iam in the process. He asked his guide, "Why? I mean…why all this for me? I'm not that important."

A boisterous laugh echoed off the walls and repeatedly bounced off Jon's eardrums. "Not that important? My dear Jon, you have no idea how important you are. Everyone up here has been watching you. They know who you are; everyone in the city knows who you are. The King especially knows who you are. 'Not that important.' Just think of this as a…birthday celebration."

Nervous and slightly embarrassed, Jon asked, "A birthday celebration? It's not my birthday."

To this Iam chuckled more and asked, "Is it not?"

As Jon tried to process everything just said, they arrived at the foot of the stairs. Twelve stairs stood in between them and the well-lit area ahead. After this last climb Jon knew he would be seeing the King. There was definitely no turning back and no regrets. He paused momentarily, still trying to collect his thoughts, while Iam waited patiently for him to take the next step. He was rechecking his clothes and hands for any dirt or mud that might have magically appeared since he checked last when Iam whispered to him, "You are not going to find any dirt."

Jon looked over to him and replied, "I was just… I'm sorry."

"It is perfectly reasonable for you to be nervous right now, but I do have to tell you something." Iam turned to face Jon. "If you keep waiting down here, the King has no problem relocating the party to this tunnel and coming down to meet you."

Another nervous laugh came from Jon's mouth as he replied back, "Okay, let's go up, but please stay next to me."

A simple "of course" spilled from Iam's lips as he put his arm over Jon's shoulder. They looked at each other, smiling, and began climbing the stairway. Every stair they climbed, Jon tried to calm his nervousness by repeatedly thinking about how the King actually wanted to see him and how everyone gathered in the banquet hall actually wanted to be there, knowing what they did about him.

They climbed to the second to last stair, unable to see in the doorway due to the blinding light emitting from it. Jon took one last deep breath before lunging off the stone into the room that awaited his arrival.

Cheering encircled Jon as he was led by Iam through the light still melting his eyesight. His eyes watered and his eyelids repeatedly batted in an attempt to regain the sight he once had. Iam led Jon across the stone floor of the vast room to where the King was waiting with an enormous, luminous smile. He had gotten up from his extravagant chair to wait for Jon and Iam's arrival. Lavishly decorated wooden tables lined the hall. Matching benches stretched the entire length of the tables, providing adequate seating for all those who had gathered. The tables were covered with an abundance of food and beverages, all of which had yet to be touched or picked at. It was probably best that Jon could not see momentarily, because every eye was following him as Iam led him between the tables to the front of the hall. The nervousness that would have formed would have dropped him to the floor with trembling knees. Everyone watched as Iam and Jon finally arrived to where the King stood in wait.

As they stood before the King, Iam bowed his head and the King did the same. Iam then looked over at Jon and quietly said, "Open your eyes."

At this statement, Jon's tears dried up and his eyelids ceased their tug of war with one another. They sprung open to reveal a blue and yellow-eyed eighteen year old. Once he realized where he stood, Jon's mouth immediately sprung open in disbelief. He was in front of the King, able to see, however, unable to speak. All he could focus on was the King's golden jeweled crown that rested neatly on his platinum hair. Just by appearance alone, Jon could tell this man was highly respected.

A long silence followed with nothing to hear but everyone's breathing and the loud beating of Jon's heart, until Iam humbly and respectfully said to the King, "This is Jon Smith, and he is ready to fight."

Jon saw the King's smile grow larger than it had already been at this statement, which caused Jon's nerves to relax tremendously. A deep, booming voice proceeded afterward from the King, himself, toward Iam, "Very good!" Then looking down to Jon, he said, "Before you get your armor, you are going to need to eat. Go and grab some food while we get your armor prepared."

He did as the King said and turned toward the long tables he had been oblivious to as he walked in. Everyone was standing and cheering. Noise collided violently with his eardrums, once again in a bombardment of joy. He walked toward an open seat next to Cay, amid a sea of faces he did not recognize. He knew they were there because they wanted to celebrate a new soldier meeting the King, so he embraced each smile with one of his own.

He sat on the bench and gathered food onto his plate, from an endless supply of various breads, cheeses, vegetables, fruit, fish, and other meats. He consumed as much as his stomach would allow him, all while many people came over to congratulate and welcome him. Most chose to hug him, while others patted him on the back. Several older men just gave a firm handshake and a nod of the head. Between all the embraces, Jon managed to make conversation with his friends, Cay and Emet. It was not long before he saw Iam approaching to, presumably, take him to get his armor on. Before he left, he made sure to say farewell to them this time. He hugged them both, and they assured him that they would be seeing him shortly.

Iam arrived and placed his hand on Jon's shoulder. "It is time to go. I hope you have gotten plenty to eat." Jon nodded as he felt the last bit of bread splashing into his stomach, filling the remaining vacancy it had. He led Jon out of the banquet hall in the direction of the tunnel they had emerged from almost an hour previous, but they took a right turn down a different hallway instead, leaving all the noise, celebrations, and loved ones to continue carrying on behind him.

As they walked down the extravagantly large and luxurious torch-lit hallway, Iam leaned over to Jon and confidently whispered, "Now it is going to start getting more interesting." Noticing Jon's worried expression, he continued, "Do not worry. It will be a good interesting. Trust me."

Chapter 2:
Our Word

Excitement kept building inside of Jon as they continued on to where his armor laid waiting. He had so many memories from when he was in the confines of his cage, memories of watching those around him fighting and training with each other. He watched their teamwork. He listened to their planning. He sat in on their gatherings and saw the encouraging looks on their faces when they told of successful battles. He saw some of them fall, but they soon got back up and continued fighting. Then there were others that, when they fell, retreated into the empty refuge of the once inhabited cages lying around. He remembered thinking when he saw this, "I'm never going to be one of them. If I get out of here, just wait." The cold bars, intertwined within each other, would not suffice any longer. Once he escaped, there would be no returning. He remembered the shimmering of the sword and the sturdiness of the shield. The armor came in different colors for different soldiers, but otherwise it was all the same.

After remembering these stories, he realized he would soon be getting armor of his own: his own sword; his own shield; his own helmet. He would soon be on the battlefield, making his own name known to the enemy. He would be able to contribute. He would be able to fight. He would be able to help. He would be able to start having fun. No more boringness or mediocrity. No more being trapped or restricted. He was not rescued to keep sitting in the dirt while others lived a story worthy to tell.

They turned left around a corridor to reveal another stone staircase, though a much farther climb than the previous stairway. Large, oak-framed windows slept comfortably along the entire wall on the right side, intermittingly allowing moonlight to accompany the torch flames in lighting the way. Matching oak doorways rested across from each window, wide enough for many people to enter at a time, and high enough to where those people could have others on their shoulders with plenty of clearance to spare. As Jon gazed at the extensive climb ahead, Iam turned to him and said, "At the top of this stairway is the armor room."

"That's where I get my own stuff, right?" Jon asked almost instantly.

With a friendly laugh, Iam answered, "Yes, you will get your belt, your boots, your shield, your helmet, your belt," an increasingly large smile grew on Jon's face as Iam mentioned every piece of armor, "...and your key."

"Finally...wait, my key? What key?" Jon asked, surprised by this new development.

"Yes your key. Everyone gets a key. The King designs a unique key for every soldier. No two are alike," Iam calmly answered, knowing it would surprise his newest recruit.

"What are they for?" Jon asked.

"Walk upstairs with me, and I will explain along the way," Iam answered, nodding his head toward the lengthy ascent. They began to climb. "Every cage has locks on it. They are scattered around the top, sides, bottom...everywhere on the outside. So the only way to get these locks off is by using these keys the King made. Everyone has their own unique key that fits inside many locks on many different cages. It is everyone's responsibility to find where their key fits, so they could remove the lock designated for them."

They arrived at the halfway point of the stone staircase, but Jon was too enthralled to realize it. He wanted to learn more. "So after I find the locks that my key fits inside of, what happens?" Jon asked.

"Well that depends," Iam answered, "you either leave and continue your travels, or you use your sword. Sometimes there is nothing else you are supposed to do, so you leave, but you must not leave when you are supposed to do more. There is a fine balance."

"So how will I know what to do next?" Jon continued his attempts to fill in as many blanks as Iam would allow before wanting to continue onward.

"Simple," Iam replied. "You ask the King. You could talk with him at any time, but you must be willing to listen for answers."

"So all I have to do is ask the King? And I could talk to him at any time?" Surprised at how simple Iam was making it sound, Jon wanted to make sure he clarified what he was hearing.

"Yes. Any time you need him, you can ask him for help. He might not answer you right away or even as quickly as you would like, but, I assure you, he knows what he is doing," Iam clarified.

"I trust you. So, you also mentioned there may be times to use my sword?" Jon asked, even more excited at how readily Iam was providing answers.

Pleasantly obliging to Jon's eagerness to gain knowledge, Iam answered, "Yes, there are times where you are supposed to use your sword to break apart the welds holding a cage's bars together. However, you cannot just beat on the cage wildly or else you could harm the person inside. While you may have noble intentions, the person inside may not see them. You have to know where to hit and how hard." Jon nodded in understanding, so Iam continued, "There have also been many soldiers that have mistakenly gotten angry at the person inside when they got hurt, but in actuality it was the jagged edges of the cage that cut them. So, instead of continuing to do what they ought to be doing, they walk away offended."

"I noticed that while I was in my cage. There were soldiers that would come by and try to get me out, but when they would get cut up by the cage, they would get angry at me. While they stormed off I would try calling out to them, 'It's not me that's doing that. It's the cage,' but they wouldn't listen. They kept walking and gave up on trying again," Jon responded.

They arrived at the top of the stairway, which sat at the end of another magnificently spacious hallway. Even more large oak windows cooperated with fiery torches to provide abundant light for the path ahead. There were no doorways lining the halls anymore. It was a single, uninterrupted hallway with the sole purpose of leading someone to the armor room. Jon and Iam stood at the top of the stairs, staring down at the fire-lit room ahead, but before they approached the entrance, Iam explained more about the cages. "There are other instances to keep in mind as well. I once arrived to help someone up whose cage was opened, but they still refused to get out. They had grown accustomed to being inside its grasp for so long that they no longer wanted to come out. It had become their home and their bed. They had been left behind so often by countless wounded soldiers, and they had convinced themselves their cages were better than what is out there on the battlefield."

To this, Jon asked, "What do you do then?"

"I wait there, patiently. Hopefully they will realize there is more to life than being in a cold, dirty, dark cage, and there is no reward and no chance at happiness while inside. I just hold out my hand, waiting for them to grab onto it. If they pull the door shut again, then I leave, and I will come back when they are ready," Iam answered.

"Why don't you just reach in there and grab them?" Jon asked.

"That is not how it works," Iam answered, looking down the hallway. "There is more to this subject, but we could discuss it at a later time. We have your armor and key to retrieve."

With a nod of understanding, Jon smiled at Iam and looked down the hallway. The torches in the distant room flickered, as though they sensed they would soon have company. Iam started walking and Jon closely followed.

They covered the entire length of the hall in minutes and stood at the grand archway of the room. A simple wooden sign was suspended from overhead with the words "Armor Room" neatly carved into it.

As they stood there, Iam whispered to Jon, "It looks like we have arrived."

He looked from the sign to the doorless entry to examine what stood before him. A large window rested on the back stone wall. Torches abundantly lit the room, exposing a massive oak table sitting in the center. As Jon stood in the doorway, he examined the contents that occupied its finished surface. Once he realized what they were, the young man with the large frame approached what had been designated for him this whole time. Iam lingered behind, observing as Jon eagerly examined his belongings. A giant brotherly grin appeared across Iam's face when he saw Jon's willingness to contribute.

Jon had placed his non-calloused hands upon the rugged face of the table. He ran his fingers along its grooves, inspecting its superb craftsmanship. Silhouettes of soldiers intertwined with vines ran down the hand-carved legs. Each plank was flush against the next with no overhanging pieces, and there were no visible nails or screws to tarnish its appearance. It was extremely sturdy and carefully measured out. As Jon bent down to further inspect the legs' art, Iam approached and knelt to the ground beside him. Also inspecting the table's trunk-like legs, he said to Jon, "Each collage tells a story of a famous battle. Everyone before you has been to this very room to get the same type of armor you are about to receive. They were able to use what they were given in an extraordinary fashion, so the maker of this table wove them in."

As Jon ran his fingers along the wooden faces and vines, he asked, "Who made this table?"

"Everyone knows him by the name 'Pneuma'. You will have a chance to see him later, after we get you suited up." Both men looked at each other, smiling. They stood up, and Iam asked, "Do you need help with putting this on?"

Jon looked down at the diverse assortment of armor resting on the table and said with a chuckle, "That would be helpful."

Iam nodded and motioned back down to the waist-high surface and asked, "Shall we see what you have?"

The Battle

Jon's attention joined Iam's to see what did wait for him. First, his eyes fell upon on a dark brown belt that had mid-sized pouches attached to it. It was perfectly designed to hold small, but useful objects when at war. Just a single hole penetrated the front of the hide that was custom fitted for Jon's waist. His eyes traveled along the table until he saw work boots neatly placed upon the table. They were a dark brown, clean-looking pair. When he lifted them up for further inspection, he discovered they were, to his surprise, featherlike in weight without compromising durability. The soles were made of tough black rubber, able to withstand impact of any sharp objects desiring to harm the wearer's feet. The interior of the boots was made of light, porous foam, waiting to be molded around Jon's foot as it entered its new surroundings. The foam was durable to provide support, porous for ventilation, and flexible to provide comfort. Next was a large, thick, feather-weighted, metallic shield. Its perfect circular shape was coated with a dark shade of green on the surface and polished silver on the underside. Its slight convex bend added structural support. Next to reach the eye's attention was a freshly polished, dark green, Spartan-like helmet, which was made of the same rare and extremely durable material as the shield. There was a sturdy strip of metal that jettisoned from the sleek cap to cover the bridge of the nose while two other pieces of sturdy metal hung down on either side of the head to cover the ears, cheeks, and jawline. The back rested at the base of the neck to provide the wearer with optimum mobility, and the interior was like that of the boots. A modest layer of the light, porous foam coated the smooth belly of the helmet. The entire outer surface was as a simple blank canvas stretched tightly over the head, waiting for the paint of war to be splattered upon it. As Jon lifted it from its well established position, he noticed its weight was also extremely light. This piece of armor appeared to be constructed from a single chunk of metal. There were no welds, bolts, or fasteners keeping it together. As he returned it to its place on the oak table, his eyes came to the last item on the table. It was a thick, dark green and white, camouflage Kevlar vest. It was custom made to adequately cover every inch of Jon's torso. Three industrial strength Velcro straps were fastened in the front to ensure Jon would be harnessed properly. As it lay there on the table, Jon peeled back the three strips to explore the innards of his new piece of equipment. He exposed the inside to see what appeared to be chainmail lining the cloth. As he lifted it up he braced himself for the weight that was sure to buckle his knees; however, he discovered the weight was comparable to the boots.

After this long silence, Iam interjected, "The chainmail on the inside is double layered and consists of a mixture of platinum, titanium, and other metals the King chose. It's tightly woven and extremely durable. There is not a single weapon that is made, or could be made, that could pierce through it to harm you. The outside is an enhanced Kevlar material that will further aid your survival for when you are around...let's say...dirty situations."

After Jon finished examining the vest, he set it back down on the table and turned to face Iam to say, "I believe I'm ready to put it all on now."

"I would agree with you," responded Iam, "but you put these on first." He tossed Jon a pair of baggy, dark green camouflage pants, a dark green t-shirt, and a pair of tall, dark green, socks and said, "I will get everything ready while you change." Jon quickly did so and hurried back to where Iam waited with his new boots.

The Battle

Iam handed Jon the belt, then knelt to the ground and fit both boots onto Jon's feet while Jon fastened the belt to his waist. His feet immediately welcomed the comfort of the foam, which began maneuvering itself around to provide support to its soon-to-be well-traveled inhabitants. With the boots taken care of, Iam returned to Jon, still struggling with the utility pouches. Iam noticed and offered some helpful advice. "There is a Velcro strap you must put through the loops first. The belt has Velcro on the inside, so you just press the two together when you have them lined up properly." This helped Jon secure it much faster and stand ready for the vest Iam held in his hands. The straps were already unfastened and the mail was exposed, awaiting the eager new soldier to pull his arms through. Jon turned around while Iam slipped the camouflage armor over his shoulders. He shrugged to secure the fitting and turned back around to face Iam. The straps embraced the mainland of the vest, as a daughter would cling to her father in an attempt to persuade him not to return to war.

With Jon's belt, boots, and vest secure, Iam reached for the helmet that rested on the table. He looked at Jon earnestly while holding it up and said, "These next two objects you must be extremely careful with. You are allowed to take them off, but only around the right people, especially the helmet. One cannot simply replace a head if it gets dismembered, so be extremely cautious." With that being said, Iam held the unblemished helmet up, and Jon bowed forward to receive it upon his head. As the helmet enveloped his head, Jon felt the foam kindly fitting itself to him. Once the helmet was secure, Iam continued, "This helmet is particularly special. The foam is designed to not allow your head to jostle around inside. Your enemy can bludgeon it as many times as they want, but it will not budge. However, being the wearer of it, you can remove it at any time you choose. I do not recommend taking it off on the battlefield or in the presence of your enemy; not even for a second. They will not hesitate to aim for your head...repeatedly, until they see it rolling at their feet, but this next piece should help you out considerably with that last part." Iam hoisted up Jon's new dark green metallic shield off of the table. There were two leather straps secured to its underbelly, so Jon could easily slip his arm through. Iam fitted and tightened Jon's left arm through the straps and stepped back to examine his work. "That shield must also be only set down in the midst of the right company. The straps are well secured to your forearm, so you could operate a weapon with that hand as well if you choose to."

Overcome with immense appreciation, Jon could only manage to say, "Thank you." The gratification expressed through his watery eyes, constant examination of his new attire, and occasional glances toward Iam showed his rescuer more than he could ever express.

After several minutes of this, Jon composed himself and looked up at Iam and asked, "Is this everything then?"

Pleased at the man Jon had quickly become, Iam could not stop smiling. After a long pause, he answered, "Oh no, you need two more things. You need your key, and you need something to attack the enemy with. You cannot expect to just sit around with your shield and expect to rescue anybody. Can you?"

With a soft laugh, Jon humbly answered, "No...I guess not."

"Well then," Iam opened a drawer on the back of the large table and pulled out a moderately sized white key. It had three solid spheres in a pyramid-like pattern on the crown of its long handle,

The Battle

and its four-sided blade had an intricate pattern of teeth on all sides. It dangled from a two and a half foot long, thin, metallic green, looped chain. He brought it over to Jon. "First, here is your key, made by the King himself. There is no other key like it." He motioned to Jon's shieldless arm and asked, "Could you hold your other arm out for me?" Jon obliged, and Iam placed the chain on his shoulder. Instantly the chain seemed to come alive. One moment it was dangling, suspended below Jon's armpit, and the next it was securely wrapping itself around Jon's right arm resting the key in his palm. "That chain will only be able to unwind itself when your part in the war is over; other than that, it is not going to move from your arm. It was made for you to use, and you alone."

Dumbfounded by what just happened, Jon's jaw dropped and he muttered, "That was pretty cool."

A luminous smile appeared once again across Iam's face as he said, "Now we need to get you a sword." Jon looked back at the table, confused. There were no other items on top or resting on the sides. Noticing Jon's bewilderment, Iam motioned toward the doorway and said, "Follow me."

He led the newly adorned soldier back across the room, to the stairway that awaited their departure. As they left the room and turned down the hallway, Jon asked, "Where are we going?"

"We are going to the eagles' room." Iam answered.

"What's the eagles' room?"

"In simple terms, it is the room in which the eagles reside, but..." Iam noticed the blank stare on Jon's face, "...after observing your reaction, you do not want 'simple terms'." Jon's face relaxed, and he grew more intrigued as they turned back down the staircase. They had arrived at the nearest doorway from where they began their descent. Jon had not peered into these rooms on the way to the armor room, because he was so engaged in the conversation he and Iam were having. This massive doorway led to a long hallway, which Jon could not see more than a few feet without light to guide him. As they stood there looking into the tunnel, Iam filled Jon in on the room's purpose. "Those of us that live in this city are able to use these eagles to reach soldiers on the battlefield."

"Why do you need to reach soldiers on the battlefield? I know you come down to get the captured out, but why the soldiers?" Jon asked.

"There are various reasons. It is mostly to deliver messages and packages though," Iam answered with a confident smile. "The other reason we use the eagles is to bring soldiers up here to the castle." He leaned over toward Jon and whispered, "This is so you do not have to get into that water anymore; it makes things plenty easier, I think."

Jon laughed and agreed that it would definitely be easier, remembering the feeling of drowning he had experienced not too long ago. "So what will we be using them for today?" Jon asked.

As they began walking down this new hallway, Iam answered, "To deliver a message. I am going to take you down into the forest."

"Is that where I'll get my sword?" Jon excitedly asked.

"Yes, it is," Iam replied with a smile.

They had arrived at the entrance to the eagles' room. Both of them grew silent as they took in the sight before them. It was a large room with an extremely high ceiling. There were two arched openings, one above the entrance and another on the opposite wall. Both were open to the outside, allowing the eagles an adequate

The Battle

amount of room to leave and return to their perches, which rested along the circular tower's walls. The eagles that inhabited this place were ten times larger than normal eagles. Their talons gleamed in the moonlight, and their beaks flashed their own brilliance. Their clean bodies had the most majestic feathers covering them, as a robe would cover a king's body.

    Iam led Jon to the center of the room, and upon clearing his throat each eagle present turned its head toward the much smaller beings calling for their attention. Once they realized who had cleared his throat, each eagle turned their body completely toward Iam and Jon. They each bowed their heads and instantly became quiet. As they were doing this, Iam leaned over to Jon and said, "I have raised them all since they were babies." He turned back to face the giant birds and bowed his head, releasing them from their positions. They went solemnly about their own tasks, occasionally glancing back down to check on the non-eagles that remained in their room. Iam and Jon stood there for a few minutes, watching birds occasionally arriving and departing through the archways. Little, newly hatched eagles played on the thatched bedding, while larger eagles played in the air.

    "So which one are we leaving on?" Jon asked as he looked around at them all.

    "It is actually coming down now," Iam replied as he stared up into the towers rafters. A large white eagle was swooping down, weaving through the wooden beams with ease. Every other eagle retreated from its flight path in reverence of this majestic bird. It circled over their heads three times before landing comfortably on the ground next to Iam. He mounted the eagle and held out his hand for Jon to join him. Iam could tell Jon was still soaking in the size of what he was about to ride on, so he said, "It is even better when you get on." Jon smiled and laughed as he realized Iam was watching the expression written across his face and under the helmet's protective concealment. He grabbed onto Iam's helpful hand and climbed aboard. Iam patted the bird's neck gently to signify all was clear, and the white eagle shot up. Jon quickly grabbed onto Iam's shoulders as they jolted upward toward the wooden archway. Every other eagle turned and watched as they crossed the threshold and left the room.

They were now outside in the nighttime sky, drifting through the cloudless air being held up against gravity by the eagle's wings. A gentle summer breeze caressed both Iam's and Jon's faces as the eagle continued its journey to their destination. Jon looked over its side to see a vast forest canopy below his feet. It seemed to be a never-ending pool of green flowing off into the distance. Birds frequently left their perches to join their flight, but soon left on expeditions of their own. The eagle took a slight left, helping Jon to see the castle they had departed from. This was the first time Jon was able to see how magnificently large it was, both in height and length. Two towers blended into each other in the front of the castle's wall. The first one he saw was cylindrical in shape and stood in front, with windows cascading down its facade. Jon could see a large wooden archway at the top where a few eagles were leaving from their room's embrace. The other was connected to the first tower's side. It was still considerably large, but rectangular in appearance unlike the eagles' tower. It had a single room at the top depicted by its simple double windows. Jon quickly realized that was where he had gotten his armor after recalling how long it took to get to the top of the stone staircase. As he stared at its structure, two things stood out to Jon the most.

The Battle

    The first was how indescribably massive the front wall was and how far it stretched. He attempted to find its corners, but he had not gotten far enough away from its wall to see where it ended to join the next. It was immensely tall, with the front tower protruding in its center.

    The second was its location. The castle sat embedded on the top of the largest mountain in the range. A steep cliff separated the castle wall from the thick forest below, ensuring no traveler would get up to its gates by accident. As he examined the castle, Jon noticed two large waterfalls that streamed from tunnels at the wall's base only to disappear into the forest's canopy below. Each tunnel sat on either side of where Jon imagined the giant center towers would have met the ground if he was able to see beyond the front wall. It was indeed a majestic view, but, by the location of the castle, Jon could not imagine the scene the King looked upon when he desired to check on his kingdom. At this last thought, Jon turned back around to see the eagle aimed at a clearing in the forest.

    It began gently losing altitude while it circled around the area. Iam remained silent, enjoying the ride. Jon looked around at everything he could before the height of the trees prevented him from doing so. All he could see was an endless ocean of trees, so he instead braced himself for the landing soon to take place.

    Just a few minutes passed before Jon found himself hovering a few feet above the landing area. The eagle flapped its wings a couple more times and softly touched its talons upon the green, carpeted ground below. Iam led the way, dismounting from the large white bird, and Jon shortly followed using Iam for support. Once they had stepped several feet away, the eagle bowed his head toward Iam and flew off toward the castle after Iam returned the gesture.

R.W. Allen

They were now alone, surrounded by trees, with moonlight giving its best effort to illuminate everything Jon desired to see. Its attempts were of little effect, as the lofty trees eclipsed a majority of the moon's brightness. Jon inched closer and closer to Iam the longer they remained there. Upon the departure of his animal friend, Iam started looking into the forest's depth in search of something Jon did not know. Jon's nerves attempted to suffocate him again, trying to paralyze his legs from moving and his lungs from breathing, but he was not having any of it. As soon as they made their presence known, he quickly fought them off and tried to focus on what Iam was focused on.

Once Iam found what he was searching for, he simply looked back, smiled, and continued on into the lush green future that awaited Jon. Jon looked up at the tall canopy above and felt extremely small. What awaited him inside was going to humble him more than he could currently comprehend. He knew this was going to be a challenging journey just by the smirk on Iam's face when he turned to look back, but this is what he signed up for. Easy was staying in his cage. Easy was sitting back and watching everyone else on the outside. Easy was deciding not to get into the water and turning back instead. No, easy is not what he expected, and easy is not what he agreed to. Jon knew that as soon as he followed Iam into the forest, his life would become a new story to be told by someone later. There are people to be rescued and enemies that need to be restrained. So into the forest Iam went, which meant into the forest Jon went as well. With a new confidence summoned from within, Jon took a deep breath, secured the shield to his left arm, and crossed the threshold into the wilderness.

Jon trailed a few feet behind as he admired the height of everything around him. When he caught up to his mentor, Jon noticed Iam's eyes were closed as he walked. He still navigated perfectly, gently ducking branches, stepping over roots weaving their way through the underbrush, and all as though his eyes were still open. Jon could not help but to watch, causing himself to narrowly avoid low-hanging branches and stumble over tree roots.

As they continued walking, they both started hearing a dull banging noise off in the distance. Their steps began to follow the rhythmic pattern as they traveled, as though they were marching along to it. They started to get close enough for Jon to distinguish the sound as being the banging of metal against metal. He looked over to Iam for clarity to find his mentor casually reopening his eyes from their rest. He stared back toward Jon and gently told him, "Well Jon, unfortunately I have to head back to the castle now. You will be taking it from here. Just head toward that noise and you will be fine."

Jon came to a complete stop. "What do you mean? You aren't staying?"

"The King needs me at the castle. If you keep walking toward the clanging sound, you will meet the next person that you have to talk to. He has something for you. Trust him; he is a family member of mine," Iam consoled Jon.

Reluctantly Jon answered, "Okay. I will trust him, but when will I see you again?"

"Soon," Iam said as he placed his hands on Jon's shoulders. "You will see me again very soon. I promise."

There was something that Jon had not noticed before about Iam as he looked down at Iam's hands before he pulled away. He had never really gotten an adequate look at them before, because the robes had covered them up. As his sleeves slid back, they exposed what appeared to be large scars on his palms.

One of the stories leaped into his mind that he had overheard while in his cage. It was the story of a great general in his final battle against a colossal dragon. Before he defeated this enemy he was pinned to a tree, being held in place with the talons of the beast. Two talons found each hand, and a third talon pierced his feet, keeping him from touching the ground. Aside from the cages scattered around and a few soldiers ordered to keep their distance, these two were alone in a forest abundantly filled with dead foliage. At one time there was a man in his cage calling out to the general asking for help. How the general reacted still resonated with Jon to this day.

Here this general was pinned against a tree, clearly incapable of moving, and then someone called out to him for help. This general simply looked down to him and said the words, "After I am free, I will rescue you." After enduring intense torture and pain the general managed to summon enough strength to get free. Once he escaped the dragon's grasp he immediately sprinted toward the trapped man and picked the lock of the cage, which kept him from obtaining his own freedom. The general quickly released many caged prisoners nearby, but there was work that still needed to be done. While unlocking captives, the general found that the dragon had retreated back into its lair. Knowing that it was gravely wounded, he went in after it, but before he did he told everyone that he would be back in three days. Sounds of pain enveloped the air as the wounded beast made it known that it was not pleased with what just transpired. The gruesome howling shook the cave's exterior walls. Nonetheless, the general plunged himself into the dark abyss beyond the cave's mouth. After he traveled deep inside the lair, its entrance was swallowed whole by the very rocks that supported its structure.

While remembering this story, clarity arose in Jon's mind. This man that had been leading him around must be the general that he had heard so much about. He was actually walking with THE general. So many questions emerged into his mind as Iam faded slowly away into the distance, but Jon could only stand there motionless. He watched as Iam disappeared, not knowing when they would meet again.

The banging of metal continued on in the distance, desiring to be heard once again. After a few moments of standing in the same place, the noise had finally pierced Jon's consciousness and plunged him back into reality. Eager to keep its audience, the noise continued like the ticks of a metronome. They had done their job to get his legs moving once again, because Jon began heading toward their origin. He had remembered the orders Iam gave him and did not want to disappoint.

Off in the distance he could see another clearing in the forest. In this clearing there was a silhouette. It appeared to be a man clothed in long robes, hammering on an anvil, with a cylindrical furnace nearby hosting flames hungry for fuel. As Jon got closer he could see a flat piece of metal, glowing red, resting upon the anvil. The man that was once hammering now stood motionless. The sound of rustling leaves and Jon's heavy breathing must have traveled to this man's ears, causing him to cease his work. This mystery man hunched over and peered through the trees toward Jon's direction. He must have seen the shimmer radiating off of Jon's shield, because he abruptly stood back up and let out a hearty chuckle. "There he is," Jon heard a gravelly voice say. "Well why'd you stop? Come on now.

Get yourself over here." He seemed friendly enough, and Jon's feet navigated him through the trees until he arrived in the clearing.

"Now there we go. What took you so long?" He asked. Jon stood motionless, now able to see this man clearly. All that lit the clearing was the moonlight and the flame still gloriously burning in the furnace. These two light sources illuminated the man's face to reveal an eerily similar appearance to Iam's. Aside from this man's scars, and the fact that he had green eyes, the two could very well have been twins. "My apologies young man, I'm not really much for introducing myself, but I'm guessing I should right about now. Everybody calls me Pneuma, but you could call me Richard if you'd like."

Trusting Iam, Jon respectfully and surprisingly comfortably, answered back, "Pleasure to finally meet you. I think I'll stick to Pneuma instead. It sounds more original."

"I'm extremely close with the King and Iam; I assure you," Pneuma humbly said, desiring to quench any doubts still lingering in Jon's overly occupied mind.

"I trust you," Jon confidently answered back.

This provoked a gentle grin to appear across Pneuma's face. While his attention momentarily returned to the flat piece of metal he had been hammering, Jon was able to gather a better look at him. Pneuma wore light brown robes with a darker brown leather belt around his waist. He had no sandals or shoes to give his feet warmth or protection. Now that Jon thought about it, neither was Iam. At this realization Jon asked the simple question, "Why do neither you nor Iam wear anything on your feet? All these rough places to be walking, navigating through the forest; don't you need something on your feet?"

Staring down at his feet, the gravelly-voiced man answered, "When you been around this forest as much as I have, you know where to step. Also I have noticed that it's kind of hard to feel the dirt in your toes when you have shoes on. It's more comfortable, you know? It makes you feel like you've arrived home after a hard day of work."

Jon slowly nodded his head with understanding, and Pneuma turned back to working on the piece of metal. Occasionally he would walk over to the furnace to heat it back up; then he would continue to hammer away at it on the same anvil. While watching intently, Jon noticed something peculiar on Pneuma's back. It looked as though it were a large leather sheath diagonally situated across the entirety of his back. A glimmer caught his eye as he moved a step closer to investigate. There appeared to be something metallic protruding from the apex of the sheath. Curious as to what it was Jon inquired of Pneuma, "Excuse me, but what is that on your back; the metal object sticking out?"

"Oh you mean my sword. Oh yeah, this old thing comes in handy," he replied, reaching above his head and producing a proportionally sized sword in his grasp. It was rather simple in its appearance, but with writings carved vertically down the blade. As Jon gazed at this amazingly constructed work of art he felt as though his eyes were deceiving him. From the angle Pneuma held this sword, it appeared that the sword seemed to have a metallic shadow attached to its back. He spun it to give a profile view, and to Jon's amazement there actually was a second piece of shining metal, mirroring the first. Watching Jon's facial expression, Pneuma divulged in his nonchalant way, "Yeah, these are two swords attached at their handle. It's pretty sweet, I know. What's really cool is that they detach, so you could use them both while fighting. You pull them apart like separating the pages of a book. They do this only when my thumbprint is detected." Pneuma then gave a quick demonstration to show Jon how it was done. After wielding them around for a short while, he fastened them back together and placed the sword on the ground, resting it against the tree stump the anvil sat upon.

After seeing and learning all of this Jon asked, "Why do you need a sword out here in the forest? Everything seems peaceful and nonthreatening out here."

"Ah, but that's where you're wrong. These trees are attacked and threatened very often, so it's one of my responsibilities to protect them. Without me defending them, they could be torn down, burned up, or made into a bountiful supply of toilet paper." Stopping momentarily to look around at the majesty of them all, Pneuma continued, "No enemy has even come close while I have been on watch. I'd like to keep it that way. That's why I have this sword." At this, both he and Jon smiled down at the object reflecting the moonlight that lay peacefully against the stump. "You see? It's napping now from a long day of work."

Looking back at Pneuma, Jon inquired, "How long have you been on watch?"

"Well, let me see." After taking a long pause he answered, "Since the first tree began growing. Yeah…I've been the only one."

Impressed by this, Jon humbly asked, "So is this all you do then? Stay in the forest and protect it?"

With a tree-swaying laugh, Pneuma answered, "Oh no! There's a lot more that I'm responsible for doing. This is just one of the tasks. Though, you'd be surprised at how many people think I only stay in the forest." He paused and looked down at the ground for a moment before he continued. "They just don't pay attention like they used to." Looking back up with a beaming smile, he finished, "But then you have some that continue to look for me, and they greet me when they do see me at work. I don't do it for the glamour or recognition, none of that stuff. It's what needs to be done regardless if anyone notices. You get dirty, sweaty, and tired, but you keep working. Just remember, you appreciate being clean much more if you have the feeling of being dirty to compare it to."

Jon stared back down at Pneuma's feet and asked, "So when is all that dirt coming off?"

Pneuma's forest green eyes joined Jon's to stare at his own feet, "They'll get cleaned the next time I go up to the castle. No worries." With a slight pause engulfing the air, Pneuma lifted his head back up and asked, "Am I right to assume that the reason Iam led you down here was so that you could be provided with a sword?"

Jon also lifted his head to answer, "Yes." He had not thought about the sword that was soon to be his for quite some time now. So many interesting visuals and so much more knowledge filled the filing cabinets in his mind, and now he had to find the one that contained his enthusiasm about his sword.

Noticing the sudden widening of Jon's eyes, a smile appeared yet again on Pneuma's face. He picked up the double sword that was resting against the tree stump and stared directly into Jon's eyes. "Well you have been led to the right place. As I told you when you first arrived, I know Iam and the King extremely well and they know what they are doing. You must know that after you get your sword you will be prepared to fight, so you will have more responsibilities. Whatever happens to you out there, please remember that we, all three of us, will never leave or forsake you." As Pneuma passed his sword to Jon, he confidently pronounced, "You have our word."

As he gripped the sword in his hands, Jon looked down in bewilderment at it and summoned the words, "But this is your sword."

"It's yours now. It answers to your thumbprint now," Pneuma proudly replied back.

"But...what will you use to defend the forest?" Jon asked, still amazed at what just happened.

"I've finished my new one." Pneuma held up two swords connected at their handles, almost identical to those Jon now held. "This is what I was working on when you came up. I thought for sure you would have predicted this would happen." Upon seeing the perplexed look on Jon's face, Pneuma added, "I guess not...well it looks like you're going to need a lot of my help." At this, they both filled the night air with boisterous laughter.

Jon turned back to Pneuma after wiping the tears of joy from his face and said, "Thank you. For everything you do, thank you."

With a slight nod, Pneuma responded, "It is my honor and pleasure. Well, now that we both have swords, marvelous ones at that, we need to put yours in its place. Could you turn around for me please...and kneel? You're too tall to be standing for this."

Jon turned away from Pneuma to face the darkened tree line that encircled the clearing and knelt to the ground. Pneuma lifted the sword with its gleaming handle pointed toward the moonlit sky, and started lowering it into the specially designed pocket that was built into the back of the vest. "May I ask how you're attaching it?" Jon spoke.

The Battle

"I assume you never bothered to look at the back of this vest, but just at the front and inside, huh?" Pneuma answered.

"Right, I didn't think there was anything there...what's on the back?" Jon asked.

"Well that's what I thought. Nobody ever does. There's a large pocket that runs down the length of your spine that'll hold your sword for you. It's designed to have the handle stick out, so you could easily unsheath it when you need to." Pneuma finished positioning the sword in its place and motioned to Jon he could now rise and turn to face him. Jon obliged, and Pneuma continued, "You also have smaller pockets built in right under both your arms as well...just in case you need them later."

Amazed at all this, Jon started lifting his arms to feel what Pneuma was describing. "I had no idea those were there! What else don't I know about?"

"Well there's something unique about your shield, but I'll show you later...you must be thirsty. We've been talking for quite a while, and I'm parched," Pneuma abruptly changed the subject. He was right though, Jon was getting extremely thirsty. He could not remember the last thing he had eaten or drunk. As he nodded at Pneuma, the gravelly-voiced man said, "Alright, shall we go see what we can find in the forest to drink? There must be something in there. Try and keep up."

Pneuma firmly grabbed his own sword and started walking toward the tree line, and in the same way as Iam, he looked back, gave a gentle smirk, and continued on into the trees with Jon close behind.

Chapter 3:
The Forest

As Jon crossed the threshold, a strong breeze collided with him, almost knocking him off his feet. He looked around to see if his surroundings had felt this rush of wind as well, but, to his surprise, nothing seemed out of place nor did the tall cedars sway. He looked ahead to Pneuma, who just continued traveling, seemingly oblivious to what had just taken place. Jon shrugged this off and sped up to try and catch up to the barefooted man in front of him.

Once he had caught up, Pneuma asked him, "Did you feel something strange when you came into the forest?"

Relieved that he was not crazy, Jon replied, "I did. Why didn't the trees or anything else move? That gust nearly knocked me over."

"It's because you're new to the forest. Take that as...a welcome gift, as though the trees were running up to wrap their arms around you...well limbs, but you know what I mean," Pneuma answered back without breaking his stride.

"Why didn't that happen when I came in with Iam?" Jon thought back to the humbling feeling he had when he entered the forest the first time.

With his eyes aimed at the majestic canopy above their heads, Pneuma tilted his head over to Jon and answered, "What do you have now that you didn't have before?" Jon motioned to the sword now resting along his back, and Pneuma nodded, "That's right. Your sword and the forest are connected. I forged it here in the forest, and then used it to protect all of this. It's a mutual relationship, and the one who possesses it is greeted by all of this around you. You felt refreshed afterward, right? I mean after you collected yourself?" Jon confirmed this assumption with another nod of his head, and so Pneuma continued, "You see, you are in an extremely different situation than you were in before. Since you came out of that cage, you are about to see and experience things that you couldn't comprehend before. I'll guide you through it all, but it'll only be at the pace you decide. I do have to warn you though, you may decide the pace, but I get to have the...esteemed privilege...of choosing what you will see." At this last sentiment, Pneuma shined a mysteriously joyful smile across his face and turned to Jon. Noticing his hesitancy, Pneuma winked, "Don't worry, it'll be fun."

Although slightly comforted by the last statement, Jon still wondered what Pneuma had in mind. Trusting that Pneuma would keep his word and help, Jon answered with a smile, "That works for me."

Pneuma's eyes returned back to the forest's canopy to gaze again at the moon through the treetops. After a moment of brief silence, his head tilted back toward Jon to ask, "Jon, have you noticed anything else...peculiar...about this forest? Look around."

Interested to see what Pneuma could be referring to, Jon's eyes quickly jolted up toward the canopy to discover what he could. He first looked to see the moon, but it was hanging patiently in its place, mirroring light down just as it always has done. He then looked around for stars, and those too were resting in their respectable places. The night sky was clear, so there were no clouds to creatively interpret. Perplexed as to what he should be seeing, he turned to Pneuma and said, "I don't know what I'm supposed to be looking at. Everything seems in its place."

"Look ahead, and tell me what you see," Pneuma politely requested, as his eyes remained transfixed upward.

At his request, Jon looked ahead to see what he could. The moonlight embraced a small pond at the bottom of a hill that was idly napping in the center of a group of palm and cypress trees. The sound of rushing water played melodiously on his eardrums, and he searched to find where the conductor resided. His eyes followed along the hill's ridge to discover a waterfall holding the baton. Water rushed past the small habitation and into the forest.

Eager to visit this oasis, Jon excitedly looked over at Pneuma and asked, "Is that where we're going?"

Pneuma gave a slight nod. Although they grew closer, Pneuma kept his gait slow and steady to be able to gaze around without missing any of the scenery they were passing. Jon, on the other hand, was so intrigued by the oasis and waterfall ahead that he grew increasingly impatient and desired to walk faster. He looked back over his shoulder at Pneuma, and, to his displeasure, Pneuma was still walking at his slow pace. At this, Jon impatiently asked, "Why aren't you moving faster? We could be there by now."

The tranquil expression on Pneuma's face did not change, but he gave a slight sigh, "Oh Jon. I know where we're headed." After a brief moment of silence, he continued, "You have to learn that it's not all about the destination. There's a reason this path and these trees are here."

Pneuma slowed to a stop, which caused Jon to grow increasingly impatient. When Jon came to a stop as well, the gravelly-voiced man suggested, "I have an idea. Close your eyes with me. Take a deep breath and smell the air." Jon hesitantly did what was suggested, but nothing happened. Pneuma, noticing the anxiety in his fellow traveler's attitude, spoke again, "Relax, just relax. Now take a deeper breath." Jon tried his best now to do what was suggested. He relaxed his arms, his shoulders, and his feet before taking a deeper breath than he did before. The smell of the night sky and of the forest around him traveled into his nostrils. "Now keep breathing in. Tell me what you smell."

Growing more relaxed with each inhalation, Jon searched for the right words to describe the aromas he was experiencing. His only reply was an honest, "I don't know how to describe it. It's just...I don't know." He did know it was pleasant and fresh smelling, but the words did not seem to do it justice.

Pneuma's voice patiently waited for its time to cut in and say, "Open your eyes and tell me what you see." Jon's eyelids peeled away, and he could see once again. This time, however, everything was much clearer. His eyes were saturated with so many new images, and as he searched around the forest the moonlight seemed to grow brighter. It exposed insects crawling along the forest bed, the funny positions the trees contorted themselves into in attempts to reach sunlight, hollowed-out logs that provided shelter for animals in need, and many more things for which words could not do justice.

"Was this stuff always here? I mean, while we were walking?" Jon's voice now broke the silence.

Pneuma nonchalantly replied, "It's pretty cool, huh? You have to understand, with someone as new as you are, you have to learn to slow down. There are so many new things around you itching to be seen, or heard, or smelled, or felt. You have to allow your senses to be more open, or else you'll miss what is being shown to you. Everything in this forest is now on display for you to appreciate and interact with. Take advantage of it." While still gazing around in awe, Jon simply nodded his head. Knowing he had gained Jon's attention, Pneuma calmly asked, "Shall we continue walking?"

A simple "Yes" left Jon's lips, and they were off again toward the oasis at the foot of the waterfall. This time they walked next to each other, occasionally showing one another things their eyes came upon. Everything was so new to Jon. Every tree was interesting. Every stone, every blade of grass, every piece of bark, every log on the ground—it all was extremely interesting to the young man who would have been content with overlooking it all just moments ago. Jon also began to understand why and how Iam and Pneuma had developed such a habit of walking barefoot along the forest's floor. Such a relaxed feeling came over Jon the more he spent time within the forest. He wanted to be able to feel the dirt between his own toes. He wanted to feel the textures of the peaceful ground he trod on. He wanted to feel the ground give a little under the weight of his body. He wanted to feel it interact with him in a tangible way, but for now he kept his boots on and traveled along the path with Pneuma, trusting he would have plenty of opportunities in the future.

After several minutes of walking, they arrived at the edge of the river. It was wider than Jon had initially perceived it to be. With no indication of a bridge being nearby, the only way to cross the river seemed to be swimming the hundred-foot distance to the other shore. The wall of water to their left filled Jon's ears with a constant reminder of the climb he had to make earlier in order to see the King. A fresh mist from the waterfall surrounded them as they gazed into its landing platform to see the many variations of fish that inhabited its waters.

As they turned around to head toward the oasis, Pneuma leaned over to tell Jon, "This is where we're getting something to drink," Jon's chapped lips cracked to form an appreciative smile, "but, since you're taller than I am, you'll have to get them down for us."

Pneuma noticed the confused look on Jon's face, so he elaborated, "You're going to have to climb this palm tree and bring down a couple of coconuts." They had arrived at the base of a fully grown palm tree with an abundance of coconuts under its leaves. Instead of arguing or complaining, Jon rested his shield and helmet at the base of the tree and began his climb to retrieve two of its inhabitants.

After getting half way up the tree, his grip slipped and down he came. The next three attempts yielded the same results with Jon rapidly sliding down after only climbing halfway up. With a frustrated look on his face, he turned to Pneuma for advice. All Pneuma said in response was, "Try using your sword to get them." Jon heeded his advice and made his way back up the palm tree, but this time, when he got halfway up, he supported himself with his legs and left arm so he could reach behind his head and pull his sword from its resting place. Moonlight glimmered off of the metal as it swung in the air to free two perfectly round coconuts from their resting places. They fell into the waiting hands of Pneuma at the base of the accommodating tree. Jon slid back down to join Pneuma after putting his sword back in its bed. As he was coming down, Pneuma peeled the outside layers away from the coconuts and drove holes into them with a knife he kept on his belt to reach the water inside. As he handed Jon his share, Pneuma smiled and said, "Drink up!"

Jon grabbed his and touched his lips to the opening. He tilted his head back, and rich, warm coconut water flowed out. It navigated through his cracked lips as though it were impersonating the river that flowed next to them. Jon lowered the shell to catch his breath and to say to Pneuma, "Thank you for leading me here. I would've never known any of this was here if it weren't for you."

Pneuma lowered his own drink to reply, "It's my pleasure." After a long pause so Jon could finish his drink, Pneuma spoke again, but this time his head was turned and he was staring solemnly out at the water. "So many people come into this forest not knowing what anything is for. They misuse and overlook many things. They come in here seeking nourishment like this, but since they don't know where to look and they don't ask me for help, they leave feeling thirsty or hungry. Then they try and fight afterwards. It's no wonder why people aren't fighting like they used to. They aren't getting nourishment, and they're running on the fumes of meals past." He turned back to Jon and said to him in a pleading voice, "You must come in here whenever you need something. Just follow the river if you need to. There is plenty in here to quench your thirst or hunger." After Jon nodded, Pneuma placed his empty coconut on a stone and motioned for Jon to do the same. He looked back to Jon and told him, "Not many new soldiers come in here as often as they should, and there are even older soldiers that are still drinking what you just drank. They don't work that hard, so they only get thirsty and drink water or milk. Always remember, when you work harder, you start getting hungry. You work lightly, you only get thirsty. Take these coconuts here. Many soldiers only think they offer water or milk, but when you really open them up," with a quick slice of his sword, Pneuma cut through both of the hollow coconuts to expose their interiors, "they offer you meat." Jon stared at the four half-shells wobbling on the stone slab before him. "Put some in your belt compartments for later." Pneuma cut smaller pieces so they were simpler for storage, and Jon grabbed them all and secured them in his belt.

    Another long pause followed after all the pieces of coconut were fastened in their new homes. A gentle breeze grazed the tree tops, which dislodged a few leaves from their branches. They fell majestically around Jon and Pneuma as they peered into the night sky. Pneuma's voice once again pierced the silence in a calm whisper, "You have to be different Jon Smith. They need you to be different. There will come times when you have to feed some of them meat when they don't want it. They have fasted from this for too long. It has gotten to the point where their stomachs are tired of being ignored so they cease to call out. Some come in here with no intention of finding anything. They aimlessly walk around with their eyes staring at the ground, and before the trees have a chance to breathe upon them, they walk straight back out. I have asked this question to many men I have led through here." Pneuma's eyes met Jon's. "Are you willing to be different?"

    Jon was staring at a man that has spent so much time watching and interacting with so many soldiers, young and old. The pleading in his voice was a drastic change from the carefree nature he had been experiencing thus far in the forest. He could tell the heaviness of Pneuma's heart was weighing him down. With a soft voice Jon replied, "I'll try."

At this reply, a slight grin appeared across Pneuma's face. It lingered there for a short while, but then faded rather quickly. A stern-faced man now stood before Jon. Pneuma approached Jon and placed both his hands on the young man's shoulders. The forest around them was eerily silent as his gravelly voice filled the air, "Don't try. Just do." After saying this, Pneuma nodded and gave him a slap on the shoulder. He then walked over to the tree where Jon laid his shield and helmet and picked them both off the moss covered ground. He walked back over to where Jon still stood, and placed the helmet upon his head. As Pneuma handed over the shield, he said, "Do you want to learn the cool thing about your shield now?"

Jon grabbed his shield and answered soberly, "I would like that."

A smile appeared again on Pneuma's face, which indicated to Jon that the seriousness had subsided. The dirt-covered man spoke again, "I figured you have had a long day, and it's getting pretty late, so I am going to show you how to make your tent."

Jon looked around, perplexed at what they could be using for this tent. There were logs nearby, and branches could easily be acquired from the trees surrounding them. However, Jon felt as though they would not be using any of these things, based off of Pneuma's abundant appreciation of the forest. Highly confused, Jon looked to Pneuma for clarification, "What are we going to use?"

Pneuma glanced down at the circular object Jon held in his right hand and said, "Your shield will serve as your tent. I know it's kind of weird, but hear me out." He saw Jon staring down at his shield perplexed, so he quickly added, "Just grab hold of an inside

The Battle

strap with each hand." Jon did as Pneuma suggested. "Then you hold the shield above your head, kneel to the ground, and close your eyes. Your shield is specially made for you, so it will be able to detect when you need rest. At the appropriate time, it will encapsulate you within an impenetrable dome. You are then free to let go of the straps and rest securely. It will also know when you are ready to wake up, so it will retract back to its original state when you grab hold of the straps again." Jon listened, and trusted it would work later when the time was appropriate. "Also, on the battlefield, be prepared to fight as soon as the shield retracts. Trust me, there are going to be creatures waiting for you to wake back up." Jon stood there, transfixed by his shield, amazed at how previously oblivious he was to its capabilities. "I will tell you more in the morning; I can see this is plenty enough to process."

It was plenty enough indeed. The young man trusted Pneuma at his word, but it was so unexpected. "This shield I've been carrying along will even protect me while I sleep?" Jon thought to himself. "What other things could his armor do?" He knew this question would have to wait, so he could rest. He looked up at Pneuma and asked, "Where are you going to be sleeping?"

With a deep chuckle Pneuma answered, "Sleep? I still have work to do. I'll sleep later. I'll come back in the morning to help you some more. Just get some rest now." They both smiled at each other, and then, in an instant, Pneuma disappeared into the waiting arms of the forest.

Jon turned back toward the river and stood peacefully in the waterfall's mist. Other than the rushing water, complete silence surrounded him. The breeze had stopped blowing, and the trees had stopped swaying. He was alone, but he felt secure. It was his first night out of the bondage of his cage. He was free.

Jon watched the flowing water for another hour. The longer he stared at it, the more it started to look as though it were alive. The way it cascaded off of the rocks, the way it hurried down its path, the way it sped off into the distance, it all started to look as though it were running an obstacle course. It had such determination to reach its destination. It would not let any object, large or small, stand in its way. Watching this river reminded him of Pneuma's words. He must be different; he must keep fighting. For now, however, he needed to rest.

Jon finally peeled his attention away from the mesmerizing flow of the water in search of a spot to make camp. He returned to the palm trees that encircled the oasis and came upon a patch of moss covering the ground. Appearing to be a suitable bed, he took his sword from his vest and his helmet off his head and placed them gently on the ground. He then unfastened his shield from his arm and knelt to the ground, as instructed by Pneuma. He grabbed hold of a strap on the underside of the shield with each hand, and whispered, "Please come through." Trusting Pneuma again, he closed his eyes and raised his hands above his head, hoisting the shield in place.

The shield neither shook, nor rattled, so Jon opened his eyes to see what happened. He opened them to see a metallic dome completely surrounding him. The shield had done what Pneuma said it would. Jon stared back at his reflection to see wide eyes and a jaw stretching toward the floor, just as his shield had done. Two straps still hung from the dome's roof, assuring Jon this was still his shield. He relinquished his grasp and could only hope this shelter would not retract and fall upon his head in its shield form. The metallic structure graciously obliged and remained in its new form. He looked around once more at it all and, overcome with gratitude and exhaustion, chose to lie down on the mossy ground beneath him. There was abundant room under the shield's canopy, which allowed him to sprawl out completely. As he laid there, he looked up to his reflection smiling back down to him. He reached for his sword's handle and the smooth dark green canvas of his helmet and pulled them in close to him for their much needed rest. The soft dirt and moss provided adequate comfort, and Jon closed his eyes and faded away into unconsciousness.

    After hours of rest, consciousness restored itself to Jon. His eyes opened once again to meet the lush green color of the forest's canopy above. His shield retracted and started falling down toward his chest to be caught by its owner's awaiting hands. He placed it on the ground beside him and lay there peacefully on his mossy patch of earth. After a few moments he reached out to wake his sword and helmet from their naps. The sounds of birds chirping filled the air as he looked up toward the sunlit sky. A gentle breeze filled his nostrils whenever he took a breath. Insects started to travel on the surface of his hairless face and in between his fingers. He gently brushed them off and sat up to view the forest in the daylight. He returned his helmet and sword to their proper locations and slid his left arm through the shield's straps.

    His eyes took in the scenery around him, coming across many things he had not seen in the moonlight. Many brightly colored flowers inhabited the undergrowth of the monstrous trees surrounding him. Jon watched a pair of squirrels and many other small animals playing amongst the branches high above as he surveyed the treetops. Familiarity showed itself when he looked down toward the waterfall, river, and oasis near him. They still looked as extraordinary as they had when the moon bathed them in its light. Minutes passed as his eyes gravitated toward the flowing water.

While Jon's attention was preoccupied, a sword-wielding, barefoot man approached on one of the forest's paths. His hands and sword were covered with a thick blackish liquid that vaguely resembled blood. Jon instantly smiled and looked up to meet this man's eyes when he heard his footsteps approaching. "Did you run into some trouble out there?" Jon asked as he noticed the bloodied sword and hands of the man that now stood a few feet away.

"Little pests tried to sneak up on you. I had to try this sword out sooner or later," Pneuma slyly answered.

"It looks like it worked well," Jon replied.

With a laugh, Pneuma motioned to both blades, "Oh yeah, it did! I used them both just for fun."

"So is that the...enemy's blood?" Jon asked.

"Yes, it's all theirs. None of it's mine," Pneuma assured Jon. "And it's about time I tell you a little bit about what you're dealing with out there, don't you think? I mean, knowing is half the battle, right?"

"Right!" Jon excitedly answered.

Pneuma walked over to the river and hunched down beside Jon. As he cleaned off his sword and hands in the running water, he replied. "They're called malorum. They work for the dragon you've heard stories about."

Jon thought about the story of Iam dismembering the dragon that Pneuma mentioned, and with a confused expression he said, "I thought the dragon was defeated. How could there still be malorum that work for it?"

Still washing his hands off, Pneuma replied, "There are plenty of different reasons. Some of them think that the dragon will roam again, some believe the war's not over; and some are just in denial. They're trying to carry out their orders despite what happened, but we know the truth. I'll tell you this, a stubborn, close-minded enemy is a powerful force, and they shouldn't be taken lightly. You must learn how to defeat them, or they could become increasingly annoying."

Allowing all of this to settle in his mind, Jon walked over and sat near Pneuma by the riverbed. Pneuma finished cleaning off his hands and sat on the moss-covered ground, sharing a moment of silence with Jon.

Jon's voice broke the silence first to ask Pneuma a question. "Where were you when that happened, when Iam defeated the dragon?"

A gentle smile appeared on Pneuma's face as he looked down at the water. He looked up and answered, "I was in the castle."

"Were you able to see what happened?" Jon continued asking.

A chuckle came from Pneuma as he answered, "Oh yeah, I was able to see it all. I tell you what; it was an awesomely fought battle on Iam's part. That dragon had no idea what it was up against."

Jon turned to face Pneuma and inquired, "So what happened?"

Pneuma turned to face Jon and said, "I'll tell you over a couple of coconuts, if you want to go get them."

In an instant, Jon excitedly leapt to his feet with his sword in hand. He sprinted over to the nearest palm tree and scurried to its midway point. He swung his sword a couple of times to relinquish two coconuts from their resting places, and watched them fall to the ground below. Jon put his sword in its own resting place and climbed down off of the tree. After picking the nourishment off the mossy ground, he hurried back to Pneuma to have him open them as he did last time. Pneuma readily did so, and he passed Jon his share to drink.

"Before I start, let's toast," Pneuma suggested.

"What are we toasting to?" Jon replied.

"It'll be a toast to Iam, for doing what no other man could've done ...so easily, I might add," Pneuma answered.

Their coconut shells triumphantly collided with each other, and both Pneuma and Jon had a drink of the milk that filled their shells.

After each swallowed a sip of his own drink, Pneuma began with the story while Jon looked on in anticipation. "I'll give you some background information to start out with, so you can fully appreciate what happened. Many years ago a small serpent grew when nobody paid it any attention or fought it back. It feasted, in a way, off of neglect. If nobody fought it, then it had time to grow.

"It had no way to get around in its earlier years, but to slither along the undergrowth of what the King created. It gained followers the stronger it became—these are the malorum. You see, the more negligence there was, the larger it grew and the more followers it had. This serpent started with two people and played into their curious nature by distracting them from what the King had told them to do. Once it was full from their disobedience, it simply moved on to seek more power. It encountered villages, towns, and great cities, setting its sights on increasingly larger populations. You see, the more comfortable people were, the less they looked down at their feet to see this serpent slithering around. Any battles it won, it also became stronger, even when its followers were the ones who won.

"We fast forward several years, and the serpent and its army had grown considerably. The negligence and disobedience they fed off of made them larger and more powerful, eventually turning the serpent into the dragon you've heard tales of. It got to the point where nobody wanted to fight it, so they hid themselves altogether; promoting neglect even more. They stopped turning to the King and stayed in their campgrounds. Meanwhile, the serpent, now a dragon, roamed around to battle the few that kept fighting. After a while people started going missing from the campgrounds and the battlefield. What the serpent and the malorum had done in their free time was build cages to contain soldiers. The cages were built to take soldiers away from fighting. The soldiers inside became prisoners. They were helpless from the inside, but there was a catch. This is all still the King's land, and even the King's worst enemy has no choice but to ask permission to do anything. Yeah, the King is that strong."

"What was the catch?" Jon inquired.

"The serpent had to include locks on the outside of the cages," Pneuma answered. "With the institution of these cages came the institution of the keys the King designed, one of which you received from Iam." He motioned to the glimmering metallic green object dangling from Jon's right hand that he seemed to have forgotten with everything else that had been going on. "Nothing happens here that doesn't go through him first," Pneuma continued.

"So why did the King allow the dragon and the malorum to build the cages anyway, if he would just make keys for them to be opened?" Jon asked.

Another smile appeared on Pneuma's face. "The sign of a true King is to allow his people to choose to either fight for him, or not fight for him. These cages weren't really anything new. The dragon thought, and still thinks, that he outsmarted the King with these "new inventions", but technically the soldiers that were choosing not to fight were already prisoners to themselves anyway. It's the same thing that has been going on since the beginning of the kingdom. It's the same problem, but there's a different face to it." Jon nodded, so Pneuma continued. "So here we have all these would-be-soldiers trapped in these cages, but soldiers on the outside are getting severely outnumbered. More are being captured while those still fighting are getting exhausted by pulling their weight. So you have men and women constantly in need of bandaging and healing. They start losing hope and forgetting their purpose. That's when the King has had enough. He can't watch all of this without becoming enraged at the dragon and its malorum for what they're doing to his people. So he starts telling them about a hero that will save them all." Pneuma leaned really close to Jon and whispered, "Secretly this was his plan all along; to send Iam down from the castle and save the captured while also healing those that were fighting. It sounds crazy to you, I know, but trust me, the King knows what he's doing." He straightened back up and continued, "So when the timing was just right, Iam descended from the castle and joined the fight. Now we get into the battle itself."

The Battle

Jon's eyes opened wider, so that the silvery blue orbs that inhabited them were completely visible. "So what happened then?" he asked.

Pneuma finished off his coconut water and put the emptied shell on the ground next to him, waiting for Jon to do the same before he continued with the story. Jon bit off a little bit of coconut meat from his shell and placed the rest on the ground beside Pneuma's. As he chewed, Pneuma continued on, "Iam spent much time with the other soldiers during the years he was down here. He healed many of the wounded and also unlocked many cages before his battle. You could tell that the dragon and the malorum started taking notice. Then one day Iam started gathering up all the remaining cages and tied them all together. Nobody had any idea what he was doing except for the King and me. He tried telling them, but nobody seemed to listen. He carried each cage individually on his back to group them all together. Each cage is lined with extremely sharp metal, broken glass, barbed wire, and anything else you could imagine that would make for an excruciating load to carry. Once he got them all together, he tied them to each other with a special rope he got from the King and me. With his back bloodied and mangled, he lifted the rope over his shoulder and started walking into the Dead Woods—I'll tell you about that place later. He pulled every single cage behind him, only receiving help from a man named Simon.

In the Dead Woods there is an entrance to a cave that leads to the dragon's lair. Soldiers have gone in before, but they have never come out. This is where Iam pulled the cages. He placed them all around the area as though it were a coliseum. He looked everyone in the eye—every caged person, every soldier that followed him—he looked at them all, and he turned to face the mouth of the cave and waited without saying anything.

"Hours passed with nothing happening, until a loud noise violently shook the ground. A cloud of black smoke emitted from its opening and the dragon finally appeared. Black scales covered the entirety of its back, its tail, and all four of its mammoth legs. Dark black talons protruded from its feet and sunk into the burnt ground underneath. Once it was completely out of its lair, it stretched its wings as though it could intimidate Iam. The dragon itself was awfully large, but Iam remained calm. No words left his lips. You could tell this upset the dragon, because it let out another bellowing, tree-shaking roar. After this happened I looked behind me to see the King laughing hysterically with water filling his eyes. We both laughed for only a moment.

"The dragon approached the ground where Iam stood, coming within just a few yards of him. He roared again and flexed his wings, creating a huge gust of wind that blew in Iam's face, but Iam just smiled and looked it straight into its blackened eyes. The King and I smiled right along with him. Then a loud GASP broke the silence, followed by a louder THUD. The dragon, in a fit of rage, threw Iam against a substantially large tree and let out another roar. The gasp had come from all of the onlookers; those in their cages and those standing among the captured soldiers. The dragon charged forward to stand in front of Iam once again, this time two cages served as its footrests, each completely covered by a massive, scaly foot. Iam smiled once again, which caused the dragon to use one of his front feet to pin Iam against the bark of the tree. Two talons went in each hand, and one talon pierced both feet, suspending Iam off the ground. Everyone around now had their eyes on what was happening. The dragon had Iam immobilized against a tree, and two caged men got front row seats to watch it all. To add insult to injury, the dragon picked up one of those cages and threw it at Iam while he was still pinned. It went on like this for nearly an hour or so.

"I looked back to see the reaction on the King's face. His head was down and he was looking down at his clasped hands. He couldn't stand to watch what was happening. I looked back to the crowded spot in the Dead Woods, and that's when things started to get interesting. The other caged man called out to Iam, asking him for help, and instead of Iam saying, 'I am kind of in a predicament here,' he said, 'I will save you, I promise.' As you can imagine, the dragon didn't take too kindly to these words, so he let out yet another roar and sank his talons in the tree's bark even deeper, causing more blood to trickle out of Iam's wounds. He just hung there after that...motionless, while I looked on in anticipation. Everyone thought he was dead, even the dragon. So it picked up a cage that was lying beneath it and pressed the sharp metal frame into his side for confirmation. There was no movement. Seconds turned into minutes. Minutes turned into hours. I have to admit, it did not look good. Then there was finally movement. Another smile appeared across Iam's face. He lifted his head and looked the bewildered dragon in the eyes and laughed for several minutes. He then grabbed each of the dragon's talons that inhabited his hands and pulled them from the hold they had on the tree. Still looking it in the eyes, Iam ripped the talons out of the dragon's foot. Black blood splattered everywhere as the dragon bellowed in pain. The King lifted his head to expose his own smile as the sound reached his ears."

Overcome with all sorts of joyous and anxious emotions, Jon insisted Pneuma continue with the story. "So what happened next?"

"Due to the understandably torturous pain the dragon felt, it fled to its nearby cave. The third talon had released its grip and retreated with its master. With one of the newly acquired talons, Iam bent down and unlocked the cage of the man he promised to rescue. Then after he looked at everyone once more, he followed the dragon into the cave, but not before he promised them that he would be back with his prize in three days. Soon after he entered, the opening collapsed; forming a scab of fallen rocks over the opening of the wound of the cave. For those three days, the fighting resumed inside only with more intensity than before.

Pneuma saw his eagerness to listen, so he continued, "After three days passed, the large boulders that covered the cave's entrance were found to have mysteriously rolled away. Iam stood at the entrance with what appeared to be a large scaly leg draped over his shoulder. Just a leg. Nothing else was attached, apart from the foot with two missing talons. The instant he stepped from the cave's gaping mouth, rain poured down from the clouds like confetti and fell down upon every cage that he had brought to watch the battle. A battered, bloodied, and soot-stained Iam confidently walked out of its mouth and into the woods, dragging his trophy behind him. He headed in the direction of the castle, which was about a forty-day walk, but stopped to talk with his fellow soldiers along the way, telling them he would be back soon for the rest of the body."

"Once he got to the castle, a giant banquet was held in his honor. The King and I gathered the entire population for this event. After what must have been days of eating, singing, and rejoicing, I had to leave the celebration and come down here. That, my friend, was the last day I was up in the castle."

The Battle

So much information filled Jon's head as he sat there. He was just with Iam a day ago, and had he known fully everything that he did now, he would have asked so many questions. He knew when the time came the conversation would arise with his general. In an effort to change the subject so his mind would keep from going insane, Jon gently said to Pneuma, "I do have another question."

"Let's hear it," Pneuma replied, turning his head to face Jon.

Jon then asked, "Could I get a lay of the land around here? Just a rough outline would do."

In an I-thought-you'd-never-ask way Pneuma responded, "Certainly!" They both stood up so the gravelly-voiced man could get his bearings.

"You see, behind us is north; that's where the King's castle is. It's noticeably mountainous over there, but his castle is on the tallest mountain, so you can't miss it especially because the lights are always on. This forest lies in the east. The Dead Woods are to the west. In the middle is the battlefield, and to the south is very diverse area. Now this is speaking all generally of course. The forest overflows at points into the battle field, and there are more battlefields and camps the farther east and west you go. The King's castle is always north, so if you need to find it just look up toward the hills."

A grateful "thank you" left Jon's lips as he looked around to get his bearings.

"It's my pleasure. So do you want to learn how to see the King whenever you'd like? No questions asked?" the gravelly voice spoke.

"That would be amazing. How?" Jon inquired with a hint of desperation.

"Well, it has to do with your shield again," Pneuma answered. "Whenever you want to talk with him, ask him something, or just thank him, you hold your shield above your head and call out for him just as though he were right in front of you. I must tell you though, do not let go of those straps... It could be bad."

Jon looked down at his shield with more appreciation than he had before. "So wherever I am, whatever predicament, I could just hold it above my head and call out to him? How will I get up there though?"

With a slight chuckle, Pneuma said, "You'll see."

Jon immediately wanted to try it out, but he still wanted to spend more time with Pneuma and learn more about the forest and this new world. Sensing that Jon was having internal struggle, Pneuma said to him, "You can always come back here. I'll be here waiting. When you come back, though, try walking around barefoot. See how it feels."

With his mind at ease, Jon bid Pneuma farewell and did what his teacher told him. He raised his hands above his head, holding on tightly to the leather of the shield's straps. With one last look at Pneuma, he smiled and called out for the King. As the last letter left his mouth, the trees began to calmly sway.

Pneuma had taken up his sword and headed back into the forest, presumably to slay more malorum, as Jon stood alone. His shield remained above his head as he looked toward the hills in hope of seeing something. To his amazement a silhouette appeared in the shape of a giant bird not far out in the direction he was looking. He whispered to himself as he waited below his shield, "Is that an eagle?" Soon after he muttered these words, he remembered what Iam had told him before he left the castle. While Jon looked up at its large flapping wings, it grasped the shield with its talons and lifted him off the ground, carrying him away in the direction of the castle's endless walls.

Chapter 4:
Eagle's Wings

His feet grew farther and farther away from the safety of the forest floor with every thrust of the eagle's wings. Jon dared not to look down out of fear. In the previous encounter he had with an eagle, he resided on its back with Iam safely guiding the bird's direction. This time, however, he just swung from his shield's leather straps, trusting his transporter would not get distracted or develop a foot cramp. Although he was uneasy, Jon still trusted Iam would not send an eagle that was misguided or inexperienced in its flight, so with this realization Jon relaxed slightly and enjoyed the summer breeze flowing around him.

After several minutes of traveling, their altitude began dropping steadily. Jon took notice and slowly opened his eyes. Sunlight illuminated everything around, exposing scenery Jon had not been able to see during his moonlit travels the night before. The forest's canopy looked similar, but he now could see bird nests and tree limbs shaking as squirrels and monkeys inventing their own obstacle courses. Then he looked toward the castle.

The Battle

    He had not been able to fully appreciate how magnificently large it was in the moonlight. The eagle had brought him within a few hundred yards of the castle walls, and Jon still could not see where they ended. The center tower, with the shorter one attached to its side, was much taller than Jon had remembered. He could see other eagles coming and going from its arched windows to rest before making more rounds. They had gotten close enough to where Jon could feel the mist of the twin waterfalls on his arms and face. They, too, were unlike anything Jon had seen before. They streamed down, deceivingly peaceful, to the ground below. As Jon flew over them, he could hear the smooth rushing of the water making it known how powerful its glassy flow was. As they flew over the castle wall, Jon estimated it to be around two hundred feet wide. If the difficult climb did not keep unwanted visitors out, then this wall would surely get the job done. The center tower proved to be even thicker, protruding on the inside a couple hundred feet farther. Jon looked down at the massive structure in awe of what he saw next. He laid eyes upon the source of the two waterfalls cascading down the face of the cliff. A sizeable river flowed toward the middle of the castle wall only to split at the plot of land the central tower resided upon. The two newly formed rivers smoothly flowed through aqueducts reserved for their departure.

    Jon's eyes traced the path of the original river to see where it came from. His followed it through the large meadow and garden below that had been divided by the river's flow. Although the land had been split by the water, beautifully constructed bridges connected the two sides in the same way spouses would hold each other's hands. Jon continued navigating through the lush grass and the acres of flowers. He maneuvered his eyes around the various fruit trees and bushes all while the eagle continued its descent.

It was when Jon hovered a couple hundred feet from the ground that an enormous tree came into view. He estimated its trunk to be no less than a couple hundred feet in diameter, and its branches sprawled out toward the sky, as someone would stretch out their arms early in the morning, reaching as much as a thousand feet high. It was a noticeably old tree, but its leaves were fresh and vibrantly green. Jon examined its base, and to his amazement this is where the river began. A wide and steady stream spilled out of a hollowed portion of its trunk and continued on toward the wall. Jon was still too high to see what resided inside and how the river began its journey, as he was still being lowered to the ground.

When Jon's boots could almost touch the grass he noticed two individuals to the left of the tree's base. Jon recognized Iam right away, as he sat relaxed on a branch a few feet from the ground. The other man was lying in a hammock to his left, suspended between two branches. They were talking to one another and laughing as they watched Jon's arrival.

The eagle slowed to a stop just a few feet away from where the two men resided. Jon's feet barely touched the ground when his carrier's talons released their grip upon his shield. His weight suddenly returned to him, which caused him to kneel before the men now standing before him. Jon looked up to see a familiar hand being held out to help him to his feet once again. This time Jon noticed the large scar inhabiting his palm as he was raised up. He tried to form one of the many questions he had thought to ask, but the presence of the second man made him speechless once he realized who it was.

The Battle

Jon knew the questions for Iam had to wait, because now he was standing before the King.

Jon attempted to bow again, but Iam placed his hands on his shoulders to assure him the accidental bow he gave as the eagle released him sufficed. So, instead, Jon stood there completely frozen until Iam said, "I will put your armor and boots by the tree for you." After noticing Jon's hesitation, Iam continued, "I assure you, you will be alright." Jon obliged and relinquished his armor, boots, and socks over to Iam, which left him in just his t-shirt and pants. Iam walked over and set them down at the base of the tree, near the hammock the King had been laying on.

Iam returned to a still-frozen Jon and the almost unrecognizable King. No crown rested upon the King's head, and the robes he was wearing were plain white and notably similar to Iam's. Jon still did not feel as though he could look at him directly in the eyes, so he stared at the ground only to notice the King was also barefoot. A second set of shoeless feet appeared in his line of sight, which was attached to Iam, who said, "I do not think the grass is more interesting to you than our company, so when you are done investigating its intricacies we have some interesting things to show you." Jon responded to Iam by looking up and giving a nervous smile, which Iam answered with a smile of his own, "There we are. Well, Jon Smith, welcome to our garden."

Jon surveyed all around where he stood to see from ground level what he had seen from the sky. Every tree, bush, and plant bore food. The abundantly large river gave nourishment to everything that had thirst. His eyes had reached back to Iam and the King to see each of them drinking from identical sculpted mugs. While the King took a drink, Iam held out his own mug for Jon to drink from. Jon took it and drank, discovering it contained the purest water that had ever touched his lips. As he swallowed it, he felt a stream flow down his throat and spread throughout the inside of his body as if it were planting roots in his organs. Jon looked down into the remnants of the mug and asked Iam, "Is this water from the river?"

"It is," Iam replied. Jon looked over at the King's lowered mug, to which Iam said, "The King is drinking something slightly different." After Jon nodded his head and tried returning the mug back to its owner, Iam said, "I will get it back after you and the King return from your walk. Drink as much as you want." After he said this, Iam casually walked over to the tree to relax in the hammock the King had left vacant.

After a short moment of silence, a deep thunderous voice asked, "Shall we walk?" The King asked as Jon nervously lowered his mug. Jon nodded, and the two tall men began to stroll along the riverbank.

Noticing that Jon was still far too nervous to say anything, the King asked him, "What's on your mind?"

Jon stared down at the water in his mug alongside the King for a couple minutes before saying, "I just continue wondering...why me."

The King asked, "What do you mean?"

Jon replied, "I mean...there are so many more out there in their cages, so why did you rescue me?"

"You wanted to come out," the King answered.

Jon was now the one seeking clarity. "What do you mean?"

"I cannot force people to come out of their cages. I have to wait until they choose to come out. Then once they do, I am there in a heartbeat." the King replied.

The Battle

"Why can't you? I mean you're the King," Jon said.

"It doesn't work like that. Love and allegiance don't work like that. I can't force people into this; it goes against the very definitions of the two words," the King answered.

"So what about the others? What about the ones that never choose to come out?" Jon asked.

After this question, Jon noticed the King slow down, his eyes staring into his mug. "All I can do is show them how much better it is on the outside. If they choose not to come out, then, out of love, I give them what they want." Jon could not tell whether it was a tear or water from the mug that was navigating down the King's weathered cheek. "It is my deepest desire that everyone chooses freedom over those cages. It's like a father watching his children. You want the best for them, but you can't make them choose it. All you could do is keep showing them the best." At this last statement, he looked back to Iam, still in the hammock beneath the tree's branches, who was staring down at his hands. The King smiled, and his eyes came back to meet Jon's as he said, "It is definitely worth the wait though. So...Jon Smith, what else is on your mind?"

Jon paused for a moment before answering in a nervous tone, "I was wondering if I could ask you for something."

The King gave a calming smile and answered, "Of course you can. What is it?"

"Pneuma told me that it was going to be extremely hard out there on the battlefield, and I know I can't do this alone. I'll get killed out there if I try and do this by myself. So I was wondering if I could...if you could...I am going to need a lot of help out there," Jon nervously said.

"So you are wanting to ask me if I could provide you with some backup, am I correct?" the King asked.

"Right." Jon replied back.

The King smiled again and said, "I want to share something extremely important with you, Jon. Nobody can fight by themselves. Everyone needs help to fight. You will receive plenty of help out there, I assure you."

Jon's nervousness subsided to give residence to the confidence filling his body. He gave a sigh of relief and answered with a simple, "Thank you."

The two men continued walking and talking throughout the garden, occasionally crossing bridges and picking berries off nearby bushes, until they ventured upon a well-traveled trail that led through a densely populated, knee-high, patch in the garden. On one side of the trail, they saw a deep purple flower, and on the other side was a plant with leaves that were the purest shade of green. The mixture of their scents gripped Jon's senses, sending him into a state of pure serenity. The King noticed Jon's gait slow to smell these plants, so he, too, slowed down and said, "I always enjoy walking on this path. The colors, the smells, they have a way of relaxing you." The King noticed Jon still sniffing the air and looking around him, so he continued talking, "The deep purple flowers are lavender, and the plants with those green leaves are peppermint."

Jon took a moment from pleasing his senses to ask, "Did you plant them yourself?"

"I did. I knew I would enjoy them to be together," He replied.

"They do smell nice together." Jon sped back up to his previous pace and resumed walking alongside the King.

After a while of walking and conversing, they eventually looped back to face the tree from which they began their walk. This time Jon could see the inside of the tree's trunk more clearly, revealing something strange. He turned to his travel companion and asked, "What is that inside of the tree trunk?"

"Ah! That is a fountain. It's what this river flows from," he nonchalantly replied.

"A fountain?" Jon could not believe this was the source of the large river flowing beside them.

"There's a spring underground, so we built the fountain over it to channel its power," the King explained. "We use it to water all of these plants, including the tree above it."

"So how is the river formed?" Jon inquired.

"We knew we mustn't contain all of the water, nor did we want to. We merely desired to redirect it. This river is a result of the fountain's overflow," the King answered.

"So how did that tree grow there?" Jon continued gazing at the vastness of the fountain and the tree above it as he asked.

"That tree," the King lifted his eyes toward its uppermost branches, "is actually composed of twelve separate trees. Iam, Pneuma, and I planted twelve seedlings around the fountain's perimeter, and over time they grew and became intertwined."

"So what grows from it?" Jon asked, still in awe of its height and girth.

"I am glad you asked," the King said. "The leaves are a story in and of themselves. They have a sort of healing property attached to them when used correctly. The fruit that grows from it, since it is still composed of twelve individual trees, is different each month. Each individual tree has its own month to yield its crop."

Jon admired the tree's majesty as he said to the King, "I think I'm ready to train now." The King smiled and walked toward the robed man calmly lying in the hammock.

"So how went the walk?" Iam turned his head toward Jon, who returned his mug.

"It was amazing. This place is incredible," Jon replied.

"He is ready to go train with Pneuma now. Could you get his armor, Iam?" The King politely requested as he motioned toward the neatly arranged green and white armor that rested underneath the hammock.

"Of course," Iam responded as he got out from the hammock's comfortable embrace to reach down and retrieve Jon's belongings. He stood up and helped Jon put everything on as he had done before.

Once Jon was all dressed, he turned to the King to clarify, "Pneuma told me I could come up here anytime; is this true?"

The King smiled and answered, "Yes. You could come back whenever you desire. He would not steer you wrong."

"Good. I will be seeing the both of you very soon. Thank you for everything," Jon responded. The King and Iam smiled as a brown eagle approached them to await the hoisting of Jon's shield.

"Do not be a stranger," Iam said as the King hugged the armor clad young man.

"Definitely not," Jon replied as he hoisted his shield in the air. The eagle noticed it glimmering and instantly swooped down to grasp its metallic frame. In just a few seconds Jon found himself staring down at the two men, the garden, the river, and the tree. He was lifted higher with each thrust of the eagle's wings, but this time it was not fear or nervousness that filled his mind. It was strength and confidence, knowing he could talk to the King at any time and ask for help. As they coasted through the clouds, Jon took deep and fulfilling breaths, stretching his chest beneath his custom armor.

    He kept his eyes open as they began their descent into the forest. The eagle maneuvered through the trees so well Jon did not feel a single branch touch his body. He just hung there, enjoying the ride, until he noticed two figures standing on the forest floor looking up toward him. He recognized them almost instantaneously. Pneuma looked at the second figure as Jon cheerfully whispered to himself, "It's Cay."

Chapter 5:
Training

The eagle lowered Jon to the ground and did not release his grip until the brown and black work boots touched the ground. Jon stooped to one knee as he landed, and when he stood up Pneuma was standing before him with a smile on his face. "How was your flight?" he asked as Cay approached.

"Incredibly refreshing," Jon looked in the direction the eagle had flown off in.

"And your visit with the King, how'd that go?" Pneuma asked as he helped dust Jon off.

"Very peaceful and informal; it surprised me," Jon answered while recalling the King's barefootedness and overall appearance.

Pneuma and Cay looked at one another and smiled before he asked, "How so?" With a large smile on his face, Jon told them of his meeting with the King.

"It felt nice didn't it?" A soft, raspy voice broke the air, and Jon and Pneuma's attention turned to their much shorter counterpart. "You go in there expecting it to be all formal and nerve

The Battle

racking, but then you realize all he wants to do is spend time with you. Kind of like a dad."

Jon smiled and nodded his head, "Yeah...I was expecting to be in the castle or something. I was not expecting it to take place in a garden."

"He enjoys doing things a different way than how people would expect. But he is the King, and nobody could really argue with that," Pneuma said lightheartedly.

The three of them laughed until Jon said to Pneuma, "So, I think I'm ready to begin training."

"Ah yes! Now it's time for you to start pulling your weight around here," Pneuma answered, almost forgetting why he had gathered Cay in the first place. "Both of you follow me." Pneuma motioned to Cay and Jon as he turned down a trail behind him. It led to a clearing off into the distance that was barely visible through the shadowy undergrowth. The two young soldiers looked at each other, smiled, and trailed after their guide.

After several minutes of walking, they arrived at the clearing. It was moderately sized with various tree stumps scattered around, ranging between one to five feet in height. The ground was level and relatively shaded, providing a perfect training ground.

"Alright, Jon," Pneuma said, "I have to warn you. Cay has a few years' experience on you, so you're going to have to learn fast to keep up."

Cay gave Jon a sly smile as he stared down at her, and he replied, "That shouldn't be a problem."

Pneuma looked at Cay with a smile of his own and replied, "This should be fun." He walked both eighteen-year-olds out to the center of the clearing, standing them back to back, and said, "Now when I say go, you may grab your swords and begin. Jon, since you're new to this, I want you to listen carefully. Do not hold back. The malorum don't hold anything back, so it won't help Cay if you do." Pneuma noticed the hesitancy still on Jon's face after he said this, so he continued, "It's not like you'd get close anyway. Cay's pretty scrappy." Pneuma smirked again toward the short brunette holding her hand behind her head, ready to grab her weapon's handle.

Jon retorted, "We'll see."

As he reached behind his own head for his sword's handle, Pneuma shouted, "Go!"

Before Jon could even get his sword from its sheath, he felt a solid THUD on the back of his helmet, causing him to stumble forward. Pneuma bellowed in laughter at this sight and still managed to yell back, "Yeah! We'll see alright."

After a few attempts at reaching for his own weapon, Jon finally managed to free his sword from its resting place. He reestablished his footing and turned to face his miniature adversary, only to find her standing on a foot-tall stump a few yards away. She was now the same height as Jon, so his advantage diminished. As he stared at her with a frustrated look upon his face, she yelled back in her raspy voice, "Aw, did that hurt?" At this taunt, Jon sprinted forward with his sword raised above his head. As soon as he was a couple feet away, Cay jumped from her perch and somersaulted over his head. Before landing, she smacked the back of his head once again with the flat side of her sword, causing him to stumble into the tree stump. He did his own somersault over it; however, his landing was not as graceful as Cay's. He laid on his back, looking up toward the forest canopy and collecting his thoughts before returning to the action.

The Battle

When he finally sat up, he realized an unusual audience had assembled around the perimeter of the clearing. Various animals looked on to see what all the commotion was about. Even though the audience was composed of just deer, squirrels, birds, and other animals, Jon still did not wish to let them down. He sprang to his feet, clutching his sword firmly in his hand, and began searching around for the raspy-voiced brunette. Little did he know, she was hiding behind a larger stump, completely covered from view.

Jon walked around, growing more impatient every passing minute, until she decided to sneak up on him. He heard the nearly inaudible footsteps approaching from behind, and before she could slap the back of his head again, he swept the legs out from under her, earning him applause from Pneuma. A smirk shot across Jon's face, but quickly evaporated after Cay jumped back to her feet, separated her sword into two, and slapped each side of his head with the sides of them. Pneuma gave louder applause for this, and Jon could not help but laugh. Cay bowed toward her audience and faced Jon, who was returning to his feet. They circled around the shaded area, both waiting for the other to strike, until they heard something rustling in the bushes nearby. The surprising noise even caused Pneuma to peer past them and into the tree line. As he started walking toward it to investigate, a similar noise from behind him caused the forest animals to scatter. Pneuma grabbed for his sword as several other noises could be heard around the clearing. Jon and Cay joined Pneuma in the center with their backs facing each other, each adjusting their grip on their respective swords. Jon looked over to his forest guide to see him smiling.

Jon nervously asked him, "What's going on?"

Pneuma looked out into the forest as he answered, "They know you're here. They can smell your fresh armor."

"Who?" Jon asked, now with his knees shaking.

"The malorum, silly. It's time to see what you've got," Pneuma said with the smile still on his face.

"What? I'm not ready yet! I just started training. I don't know how to fight!" Jon started nervously looking all around, hoping this was just some sort of initiation.

"If you've got the armor, then you're ready. The King wouldn't waste all that on somebody he didn't trust. Just trust your instincts. I'm here to help," Pneuma calmly answered back.

Instead of raising a rebuttal, Jon closed his eyes and took a deep breath. He remembered that this is what he volunteered for. The armor he wore was not for show; its purpose was to get dirty and have blood painted on it. As he breathed, every sound around him faded to background noise. All he could hear now was the sound of air entering his nostrils and leaving past his chapped lips. As he relaxed, the sound of his heart beating against the chainmail blanketing his chest began to fill his ears.

He opened his eyes to see shadows, slightly smaller than Cay, emerging from the tree line. Jon pressed his thumb against the sword, where Pneuma had showed him, and peeled the two finely crafted weapons apart. He held their handles tightly and stood relaxed with Pneuma and Cay. The leather straps of his shield fastened themselves tightly around his forearm, freeing his left hand to fully grasp the sword's handle.

"Here they are, Jon. Kill or be killed," Pneuma's gravelly voice drummed the war anthem on Jon's ear drums as the malorum came into view.

The Battle

They stood no higher than five feet tall and were covered in the darkest shade of black anyone could dream up. There was a total of nine malorum standing at the edge of the tree line, surrounding the three of them. Long, black, oily hair came from their heads, slightly covering their human-like faces. At the tops of their heads, resting on their stringy hair, were crowns made of fool's gold that resembled the princes or kings they never were. They had bodies of men, some appeared malnourished while others were stoutly built, with armor embedded in their chests. Their mouths hung open, exposing their sharp black teeth. On their backs were tattered wings with all sorts of foliage stuck to them, rendering them incapable of flight. Some of them had scorpion-like tails protruding from under their wings, all of which had their tips broken off. They stood on two legs, hunched over and panting as they surrounded the three warriors that volunteered to kill them.

"It looks like we each get three," Pneuma said, sounding as though he wished for more, as they slowly approached. Jon and Cay both nodded, each with a smile confidently displayed on their faces. "Go for their hearts."

The first malorum broke the ranks and sprinted toward Jon. An overcast sky darkened the clearing. The rogue malorum was fifty feet from Jon, snarling more loudly the closer it got. However, Jon was unfazed. He whispered to his forest guide, "Trust your instincts, eh?" before he smiled and ran full speed toward the beast coming for him. When they were within a few feet of each other, Jon jumped to the side and, with one motion, decapitated the enemy. Its momentum carried the headless body a few more steps before colliding with the ground.

"Remember its heart, Jon," a raspy voice said behind. Jon obliged and thrust his other sword through its back where the heart was located. "Good job," Cay said, and Jon smiled back at her.

Jon looked down at both of his swords to see black liquid like he had noticed on Pneuma's blades earlier in the day. He could not inspect it for long, because the fallen malorum's reinforcements were quickly approaching to avenge its death. Jon did not have time to return to where Pneuma and Cay stood, so he planted his feet and readied himself for the next attack, hoping his instincts would kick in. As soon as Jon repositioned his hands, the next malorum was in the air. Jon waited for it to get closer before acting.

Just when it was right in front of him, Jon raised his shield to pummel the muscular enemy across the face. It was knocked to the ground and lay there unconscious before Jon forced his sword underneath its breastplate, into its heart.

The next two arrived in the same manner. They propelled themselves off of nearby tree stumps into the air toward Jon. His back was turned to them, still making sure the second one was dead. They hovered over him, about to land on his shoulders, but at the last moment Jon, with his back still turned, held both his swords up in the air to impale both malorum. Their breastplates had been cracked from previous battles, making it easy for Jon's swords to go right through. Their bodies slid lifelessly down to the swords' hilts as their blood streamed down to cover his once-glimmering weapons. Jon disposed of them by lowering his arms and sliding his painted weapons from his enemy's chests. Jon stood there with his blackened swords and his smudged shield, ready for the rest of them to arrive. He felt an abundance of confidence rush over him. It was a culmination of all the years he spent observing the soldiers from within his cage's confines. He no longer had sticks to practice with.

The remaining five malorum seemed to learn from their fallen comrades' rash decision making, because, instead of sprinting or leaping toward Jon, they surrounded him before attacking. Unfazed, Jon stood there with a smile still plastered across his face, aggravating the malorum even more. Jon lowered his swords and placed them firmly in the ground, provoking the enemy behind him to attack. As it rushed forward, the straps on his forearm loosened. Without hesitation Jon slid his arm out, grabbed hold of his shield with both hands, stepped to the side, and smacked the stumbling enemy on the back of the head. To Jon's convenience, the enemy fell forward onto one of the swords' handles. The sturdy metal went straight through its chest to leave it lifelessly hunched over where it landed.

Jon looked at the enemy straight ahead of him, re-secured his shield, and began running toward it. He rolled over top of his recent kill and grabbed hold of the free sword still planted in the ground next to him. As he came up to face his enemy, he flung his sword toward it, lodging it within its breastplate. Unlike the rest of his attempts, the sword did not go completely through. The enemy's armor held it in place. Jon panicked as another malorum began running at him. He ran over to the enemy which was attempting to dislodge his sword from its chest, grabbed hold of its handle, and swung the enemy around to provide himself with a barrier from the newest challenger. Jon used his shield to knock the malorum, out and finished pushing his sword through its chest until the metal protruded from its back. He then sprinted toward the approaching enemy and pierced it, too, with the exposed metal, making a malorum shish kabob on his sword.

Two now remained from the original nine, and they were cautiously approaching Jon, whose swords were both incapable of being used. Every attempt he made to dislodge his sword from the two malorum proved to be inadequate. He turned around to face the remaining enemies with his hands still firmly grasping his handle. They seemed to notice he was having difficulty, so they began running toward him. Jon, whose confidence was steadily decreasing, would occasionally check over the dead malorum's shoulders to check how close they were as he continued trying to retrieve his weapon. They got within feet of him before Jon conceived a brilliant idea. He grabbed hold of the sword's hilt firmly with both hands, jumped into the air, and dropkicked both of the lifeless bodies from his blade, sending them into the oncoming enemies. Everyone fell to the ground just a few feet from one another. His sword was now free, and Jon was the first to his feet, frustrated that it took so long to retrieve the gift Pneuma had given him the day before. The treasured gift was no longer shining, glimmering, or clean. Deep black, sticky blood covered every part of it.

As he looked down at his sword, the two remaining malorum were pushing off their fallen comrades and returning to their feet. Jon walked forward with a cynical grin on his face. The malorum froze where they stood, unsure of what to do. Jon could tell they wanted to run away, so he ran toward them. His assumption proved to be correct, as they turned to run for the tree line. Not wanting them to escape, Jon ran harder. Both of their broken tails were flailing behind them as they wove between tree stumps. Jon continued until he got close enough to reach out and grab one of their tails. The enemy made a terrible sound as Jon immediately slammed on his brakes, coming to a screeching halt. Its partner turned to see the next scene unfold before its eyes.

Holding its tail in one hand, Jon used his free hand to grab his sword, point it at the fleeing enemy, and then drive it through the captured malorum's heart. After watching his partner fall lifelessly to the ground, the remaining enemy scurried off into the forest and out of view.

As soon as it left, the clouds opened up and let their contents spill down upon the forest clearing. As soon as Jon closed his eyes and lifted his face toward the sky, he felt a metal object be lightly placed on his shoulder. It was his second sword's handle. He grabbed hold of it and smiled at its return. He turned around to see who retrieved it for him, and to his amusement he saw Pneuma standing there eating a snack.

"Way to leave some for the rest of us, rookie," Pneuma playfully said.

"Where have you guys been?" Jon exclaimed in return.

Cay joined them, holding a coconut in her hand, and answered, "Well I got thirsty and Pneuma got hungry, so we sat and watched."

Jon could not believe what he was hearing, so he tried to dislodge any possible water that was clogging his ears. Trying to understand what Cay said, he asked, "You were thirsty? What do you mean *you were thirsty*?"

"And hungry," Pneuma motioned to the food in his hand.

"Please accept my apologies; *and hungry*," Jon sarcastically added.

"It looked like you were having so much fun," Cay politely answered back.

"But I could have died!" Jon failed to see their logic.

"Ha! Yeah you could've! But you didn't. Right?" Pneuma said in a matter-of-fact kind of way. "And besides, if you were in any real trouble, we could have easily put down the coconut and berries to help you out."

"I don't even know what to say right now." Jon began trying to fit his swords together as he walked away, murmuring something under his breath.

"Hey, Jon!" Pneuma yelled after him. Jon turned around to see Pneuma and Cay nonchalantly smiling and holding up their lunch. "That was really fun to watch! Good work!"

"Yeah! Good work!" Cay hollered as well.

Jon raised one of his swords, gave a slightly frustrated smile, and answered back, "Thanks!" He sat on a nearby stump and continued trying to fit his swords back together as Pneuma and Cay patiently went over to join him.

"We got you some lunch, too." Cay reached into one of her utility belt pouches to pull out a handful of blackberries and passed them to her fellow soldier.

"Thank you." Jon accepted the gift and began to calm down and appreciate that he was indeed still alive. Cay smiled and sat on the ground next to him while Pneuma passed him a coconut.

After he guzzled down some water and berries, Pneuma asked Jon, "So, how'd it feel?"

"Relieving," Jon replied back almost instantaneously.

"Really? How so?" Pneuma asked.

The Battle

Jon looked up from his snack and said, "I just…I mean…I've never done anything like that before. I've only watched other people fight while I was in my cage, and that is all I could do. Occasionally those things would run into my cage and get hurt, but I was never actively fighting. It just felt relieving to know…that the King didn't make a mistake thinking I could contribute."

"You looked so natural out there," the girl with the raspy voice chimed in while Jon's head was still raised.

Jon smiled at her, said thank you, and dropped his sights onto the coconut in his hands. "It felt really good," he continued with a laugh. "I didn't want to stop, but also what motivated me more was that I didn't want them to hurt either of you."

Silence filled the air for a moment until Pneuma playfully nudged his arm and said, "Well, you *did* let one get away."

After the three of them filled the forest's clearing with laughter, Cay added, "Well you had to leave one. Didn't you?" Jon's laughter came to a halt when he heard this and asked for clarification. "What I mean is, how are the rest of the malorum going to know who you are if there's not one to tell the story?"

Pneuma nodded and looked over at a somber-looking Jon. "I can hear him now, 'Everyone listen! There's a new guy out there. He's fresh from the cage. Goes by the name Jon Smith. Watch out for this guy.'" The laughter started back up again as Jon thought about what they were saying.

Several minutes passed before the laughter ceased, which gave Pneuma a chance to whisper in Jon's ear, "Make the enemy remember you in the right way." Jon nodded in understanding, and the three of them got to their feet. "Let's go find some water to drink. You look thirsty, Jon." Pneuma looked at Jon and motioned to the trees behind them. "Everyone have their shields?" Pneuma asked. Jon and Cay raised theirs to show their guide. "Very good. Follow me." The three of them ventured off into the forest with rain still pouring down on them and everything within close proximity. Along the way Jon and Cay did not really say much to each other, since they were transfixed on what was happening around them. Trees were swaying. Birds were singing. Animals were playing with their siblings, paying no attention to how drenched they were getting. It was simple and relaxed. There were no malorum around, and Pneuma's sword was quietly taking a much needed nap.

  They walked a while until Jon could hear the faint sound of rushing water ahead of them. Cay seemed to hear it at the same time, because she looked over to him with a smile on her face. Jon remembered that last time this occurred as he followed behind Pneuma. This time he knew to appreciate the remainder of their walk instead of sprinting forward. Pneuma turned around to face Jon and, almost as if he knew the decision Jon made by not running forward, said, "Well done, Jon." It was as though the roots the water made previously inside his chest began sprouting, filling Jon with a sense of accomplishment.

  They had reached the waterfront just as the rain subsided, and to Jon's bewilderment it was the same location as he had been in the night before. The waterfall was on his and Cay's left, and the oasis was to their right. Pneuma stood facing them with a bright grin on his face and his arms out wide, as if to say, "You remember this place?"

  Jon smiled and answered, "This is where you took me last night." He turned to Cay and excitedly explained, "This was where I slept last night, under my shield. When I woke up this morning, he was here with the enemy's blood on him."

"You probably can't tell since it was a lot darker, but that was the same path we took last night." Pneuma motioned down the path they just walked.

"Was that the clearing that I saw you working on my sword in as well?" Jon asked as he looked back into the trees.

"It is. I wanted to see how differently you'd act this time around," Pneuma answered.

While this conversation was happening Cay was smiling the entire time. She looked around at all the places Pneuma and Jon pointed to and said, "You should start making a list of all these 'coincidences', Jon."

Jon laughed and said, "I'll probably not be able to keep track of them all by the time the battling is over."

Pneuma agreed and started helping Jon remove his helmet.

Jon rested his sword, shield, helmet, and his boots on the moss-covered ground by the river as Pneuma and Cay turned to watch him take of his socks. He removed them one by one, so nonchalantly, seemingly unaware of what he was doing. It was not until his feet touched the ground that he realized what he had done.

"How does it feel?" Pneuma asked as Jon stared blankly at his feet wiggling on the ground.

"It feels…like I'm home." Jon smiled and looked up at Pneuma and a tear stricken Cay. She too had taken her helmet off, showing off her long brunette hair. Jon stood up, and she smiled. "Why are you crying?" he asked her.

She could not speak, so Pneuma answered for her, "She spent a lot of time doing everything she could do to help you out of your cage."

Jon walked over to her, hugged her tightly, and whispered in the most heartfelt way, "Thank you."

She nodded in return, dried her tears, and playfully said, "You smell awful." The three of them each bent over laughing as Jon released his grasp and stumbled toward the river to clean himself off.

"I'll take that as a 'You're welcome' then, I suppose," Jon playfully said back as he stood next to Pneuma.

As Jon stooped down to clean his armor, Pneuma asked Cay, "Could you get down three coconuts and get them ready for us please?" Cay nodded, walked over to the same tree Jon had climbed earlier, and gave it a slight nudge. The palm tree barely shook, and three full coconuts fell gently to the ground.

Jon glanced over just in time to see this happen, to which he exclaimed, "What was that? You mean...I could have just nudged it?"

Pneuma smiled at him and answered, "You have a lot to learn." Cay picked their drinks up and walked over, winking at her fellow soldier with the look of astonishment on his face.

"So what else have I done wrong?" Jon humbly asked, still washing his sword's hilt.

"It's not that you've done anything wrong, just...made things harder than they needed to be," Cay said as she sat down and passed out their shares.

"Ok, so what could I have done better?" Jon looked at the both of them with an eagerness to learn.

Cay looked at her forest guide as he answered, "Well, during that fight back there, you could have waited for them to come to you

The Battle

instead of chasing one down. Don't get me wrong, it looked sweet and all, but you're going to start seeing bigger malorum on the battlefield that you'll need help to defeat. It also doesn't make much sense to run away from those that are there to help you. It leaves them with blind spots they thought were covered."

"I didn't even think of that. I'm sorry," Jon apologized.

"It's alright...this time," Cay playfully answered.

"So what are these 'bigger malorum'?" Jon asked after nudging Cay over.

"Well those ones that you defeated are average-sized ones. They could be anywhere from slightly shorter than those to a couple hundred feet tall," Pneuma said.

"There are also flying ones," Cay chimed in, sticking her tongue out at Jon.

"Flying ones?" Jon nervously asked.

"Yeah, they are smaller than the dragon Iam claimed the arm of," Pneuma answered.

"So there are other dragons out there?" Jon, even more nervous, asked.

"Yeah, they breathe fire and everything!" Cay answered back, trying to intimidate Jon.

"I can't kill those!" Jon exclaimed.

"Iam did," Pneuma said nonchalantly.

"Well he's Iam. I can't do that!" Jon answered as he moved on to clean his dirtied shield.

"The thing about Iam is that he didn't defeat anything that we can't defeat. If he killed a monster, then we can too. It's simple," Cay said with a more sobered look.

"But how am I supposed to know how to kill one of those?" Jon asked.

"It'll come to you when it's time." Pneuma began drinking his coconut milk as he watched Jon process this information.

Jon finished cleaning his armor and boots after drinking the last drops of his milk. Jon and Cay passed their shells to Pneuma so he could crack them open as the three of them sat along the riverbank with their feet dangling in the water. They stayed there until Jon turned to Pneuma and asked, "What should I expect on the battlefield?"

"Good question." Pneuma stood up and discarded the remainder of the coconut shells. "Expect everything that's not good. Smells, tastes, sights, sounds, you name it...it's out there. Every malorum wants you dead or in your cage. They don't care what time of day it is or where you are. They have their orders. You have to remember; they failed to keep you in your cage, and this does not make their boss happy. Also keep your eyes open for help. There are a lot of soldiers that need help fighting, but they either run from you or refuse your offers. It's much different out there than it is in the forest."

Jon nodded his head after he and Cay stood up and said, "Thank you."

"There are more things that I'll fill you in on along the way, but that should be it for now. Just remember that you all have the same mission and the same enemy. Good?"

"Good." Jon nodded.

"Make sure you keep your eyes open. I'm going to go back on patrol, but I'll be around." Pneuma firmly shook Jon's hand, hugged

Cay, and turned back into the forest just as he had done the previous night.

    Jon stood with Cay by the river as he looked around at the trees swaying westward in the wind, motioning in the direction he was to travel. Cay smiled up at them to give thanks and led the way onto a dirt-covered path nearby. As they traveled Jon occasionally checked behind him to watch the oasis fade away until the sound of the waterfall could not be heard any longer.

R.W. Allen

Chapter 6:
The Battlefield

They walked until they could see the end of the tree line. After standing motionless for several minutes Cay turned to Jon and said, "Make sure you have a tight grip on your sword Jon, and keep your shield up." Jon, standing to the right of Cay, dried his sweaty hands on his pants and gripped his sword as tightly as he possibly could. Cay could tell his hands were shaky by the sound of his key vibrating on the side of the sword's hilt, so she continued, "Don't be afraid. There are more on our side than they have on theirs. Trust the King."

At this Jon proceeded forward with Cay at his side. They stood at the imaginary threshold which separated the forest from the battlefield. While his eyes were closed, Jon repeated Pneuma's words to himself, "Kill or be killed." He opened his eyes and looked at Cay before they took the next step forward together.

As Jon's foot touched the much harder, rockier ground of the battlefield, a single poison-tipped arrow grazed the right side of his helmet, leaving a trail of black liquid smeared on his freshly cleaned equipment. The screaming noise it made caused Jon to focus his attention on what was in front of him. The phrase "keep your eyes open" seemed to carry plenty of weight at the moment as Jon frantically started looking around for the enemy that had aimed for his head. His heartbeat was the only thing he could hear as Cay rushed him behind the nearest boulder. He stood there staring back at the trees, which were still in the breezeless atmosphere. He wished to be back where he felt so secure. Meanwhile, Cay was attempting to shake him back into consciousness, but her attempts were of no avail until she raised her sword above her head to give a solid "SMACK" on the top of his head. This seemed to do the trick, because Jon could hear more than his heartbeat again. "What happened?" he asked.

"You're in a war, remember? Get up!" Cay hollered at him over the sounds of explosions, yelling, and clanging of metal around him.

"So what do I do?" Jon asked, still trying to get his bearings, occasionally being interrupted by the potent smells of sulfur and other noxious fumes.

"What do you think? You fight," Cay sarcastically said as she was looking toward the battlefield. "Oh! There he is. Follow me."

"There's who? Where are we going?" Jon struggled to his feet.

"Keep your shield up!" Cay exclaimed as another arrow bounced off the large boulder they took refuge behind. Jon kept his head down, raised his shield, and sped off after Cay. She led him behind other boulders, just like the one they had been behind before, on a quest to reach someone Jon did not know.

"Are we almost to him?" Jon yelled amidst the noise surrounding them.

"Yes! He's just right over there!" Cay pointed around the boulder they crouched behind. "Odas! Hey Odas! I need your help over here when you get a chance!" Cay hollered out.

In a matter of seconds Jon could feel a slight vibration in the ground preceding a deep voice asking, "Is he here?"

Cay answered, "He's with me behind this boulder. Something is shooting arrows at his head. Could you please help?"

"I see it over there on another boulder." Not even a second passed after Odas replied that the large boulder Jon was taking shelter behind lifted off the ground and was hurled through the air in the direction of the malorum shooting the arrows. The large rock collided violently into the malorum, sending it off its perch and into a crowd of its friends—killing them all. "That should do it." Odas dusted his hands off over Jon's helmet, getting it even dirtier than it had been, and said, "So this is him…with all his armor on and everything." Odas was smiling down at a hunched-over Jon, still with his shield raised while the sound of arrows hitting metal filled the air.

Odas was a massive, powerfully built man with a full, unkempt, red and brown beard. He was a couple of inches taller than Jon and had little body fat to account for. His vest, helmet, belt, pants, and boots were the same colors as Jon's, but he instead chose not to wear a shirt underneath his vest, exposing arms as big as Jon's midsection. He, too, had a tightly wrapped keychain around his right arm; however, neither of his hands was holding sword. They were wrapped tightly with his tattered and dirtied cloth that matched his shirt, from which the sleeves were missing. His dark green helmet, which snuggly covered his head, was deeply stained with blackened dirt and blood he collected from battle. His sword, which also resembled Jon's—only slightly larger—was tucked away behind him while his shield was fastened to its handle. The sounds of arrows being deflected to the ground rang melodiously through the air. "Are you going to stand up then, bud?" he asked.

Jon lowered his shield and stood up to face this colossal man. The large shadow that he cast allowed Jon to gain a full appreciation of the man whom disposed of the malorum that had attempted to put a poisonous arrow though his head. Upon seeing Odas's full stature, Jon's jaw dropped, provoking Odas to say, "Don't worry, bud. I'm on your side." Jon smiled while Cay and Odas's laughter drowned out the sounds of the arrows deflecting off the large man's shield.

"I remember you," Jon softly said.

"What was that?" Odas and Cay had both stopped laughing to give attention to Jon.

"I remember you…from before I got all of this." Jon thought back to his days of being in his cage. "You helped me."

"You're right, bud," Odas smiled cheerfully, "so you goin' to give me a hug or what? We gotta hurry because we got some killin' to do!" Jon approached Odas cautiously, only to have the large man lift him a couple feet off the ground in a moment of uncontrolled excitement. His vest absorbed much of the force, but there was still a considerable amount that reached Jon's ribcage. The sounds of the repetitious clanging of the arrows seemed to be playing an annoying tune on Odas's eardrums, because after he returned Jon to a standing position, he instantly turned around and caught the next two arrows by their stems and hurled them back at their shooters, piercing their throats. "They really do have awful aim. I mean, how big am I and they can't hit anything but my shield?" He turned back to Jon, "They are not very intelligent creatures, bud."

"They still follow orders from a one-armed boss, what does that tell you?" Cay added as she watched around their perimeter for any other malorum with ill intent.

Odas nodded in agreement and turned back to Jon. "Well now that you're here, and we established they need some sense driven into them, we can go kill things." As the last word left his mouth, the bearded man turned back around to catch a mid-sized boulder being hurled in their direction. He threw it back at its sender, decapitating it. "I will teach you many fun ways of dismembering these filthy things. Just keep your eyes open and you will learn tons." Jon smiled, nodded, and turned to Cay to see if he was making the right choice.

She whispered to him, "He may have an unconventional way of doing things, but for the most part," she looked at Odas's hands bleeding through their cloth bandages, "they are effective."

Just after she said that, a poorly assembled grenade was on track to land in their midst. Odas noticed it in time and caught it in his hands, clasping them tightly around it. A couple of seconds passed, and Jon heard a faint explosion accompanied by a puff of smoke escaping from Odas's grasp. He opened his hands, dusted off the metal shards from his cloth-wrapped palms and turned back to survey the land after exclaiming, "You have got to be kidding me! They're playing with kids toys." He turned his head toward Cay and asked, "Are we ready to go, madam?"

She looked over at Jon, who was now smiling, and answered, "I do believe so, sir."

"Alright follow me." Odas led Cay and Jon from where they were standing to a different section of the battlefield on a fairly large hill.

The Battle

Jon could now see the field since he did not have his shield covering his face. He could see how vast and almost endless it truly was. There were hills and shallow valleys throughout the land, as well as random patches of trees and ponds. Many individual and group battles were being fought all around where Odas, Cay, and Jon walked. There were malorum running around and stealthily peering over embankments, unaware of the soldiers that waiting for their grotesque heads to rise just a few more inches into their sights. There were also dead and dismembered enemies scattered all around, providing the land with a less than ideal form of fertilizer. The amount of limbs no longer attached to their owners was only outnumbered by the amount of decapitated malorum heads lying around unattended.

As they trod along, Jon also noticed many pieces of armor scattered and covered in dirt and blood, belonging to both human and malorum. Discarded swords shone in the muted light of the overcast sky, while shields of various sizes wobbled freshly on the ground. Jon was beginning to notice that this was not only a land of fallen malorum, but it was also a land of fallen soldiers.

Odas and Cay knew how important it was for Jon to know his surroundings, so they provided him with cover so he could get a lay of the land. They were once in the same place he had been, a day removed from the binding construct simply referred to as a "cage", so they could understand how much of a shock the smells, sounds, and sights were after being totally submerged in the culture of the forest.

It was a different place out on the battlefield. Jon could hear screams around him, provoking his head to whip around toward their origins. He heard war cries and the sounds of slain malorum mixed throughout. The smells of fire and sulfur filled his nose, less potent than before. The sights of death and small victories filled his eyes and were being filed away as memories as he absorbed the physical appearances of his new playground, but there was something that stuck out to him as he marched along.

    He had seen cages littered around the battlefield while he walked, but there was one that stood out. Its appearance was relatively similar to those surrounding it, although it could have possibly had a few more spikes and shards of glass welded to it, but Jon could not keep his eyes from going back to it. It was as though it were magnetically bonded to his attention. Odas and Cay were too busy to notice that after walking several feet they would have to slow their gait slightly so Jon could catch back up. He wanted to go up to it and see who the shadowy figure inside was, but he was not yet mentally prepared enough to venture from his fellow soldiers. For now all he could do was to try to stay focused on the task at hand, and that was to absorb the sights around him—without putting Odas and Cay in the precarious position of having to unnecessarily get stabbed or shot while protecting him.

    The three of them had finally reached the base of a fairly large hill, which had been flattened on its pinnacle, to provide the King's soldiers a much-needed vantage point. "We'll be able to rest for a short while up there." After the large, bearded man pronounced this, they climbed the rocky face of the hill to gain temporary relief from the arrows and rocks being hauled in their direction.

    After a relatively simple climb, Jon was able to see more of what he had just walked through, since a majority of his time was spent focused on the mysterious cage he had hoped to investigate more of later. He was truly on a battlefield. The stench of decay lingered in his nose while the sights and sounds of war surrounded him. The most horrible noises were coming from just a few hundred feet away causing Jon to have a death grip on his sword. He could see individual soldiers quivering under their shields while dozens of malorum relentlessly banged on them as though they were drums. Small groups of soldiers were being chased around, stumbling over each other, trying to reach some sort of sanctuary. He could see extremely large monsters, some as big as fifty feet tall, terrorizing groups of unprepared warriors. All the while, patches of rain fell upon the field below in attempts to aid those that were fighting, by washing away the malorum, while also providing the soldiers with momentary refreshment. Several times Jon scanned parts of the battlefield to find what appeared to be vast stretches of shadows covering the land, but upon further inspection he realized these were actually large groups of mangled metal cages, each one with its own occupant.

    It seemed as though his eyes would have no relief from the torturous sights he was witnessing until he turned toward the vast mountains behind him. Just as his shoulders were beginning to slouch, Jon could just barely piece together the silhouettes of large eagles dispersing from their tower and throughout the land. He watched as one of them swiftly flew over his head, swooped down the side of the hill, and hovered over a soldier kneeling beneath his shield. With a few flaps of its wings, the brown and white eagle brushed away the surrounding malorum and reached down to grab hold of its cargo.

    In the same way as it arrived, it left by soaring toward the sanctuary within the castle walls. With a smile beaming across his face, Jon's eyes navigated throughout the land to see more of the same. Soldiers were being carried off toward the garden to meet with their King, leaving the malorum dumbfounded and sprawled out on the ground. They were rescued, even if it was just for a moment. The malorum that were left soon got their wits about them and moved on to the next soldiers to fight. Some of them wound up being defeated by their new combatants, while others experienced the same result as they had before with their enemy flying away to be temporarily in the King's presence.

"This is actually it, then," Jon silently uttered the words under his breath while taking a panoramic view of all that was happening.

"This is it," Odas responded.

"It's like we're in a movie, isn't it?" Jon asked while he soaked it all in.

"Or a book," Cay said in a quiet voice as the three of them stood around, looking out at their comrades pressing on.

"Well by the looks of it, this story is about to get a little bit more interesting." Odas's face lit up at the sight of nine malorum ascending the hill toward them. The enemies encircled their small camp, just as nine others had done in the forest earlier in the day.

When Cay had noticed them as well, she turned to Jon and said with a sheepish grin, "Now remember, don't you go running off again."

Jon playfully stuck his tongue out at her as one of the malorum lifted his head into view. The battle started off with Odas reaching over his head for his shield, grabbing it with both hands, and smashing it down over the first malorum's head. The enemy's head became lodged inside its chest, instantly dying, as it slid down the hillside and past the others on their way up. Odas stepped back to rejoin Cay and Jon, bellowing, "That had to hurt!" Although Jon would have liked for that to deter the other malorum from their pursuits, it only seemed to encourage them to avenge their fallen comrade.

Jon reached behind his back for his sword and separated it just as three more scampered up to surround them. Without hesitation, Cay easily disposed of them in three swings of her sword, which she had just gotten from its holster a few seconds before Jon thought to reach for his. The five remaining malorum arrived at the top of the hill as the three Cay slayed fell to the ground below.

The overcast sky loomed above, waiting to shower the soldiers with its tears the moment the final malorum tumbled down the face of the rocky hill. Odas noticed its rumbling and motioned to Jon, "You don't want to keep our audience waiting, bud. We've got five more 'til we can celebrate."

Jon looked up at the light show occurring within the clouds waiting to release their contents upon the victorious party. "Kill or be killed, right?"

"Right! Watch your back; one's trying to sneak up on you bud!" Odas shouted as he claimed another malorum's life with another swing of his shield. He sent its head sailing upward and out of view while its body lay lifeless at his feet.

Jon turned around to find the culprit creeping toward him with a rusted dagger in its grasp. He secured his two swords together as the malorum quickened its pace. The leather straps holding the dark green shield on Jon's left forearm loosened, and the shield slid down to his hand, ready to be used. The malorum ran toward Jon with the dagger held tightly in both of his hands, coming within arm's length of Jon. Once he noticed it was close enough Jon swung his shield upward, just as Odas had done moments before, to cause the malorum to fall backward and send the rusted dagger skyward. The malorum rolled on the ground, dazed and confused, until its own dagger returned to stab it through the chest. It was not the same effect Jon had been hoping for when he visualized the attack in his mind, nonetheless it was effective in accomplishing the task at hand.

As Jon stood there, looking down at his kill, he heard a voice shouting, "Duck!" He fell to the ground as fast as he could to see Odas's giant hand swat a smaller malorum away from behind him. It was silently approaching with its own dagger, ready to stab Jon in the neck until Odas interfered with its plans. The smaller enemy flew through the air with greater ease than then previous two the giant man had disposed of. Jon nervously glanced up at his fellow soldier to hear him say, "You gotta keep your eyes open, bud."

Just as Odas began to tuck his shield away behind his back Cay plunged her sword through the malorum creeping up on him. The large man felt the splatter of blood reach the back of his neck, and he whipped around to watch the enemy fall to the ground. "You gotta keep your eyes open, *bud*," the raspy-voiced girl said in a playful tone. In an ironic manner Odas suddenly thrust his fist past Cay's ear to punch a malorum's head. It had its dagger raised, ready to thrust it into her neck, until Odas saved her. He lifted it from the ground as it dangled lifelessly from his clenched hand and threw it down the hillside to join its other fallen comrades.

Odas smiled back at Cay and agreed, "That is very good advice. Thank you." Cay, less than amused but also terribly grateful, nodded back toward Odas to express her appreciation.

The only bodies left standing atop the hill were the three soldiers, slightly dirtied, but none of the blood they now wore was their own. As Jon returned to his feet to join Odas and Cay, the heavy

The Battle

gray clouds above released their contents in a congratulatory fashion, instantly refreshing the soldiers as it touched their skin. Each drop of water set out to clean their hands and armor from any dirt and blood weighing them down. Cay looked skyward, allowing the rain to wash the exposed portions of her face. Jon wiped clumps of mud from his pants and arms while occasionally glancing over in Odas's direction as the large man stared heavily down at his bloodied and poorly bandaged palms. Jon walked over to his larger counterpart and asked, "What's the matter with your hands?"

Before he could answer, Cay walked over and answered on his behalf, "He doesn't use his sword as much as he should." Odas rolled his eyes and let out an occasional groan as the rain fell upon his wounds. "We keep telling him that if he used his sword more, then his hands wouldn't get bloodied so much, but he still doesn't listen."

"It's still effective, isn't it?" Odas shrugged as he winced in pain.

Cay looked over at Jon and whispered, "It's not always effective in the long run."

"I heard that," Odas bellowed before dusting his hands off and continuing, "Look, it got the work done, and I caught that one sneaking up on you."

"I'm not saying, 'always use just your sword,' I'm saying you don't always have to use just your hands. You won't be able to keep it up for long," Cay boldly answered her much larger comrade.

"Alright…well we can continue this later. I have to go help someone near the Dead Woods." Odas bid farewell to Cay and turned toward Jon to say, "Jon, I am honored to fight alongside you. I look forward to seeing you soon." Jon smiled in gratitude as Odas waved to the both of them and walked down the hillside and out of sight.

"He doesn't really like talking about it, does he?" Jon asked Cay as the rain began to slow.

"It's not one of his favorite topics," Cay answered while the two of them began their decent from the hill.

"Why is that?"

"He doesn't think he's as good with his sword as other soldiers," Cay answered.

"So he doesn't even try?" Jon asked as they approached the bottom of the rocky face.

"Well, think about it. With how big he is, I think he's worried he might hit another soldier by accident," Cay answered as the wind began to pick up around them. "I wonder what this is about." She said as she watched an eagle land near them.

Jon curiously whipped his head around in the direction Cay was looking. He stumbled back as the majestic animal came to a stop mere feet from where he stood. Cay took his hand and led him to the side to greet the dark-skinned rider clothed in the same robes Iam wore.

Jon leaned over to Cay and whispered, "Who is this?"

Cay whispered back, "You'll see." She then turned to the rider, who was reaching in a considerably large pouch, and asked with eagerness, "Who is this one for?" He held out a moderately-sized white box to Jon. Jon looked to Cay, unsure whether or not to trust this hooded man. Cay smiled, so Jon reached up to retrieve the box. The rider did not leave immediately, but instead seemed to wait for Jon to open his package. Cay noticed his eagerness to see what

The Battle

the contents were, so she informed Jon, "Go ahead and open it. They never leave until the packages are opened."

"A gift?" Jon thought briefly while he stared down at the plain white box that was no larger than the length of his forearm. After he inspected it for any noise, he flung open its lid to reveal a long brown rope laying down inside of it. Upon realizing what it was, he turned to the rider and Cay and announced, "It's a rope." At this proclamation the rider smiled and lifted into the air. Jon stared at his departure with a puzzled look on his face before going back to the package's contents. "Why do I have a rope?"

"Well take it out and look at it," Cay said while motioning to her fellow soldier. Jon unraveled the rope from its resting place to reveal that it was several feet long and intricately braided. "I remember when I got mine," She continued. "It doesn't look like much, but I assure you it is crazy strong."

"Where's yours?" Jon asked while trying to see if she had it with her.

"I keep it under my vest for whenever I need it," Cay kindly answered back. "You've seen me use it before."

"When am I going to use mine?" Jon stared back down at his newest acquisition while he tried to wind it up.

"You'll know when the time comes. That's the way I was taught." Cay smiled as her confused comrade still trying to wind his rope up.

Finally getting the rope to stay in place, Jon put his head and right arm through its loop and rested it upon his other shoulder. After he figured that out, he turned to Cay and asked, "So who was that?"

"That was a castle messenger. They occasionally visit to bring...well...messages," Cay answered as she surveyed the land around them. "It's getting late. We should go up to the King before going to sleep."

Excited at the idea of going to see the King twice in one day, Jon's face lit up with a smile and exclaimed, "I agree!" After he thought about it for a moment he asked, "So do both of us raise our shields or just one?"

"Both of us do," Cay kindly answered. So they each raised their shields above their heads and closed their eyes. Within moments two large eagles swooped down to retrieve their own packages. Jon and Cay were carried away in the direction of the King, Iam, and the garden.

They arrived within the castle's walls as the sun's glow disappeared under the horizon, but to Jon's amazement he could still sense a light brightly shining through his closed eyelids. He opened them just as the two eagles arrived at the base of the massive tree. The light was coming from tree itself. Lights were neatly strung throughout the branches as well as within the tree where the fountain was located. Jon's face became illuminated as he looked over at his travel companion, who was staring back at him with a glowing face of her own. The entire garden had been lit by lanterns and intricately designed torches. It was as though it was still daylight within the castle walls, although you could still look up and view the stars if you desired. A gentle breeze pushed Jon's attention toward the man he had come to see. Iam stood before the two of them to retrieve their armor as the King left his hammock and walked over to join them. Before leaving them in the King's care, Iam whispered to Jon, "I am glad to see you again." Jon smiled, and Iam walked toward the vacant hammock to place the armor at the tree's base.

"Twice in one day? I could get accustomed to this, I suppose," the deep voice spoke from the mouth of another smiling man. The King now stood before Jon and Cay. "Shall we walk?" The two soldiers nodded their heads as the King passed them each a mug of water. He caressed his own unidentified drink as the three of them navigated along the same path Jon had traveled with him before.

Iam looked on as the three of them strolled through the batches of lavender and peppermint, each taking a moment to smell the clean air. While they talked and laughed, they moved on to briefly view the extraordinarily large vineyard next to the bushes of blueberries. As Jon looked out over the various fruits and vegetables, he asked, "Who picks them all when they're ready?"

"Iam and I do," the King answered.

"Doesn't that take a while?" Jon asked to satisfy his curiosity.

"When you enjoy doing something, you don't pay so much attention to the time. It's as though time doesn't exist." The King smiled as he examined a nearby tomato plant and whispered slightly under his breath, "This one isn't ready yet. Still plenty green." At this answer Jon nodded his head as Cay smiled.

"I have another question," Jon stated.

"You want to ask about the rope you just received?" the King correctly guessed.

"Yes. How did you know?" Jon asked, slightly perplexed. Cay could not help but to laugh as she looked at his confused face.

"I am the one that sent it, you see. What kind of King would I be if I didn't know what was happening to my people?" the King answered.

"So what do I use it for?" Jon figured there would be no harm in asking.

"You will know when the moment comes," the King answered as he plucked a ripened strawberry and handed it to Cay. "I assume she had already told you that much, but there is no harm in double checking." The three of them wound around back toward the river bank and the tree as the King continued, "After you leave here, I am going to send you both to separate places. I need Cay to go somewhere for me tonight."

"Where will I go?" Jon became slightly nervous at the thought of returning to the battlefield alone.

"I will send you back into the forest with Pneuma for the night," the King answered.

Jon's nerves suddenly calmed at the thought of returning to spend time with Pneuma. "I would very much enjoy that."

"Is that alright with you, Cay?" The King asked the raspy-voiced girl. She nodded after looking over at Jon. "You both will know what to do in the morning, but for tonight just get some rest." The three of them had arrived at the base of the tree again to see Iam waiting with their armor in his hands. After a few final words and laughter, Jon and Cay re-equipped themselves with Iam's help and hugged their King.

After grabbing their shields, Jon and Cay hugged one another and raised their hands above their heads. The two eagles, which delivered them moments before, returned and grasped their respective soldiers' shields to raise them off the ground. Jon and Cay both looked once more at the King and Iam before they were carried away toward the castle wall. Jon watched the abundantly lit ground pass by under his feet, completely in awe of its beauty. He looked

The Battle

over at his airborne comrade, just before their eagles were about to diverge into their appointed directions, and smiled. The gesture was returned as the two of them waved and were carried out of each other's view.

R.W. Allen

Chapter 7:
The Prisoner

"Hey! You've come back." Jon could hear Pneuma's familiar voice as he landed on the mossy forest floor. He looked up to see Pneuma standing before him, propped up against a tree. "You know, I could get used to seeing you this often." Jon walked in his direction as he gazed into the sky and watched the eagle soar away. Pneuma could sense Jon was slightly preoccupied, so he asked, "You miss her, don't you?"

"What do you mean?" Jon's attention left the night sky to answer his guide's question.

"Well I mean, you miss Cay don't you?" Pneuma repeated with a slight grin. Jon shifted slightly, giving Pneuma the answer he was searching for. "She's doing the King's work. Don't worry about her." The night air remained silent as Jon looked out into the trees around him, occasionally tugging at his newest acquisition, which still rested across his chest, to ease his mind. "Well that's new!" Pneuma had noticed Jon's rope. "When'd you get that?"

"Just a few moments ago," Jon answered as he sat down on a log near where Pneuma stood.

The Battle

"So it must've been after a nicely fought battle, eh?" Pneuma took his place next to Jon.

"What does that have to do with it?" Jon obliviously inquired.

"A bunch of stuff really, but that means you saw the castle messenger, too, right?" Pneuma subtly steered the conversation in a different direction.

"Right, but..." Jon was still eager to learn how the battle he fought was connected to acquiring the rope.

"All in due time, Jon." Pneuma said. "Those messengers are a curious group of people, aren't they?"

Wondering what he meant, Jon replied, "What do you mean?"

"They never want to leave until they see what the King has them deliver. I only pass by them occasionally now, but I remember when I'd see them all the time when I traveled around. People just aren't fighting like they used to." Pneuma was the one now staring out into the tree line, while Jon hoped he would still share more of their connection.

His hope was to no avail as the two of them sat in silence until Jon asked, "Do you know when or how I'm supposed to use this rope?"

"I do," Pneuma answered.

After moments of waiting for him to elaborate on his answer, Jon impatiently asked, "Could you tell me?"

Pneuma laughed and suggested, "I'm almost certain that you might already know." Jon sat there, examining the inner workings of his mind for a moment, as a gentle breeze picked up around them. It began swirling leaves around at their feet, causing rustling to occur in the branches above their heads. Jon's attempts to answer his own question returned unanswered as Pneuma suddenly rose back to his feet. "Jon, I must go. I'm going to leave you here tonight to lodge. Try not to wander too far off from this spot."

Jon could sense Pneuma felt danger in the area, so he nodded and said, "I won't."

"Good. I'll meet back with you in the morning. Get some good rest." Jon nodded once more, and Pneuma swiftly walked into the wind-blown forest with his sword drawn.

As Jon settled down next to a group of logs, a pair of eyes peered through the trees at him. They belonged to a menacing hooded figure just outside the perimeter of the clearing. Jon was oblivious to this malorum lurking around just few hundred feet from where he decided to make camp for the night. The wind violently rushed in the malorum's direction, causing it to break its gaze and scurry off into the battlefield. The loud wind led Jon to look in its direction, but only after it had already left, so he returned to removing his boots and socks and laid them next to his sword. Jon raised his shield over his head, and, as it had done the night before, it surrounded him in a protective dome to assure him a well-rested night.

The next morning Jon had been awoken by the sound of clanging metal. His shield had been retracted and placed by his side along with his sword, boots, and socks. He looked around for the origin of the noise to find Pneuma sitting on a nearby tree stump sharpening his sword. "Good mornin' to ya! It's about time you opened your eyes."

Jon smiled, searched for his socks, and mumbled, "Good morning."

"I've gotten you some berries, but you were asleep for so long that I got hungry again. Don't worry though, there's a bush a couple hundred feet that way." Pneuma pointed into the forest along an overgrown path.

"Thanks, I think." Jon finished putting on both socks and boots and stood up to stretch. "How was your night?" he asked while yawning.

"It went exceptionally well. There were some malorum disrupting a group a deer by the river, so I had to handle it, but that's usual," Pneuma responded as he checked the sharpness of his blade.

"So the malorum don't just attack the soldiers?" Jon asked as he reached down for his shield.

"Oh no, they like to go after everything in the forest they can get their claws on. I think I've even seen them attack a boulder... Yes, a boulder. Stupid little things they are," Pneuma replied.

"They do seem that way." Jon laughed as he secured his sword behind his head.

"Don't let that fool you though. They are determined to follow orders," Pneuma added before suggesting, "Shall we go get some more berries then?"

Jon nodded, and the two of them headed along the overgrown path to a collection of bushes. As they walked, Jon said to Pneuma, "After we get some food, I want to go see the King."

"That's convenient. He wants you to go up to see him, too," Pneuma responded as they reached a bush abundantly decorated with raspberries. "He has plans for you today."

Several berries fell out of Jon's mouth as his jaw hung open. "He has plans for me? What are they?"

"He'll tell you when you get up there. Don't worry about it," Pneuma nonchalantly replied.

The two of them finished their morning snack before Jon decided his curiosity needed to be quenched. "I think I'm going up now. I want to find what he wants me to do."

After laughing, Pneuma said, "I figured you wouldn't be able to wait long. Don't worry, we can keep talking later." Pneuma smiled as Jon hurriedly shoved a few remaining berries into his mouth. Jon smiled, and they said their goodbyes as he raised his shield in the air. Soon he was being carried off into the morning sky in the direction of the castle.

As was the custom, Jon landed in front of Iam, handed over his armor while Iam handed him his mug of crisp water, and departed with the King, who was sipping his own unidentified drink. The two of them walked and talked for several minutes before Jon asked, "Do you really have something for me to do today? That's what Pneuma told me when I woke up."

The King continued walking at his regular leisurely pace and answered, "Yes that is correct. That is, if you want to go through with it."

"Of course I do!" Jon answered excitedly. "What do you want me to do?"

"Alright then," the King smiled at Jon's enthusiasm and continued, "do you remember that cage you saw yesterday? The one you could hardly take your eyes off of?"

"Yes," Jon curiously but excitedly answered.

The King took another sip of his drink before saying, "Well I would like for you to go back to it for me and help the person who is

The Battle

inside. I care immensely about him, and I would very much enjoy seeing him out again."

"Who is it...on the inside?" Jon asked as the two of them walked along a path Jon had not been down before.

"You will recognize him when you get closer, but I do have to ask you to be patient," the King answered.

"How do I get him out?" Jon asked.

"You will know when you are closer. Please just be careful not to harm him," the King answered as the two of them arrived back at the tree's base.

Iam walked up to return Jon his armor as he said, "I will do my best."

"That is all I ask, but do not underestimate what that is." Jon began processing those words as he secured the last piece of armor around his waist and lifted his shield to await an eagle to carry him away. "The eagle is instructed to carry you to where you need to go, so, as always, hold on tightly to your shield." After this final statement, Jon bid farewell to Iam and the King as a majestically large eagle swooped down and carried him out of view.

Jon did as was suggested and held on tightly to his shield as his carrier flew over the sunlit garden, over the castle wall, and over top the forest's canopy, before it steadily descended toward the tree line of the Dead Woods. Upon realizing where he was headed, Jon grew exceedingly nervous, rendering it more difficult for him to heed the King's advice. He had not been in the Dead Woods since his walk with Iam a couple days earlier.

As he touched down upon the hardened ground the eagle departed, leaving Jon standing there alone just a few feet from the tree line. As Jon watched the silhouette of the eagle fade away, he realized how alone he was this time around. Iam was sitting in his hammock, and Odas and Cay were off doing their own tasks, leaving Jon to feel the cold breeze being emitted from the gray, leafless trees.

    As Jon stood in the midst of all the fighting, he could not help but feel that, on top of everything already happening, he was being watched. Unbeknownst to him, he was right. The same hooded figure from the night before stood against a tree, sharpening tips of arrows while he watched his prey nervously looking around for some sort of comfort. As Jon began running his hand over his helmet's surface he remembered that, while he was alone, he was not unequipped to handle what the King entrusted him with. A confident smile formed across Jon's face as he peered down at the rest of his armor, which caused the malorum to cease sharpening his arrow and slip away unseen in the wood's embrace.

    His nervousness and anxiety quickly faded away, and Jon began looking around for the caged man he was sent to help. He was farther west than he had been the previous day, so he was left to assume the cage had somehow moved closer to the tree line in his absence. Nevertheless, Jon finally located the mangled metal cage amidst a large group of ones just like it. He walked toward it, bypassing many downtrodden people staring blankly at the shards of glass and barbed wire that kept them captive. Many of their cages looked weathered and possessed many scratches, while others appeared untouched from the lack of attempts made to rescue their inhabitants. Jon did not know whether to stay with them or keep pressing on toward the person he was sent to help. He secretly wanted to do both, but he chose to keep walking instead.

    After walking for what seemed to be a couple hundred yards, Jon finally stood before the cage that magnetized his attention for the past twenty-four hours. He inspected the exterior of the cage to discover old wounds that had been carved carelessly into its bars, some of them coming close to damaging the only golden lock Jon could see fastening it together. He leaned over to examine the craftsmanship of the lock only to discover the key dangling from his right hand was levitating toward its keyhole. Without much hesitation Jon obliged its curiosity by placing it into the hole. It was a perfect fit. This was a lock Jon's key was made to fit. He turned the four-sided key gently, causing the lock's grip on itself to loosen. He reached out, took the lock off, and dropped it onto the rocky ground beneath his feet. He did not know what to expect next. Part of him wanted the cage to explode open, rescuing the person inside, while another part of him expected Iam to show up and do his thing. Either way Jon grew increasingly disappointed, as he waited several minutes without anything happening. The only thing which appeared to happen was that a slight breeze blew across his face, seemingly to slap him back into reality. Jon then realized he had to do more. He vaguely remembered the conversation he had with Iam in the castle's tower, reminding him he had to use his sword to break up some of the shrapnel holding the bonds together.

    At this sudden epiphany he began swinging away at its defenses. He continued like this for several minutes, only to grow more frustrated at the lack of progress he was making. Exhausted from his work, Jon found a nearby boulder and sat down against it. He opened one of the pouches on his belt and pulled out a handful of berries he had saved for an occasion like this. As he sat there he looked back toward the cage resisting his attempts. A vacancy showed in its shell to give Jon a glimpse of the person inside. He had realized where he knew this person from. Jon's own cage sat next to his for several years, occasionally to be dragged away now and then by Cay and a couple other soldiers. They made their attempts of rescuing him as well, only to be rejected and cut by the cage's daunting façade. Jon had seen many soldiers approach the man inside, only to be met with the same result.

Jon approached the cage after finishing the remainder of his food and peered through the vacancy closer than before. Inside of it malicious structure lay a middle-aged man dressed in dirt- and blood-stained robes. He stared blankly back at Jon with the same colored eyes and similar facial structure. His muscular arms were folded, showing Jon the multitude of cuts and scars inhabiting them from the carelessness of other soldiers' past attempts. The man's face was no different with the amount of punishment that had been endured. Jon remembered back to the days when his cage sat next this man's. Many conversations were had about the carelessness and the lack of compassion which was shown toward him over the years.

As he sat there remembering the last time he had resided next to the man, a large gust of wind nearly sent him to the ground. Jon mustered the strength to look out toward its source, after shielding his eyes from the debris that was loosed into the air, to see a large eagle descending toward him. Bewildered by this, Jon thought to himself, "I didn't raise my shield. Why is the eagle coming toward me?"

A figure Jon could not see clearly through the haze came into view as the eagle settled itself onto the ground a few feet from where Jon huddled next to the prisoner's cage. The figure, adorned in the same manner as the messenger Jon had received his rope from, dismounted the giant bird and walked toward Jon with a rolled up paper in his hand. "This is from your fellow soldier, Cay," were the

The Battle

only words spoken before the messenger turned around, mounted the eagle once again, and flew off, kicking more debris toward Jon and the man inside the cage.

The eagle soared off toward another area of the beautiful, vast battlefield, seemingly to deliver more letters to their desired recipients, as Jon stood motionless, looking down at his delivery. He finally looked over at the man inside the cage to whisper in a joyous tone, "This is from Cay. I wonder what the King has had her doing." The man, however, did not seem as enthralled. He only stared blankly at his hands. It did not seem to faze Jon, because the next moment he was separating the hardened-berry seal to see what Cay had sent him. It turned out to be a letter, updating Jon with everything she had been sent to do. Jon sat on the boulder he had rested against earlier to read its entirety. He learned that Cay was with a group of soldiers battling a couple dozen malorum near a random patch of forest on the battlefield. Jon read the letter several times before laying it on the boulder beside him. "Cay is fighting off over twenty malorum with a group of soldiers right now. She took a little break to write me this letter letting me know she's doing well and she'll see me tomorrow at the campground if the King permits," he spoke toward the cage to update the prisoner on its contents. However, the man inside the cage was not listening but still staring blankly around. Jon seemed not to notice, because he continued, "She'll see me at the campground tomorrow? I think I remember where that is. I have only been there in the cage before, though. I'll have to ask the King how to get there."

Jon continued rambling on to himself for several more minutes until he was interrupted by the ground slightly vibrating. He instantly stood back up to look for where the source was coming from only to see Odas rushing past, yelling, "Move!" Jon fell back to the ground to witness Odas tackling a group of three malorum sneaking up on him. After violently disposing of all three he walked back toward Jon, dusting the dirt from his hands. "You really have to start keeping your eyes open out here, bud. You're going to wind up hurt real bad if ya don't."

Shocked by Odas's sudden appearance, Jon slowly returned to his feet with wide eyes. "How long had those been there?"

"I only saw them for a little while before rushing over," Odas answered while he re-bandaged his hands.

"How did you know...I mean..." Jon stammered while collecting himself.

"I saw the eagle leave. You can't really miss it, and I saw those three coming toward you after the wind settled," Odas answered before Jon could finish collecting himself.

"I had no idea," Jon started looking around as he clenched his letter tightly. "Thank you."

"I'm glad I was still in the area, or else I would have been seein' ya in the infirmary later." Odas directed his attention toward the paper being held tightly in Jon's hand, "What do ya have there?"

Jon opened his hand and straightened out the letter, "It's a message from Cay. She was telling me of what's been happening with her."

"I think I saw her and a group of soldiers fighting a bunch of malorum as I flew back from the castle. I wanted to join them, but it looked like they had everything pretty much covered." Jon smiled at this second reassurance that Cay had been doing well. "Well who do we have here?" Odas turned around to see the cage Jon had been spending his entire afternoon around.

"The King sent me here to help him. I remember him from when I was in my cage." Jon answered as he folded up his letter and secured it away into an empty pouch on his leather belt.

"Oh! I remember him!" Odas exclaimed while he peered through the gap Jon had been communicating through.

"You do?" Jon sought further elaboration.

"Oh yeah! That is one stubbornly sharp cage," he answered as he looked down at his hands. "How far did you get with it?"

"Not very far; I mostly just made shavings fall down on him," Jon answered as he looked back at the man apologetically. The man still was staring blankly at his hands, paying no attention to the conversation occurring around him.

"It looks like you've gotten the lock off though. That's a good start." Odas said as he kicked the golden object from under his foot.

"That was the easy part. The key really did all the work," he retorted as he held it up to the sunlight.

"No worries. It got done," Odas said as he patted Jon on the back with his enormous hand before he turned to head back into the Dead Woods.

"Wait! Where are you going?" Jon exclaimed after him.

"I have more killin' I need to do! I will see you at the campground tomorrow though, if the King permits." After nodding goodbye, Odas slipped away into the neglected tree line and out of view. Jon stood alone again with only the man inside the cage as company. He sat back down against the same boulder and pulled out his letter again to re-read it for company, occasionally looking back up to observe the man to see if he decided to do anything but stare at his hands or the cage which contained him. To his dismay, the man continued more of the same activities as though he was oblivious to Jon's newfound freedom.

    As the sun began to set Jon grew tired of staring at the same inactivity, so he stepped away from the boulder he sat against, raised his shield, bid the man goodnight, and called out for an eagle to retrieve him.

    It was only seconds until Jon was being carried away from the Dead Wood's perimeter and toward the sanctuary the castle provided. Jon watched the cage fade away as he soared above the cloud's misty embrace. He continued thinking about the man and the vacant expression on his face while he stared down at his own hands. Jon could not prevent himself from wondering if he did what he was sent to do while he had the chance.

    His transport began its usual descent back through the clouds as it flew over the castle walls and toward the tree which inhabited the center of the garden. Jon's shoulders abruptly emerged from their slouched state once he caught a glimpse of the King and Iam awaiting his arrival. Soon he would be able to talk with the King and drink the water Iam had prepared. He wanted to get a head start on loosening his shoelaces, but his hands were already preoccupied with keeping him attached to his shield and preventing him from plummeting to the ground. So he tightened his grip until his feet were on the ground before the King.

    Upon landing, Jon squatted down to untie his boots in preparation of relinquishing them to Iam. He sprung to his feet, boots in hand, eager to remove the rest of his armor and begin his walk with the King. However, the King did not appear to be in as much of a hurry. He slowly took a sip of his drink and calmly assured Jon, who was hurriedly trying to remove his vest, "Slow down Jon.

The Battle

We have plenty of time to talk." Jon heeded his words, took a deep breath, and slowly handed a smiling Iam the remainder of his armor. "There, now isn't that better?" Jon nodded as Iam passed him his drink of the clean fountain water and left to place his belongings by the hammock he then laid in.

After taking a sip of water, Jon said, "I'm sorry for hurrying. I was just so anxious to talk with you."

"That's quite alright, Jon. You have had a long day. Shall we walk?" the King motioned to the abundantly lit garden surrounding them. Jon nodded his head, took another drink, and the two of them began walking. They followed their usual path, occasionally detouring to cross a couple bridges and look at plants Jon had not seen before. They talked for several minutes about his day and the frustrations Jon had with the man inside the cage, which provoked the King to say, "I have spent many years trying to show him what else there is outside of that cage. There is so much to explore and experience, but, as you have witnessed, he chooses not to listen or see what is around him."

"So what do I do?" Jon asked as his shoulders dropped. "If he won't listen or look around, what can I do?"

"You be patient," the King answered. "You have to wait for him to be ready."

"How much time will that take?" Jon impatiently asked.

"Don't worry yourself with time. Be patient for as long as it takes. You are not the only one waiting for him," the King assured Jon.

"But what if...I do something wrong, and he stays in there longer because of it?" Jon asked.

"If he desires to be free…if he really desires to be free, then it won't matter. Trust me; I want him out more than you do, and I won't allow him to be trapped if he desires to be out. Just remember to be patient." The King took another drink from his mug as they sat down upon a patch of the greenest grass Jon had ever seen before.

The two of them continued talking well into the night. They occasionally broke the silence with laughter that echoed throughout the garden, providing music to Iam's ears as he sat comfortably in his custom made hammock, carving something from a tree branch. The torches around them flickered and the grass beneath them swayed at each passing breeze, providing its own form of laughter, as Jon slowly drifted off into an exhaustion-induced sleep. The King slowly returned to his feet and located a moss-covered rock to place under Jon's head as a pillow. He knew that Jon needed plenty of sleep if he were to carry out the plans he had for him the next day, so he remained there with Jon for the night, drinking from his cup and watching the stars shooting across the sky.

Chapter 8:
The Campground

After an entire night of rest Jon finally awoke at the sight of the King sitting next to him, drinking from his cup. "Where am I?" he stammered while he looked around at the rest of his surroundings.

"You are still in the garden," Iam's friendly voice sounded. Jon looked in the direction it came from to see Iam holding all of his armor.

"You fell asleep mid-sentence," the King politely added.

"I must have been really tired," Jon said as he began standing up.

"More than you know. Let me help you with your armor," Iam insisted as Jon reached for his boots.

"How was your rest?" the King asked after he stood up.

"That was probably the best night of sleep I have ever had," Jon answered with a well-rested smile inhabiting his face.

"Very good then," the King answered with another sip of his drink.

After Jon was suited up, Iam left to collect some jerky from a basket that lay nearby and a handful of fruit from a few surrounding bushes. Upon returning he passed them to Jon and said, "Here is some food for your journey, Jon."

After Jon had finished eating, Iam gave him a mug of water to wash it all down. "Thank you for all of that. I really needed it." Jon finished the remainder of the mug and turned back toward the King. "Thank you for allowing me to sleep up here and for watching over me while I did."

"You are welcome any time," the King said as he and Iam beamed at Jon. "It looks as though you are ready to go back down." The King looked at Jon standing confidently before the both of them.

"I believe I am," Jon said as he re-checked himself.

"We will be seeing you shortly then. You will be coming back up with your fellow soldiers when you meet with them." The King, noticing a question forming in Jon's mind, continued, "Do not worry. I will make the arrangements so you get to the correct place."

Jon's concerns were answered, and he commenced with raising his shield and bidding the two of them a farewell. In moments a large eagle swooped down and grasped the glimmering shield's edges to soar off into the cloudy sky before them. Jon eagerly looked back toward his King and Iam as he sailed over the castle wall, trusting that he would be returning soon.

The eagle released its grip on Jon's shield and flew away to leave him by himself once again. Jon returned to the boulder and peered inside of the man's cage to see if anything had changed. To his dismay, the man was still staring down at his hands, unresponsive to any of Jon attempts at a conversation.

As Jon sat there on the boulder, an eagle abruptly landed several feet beside him. Jon turned his head toward it to see a castle messenger standing near, holding a letter for him to take. After Jon took it the messenger returned to its eagle and flew away, kicking up dust and debris as it had done before. Curious at his new letter, Jon ripped apart its dried-berry seal and unfolded it to read what it said.

After just a few minutes of reading its contents Jon sat up and proclaimed, "Cay is coming to get me!" The man inside the cage was unresponsive, so Jon whispered to himself, "So that's how I'm getting to the campground."

Jon sat there for several minutes, basically talking to himself, while he stared at the caged man until a gust of wind nearly knocked him from atop his perch. Jon looked toward the dust cloud to see Cay energetically walking toward him. "You ready to go?" her raspy voice asked.

"Definitely!" Jon sprung to his feet and joined Cay.

"Does he want to come?" Cay asked as she bent down to look at the caged man.

"He hasn't been responding whenever I try to talk to him. All he does is look at his hands," Jon answered as he shrugged his shoulders.

"Try asking again next time; we have to get going now though. They like to be punctual," Cay said as she began walking with Jon following close behind.

"So how far do we have to walk?" Jon asked as he started noticing the assortment of skeletons and abandoned armor laying empty along the path.

"It's only just over this hill and down in the valley by the river," Cay answered as the two of them skipped over piles of rocks stained with the blood of the malorum.

"I have another question," Jon said as he noticed more skeletons draped across their way.

"What is that?"

"I was just thinking about yesterday and looking at all of these dead malorum around here, and I was wondering why I wasn't attacked yesterday. I mean I was, pretty much, all by myself and there were no malorum around that I could see." As Jon answered, Cay smiled and chuckled. "You know why, don't you?"

"I do." Cay continued smiling and laughing while Jon's curiosity grew exponentially.

"So...?"

"You had a lot of people watching out for you," Cay indulged an answer.

The much sought response only intrigued Jon further. "What do you mean? How did anybody know where the King sent me?"

"You don't know do ya? Makes ya wonder doesn't it?" Cay playfully answered as Jon grew impatient.

"You are a cruel." Jon smirked.

"Oh alright then, I'll tell you. The King knew that you'd be too preoccupied with the task he had you do, so he sent a few of us to watch your back. You were, however, able to spot Odas—being the large person he is—but the orders were for us to go unseen," Cay answered as they came upon the base of a dwarfish line of hills.

"It doesn't feel like I did much of anything though. The man inside the cage just sat there and hardly ever looked at me," Jon said as he stared up the face of the hills. "May I ask how we get over these?"

"There's a pass over here," Cay answered as she led him to a gap in the shortened hill's façade. "And you did what you were supposed to do. He now knows you're out. Don't overthink it." She knew Jon well enough to know he had a habit of overthinking situations more often than under thinking them, so she quickly changed the topic. "It won't be long now until you'll be able to see the campground. Do you remember anything about it from your days before?"

Memories of the campground flooded his mind instantly. "I remember that it sat atop a large hill that had been flattened, and there was a really big tree which grew halfway up the slope." Jon was correct with his recollection. A three-acre plain rested on top of a hill slightly larger than the one on which he, Odas, and Cay recently fought the group of malorum. It had a steep hill interrupted only by a large oak tree. It was not until he and Cay emerged on the opposite side of the hills that he remembered the nine-foot wall, which had been made from decaying tree trunks with sharpened ends, surrounding the small village. "There it is!" He exclaimed as he motioned downward toward the campground several soldiers were making the pilgrimage to.

"It looks like we're arriving just in time. Let's hurry inside," Cay excitedly said as she began sprinting down the hillside. Jon continued after her and across a bridge, which had been constructed over a small river, to the base of the steep hill left to be climbed. "I do have to warn you," she stopped and looked over at Jon, who was breathing heavily from the spontaneous exercise "there are going to be a lot of people excited to see you out of your cage, so brace yourself."

Jon nervously smiled as she slapped the side of his helmet. The words, "Thanks for the heads up…" trailed after her as she began her ascent up the hillside. After a few more deep gasps of air, Jon, too, began his climb after Cay and toward the campground's awaiting embrace. As Jon passed by the large oak tree he noticed several tally marks and greetings meant for travelers carved into its weathered bark. He made a mental note to ask of their meanings at a later time, for he was falling well behind his traveling companion, who had already reached the door to the campground.

"I beat ya to the top!" She hollered as she began her congratulatory dance.

Once Jon had finally joined her, out of breath once again, he joked, "If somebody told me it was a race then the results may have been a little different."

"I'm sure," she retorted as she began walking toward the substantial wooden door, which guarded the entrance, presumably, from any unwanted intruders. "Shall we?"

"After you," Jon answered as the two of them entered through the gate and stepped onto a path which ran down the center of a rather large, yet poorly maintained garden. If it had not been for the impressively large mead hall straight ahead, Jon would have noticed the poorly maintained garden and slightly smaller building on either side of him. Instead of asking about the malnourished bushes and wilted trees peering over the man-made walls he motioned ahead and asked, "Is that where we're heading?"

"It is," Cay answered with elation as she hurried toward the entrance. The door had partially been left open from the previous soldier, so with a nod and a smile Cay led the way through its protective façade and into the great hall. What Jon saw next was nothing he had not seen before; however this time he was able to see everything in a new light.

There were three columns of benches, all facing toward the back of the room, where a single podium stood next to a long and slender table. Each bench had a peculiar look to it. They all appeared

The Battle

to be modified picnic tables made of wood similar to the head table. However, these tables had been cut long ways and arranged to face the same way. Wooden boards had been nailed in place to provide the soldiers a back rest while they sat. None of the soldiers seemed to mind this odd arrangement, so neither did Jon. He moved on to notice the bearskin rugs, the stone floor, the stone columns—which held up the thatched roof—adorned with unlit torches, and the colorful array of armor being worn by the three hundred or so soldiers conversing amongst one another. Just as he had gazed upward toward the windows, Jon heard a familiar voice behind him. Odas had just arrived and greeted Cay before breaking his concentration with a heavy pat on the back.

"Glad to see you found the place!" he bellowed.

Jon turned around into the outstretched arms of his much larger comrade to receive a similar bear hug to the one he received upon their first meeting. "I had quite a bit of help from this one," he said while motioning his flailing arm toward Cay.

"She already told me all about it." The large, bearded man answered as he removed his dark green helmet, revealing his bald head. "It feels good to feel the breeze through your hair sometimes, doesn't it?"

"Yeah, I'm sure you know what that feels like," Cay snorted in response to Odas running his cloth-wrapped hand through his invisible field of hair.

"Oh...would you look who it is." Odas had lowered his hand and developed a more serious look on his face.

Jon and Cay had ceased their laughter to see who Odas was referring to. An older man in silver and gold armor was approaching the platform where the three of them stood. "I had hoped to see you before we started!" Emet had approached and held out his hand for Jon to shake. "I see you have already met Odas." He turned toward the much larger man and only nodded his head in his direction. "Good morning to you sir."

Odas instead retorted by holding out his own hand and asked, "What? You don't wish to shake my hand, too?"

Emet glanced down upon the blood- and dirt-stained cloth not-so-neatly wrapped around his massive hand and sneered, "I would have to...politely...decline."

"Aww!" Odas bellowed, "When are you going to get your hands a little dirty, Emet?"

Emet turned his head, ignoring the question, and said, "Well it looks as though we are about to begin our meeting. We shall talk again afterward, Jon. Cay, it is nice to see you here as well." Jon and Cay both nodded their heads and smiled as Emet turned away.

Odas, however, called out after him, "You want to make sure to get your seat at the head of the table now...sir. You can't be late." This was followed by a few muffled words under his breath. After he realized Jon and Cay stood looking up at him with confused looks upon their faces, he returned to his much cheerier tone and said, "Well I guess we had better go find our seats."

Jon looked toward the once uninhabited podium to see an older, helmetless soldier standing behind it. "Sounds good to me."

The three of them scurried down an aisle and found three vacant seats at the end of a row and removed their armor just as the man at the podium began speaking. "Welcome back everyone! It is good to see all of us stayed safe to return this morning." After this was said Odas shifted slightly in his seat, but he remained silent. "Before we have Collin get up here, I have a few announcements to start the meeting off." The gray-haired man went on for several minutes announcing concerns, updates, and general information, all of which fell on Jon's deaf ears. Instead, he had been looking around the room at all the wounded soldiers, some of which were barely able to sit up at all. Although it was peculiar to him to see them being unattended to, he thought it was more peculiar that nobody else seemed to notice except for the occasional straying eye.

His concentration was broken by the eruption of sound which filled the mead hall. Everyone had started singing in unison, and the man that stood at the podium once before had been replaced by a younger gentleman. The words being spoken were unknown to Jon, so he just sat back and listened to all three or four of the songs until another man stood up, who he remembered from his days in the cage, and stood in front of the podium.

The singing had stopped and the mood was timid once more. Jon looked back at the people he had seen which were wounded, and they were now sitting up straighter in their seats with a not-so-mortally-wounded look on their faces. This eased Jon's nerves, so he turned back around and began listening to what the man standing in front of the podium had to say.

He was speaking passionately of the forest and how some of the animals, fruits, and water interacted with one other. Jon understood the imagery being presented, since he had spent the past couple days in the forest with Pneuma. It was an extensive contrast to what Jon understood while he sat in his cage just a week before. After forty or so minutes of teaching, Collin stepped aside, and Emet took his place at the podium. "As it is our custom in these meetings, could I have you all grab your shields and follow me outside?"

Obliging to his request, just about everyone stood up and followed after Emet confidently marching out of the mead hall. Jon turned to Cay as he walked and before he could ask where they were going, he witnessed a marvelous sight ahead. He saw a multitude of eagles hovering above the garden outside. Once they were gathered with the door at their backs, Emet announced, "Everyone raise your shields!" They cooperated once more, and in a blink of an eye Jon saw nearly three hundred soldiers lifted into the air. Everyone besides Odas got paired with the person next to them, for he required his own due to his heavier than average frame. Jon was fortunate he had been paired with Cay, because he got to ask her as they lifted off the ground, "Are we all going to see the King?"

"Yes!" Cay smiled and snorted as she looked over at her flying companion.

"All of us...at once?" Jon could not believe his eyes as he watched a rainbow of colors fill the sky and head north toward the mountains. He had questions in his mind about how the King would be able to spend time with each of them, but he involuntarily chose to ask later due to the speechlessness he was experiencing.

The two of them traveled silently through the sky until they soared over the castle wall. "Keep your shield on your arm while we walk around. There will be another place to set it down." Jon nodded as every eagle descended toward the tree Iam and the King stood at the foot of. Before having his vision obscured by feathers and the glimmering of shields, Jon could see a multitude of mugs resting on the ground by Iam's feet.

As soon as everyone had landed and obtained their mugs Emet approached the King as if he were greeting a father figure. After exchanging pleasantries, the King took a sip from his mug and said,

The Battle

"I see you all are ready for the feast. Iam has everything prepared. Just follow him." The King warmly scanned the crowd as Iam led them to the other side of the tree. After Jon passed by the King and returned his own greeting, he could see what appeared to be an immense building on the other side of the massive tree. As he got closer he realized the King had a mead hall of his own, however it was slightly different. This one did not have any walls, windows, or a door at its entrance. It was a lot simpler. It had a thatched roof, which was supported by numerous stone pillars that were adorned with unlit torches. To Jon's estimation, he counted twelve posts on each of its four sides. Instead of having rows of benches occupying the inside, there were a multitude of round tables, plenty enough to seat the three hundred or so soldiers which Jon was numbered amongst.

    Upon arriving at its threshold Jon noticed the soldiers ahead of him remove their shields and rest them on hooks which resided on every side of the stone pillars as if it were a requirement to do so before entering. Jon found a vacant hook and placed his green shield on it the same time Cay placed her pink shield on the one next to it. She silently laughed at the overwhelming excitedness displayed on his face as she grabbed his arm and led him across the stone floor to a couple vacant seats at the center of the simpler mead hall. "It's pretty cool, huh?" She leaned over and whispered to Jon as he sat gazing toward the wooden beams overhead.

    "How did I not see this place during the times I've been up here? Jon marveled at the hall's grandeur.

    "Well for starters, there *is* a big tree in the way. Also, it just wasn't time yet." Cay smiled as Odas took a seat at their table. "You fly here alright Odas?"

"Oh yeah! A bit later than everyone else I suppose, but I got here nonetheless. Aww, look at him!" The bearded man's attention was now directed toward Jon, still aimlessly gazing around. "You'd think he wasn't even hungry."

Jon, however, was not entirely zoned out for he heard what Odas had said. "What are you talking about?"

"Well, you've looked everywhere but down at your plate," Odas elaborated.

"My what?" Jon's peripheral vision barely caught a glimmer of light reflecting from below his stubbly-haired chin. He looked down at the table and immediately felt his stomach leap for joy. There were seven silver plates resting on the table -each one belonging to its own occupant- and on each plate there was a custom grilled steak prepared exactly the way everyone preferred. A barely audible "Oh" left Jon's lips as he sat amazed at how he had not even smelled it upon his arrival.

"That's more like it. I guess he hadn't even bothered looking what was in his mug yet, has he?" Jon had just assumed it was water, just like every other time he had received a mug from Iam, however, upon looking down at its contents Jon realized it was a bit redder in color.

He looked back up at Odas to ask what it was, but Emet was now walking by and clinking his own mug to call everyone's attention. "I would like to propose a toast to the reason we're all able to be gathered here today. If it was not for Iam's bravery we all would still be residing in our cages. He has provided us with this food and these chalices which overflow with wine. To Iam!"

With one accord each soldier raised their respective mugs and announced, "To Iam!"

The Battle

Now knowing the contents of his mug, Jon raised it, toasted with everyone at his table, and swallowed a mouthful of the wine. He looked around the room, as Emet took his seat, to notice everyone almost finished with their steaks. Without any more hesitation Jon picked up his fork and knife and began eating the perfectly cooked steak in front of him, only coming up for air a handful of times to have some wine.

The soldiers continued eating, drinking, and conversing until there was no more food or wine to be had. As Iam passed by each table, to collect the plates and mugs, he smiled and nodded as each soldier thanked him for what he had done. After every dish had been collected and each table had been cleaned, the soldiers returned to their feet, collected their respective shields, and exited the King's mead hall. Jon, Cay, and Odas walked together back to the place of their arrival to see the eagles patiently waiting for their passengers. Just as they had done a few moments before, the soldiers raised their shields to be grasped by an eagle's talons after bidding farewell to their King. Jon and Cay had been paired together once more, and the two of them—with Odas following close behind—joined their other comrades in flight. The colorful band of soldiers stretched across the sky as they returned to their own mead hall.

Jon's heart sank a little as he looked down toward the man-made walls, its poorly maintained garden, and wilting trees. He wanted to be back around the table under the thatched roof. While he reminisced about the juicy steak and wine in his mug, the raspy-voiced girl accompanying him whispered in his ear, "A bit different than eating berries and drinking coconut milk, wasn't it?" To answer the "how did you know I was thinking about that" look on Jon's face,

Cay continued, "You were drooling. I think a glob of it actually landed in a malorum's eye down on the ground."

"I...I meant to do that," Jon stammered as he wiped off the remaining saliva from his lip.

"Sure you did," Cay facetiously answered as the two of them began their descent to the campground.

"So what are we doing when we get back?" Jon noticed he was only a couple hundred feet from landing.

"We go to fight. Emet and Odas will be coming with us, so don't worry," Cay replied moments before she touched the ground and the eagle released its grasp on her shield. Jon landed moments after, and the two of them waited for Odas before returning to the mead hall.

As they stood there, Jon noticed something peculiar to the right of the pathway, "What is that place for?" Jon had noticed a moderately sized building with shuttered windows and a large wooden door occupying a space by the wall. He must not have noticed it before, since his gaze was transfixed ahead.

"Odas, you want to take this one?" Odas had only just gotten there before Cay asked his assistance.

"Ah! I know all about that place, unfortunately. That right there is the infirmary. If you get too beat up and mangled out there on the battlefield, this is where you go to get fixed up." Odas turned to show Jon a rather large scar on the back of his left shoulder. "It took a few stitches to get this one sealed up." Before Jon could ask how Odas got the wound, the three of them were being hurried back inside the mead hall.

Once everyone was back inside Emet returned to the podium and announced, "Thank you all for gathering this morning. I look forward to seeing you all again tonight. Good day to you all." After the announcement was made every soldier returned to their feet and began conversing amongst themselves.

    As Jon began observing the groups of people, Cay lightly tapped on his shoulder. "You remember what I said as we walked up here this morning, right? About how there are going to be a lot of people wanting to see you?" Jon nodded. "Well you might want to turn around." Although the excitement of the morning deterred him from thinking about it before, there was no escaping the large crowd which was flocking toward the unassuming soldier. Just as Jon turned around he was met with a hug by a female soldier in yellow and white armor. "You remember Mel, don't you Jon?" He nodded his head as he recalled the integral part she played in getting him out of that restrictive cage. Jon expressed his gratitude with a much firmer hug of his own. For several more minutes the greetings, handshakes, and hugs continued. Jon remembered most of the people that came up to him with only a few getting lost in his memory.

    The crowd soon dissipated, and Jon was left with Odas and Cay once more. "Well that was fun," he joked and turned to the bearded man, "Are we all ready to do some fighting?" The others agreed and they reequipped themselves with all of their armor. Before they headed out of the door Jon turned to take another mental picture of the mead hall.

    This was the first time he was able to see it without shards of broken glass and barbed wire blocking his sight. Everyone looked at him differently now that he was out. He was instantly a part of something bigger than himself, even with his taller-than-average frame. It was as though he received many family members through a marriage. He had a responsibility to these people; to help them whenever they need it, even if they do not realize they need it. Especially if they do not realize they need it. As his eyes scanned the room, he saw that everything was quiet and empty; everything except for a few stragglers still sitting at their benches and the gray-haired occupants of the long, skinny table resting beside the podium.

    As Jon turned to join his comrades, a peaceful smile emerged across his face. He wanted others to feel what he felt. He wanted to rescue those inside their cages so they could feel the freedom and realization of purpose he was experiencing, so he left the building and joined the others outside.

Chapter 9:
The Infirmary and the Door

Once outside, Jon only saw Odas standing before him. "Where did Cay go?" he asked.

"She went into the infirmary to get me some fresh bandages and wash the blood off the ones I did have on." Odas replied as he stared down at his hands. "You want to see 'em?" Before Jon could reply, Odas showed him the cuts and scars he had sustained in battle.

"Those are very desirable to have indeed, Odas." Emet had joined their company and began critiquing Odas's wounds. "What was it that you inquired of me earlier? I believe you asked me when I was 'going to get my hands a little dirty.' I will tell you this, my good fellow. The moment you begin to use your sword is the moment I will 'get my hands a little dirty.'"

Just as the awkwardness had reached its peak, Cay showed up with the fresh bandages and the much cleaner cloth. "Thanks Cay." Cay nodded and began to treat Odas's wounds as Jon looked on.

After the four of them were ready to go, Jon asked, "So where are we going?"

"Just follow after me, young Jonathan," Emet answered as the four of them began their walk toward the gate of the man-made wall. Annoyed at the lack of transparency, Jon looked to Cay for comfort. She patted him on the head, and the four of them scaled down the side of the hill. Emet was in front, Cay followed next, and Jon traveled in front of Odas as the large man watched everyone's backs for any surprises along the way.

As they traveled throughout the land they encountered many cages and remains of fallen malorum. Each soldier found the locks which their keys fit inside, discarded them onto the ground, and followed behind Emet as he led the way. The entire afternoon went this way. They occasionally encountered small groups of malorum, but the expertise of both Emet and Odas deemed too much for the enemy. Cay proved to Emet that she could hold her own; however, Jon was not as fortunate. The veteran soldier had not been around for Jon's two previous battles, so –needless to say- Jon was restricted to the much smaller and already partially wounded malorum. He did gain plenty of useful knowledge as he observed the other three fight and asked many questions as to what they were seeing or thinking while they did so, so it was not too disheartening for the newest soldier.

Once or twice throughout the day they decided to take a brief rest along a creek bed to regain their strength with the food they kept secured in their belts. The water they drank came straight from the creek running alongside of their rest areas. Emet would filter it through a piece of cloth, Cay and Jon drank from their hands as they cupped the water, and Odas just simply climbed down into the creek and opened his mouth. Every time he came up for air, there was a mixture of moss, twigs, and—in one instance—a small goldfish

The Battle

trapped in his unkempt beard. Anything that wandered into his mouth he either picked out or ate. He clearly was not as picky as Emet was, flinching with disgust at the sight of Odas even getting in the water. The rhetorical question of, "Is that really necessary?" seemed to come out of the veteran's mouth quite often throughout the afternoon.

"It gets the job done, doesn't it?" Odas would reply each time before taking one last gulp of water or ripping one more limb off the enemy. "You should try it sometime, bud. Oh, that's right! You don't want to mess up that nicely trimmed beard of yours, do ya?" Odas knew his words had been falling upon deaf ears, but he continued nonetheless.

As the two seasoned warriors continued their prodding, Cay gave Jon a smirk and whispered, "You get used to it after a while. The water is good though, isn't it?" Jon nodded as he tried to ignore the other two's conversation.

After each of them got their fill of nourishment, they continued traveling around until the sun was barely visible. Right before it began to sink below the tree line, Emet turned to the other three and said, "It appears as though it's almost time to gather with our number once again. It is a good thing we have not wandered too far away from the hill. Follow me everyone."

All four of them arrived at the top of the campground's hill several minutes after the sun disappeared under the forest's tree line. As they entered through the heavy wooden door, Emet sped off toward the mead hall to perform his duties as scheduled. Spots of blood were showing through the bandages on Odas's hands once again, so the three of them hurried toward the infirmary. Jon waited outside in the small courtyard as Cay went in to help Odas. He tried to look in at his companions, but with the door being shut and the shudders closed his efforts were in vain. Several minutes passed before the two of them emerged with fresher bandages in place. "Sorry for leaving ya out here like that. We only thought we'd take a minute," Odas apologized.

"Yeah, we ran into an old friend that was lying down on one of the beds," Cay elaborated.

"No worries. It feels nice out." The summer breeze and a light mist kept Jon company as the others were inside. "So, shall we go inside the mead hall now?" The other two agreed, and the three of them headed toward the much larger building.

Upon entering they were warmly greeted by their fellow soldiers, as well as the torches, which were now lit. Most people had already gotten to their seats, and Emet was walking toward the podium. As the three of them found adequate room on a bench and removed their armor, Jon gazed around the room as he had done during their earlier visit. He found that each window was now open and each torch was lit, which provided the room with plenty of light.

As he began meeting the eyes of his fellow soldiers, Emet's voice filled the air. "We would like to welcome everyone once again, and express our appreciation that all of you have returned." The gray-haired veteran looked around at the half-depleted crowd. "Our first order of business is to ask for more volunteers to assist those already appointed to help with the garden. If you could help, please speak with one of us afterward." After making a few more announcements, the gathering continued on as it had done earlier in the day. There was a mixture of singing and teaching—regarding the forest and how to effectively fight on the battlefield—before Emet returned to the podium. "If those that were not here this morning could stand up and follow me outside, we will go up to the castle for the feast."

Jon watched on as a few soldiers stood up and headed for the door, "What do we do? I mean...the ones that are left," he whispered to Cay.

"I guess we wait until they come back. That's what I've always done," she answered as Odas impatiently shifted in his seat.

"What's wrong with him?" Jon noticed Odas picking at his hands.

"He doesn't see why we all can't go with them." Cay nudged the much larger man as he began to discard dead skin from his hands onto the floor.

"Well...what else is there to do?" Odas whispered. Cay responded by shrugging, and Jon began to laugh under his breath.

After several minutes of waiting, Emet and the small group of soldiers emerged through the door and returned to their seats. The meeting only lasted for another twenty minutes before concluding. Odas was one of the first people up and with his armor back on before he hastily made his way toward the door. Jon and Cay pursued him after returning their own armor to its rightful places.

They found Odas waiting in the courtyard, rewrapping his bandages. "You alright, Odas?" Jon asked.

"I'll be alright. I just need to go kill some malorum, is all." Odas gave the two of them each a lung-deflating bear hug and walked away. Jon turned back to Cay just before hearing a sound echo throughout the garden. The two of them turned to see the door of campground's entrance lying on the ground with a cloud of dust kicked up around it.

"So you ready to go?" Cay asked Jon as he stood there with his mouth wide open.

"Uh...I think so. What was...?" Jon stammered.

"Alright then. Let's get going." Cay said as she lovingly waved at the soldiers venturing around outside the mead hall. She raised Jon's hand to do the same as he stared at the unhinged door. As the two of them walked through the now vacant doorway, Jon continued in his silence.

Cay led him down the hill and to the bridge before he muttered his first phrase. "Um...what was that about?"

"He never really liked that door...or doors in general for that matter."

"Ah! So ripping it off its hinges makes sense." Jon looked back to see a group of elderly soldiers fitting it back into place.

"Well I'm not about to question him. You have at it all you'd like though," Cay responded.

"I'm sure he had a good reason," he nervously rationalized since he did not want to be the one to confront his bearded comrade. "So what do we do now?"

"You want to go up to the castle?" Cay suggested, to which Jon's eyes lit up immediately. In an instant both of their shields were raised in the air to call for a pair of eagles to wrap their talons them. After waiting for only a few more seconds, the majestic birds swooped down, retrieved their packages, and began their return flight toward the castle walls. Silence fell upon the young soldiers as they enjoyed the sights below and felt the breeze slip underneath their helmets. The trees swayed and the clouds rolled as the sounds of chirping could be heard off in the distance.

The Battle

They flew over the castle wall to come within view of the large tree, to which Jon instantly smiled brighter. "It always looks so peaceful up here." The garden was illuminated by a wide assortment of torches, lanterns, and every other light-emitting object one could imagine. Even the tree and each of the bridges had their own lights being shone on them. It was a much different place than where Jon and Cay had spent most of their day. Within the walls there was no fighting, bickering, or sarcastic remarks meeting their ears. Instead, the wind blew, the birds chirped, the river flowed, and the King sat in a hammock experiencing it all as well.

They landed in their usual spot, gave their armor to Iam in exchange for mugs filled with the cleanest water, and began their walk with the King throughout the garden. "So what is on your minds?" The King asked before taking a drink. Jon began by thanking him for everything he had experienced that day while Cay joyfully echoed the same feelings. They continued their conversation as they walked along the river, occasionally veering off to pick some fruit from nearby trees.

As they wound back to the center tree, Jon asked, "So what's next for us?"

The King looked at the both of them to answer, "I need Cay to help another soldier out again. As for you, Jon, I need you to go back to where I sent you this morning."

"You mean that cage?" Jon asked as he hoped for something a bit more exciting.

"Preferably the focus being more on the man inside the cage than the cage itself. However, first I'm going to send you both back to the forest, but in different parts," he added. Jon and Cay both nodded, and the three of them continued their walk toward the tree and Iam. After saying their farewells, the two young soldiers were retrieved by their own eagles and began their flight over the garden.

Before they got over the wall Cay turned and shouted over to Jon, "Remember to keep your eyes open when you're out there! They don't wait for you to be ready!"

"OK!" Jon yelled back. "When is the next time I'll see you?"

"I don't know yet! We could always write though!" she added with a smile.

"True! I'll see you later!"

"I'll look forward to it!" After Cay smiled, their eagles swooped down into the forest—in different places—and they were out of each other's sights.

Jon was still smiling as his eagle dodged tree branch after tree branch to reach a clearing Jon had not been to before. Pneuma was already sitting on a waist-high stump, waiting for the stubble-faced soldier to arrive. "Well there ya are!"

The eagle released its grip on the dark green shield and ascended back toward the castle, leaving Jon with his guide. "It seems like it's been so long since I've seen you," Jon said as he gave Pneuma a stronger-than-usual handshake.

"You've gotten stronger since we last met," Pneuma said with a grin.

"I have?"

"Oh yeah! You got some meat in ya, huh?" Pneuma asked.

Jon remembered his time in the castle's mead hall. "It was amazing! I got to see what was on the other side of the tree."

"I'm guessing ya liked what ya saw then?" Pneuma remained on his stump as Jon sat upon the lush grass.

The Battle

"I had no idea that mead hall was there! We all are going around the tree, and there it is. It was a lot simpler than the one we have in the campground. Also, that one had tables instead of benches," Jon explained.

"So ya like that one better then?" Pneuma reached in his pocket, pulled out an apple, and began eating.

"Yeah. We got to see each other better, but I still like the way the campground's mead hall is set up too, I guess."

"I see," Pneuma replied in between taking bites.

"So what have you been up to since I last saw you?" Jon asked.

"I've been walking around for hours doing a bunch of stuff. It feels great to finally sit down." Before Jon could ask where Pneuma had been, the gravelly-voiced man continued, "I guess I do have to get back out there. I have a lot to get done."

"Alright. Will I see you in the morning then, before I head back up to the castle?" Jon asked.

"You will. Feel free to sleep here. The moon is remarkably bright tonight, so it might help ya see better." Pneuma looked around the clearing before he returned to his feet and headed back into the tree line.

The moon was, indeed, exceptionally bright that night. Jon could easily see groups of deer at the far end of the clearing, as well as a raccoon or two emerging from a nearby log. What he could not see, however, was the pair of eyes peering at him from underneath a black hood far off into the forest behind him. A chill came over Jon as he sat there on the grass. He reached behind his head to grasp the hilt of his sword, completely naïve to the fact that this action sent the hooded being away. Jon knew that if he was going to have any energy for the next day he had to get plenty of rest, so he placed his armor on the ground next to where he sat, held his shield toward the sky, and drifted off into a deep and refreshing sleep.

The following morning, when Jon awoke, he opened his eyes to see Pneuma holding out a large bowl of oatmeal, a banana, and mug of water. "Good mornin' Jon!"

"Good morning to you, too," Jon mumbled back as he stared at the food in confusion. "What's this?"

"I got some food for ya. I figured it'd be a break from eatin' berries. Eat up!"

Pneuma handed the food over to Jon, who instantly consumed it all. "Thank you. I needed that."

"You are welcome. You have to have plenty of food in your stomach if you're goin' to do all the King wants you to do today." Pneuma reached down and took the empty bowl and mug.

"What do I do with this banana peel?" Jon asked as he began putting his boots back on.

"Just throw it into the forest. Something will use it," Pneuma started helping him with the rest of the armor.

"Thank you again, Pneuma." Jon shook his guide's hand.

"It's my pleasure. Now get your shield in the air and go talk with the King," Pneuma suggested.

Jon grabbed hold of the two leather straps, said another "until next time", and raised his shield—now returned to its smaller form—toward the sky. Seconds later, dust was kicked up into the air, and Jon was lifted from the ground. The next few minutes were occupied by Jon effortlessly flying through the air toward the castle.

"I see more meat on your bones, Jon. It appears as though you are getting plenty of nourishment," the King began.

The Battle

"Pneuma has been helping a lot with that. I wouldn't know where anything was if it weren't for him." Jon smiled.

"Very good." The two of them continued their conversation by the river not far from their starting location.

After several minutes Jon decided to ask, "So what do you want me to do at that cage today? It doesn't seem as though the man inside it is listening."

"Be patient with him. It has taken many years for his cage to get to the point where it is now. Do not lose hope. I have been watching him for many years," the King replied as he took a sip from his own mug.

"I will, but I need your help. You know him better than I do," Jon requested.

"And you will have it." The two of them finished their conversation and returned to Iam, who had Jon's armor already prepared. "Remember Jon, you can return at any time." Jon nodded and thanked the King before he lifted his shield and soared off over the garden.

"Don't mess it up, Jon." He whispered to himself as the eagle climbed over a group of darkened clouds. "He wants you to do this. Just don't mess it up." For the remainder of the flight Jon closed his eyes and felt the warm breeze on his face. He reopened them when he felt his flight come to a stop, realizing he must have returned to where he was the morning before.

The eagle brought him close to the boulder in front of the cage and released its grasp before it made its return flight back to its perch. Before Jon could climb the rock to see the cage's prisoner, another eagle arrived with a castle messenger riding atop it. The messenger approached Jon and placed a folded letter in his hand.

Jon recognized the seal from before and knew it instantly was from Cay. He peeled it open and excitedly read its contents.

At the conclusion of the letter it read, "I left a place for you to write back. Pneuma told me he slipped a pencil inside one of your belt pouches. The messenger should be waiting for your reply."

Jon instantly reached around inside his belt's many compartments and found a freshly sharpened wooden pencil. "He must have snuck this in before I went to the castle," Jon thought as he began writing about how his morning had gone. After he finished, he folded the letter, and returned it to the messenger. Jon watched as the eagle lifted off the ground and disappeared from view.

After the dust settled back down around him, Jon remembered the reason he had been sent to this location. He turned and climbed on top of the boulder he had already spent much time sitting on and saw the mangled steel of the cage. Its condition had not improved, and actually looked to be worsening. It appeared to have additional metal barbs welded onto it in places where Jon could previously peer through to see the man inside its confines. As he approached it to investigate, he noticed the man inside shifting around. Jon managed to say a "Hello" in his excitement, but it fell upon deaf ears once again. After his failed attempt at conversation, Jon withdrew his sword from its sheath and began letting his frustrations out on the cage's exterior. Shards of glass and barbs of metal flew off every time his blade would collide with it, narrowly avoiding his face more than a few times, but it was of no use. The man inside of its confines put his hands up to shield his own face from the barrage of sharp pieces raining down on him.

It took a while for Jon to notice, but once he did he backed away and returned to his resting place upon the rock. Frustration

The Battle

overwhelmed him the longer he sat there. As his hands got heavier and heavier from the increasing weight of his sword and shield, Jon made the decision that there would be no harm to set them on the ground by his feet. This proved to be one of the worst decisions the young soldier could have made, for there was an enemy approaching calmly behind him.

Now that Jon's guard was down the hooded figure was able to successfully get close enough to almost touch the back of his dark green helmet. Everything grew eerily silent. The only reason Jon had gotten the inclination to turn around was because he felt cold air crawl down the back of his neck. He was not able to see much, because the moment he turned his head a dark metal club met the right side of his face. It sent Jon clear off his perch and onto the ground where he laid unconsciously vulnerable.

"What happened?" Jon stammered as he awoke. "Where am I?" He was no longer on the battlefield or anywhere near the cage he had been sent to watch over. Instead, he was lying on a bed in a dark room, armorless.

"Everything is alright Jon. You're ok," A calm female voice spoke which Jon did not recognize.

"Who's there?" His panic increased as his eyes darted around in the darkness. "I can't see anything!"

Nearby to where Jon laid a lantern flickered on. The one who had lit it was a much older, and shorter, female soldier Jon had not met before. "You are in the infirmary, my dear. A barefooted man in dirty robes brought you up here."

Jon instantly reached for his head, remembering the blow he had taken before he passed out he asked, "Where's my helmet?"

"All of your belongings are on the shelf at the foot of your bed," the lady calmly answered.

Jon could barely see the foot of the bed now because of the dim light. "How do I know you aren't tricking me?"

"Look around you dear." She quietly chuckled. "I knew I hadn't seen you in here before. You must be new."

Jon looked around and saw many beds lining the walls, none of which were occupied at the moment. "Am I the only one here?"

"At the moment…yes. Though, sadly, it won't stay this way for long."

After pausing for a moment to collect his thoughts, Jon asked, "So what happened to me? Last thing I remember was being knocked to the ground by something."

"I don't know exactly, but by the looks of it it appears as though something hit the side of your head pretty hard. Your helmet wasn't damaged at all…though I can't say the same for your face." The old lady brought a mirror for Jon to look into. The right side of his face was indeed damaged. Scabs were forming over the slices by his eye, and his top lip appeared to be stitched together in one area.

"So are you a nurse?" Jon asked.

"In a manner of speaking…yes. There are a few of us who volunteer." The calmness of her voice and mood were significantly helping Jon with his confusion and anxiety.

"Why is it so dark in here?" Jon looked around at the shutter-drawn windows and the large wooden door at the entrance.

"We thought it'd be a little…too embarrassing…for those that are in here if other soldiers were able to see inside." She answered.

After trying to process this answer for a while Jon said, "Well it'd be nice if we could see around while we're in here."

The Battle

"Your eyes will get used to it after a while. There are more that prefer it this way."

"Like who?" Jon asked.

"Many of the older gentlemen. We do have these lanterns for those that ask for more light though." She smiled as she motioned toward the dimly lit canister in her hand.

Jon looked around, still barely able to see anything too far around him. "That still isn't enough light. How do I know if anybody needs help in here if I can't *really* see them?"

"You're still young. You'll get it later dear. Besides, you're the only one here at the moment." The older lady set the lantern down on a nearby table and shuffled off toward the back of the room and out of Jon's view.

"I'm still young?" Jon thought to himself as he began to put his armor back on. "What is that supposed to mean?" As Jon looked down at his helmet, ready to put it back on his head, he noticed the large black mark the club must have left. He stood up and wondered how a blow like the one he sustained left no indentation or scratches. Unable to think of a reason Jon placed the helmet back on his head and headed for the door. "Can I leave now?" Jon, still frustrated at the explanation he was given pertaining to the light, shouted toward the back of the infirmary. After waiting for several minutes, with no answer, he proceeded to push against the door to open it. He tried several times, but the door did not budge. He knew from before that the door opened outward so he turned the knob as hard as he could as he pressed all his weight against it. Nothing happened.

Something the young soldier did not know was that the door was not made for the infirmary but was added later during a renovation, so it always had a habit of getting stuck. Also the hinges on it were not fastened securely enough to the stone structure of the building, so every time Jon pressed against it the hinges would get looser from the wall. Making one final effort, Jon mustered the rest of his strength in his one hundred eighty-five pound, six-foot-three-inch frame and pressed against the stingy door one last time. This time it budged. Unintentionally, Jon sent the door to the ground as Odas had done to the campground's front entrance the night before.

  A small cloud of dust flung in the air as Jon stood there in an apologetic silence. "That's the spirit! See nurse? I'm not the only one!" Odas was standing a few feet from where the door fell and was hollering toward the infirmary's nurse that had remerged at the sound of the ground shaking.

  Jon turned and met the infuriated glare of the nurse now standing behind him. Making matters worse, Jon wanted to provide his own comedic relief to the moment and sarcastically muttered, "At least there's more light inside the infirmary now." Even though it had become nighttime, while Jon was unconscious, the moon was still providing more light for the infirmary than the lantern was.

  Odas stepped between him and the nurse to receive the brunt of the physical punishment he was about to endure. "It *is* better than that silly little lantern, nurse."

  "I do apologize for knocking it down. I can put it back up if you want." Jon stooped down and struggled to lift it even a couple of inches off the ground.

  "Don't worry about it dear. It'll take about four of you to even lift it. It would only take one of Odas though, but he always has something else to do." The nurse looked over at Odas inspecting the bruises she had given him.

The Battle

"I did come up here to get some help from you. I got a little cut on my forearm." Odas lifted his arm to reveal a good-sized gash running down from his elbow.

"That's a bit more serious than a 'little cut', dear. Let me go and get a few men from the mead hall to fix this door then I can fix that right up for you." The little old lady scurried toward the mead hall and out of view once again.

"There are people still in the mead hall?" Jon turned to Odas, who was blowing on his wound, and asked.

"Oh yeah! Some people hardly ever leave," Odas answered with an annoyed tone. "They aren't real big fans of fighting, but they are fans of eating."

"At least they can help us with the door," Jon tried to reason.

Odas snorted as the nurse returned with five overweight helmetless soldiers, all with gray hair neatly trimmed and parted on their heads. "Look who it is! Come to fix the door again, have ya?" Odas said.

"Well we wouldn't have to if you'd leave it on its hinges, Odas," one of the older men answered.

"It wasn't me this time, bud, but thanks for the flattery." Odas motioned toward Jon.

"Ah! Showing the youngins how it's done then?" The men sneered toward the apologetic soldier.

"I'll have you know, it was already like that when I got here." Odas lifted his arm and showed the five of them the gash on his forearm. He continued after he noticed all of them wince, "This is what happens when you leave these walls gentlemen."

"We're quite aware, thank you."

"Are ya now? Quite aware of where the food is stored as well I see," Odas retorted before the nurse charged into the conversation.

"Now gentlemen, let's quit bickering." She turned to address the men that followed her from the mead hall. "If you please, could you help me with this door?" The men nodded and lifted the door back into place. "Thank you kindly." All five of them gave a slight nod to the three of them before they walked off toward the hall. "Odas! Why must you start things?" After they left she turned her attention to the bearded soldier still blowing gently on his wound.

"Now that much more important task is finished, could I get a little help now nurse?"

In a frustrated tone she answered, "Come inside Odas. Let *me* open the door. I don't want to go back and ask for their help again.

Before he joined the nurse inside the infirmary Odas said to his younger comrade, "Keep fighting, bud. I will see you later." The two of them shook hands, and Odas went inside to get his wound treated.

The moment the door closed behind Odas clouds moved over the moon to block its light from reaching the ground. As Jon began walking toward the campground's front door rain began to fall. Jon traveled through the downpour toward the oak tree halfway down the now-muddy hill outside the wall of the campground. He rested against the tree to gather his bearings as all of the dirt and blood inhabiting his clothes and armor washed down the hill. The black mark the malorum's metal club left was also washed away as if it had never happened. "How did I get up here?" Jon thought to himself as he looked out toward the swelling creek below. "I need to go see Pneuma." Jon remembered the nurse said something about a

The Battle

barefooted man with dirty robes before. After soaking in the scenery for a few more minutes Jon jogged down the hill and walked along the creek toward the forest nearby. The rain began letting up as the clouds rolled away. The moonlight reemerged to help the young soldier find his way toward the tree line.

"Wait for me, bud!" A familiar voice filled Jon's ears as he pressed on. Odas had apparently gotten his forearm patched up well enough to be able to slide down the hillside. Jon turned around to see Odas running toward him. "I'm coming with you. I heard that Pneuma and the King both want to talk with you." He took a moment to catch his before continuing, "They want me to hear it, too."

"Do you know what it's about?" Nervousness fell over Jon like a waterfall. He instantly began to think he was in serious trouble for what happened at the cage earlier. He was told multiple times to keep his eyes open and to be patient with the man inside the cage, but he did neither of them. He got frustrated and paid no attention to his surroundings, and now he was sure to hear about it from the two people he did not want to disappoint.

"I have no idea. I guess we're about to find out, huh?" They arrived at the edge of the forest, and upon crossing its threshold they could both hear a faint sound in the distance of clanging metal.

As they got closer the noise got louder and they could see a faint red light flickering in the area the sound was coming from. "Well...it doesn't sound like Pneuma wants to be stealthy." Jon nervously laughed. The two of them pressed on until they reached a small clearing in the forest; much like the one where he had met Pneuma upon their first introduction.

"There you are!" Pneuma shouted. "I was just working on this weapon until you both got here." Odas and Pneuma shared a handshake as Jon wondered if he was in trouble. "Well it looks like you got a little scar on your lip, Jon. You get to meet the nurse, did you?" Pneuma asked.

"He also took the door off the hinges. Didn't you, bud?" Odas added before Jon could answer.

"That one was an accident!" Jon quickly spoke up before Pneuma could look back over at him.

"Did he now?" Pneuma returned hammering away at what appeared to be a curiously large rectangular chunk of metal as though he did not hear Jon's words. "I never cared much for that door, as you already know, Odas. You see Jon, your large comrade and I share the same dislike for that door. We both think it's relatively...what's that word we came up with earlier, Odas?" Pneuma paused for a moment as he looked over at Odas. "Ah yes! We both think it's relatively stupid. That's the word. You both want a turkey leg?"

"I believe you already know the answer to that question." Odas chuckled.

Pneuma reached down to a stone slab by the furnace he had there and grabbed two large turkey legs. He gave one to each of them and continued talking. "We aren't very big fans of doors, as you have already seen with Odas."

"Why not?" Jon asked as he reluctantly bit at his food.

"They get in the way more than they help." Odas answered before he bit off half the meat from his turkey leg.

"For instance, if someone is carrying a soldier up there to get fixed, they have to go through the trouble of situating how to open the door with them on their shoulders. It was a poor renovation in

The Battle

my mind." Pneuma added as he set the large chunk of metal on the stone slab the turkey legs were previously on.

"So it was you then?" Jon asked. Pneuma smiled and nodded. "So how would you carry someone Odas's size if he got knocked out?"

"Well I'm fortunate he hardly ever does, to be honest." Pneuma laughed.

"He's also a lot stronger than he looks. I remember one time..." Odas began as Pneuma humbly tried to stop the story from being told. "This one time, many years ago mind you, I got completely blind-sided and fell to the ground. I was told later that the ground shook as if a tree fell from the mountains. I woke up and looked down to see the ground moving and Pneuma here was carrying me up the hill. He kicked down both doors and took me in to see the nurse. That right there is a good friend," Odas concluded by taking the rest of the meat off his turkey leg and patting Pneuma on the back.

"I see what you mean by the doors getting in the way." Jon sat there completely stunned.

"When you really need to do something it doesn't matter how big the obstacle is that's standing in your way. There will be a way to get it done. In this case it was that Odas needed help." Pneuma joined them by sitting on his own stump. "There are other times where the enemy will seem larger than what you've ever experienced. The point is that if something needs to get done, then get it done."

"Here's somethin' Pneuma taught me a while back. He told me that if I'm asked to do something then I better make sure it's worth remembering later." Odas added to the conversation.

"Do something worth remembering, so you'll have the story to tell later." The gravelly-voiced man said. The three of them sat there in complete silence for several minutes. The words echoed in Jon's head, trying to fill every inch of available space. When he had arrived earlier he thought he was about to get rebuked for something he did wrong, but instead the youngest soldier of the three learned he was not the first to be in need of someone carrying him to the infirmary. Pneuma's voice broke the silence as Jon looked upward toward the stars, "I do believe it's getting late, Jon. I'm going to need Odas to do something, but you should rest here. We'll be back before you go see the King in the morning, though."

Jon wanted to object and ask if he could go with them, but he reluctantly kept his objections at bay and nodded his head in agreement. He gave them each a handshake and hug before they exited the clearing. Jon was feeling a bit apprehensive about staying there alone, so after they left he quickly removed his armor, held his shield toward the sky, and drifted off into a deep and refreshing sleep.

Chapter 10:
The Next Mission

When Jon awoke the following morning he met the gleaming eyes of Pneuma staring down at him. "You sleep well?"

"I slept great," Jon yawned and stretched as he began to put his armor back on.

"The turkey will do that to ya bud. I almost fell asleep myself while we were walking." Odas effortlessly helped Jon off the ground.

Once Jon got his bearings he asked Odas and Pneuma, "So where did you guys go?"

"You'll find out later, but as for right now you need to go talk with the King," Pneuma vaguely answered.

"You can't just tell me?" Jon pleaded.

"It's not the right time yet." Pneuma smiled as he helped Jon raise his shield. "I like your curiosity though." Just then an eagle swooped down and plucked Jon from their company.

Jon looked down to see them cheerfully waving at him through the forest's canopy. "Oh patience…I have a feeling we are going to get very well acquainted," Jon muttered to himself as the eagle soared through the pure white clouds.

In a matter of moments Jon landed and was walking with the King. "I see you got a little beat up down there." The King noticed the scar formed on Jon's top lip.

"Yes. I got so frustrated that I didn't keep my eyes open." Jon bowed his head.

"It's a war out there. I wouldn't be much of a King if I didn't know what I was asking of my soldiers." Jon raised his head, and the King continued. "I am not going to ask you to do anything you are not capable of doing. Just keep fighting."

"I will," Jon answered with his head a little higher than it was before.

"Very good. Now there's an important matter I mean to discuss with you Jon." Jon's ears perked up as the King turned to face him. "There's something I want you to fight south of where I have been sending you. It is a much larger malorum than you're used to, but nonetheless I want you to do this for me." Jon joyfully accepted the new mission in hopes he could redeem himself. The two of them talked about what to expect and what the King wanted to be done until Jon was clear of the goal.

Once they finished their conversation they both returned to the tree and joined Iam. As he has always done, Jon retrieved his armor, bid his farewells, and soared away underneath an eagle. He returned to the place he had come from earlier to see Emet now standing with Pneuma and Odas. Jon landed softly upon the moss-covered ground and greeted his fellow soldiers. "So what'd the King say?" Odas asked as he snacked on a handful of berries.

"Well...he wants me to kill a large malorum south of here," Jon answered as he grabbed his own handful from a nearby bush.

"Did he say when?" Odas excitedly asked.

The Battle

"He told me I will have a couple more weeks up here before I have to go." Jon turned to Pneuma. "He also told me that you have more information about it."

"Ah yes! Odas and Emet will be going with you. I thought it'd be best for your sanity if you got to listen to their friendly chatter for a little while longer." Pneuma nudged the two soldiers he was standing between.

"Would Cay be able to go?" Jon eagerly asked as he began to envision his head exploding from the banter.

"The King has a separate mission for her to do west of here." Pneuma could tell he deflated Jon's hopes with his answer. "Since you'll be leaving from this place soon, we have much work to do in the training department. Odas and Emet both have plenty to teach you."

"Where will you be?" Jon anxiously asked.

"I'll be around, don't you worry," Pneuma answered, re-inflating a part of what he had previously deflated.

"Shall we get started then?" Emet chimed in as he finished the remaining contents of his coconut water.

"Train him up men. I'll be back later to see his progress. Oh…and Jon, try to take it easy on these guys. They're getting pretty old, especially Emet.

"You're one to talk," Emet playfully retorted before Pneuma made his way back through the trees.

For the entire day the three of them trained, only to stop momentarily for food and water breaks. Emet taught him a variety of sword techniques that Jon picked up almost instantaneously. Not to be outdone by his fellow soldier, Odas took the opportunity while Emet rested to teach Jon effective ways to use his shield and the rest of his body during combat. Back and forth the two of them argued as to which way was most effective only to be silenced by the sounds of footsteps quickly approaching from a distance. "Did ya hear that, bud?" Odas said to Emet.

"I did. I hesitate to think we are alone anymore," Emet replied, gripping his swords.

"They probably heard your yelling," Jon chimed in.

"Nonetheless, we get to settle this dispute through a little target practice." A smirk grew on Emet's face as he moved to the center of the clearing.

"Let's just hope there's plenty to go around, eh bud?" Odas wrapped his bandages a little tighter as he prepared for the fight. "You ready, Jon? Show us what you've learned."

Jon wiped the sweat from his hands and separated his sword into two. "Try and keep up, guys." Jon's confidence grew knowing he had the help of both men.

The sun disappeared under the treetops and cast a large shadow over the entire field. Birds flew in and nestled themselves on nearby branches to watch the action about to take place. In the distance a large group of about thirty malorum was sprinting toward the three of them, each possessing a weapon ready to have blood upon it.

Once Odas could see the outlines of their eyes, he picked up a nearby boulder and effortlessly flung it through the air toward the trees. It nastily collided with the first of their number, killing three of them upon impact. "That oughta give us a head start." Odas smiled as some of the malorum tripped over their fallen comrades. This seemed to provide them with more motivation, since they started to move more quickly toward them than before.

The Battle

Just before they reached the tree line, Jon saw four knives fly through the air toward them; each of them found a way into separate chest pieces and pierced a heart of their own. "I believe that puts me ahead, Odas," Emet said, not wanting to be one-upped.

Not having any of his own knives or strength enough to pick up a boulder, Jon found a small log nearby and slung it toward the trees just as the others had done. His attempt was not as successful, since the log collided with the trees instead and fell to the ground. The failed action caused the other two to look at him with puzzled looks on their faces. "Hey! 'A' for effort, right?" Jon tried to reason with the men now shaking their heads.

Before they could provide any consolation pity-applause for Jon, the moderately sized group of malorum left standing emerged from the trees. The next several minutes were filled with the most skillfully intense fighting Jon had ever seen. All he had to do was sit back and watch the other two showcase their skills. Odas used his body and shield while Emet used both of his swords. Although he had a strong desire to climb a nearby tree and watching the experts work, Jon still wanted to contribute. He went around and used anything he could to help out. It did not seem to matter to him if it was a shield, a sword, his helmet, or logs sitting there minding their own business. It was all the same to him. He just wanted to help out.

The three of them fought until Odas had killed the last malorum by punching through its breastplate. After it fell to the ground in a heap the large man announced, in a breath-catching voice, "So I guess we tied then, Emet?"

Emet, who was also out of breath, answered, "Unfortunately so. Although if style points were awarded..."

"Then I would win…" Odas interrupted as he caught his breath more quickly than his slightly older comrade.

"So…what happens with all these bodies?" Jon asked as he looked around at the field.

"Yeah…there're kind of a lot, huh?" Odas answered. "I usually just leave 'em."

"We, however, do need to find a creek to wash off. I know of one around this area." Emet finally caught his breath and looked down at the dirt and blood that had accumulated on his armor.

"I'll actually agree to that. My fingers are sticking together," Odas agreed as he dropped the malorum's heart and looked down at his hands. After Jon nodded in agreement the three of them walked off into the forest in search of the nearest creek.

After only walking for a short while the three of them reached a creek with a small bridge stretched across it. "This is it, gentlemen," Emet announced, and they each took off their boots and armor to wash off in the creek's clean water.

"There you are! I figured you'd be coming here." A gravelly voice spoke through the trees. Pneuma had emerged through the brush with dirt and blood caked on his sword as well. "Mind if I join you?"

"Not at all, bud. We just got done fighting off a group where we were training," Odas answered.

Pneuma pulled up alongside the creek bed and began washing his feet. "I know it. I walked up on the remains. I have to tell you. That was a large fire they made. I'm surprised you all didn't see it."

"What do you mean?" Jon asked as he pried his head out from his helmet's tight grasp.

"I threw them all in the furnace of course. Quickest way to clean that I've found."

"Oh yeah...of course! Why didn't I think of that?" Jon rhetorically asked Pneuma.

"It's best if I do it. No worries," Pneuma nonchalantly answered. Jon laughed it off, and the four of them finished cleaning the remaining residue from their equipment. "Well...it looks like you both are watching out well enough, so I guess I will get back to work. I'll still be around though," Pneuma added after everyone had returned their armor to their rightful places. They all shook Pneuma's hand again as he headed back into the forest with his sword drawn and freshly cleaned.

"So what do we do now?" Jon asked the two left with him.

"We could explore the forest before it is time to rest," Emet immediately requested and the other two agreed.

For the remainder of the night the three of them continued their training throughout the forest. They stopped occasionally to get something to eat from the trees and bushes around them, and they got something to drink from a creek they came upon. As they walked around with their nourishment Emet and Odas took turns showing Jon different things about how the forest worked. They explained to him how everything was connected and how everything had a purpose. After only a couple hours of doing this both Emet and Odas announced that they needed to do something else for the King, so they would be leaving Jon alone. They said their farewells and faded off through the trees just as Pneuma had done earlier.

Jon was alone in the forest once more, but this time he felt more prepared. His nerves had been calm the entire day, and he did not think about the next mission the King had prepared for him. He calmly meandered around the forest where Odas and Emet had left him until a chill traveled up the entirety of his spine. The last time he felt this surge was right before the side of his face met the unforgiving impact of a metal club. He instantly grabbed the handles of both swords and frantically peered into the moonlit forest. He stood there motionless as small animals were scurrying off in many different directions. Jon knew there was something watching him, but he just did not know where it was until he heard a branch snap some fifty feet from where he stood. "I'm ready for you this time!" He shouted in an attempt to scare the hooded malorum away.

  Another crack was heard about thirty feet from him, but coming from behind him. A faint laugh came next, as if to mock Jon's readiness. Jon peered through the trees and saw the dark silhouette of the malorum lurking between trees. After summoning a bit of courage Jon made sure his shield's straps were secured on his forearm and began to walk toward it.

  More laughter filled the air as he got closer, so he called out after it, "Are you going to stop walking away and face me already?" The taunt seemed to work, as the malorum did stop walking and faced Jon. Its face was still mostly covered, although a sharp-toothed smile appeared below the edge of the hood. "That's better, isn't it?" Jon continued, but the malorum only laughed a little louder this time. Jon held his ground, waiting for any sudden movements from this enemy, but there were none. All it did was laugh as it slowly trekked backward through the trees. A false sense of confidence tried entering Jon's mind as it disappeared from view, but he knew better than to believe it. He knew that he did not scare or frighten this enemy off by the way it smiled and laughed. He also knew he would be seeing it again later. All Jon could be grateful for now was that he did not have to wake up in the infirmary, and he did not have to be carried up there by his barefooted guide. The young soldier eased his nerves by sitting on the ground by what appeared to be a man-made campfire. Not knowing who it belonged to Jon shrugged it off and found a comfortable spot to rest for the night. He removed his armor, as he observed his surroundings, and then drifted off into a deep and relaxing sleep.

He woke up the next morning at the sound of trees swaying in the strong breeze. He looked around, expecting Pneuma to be watching over him, but his guide was not there. The only things Jon could see as he put his armor back on was what appeared to be a pack of white wolves off in the distance and a family of bluebirds flying around nearby. Jon stood up to search for food as his stomach grumbled for attention. Pneuma had usually greeted Jon when he awoke with a handful of food, but this time he had to scavenge for his own.

After walking around for several minutes he came across a fruit tree and picked a few things from it. The wolves he had seen earlier had moved on out of Jon's sight, and he felt alone once more. He leaned against the tree he had plucked his food from and began eating only to be interrupted by the sounds of hurried footsteps coming from behind him. He quickly took his last bite, discarded the remains of the fruit, and whipped his head around to see Odas sprinting toward him. "There you are, bud!" the large man panted.

"What's wrong?" Jon had never seen Odas run so fast.

"I need your help over here. King's orders." Odas had arrived at the tree Jon stood near with his lungs begging for air.

"Lead the way," Jon quickly replied, and the two of them were off into the forest's dense undergrowth. "What's happening?" Jon asked as they hurried along.

"I just came from the castle and got dropped off around here. The King wanted me to find you before I went to fight, but I don't know the forest as well as I ought to."

"Fight who? You mean malorum?" Jon persisted as they dodged branches and jumped over logs.

"There's a group of 'em in the forest, trying to mess with a couple of people in cages," Odas answered. "It's just a small group, but the King said they're tough."

Thinking of what Odas meant by small he asked, "So you mean there's about ten of them, right?"

"More or less. I have a plan though, so no worries." Odas shrugged off a falling tree branch as he persisted through the trees.

"Where's Pneuma? Is he going to help?" Jon was hoping he would see the much more experienced warrior once he got there.

"Don't know yet. I guess we'll find out, huh?" After he said this Odas came to a sudden stop and held out his massive hand to help Jon to do the same. Jon skidded to a halt as Odas's hand caught the collar of his vest. "They're right up there, so we gotta be quiet."

Jon looked through the trees and saw a group of about thirty malorum gathered around a small number of cages in a large clearing ahead. "Um...that looks a bit more than ten Odas."

"I did say 'more or less', right?" Odas shrugged.

"You also said you have a plan, so do you want to share it right about now?" Jon asked as he considered the difficulty of the fight which was about to take place.

"Come over here. I made something." Odas led the way to a row of trees nearby.

Jon noticed something slightly peculiar about the trees once he got closer. "What is that tied between them?" Jon saw what appeared to be a rope stretched between two tree branches with something situated in the middle of it.

"Ah! That's the plan I thought of," Odas innocently answered.

"And what does this plan entail?" They had arrived at the object situated in the middle of the rope and Jon began investigating it. "Is this a seat?" Jon stared wide-eyed at a rough-cut square of leather tied in place.

"How do ya feel about flying?" Odas had a suspicious grin upon his face.

"Are you serious?" Jon exclaimed almost loud enough for the malorum to hear.

"Sometimes," Odas nonchalantly replied as he picked Jon off the ground and placed him on the leather seat. "I'll be right behind you. Don't worry."

Before Jon could ask if it was safe, Odas was pulling back the elastic rope he had tied between the trees. When it reached the point before breaking he whispered into Jon's ear, "Remember to hold your shield in front of you," and let go. In the blink of an eye Jon became a blur through the row of trees passing him by. He expected one of them to reach out one of their branches and stop him, but much to his chagrin he continued gaining speed. As he neared the edge of the tree line he realized he was heading right for the large group of malorum in the clearing ahead. He remembered Odas's parting words and quickly huddled behind his dark green shield, trusting it would provide some sort of protection from the malorum's sharp weapons.

    In what seemed to be only a couple of milliseconds, the shiny exterior of Jon's shield met the side of an unsuspecting malorum's face and carried Jon into the center of their huddled group. Jon managed to put a dent in the gathering by knocking ten of the malorum to the ground. He would have continued through the entirety of them if he had not collided into the few cages resting in the midst of the now broken circle. He stumbled to his feet, dusted the metallic remains that had been broken from the cages from his shield, and apologized to their occupants for flying into them.

    Just as he had gotten his footing he heard a familiar voice shouting from the trees. "Watch out!" Jon had barely moved out of the way to see Odas flying past him and into ten more of the malorum. Apparently the larger man had a harder time accommodating for his size, since he continued past the large group and skidded to a halt several yards away. Jon sprinted over to help him to his feet as the malorum stared around in confusion at what just happened. "Thanks, bud," Odas muttered as he got his footing and dusted off the dirt and blood from his armor.

    "Was that part of your plan?" Jon asked as the malorum began to angrily stare at the two of them.

    "It actually worked better than I thought. You ready to fight? I figured we killed about half of them." Odas was correct in his assessment. Just by knocking into the group they managed to kill fifteen malorum by forcing them onto each other's weapons.

    "You got any more bright ideas?" Jon asked as the remaining malorum began walking toward them.

The Battle

"I didn't really plan this far ahead. I guess we could just kill them the normal way now." Odas shrugged as he tightened the bandages which had been coming undone on his hands.

Without any more hesitation Odas sprang forward with his shield clasped in both hands, ready to dispose of the remaining malorum. Jon quickly followed after him but with his sword firmly embraced in both of his hands. That morning the two of them, with more credit going toward Odas, fended off the large group of malorum from terrorizing the small group of people sitting helplessly in their cages. After the last enemy fell Odas and Jon checked the damage done and found the locks which suited their respective keys. Although no one emerged from their comfortable prison cells that morning the two soldiers were still greeted by the rain, which fell from the sky like confetti.

They congratulated each other on a job well done but were interrupted by a familiar voice. "That was fun to watch." Pneuma had emerged from the direction the custom slingshot resided. "That sling shot chair worked out very well, I must say, Odas."

"Where have you been?" Jon turned to see Pneuma inspecting the area where Odas had skidded to a stop.

"I was hungry, so I sat on one of those branches and watched. I figured you wouldn't mind that I didn't ruin your fun." Pneuma finished the remainder of the food he had been snacking on.

"You liked it, did ya?" Odas asked with his chest slightly more puffed out than usual.

"Oh yeah! I looked at it before I walked over here. Very good craftsmanship," Pneuma answered as he patted Odas on the back.

"I learned from the best, bud," Odas returned the gesture.

"How are you going to clean this mess up?" Jon asked as he surveyed the carnage.

"I untied the rope from the trees, so I guess I'll just drag it all to one of the furnaces I have set up. There's one around here somewhere." Pneuma answered as he started to gather the dismembered limbs and torsos of the malorum left scattered on the ground.

"So what do we do now?" Jon asked.

"Have you gone to see the King yet? I'm sure he has something for you to do," Pneuma answered as the rain ceased falling.

"Not yet. I need to hurry and get up there," Jon excitedly said. After taking a moment to wipe the water from his shield Jon was in the air and being carried toward the castle.

The trip there was short lived due to the King having immediate plans to be carried out, but Jon still enjoyed the time he got to spend walking and talking in the garden. The King had asked him to return to the prisoner once again, and so that is where the eagle had carried him. He spent the remainder of the day trying to figure out how to strike it without doing harm to the man inside, but it was to no avail. Every time he tried something new shards of glass and metal barbs would rain down upon the man.

He eventually got so exhausted that he sought out the cold security of the boulder he would routinely sit upon in times like this. He blindly reached out for it, only for his hand to be met by a warm clumpy substance. He held his hand up to inspect what it was and found it to be blood. It was not the black sticky kind he saw earlier in the morning, but it was red and mostly dried. He remembered the blow which landed him in the infirmary and concluded the blood must be his own. After this realization Jon stood atop the boulder and surveyed the field surrounding him in hopes of finding the hooded malorum lurking around. As evening approached, Jon looked down to the boulder to see a smudged smiley face, drawn in his own blood, staring up at him. The tattooed marking had been carved into the stone in hopes that it would last long enough for the intended recipient to see it.

"There's no use in hiding! I'm going to kill you sooner or later!" Jon nervously shouted into the unoccupied space around him.

"Who are you going to kill, may I ask?" A raspy voice was faintly heard behind him.

Cay had arrived and was standing next to the boulder Jon was still standing on top of. "Who said that?" Jon looked around and could not see the short brunette looking up at him.

"Does your peripheral vision not come down this far?" Cay playfully answered back.

Jon looked down to see her arms folded and an eyebrow raised. "I didn't even see you there. You should carry a stepstool or something." After saying this Jon could have sworn that he heard a peep of laughter coming from inside the cage, but he could not see through its obstructions from the standpoint he had.

"Very funny. You ready to go?" Cay asked.

"Where are we going?" Jon stood there confused.

"We have a meeting in the forest with other soldiers. So are you ready to go?" Cay elaborated.

Jon hopped down from his post to join her and asked, "Is there a faster way to get than walking?"

"I was hoping you'd ask." Cay's face lit up. She put her fingers up to her lips and let out an extremely loud whistle. Almost instantly a large brown and black Arabian war horse galloped up to her with its head bowed. "Is this what you mean?" She began to pat its large frame. "Her name is Esvia."

"She'll work! Nice to meet you, Esvia," Jon exclaimed as he got acquainted with the muscular animal. The two of them used the boulder to mount their new form of transportation and rode off toward the dense line of trees ahead of them. As they got closer the sun began to fall behind them, which provided Jon a glimpse of their destination. A fire had been lit just inside the forest's outer shell. Cay nudged Jon to indicate that was where they were headed.

"It looks like people are getting there early."

"I see Odas!" Jon exclaimed as a much larger silhouette joined the company that was already assembled.

"Can you hear that?" Cay asked Jon during a brief moment the wind had stopped whistling.

The soldiers had gathered around the campfire and began to sing a song he remembered from his days in his cage. The pleasant noise only grew louder as they approached.

Upon arriving at the edge of the forest Cay whispered to Jon, "When we walk up just join in…obviously only if you know the song." The two of them dismounted Esvia and sent her on her way. They then walked into the forest and journeyed toward the campfire.

As they got within thirty or forty feet of the others, Jon noticed something peculiar. "What are those on the ground?"

"I think you know that answer already." Cay smiled as she pressed on toward the small gathering.

Jon had indeed known what the objects were that sat undisturbed upon the ground. They were black, waist-high, metal cages. Each one of them had a person which sat inside and watched

The Battle

the campfire flicker toward the sky. Jon joined Cay as they found an open spot by the fire, and both of them were passed an opened coconut shell filled with milk. Cay joined the singing immediately as Jon, not yet familiar with the song, listened and watched the faces of the soldiers that stood around the makeshift pit in the ground.

This continued on for about fifteen more minutes until one of the older gentlemen made the announcement, "Let's all go up to see the King." The request was met with smiles as each soldier stepped away and raised their shield into the air. Cay urged Jon to do the same, and the large group of soldiers was all in the air.

"Are we all going to talk with the King?" Jon turned to ask Cay, who he got paired to fly with once again.

"Yep!" She joyfully answered as they rose above the treetops and soared toward the garden.

"How will he hear us all?"

"You'll see when we get up there. Just talk to him like you normally would," Cay answered. For the remainder of the trip Jon silently enjoyed the breeze and processed what she had said.

They came to their usual landing spot before the King, and everyone received their own mug of water just as they always have before. Iam, as usual, took everyone's armor and placed it by the base of the tree. One of the older men that Jon had flown in with approached the King and began talking. The two of them had a conversation as if nobody else was there, and after they were done he stepped aside for another soldier to express thankfulness for what the King had done. Jon watched as the King treated everyone equally. He listened to their appreciation, their concerns, and their excitedness with fresh and open ears. Everyone wound up getting a turn to converse with him, including Odas, Cay, and Jon. After they were all finished, the first gentleman emerged from the group once more to say the parting words. As he did this Iam returned everyone's armor and gathered each mug from their friendly hands.

Once they were all adorned with their colorful uniforms, shields began to be raised in the air. Eagles gathered them, two by two, and carried the soldiers over the garden's expanse. Jon and Cay shared another flight as they smiled back down toward the waving arms of their King and friend. The eagles flew back toward the campfire from where they originally gathered.

"That was amazing," Jon said as he dumbfoundedly stared back toward the mountains.

"I know, right?" Cay joyfully answered. "It looks like they're ready to go." Cay motioned toward the group.

While Jon and Cay had been talking a few of the older soldiers had somehow acquired torches and were separating everyone else into groups. "Whoa! How'd Odas get a torch?" Jon asked as he joined Cay in the bearded man's group.

"The King gave it to him," Cay explained as Odas waved at them.

"Why didn't we get one?" Jon asked as his group began their journey into the forest.

"We're not ready yet," Cay replied.

"Ready for what?

"Odas is going to show us around the forest. Don't you remember from before?" Cay answered as she pointed toward a cage that was moving along the ground. At first Jon was confused at how the cage could be moving, but once his eyes fell on a rope stretched between the cage and another soldier his memories returned to him.

The Battle

"I remember. You used to drag me around while I was still in my cage. How were you able to do that?" Jon was watching a soldier, about their age, ahead of him dragging a cage which must have weighed twice as much as them.

"Ha! I may be small, but I got the job done." Cay smiled brightly. "Also, remember the last time you were doing this was a week ago. It was the day before you got out."

Jon watched the caged person closely for the rest of the journey. Less than a week ago he was in the same predicament they were in now. Jon wanted to go up to the cage so badly and just plead with the person inside to come out, but he did not. He just walked with the group. He would occasionally hear something Odas would say, but his main focus was on the individual that had yet to experience the freedom he now felt and understood. It was the same frustrated feeling he had toward the man near the boulder, but there at least seemed to be more hope in the eyes of this person. All Jon managed to do in that half hour was find the lock his key fit inside and discard it into some bushes while they stopped for a moment.

Jon was indeed mesmerized, which caused Cay to ask multiple times, "So are you ready to go?"

After he received a light slap on the arm, Jon replied, "I'm ready."

Cay peeled him away from the cage and brought him over to the large man still holding the well-lit torch. "So did ya enjoy it?" Both of them nodded their heads and thanked him. After he gave them both a hug, Odas went over to the cage which Jon had been transfixed by, bent down, and began picking off some of the metal barbs with his hands. Jon and Cay returned to the campfire to see the other soldiers before they all went their separate ways.

After more hugs and handshakes Cay asked Jon, "So, where do you want to go now?"

He thought of the caged man he had been spending so much time around. "Could you take me back to where you picked me up from?"

Cay politely answered, "Of course," and the two of them walked to the same spot the majestic horse had delivered them to before the meeting had started. She put her fingers to her lips, as she had done before, and whistled loudly into the cool night air. Seconds later Esvia came galloping up, ready to carry them back to the caged man.

They mounted the horse with little difficulty and rode off toward the west. After they arrived at the blood-stained boulder Jon asked Cay, "What are you going to do for the rest of the night?"

"The King wants me to help someone that's about an hour's ride from here," Cay answered as she ran her fingers through the horse's black mane.

"Will I see you tomorrow, then?" Jon asked as he sat against the boulder.

"I don't know yet. We'll have to see what the King has planned."

"Alright...." As Cay began situating herself for the journey Jon added, "I just wanted to say thank you."

"For what?" Cay asked.

"I know it must not have been easy to drag me around everywhere, but thank you for being patient with me," Jon answered his raspy-voiced friend.

The Battle

"It was my pleasure," Cay answered before she jokingly added, "I'm pretty strong, remember." Jon laughed, and the two of them said goodnight before she rode out of view.

Jon walked over to the cage to see the man still staring down at his hands. The cage looked the same as it did before he had left to join the other soldiers at the campfire. "I'm here if you ever want to talk." Jon kindly whispered between the jagged bars. The man did not look up, but he did shift around, which told Jon he had heard him.

Jon kept his eyes open for any sneaky malorum for the remainder of the night, although not much happened. The wind picked up a few times, which gave Jon the uneasy feeling of being watched, but there were no attacks made by the enemy. Since there did not appear to be any threats around him, nor did it seem as though his eyes wanted to remain opened any longer, he said goodnight to the man and decided it was time for some much needed rest. He kept his armor on as he laid down near the boulder, but far enough away for his shield to surround him, and allowed his eyelids to close.

R.W. Allen

Chapter 11:
Into the Canyon

    The next morning was unlike any other morning Jon had experienced thus far in his travels. A loud ringing noise echoed through his ears, preventing him from hearing anything that went on around him, all the while clumps of dirt and debris fell upon his face as he struggled to open his eyes. It was the first time he had fallen asleep on the battlefield. Every other morning he had either woken up in the King's garden or in the peaceful embrace of the forest. Jon's hands scurried across the ground in search of his shield and sword as more dirt and explosions filled the air around him. He stumbled to his feet after obtaining his equipment and walked into a rather large divot where his always comforting boulder used to be. The smell of sulfur filled his nostrils as more dirt flew up into the air.

    The ringing in his ears momentarily subsided, which allowed him the opportunity to remember where he had fallen asleep the night before. Still dazed from the chaos that surrounded him Jon secured his shield back on his forearm and firmly grabbed his sword. "Where is the cage?" His thoughts frantically ran through his mind. His eyes finally jolted open, and he raised his shield just in time to deflect more debris flying toward him.

The Battle

After he took a panoramic view of his surroundings Jon's eyes located what they were in search of. The cage, with the man still inside, was sitting in the same place it had been when Jon closed his eyes the night before. Fearing that the man was injured, Jon darted over to the cold metallic prison only to find that the man was totally oblivious to what was happening outside. More ringing filled Jon's ears as grenades formed divots on the ground around them. "I need to get him out of here," Jon thought as he searched for some way to help the man still absentmindedly staring down at his own hands. As more sulfur filled the remaining vacancies of his nose, Jon's hand came across the rope he had wrapped around himself. Smiling at his sudden revelation of what to do with it Jon quickly tied it around the cage with a poorly fastened knot and began to drag it toward a patch of trees far off in hope of some sort of sanctuary from the explosions.

He did not get too far before he noticed a small group of six or so malorum following him. After he became aware of the fact that he was not yet strong enough to run with the cage dragging behind him, Jon stopped and realized he was going to have to fight. "I'll be right back," Jon whispered to the man still unaware of anything not having to do with the dirtied palms in front of his face.

Jon set the rope on top of the cage, resecured his shield onto his forearm, separated his sword at its handle, and marched toward the small group of malorum. Their last grenades flew through the air only to be shunned away by the dark green exterior of the soldier's shield. They exploded in the air several yards away, causing Jon and the caged man no harm.

Jon knew this was what he signed up for. He was not going to have Odas, Emet, or Cay always around to wean him into battle. He knew he had to be able to do it himself. It was at this moment he was reminded of the magnitude of his choice to crawl out of that cage just one week ago. He knew that the malorum were not going to stop until he was dead, and the caged man grew even more hesitant to leave his prison, so he fought.

Every doubt Jon had about his skill and ability to fight was temporarily suppressed. Every feeling of inadequacy which attempted to make its way inside his mind was met with fierce opposition. He was committed to protecting the man whose cage he had tied his rope to. The next several minutes were unlike any Jon had ever experienced before. Every breath he took seemed to give him new life, and he used it to successfully defeat every malorum who persisted in their plans of triumph. He stared down at his fallen adversaries, hoping one of them would spring back to life so he could use the remaining adrenaline still coursing through his veins.

"Well, what happened here?" A familiar voice ran through Jon's ears as the rain began to fall down upon the scene before him.

The rain calmed the over-excited soldier enough to lower his swords and turn around to see a bearded man standing next to the cage. "Oh hey, Odas."

"It looks like it got a little messy over here. Who's this?" Odas looked down at the man looking up at him from inside his cage.

"Oh...so he looks up for you!" Jon exclaimed in a slightly frustrated tone.

"What do ya mean?" Odas stooped down and found a lock his key fit inside of.

"He's just been looking down at his hands whenever I'm around." Jon caught his breath and walked over to where the large man stood.

The Battle

"Well...ya just gotta be patient with him." Odas removed the glimmering lock and launched it through the air. "It's not going to be pleasant for whoever that hits." He watched as the lock sailed out of view.

"What brings you here?" Jon asked as his nerves calmed down and his breathing steadied.

"It's time to go train. I thought I'd come get ya."

"Can we bring him with us?" Jon asked as he looked down toward the caged man.

"I'm sure he'd be fine here. We have to get a move on," Odas replied and started walking east toward the forest. "Are ya comin'?" Jon nodded his head, untied his rope from the cage, and followed after his comrade.

For the remainder of the day the two of them trained extensively throughout the battlefield as well as inside the forest. They occasionally took breaks for food, water, and flights to talk with the King. During their momentary rest periods, Jon received a couple letters from Cay and returned his own after he eagerly read through them multiple times each.

This routine continued for about the next week and a half. There were a few trips made to the campground, which Jon greatly enjoyed, but much of his time was spent with his forest guide and Odas. Emet and Cay would also occasionally stop by to train with them on their way to get their own training sessions with Pneuma, supplying Jon with a little sanity and comedic relief when Odas and Emet would bicker. Jon grew tremendously during this period of time, both in ability and knowledge. A few more sprouts of facial hair grew on his chin the more he fought off the enemy and spent time with those training him. Odas would flaunt his own beard occasionally when Jon was caught spending a little too much time staring at himself in the river, but the younger of the two knew it was all in good fun.

After another night of rest inside the forest, Jon awoke to Odas staring off into the distance. "What do you see out there?" Jon hurried to his feet after putting his armor on and looked in the direction Odas was transfixed on.

"Did ya know that you've had a hooded thing followin' ya around this past week?" Odas grumbled with his arms folded.

"I figured it was around here somewhere. Why? Do you see it?" Jon reached for his sword that he had rested against his leg.

Odas squinted his eyes and pointed forward, "It ran off that way when I woke up. No matter... Today's a big day, bud." The large man turned and excitedly grabbed Jon by his shoulders. "It's about time ya saw what Pneuma and I have been working on."

"Really?" Jon eagerly awaited more information.

"Sure is! He's there already waiting for us. It's a long walk from here, so make sure your boots are tied."

"It's about time! Wait...I need to write a letter to Cay." Jon frantically searched through his belt's pouches for a piece of paper.

"It might take too long to get to her," a raspy voice came from behind Odas.

"You're here! I guess I don't need to write a letter now," Jon joyfully said as he ran over to hug his fellow soldier. "What do you have behind you?" Jon noticed a dark metal object at the other end of her rope.

"I came across him while I was walking here. I thought you'd want him to come along," Cay answered as she pulled the familiar cage closer to where they were standing.

The Battle

"Thank you! I was wondering how I'd be able to find him before we left," Jon said as he stooped down to see the man inside.

"Well now that everyone's here, let's get a move on, shall we?" Odas asked the young travelers. They both agreed and were on their way northward after Jon replaced Cay's rope with his own.

The next few hours of traveling toward the mountains were filled with many pleasant aromas as well as many sights pleasing the soldiers' eyes. Many flowers were in full bloom along the way, which attracted many of the forest's nearby inhabitants to stop and smell what they had to offer. Odas, Jon, Cay, and the man inside the cage were not alone as they walked along their path. There were a few groups of young soldiers, around Jon and Cay's age, traveling in the opposite direction. A brief greeting was shared before they wished each other well and continued on their respective journeys.

While it was still daylight they began to hear the faint sounds of a waterfall in the distance. A smile became noticeable on Jon's face as he asked, "Is that what I think it is?"

"If you think it's a waterfall then you'd be right. We're getting' closer, bud," Odas answered in a slightly anxious—but also joyful—tone. After walking a little farther and encountering a tree with an unfamiliar engraving carved into it, Odas grumbled and began to head east. "I'm not as familiar with this area as I'd like to be. Just give me a minute to figure this out," Odas asked of the other two as he began to search for another recognizable feature in the landscape.

"What did that tree say?" Cay innocently asked.

"Well..." Odas began while trying to keep his composure about him "It basically said that I made a mistake. We're not too far off though. Pneuma said he'd leave something around here just in case I got lost." The large man began straining his eyes as he stared between the trees. "Ah! There it is!" Odas saw a piece of black cloth tied to a tree branch a few paces from where they were standing. "He knows me all too well." After his mood lightened because of that subtle redirection, Odas motioned to the others and they all continued in the appropriate direction.

After several more minutes of walking they heard a rustling of leaves and cracking of branches. "Is that Pneuma?" Cay's voice cracked in excitement as she looked through a row of trees.

The gravelly-voiced man must have heard her, since he immediately stopped what he was doing and waved at the small group going toward him. "Judging by the way you all came I trust you saw the cloth I left for you Odas?"

"I did. Thanks for that!" Odas beamed.

"It was no problem at all. So, Jon, are you ready to embark on your next mission?" Pneuma asked the eager soldier.

"I think so!" Jon grabbed hold of his sword and looked around for what awaited him. "So...what is it?"

"Follow me." Pneuma led the way farther east as he continued, "I trust you've emptied your bowels or else this could get interesting." Jon gave a worried look toward Cay and silently followed after his guide and Odas. The four of them walked along an overgrown path until they reached a site only familiar to the three men.

"What is that?" Cay inquired.

"It is a device used for...how you say...achieving flight. I believe you've used something like it before, Jon?" Pneuma smiled at the young soldier.

"I have." Jon gulped as he remembered the rope Odas had stretched between a couple of trees about a week and a half ago.

"Don't worry, bud. This one is a lot better." Odas tried his hand at consoling Jon.

"How do you know this?"

"I've already tested it, of course...multiple times, actually," Pneuma politely interjected.

"So how does this actually work?" Cay asked, since she had not seen the previous episode of Jon and Odas being shot into action.

"It's simple. Young Jon over here simply sits in this exceptionally well-made leather seat, Odas will use his...uh...talent in pulling Jon far enough back, but not too far or else he'll end up as a nasty stain on the opposite cliff, and will let go to send Jon soaring through the air." Pneuma demonstrated with his hands.

"Wait! What cliff?" Jon exclaimed at this new revelation.

"Oh yeah...we haven't really told you what you'll be doing, did we, bud?" Odas said as he began to put Jon in his seat.

"I don't think you've humored me with that bit of information yet," Jon said as he tried to squirm free from Odas's bandaged hands.

"Well you see, there's something down there in the canyon that the King would like for you to kill. It's not *too* big, but we figured you'd fare better if you came from above." Pneuma's answer did not ease Jon's nervousness.

"How big are we talking?"

"Don't worry; it's no taller than five of you," a raspy voice chimed in.

"You know about it too, Cay?" Jon was too exhausted from struggling against Odas, so he gave in and collapsed into the leather seat, which had been prepared. "What else can you tell me?"

"Odas, here, is going to release you into the canyon that is just beyond that tree line ahead. There's a river at the bottom, and the thing you need to kill is going to be walking along it," Pneuma calmly answered.

"You said that you've tried this out before, right?" Jon asked.

"Many times."

"What did you land on if I'm the one to kill this thing?" Jon continued his attempts to relax his nerves.

"That river is fairly deep, and it has caught me many times. I've also had the help of an eagle or two whenever Odas has overshot the mark." Pneuma shot a glance at the bigger man in their company.

"So what do I do when I land on it?"

"We have that taken care of as well. Just keep your sword and shield in front of you and let them do the work," Pneuma answered again.

"So why hasn't anyone else done this if it's that simple?" Jon asked as he had not yet wrapped his mind around the task at hand.

"Well, for a couple of reasons. First, there aren't many soldiers out there nowadays with the...uh...guts to get shot into the air like this. They much prefer their feet to be on the ground instead of leaping through the air. Secondly, this is a task the King has sent aside for you to do," Pneuma plainly stated.

"But...why me? You've done it before, so why can't you do it?"

"You can ask all the questions that you want, but really, if the King wants you to do something, then as a soldier of his this is what you agreed to. I'm sure he'll be happy to explain it to you later though." Still noticing a little apprehension on Jon's part, Pneuma gently approached him and continued, "I wouldn't ask you to do anything that I haven't done myself. It comes with the territory of being a 'guide'." Pneuma casually shrugged his shoulders and smirked.

During this entire conversation there was something peculiar happening between the bars of the nearby cage that was unseen by the young soldier. The prisoner inside had his head raised and was listening to the entire conversation. He looked down, before anybody could notice this development, just before Jon turned his attention to him, "Would you watch him while I'm gone, Cay? I don't want any malorum to sneak up on him."

"You know I will." A confident, beaming smile stretched across her face as she looked between the metallic bars.

"And, both Odas and I will resume watch over him when Cay has to leave." Pneuma reminded Jon that the short brunette had her own orders from the King to carry out.

A slightly audible, "Thank you" left Jon's lips as he looked at the man once again staring down at his own hands.

"So are there any more questions before I have Odas sling you faster than the speed of sound?" Pneuma broke the uneasiness permeating through the air.

"I know you've addressed this already, but I just wanted to ask again. What if..." Jon had a difficult time finishing his question.

"Spit it out, bud," Odas urged him on as he took his position behind the seat.

"...What if I die? I know you've already said that you've tested it out before and you guys have been calibrating this, but there's always the possibility of something happening. I just..." Jon nervously stammered.

Pneuma looked at him with a serene look on his face and answered, "I know. There is always that chance, and it might not mean much to you right now, but if I deem it as good, then it is good. You have my word, remember, and out here," Pneuma glanced at the cage nearby, "that means a lot." He noticed Jon's face relax and his body sink back into the leather, so he added, "After all, what's the point of dying if you've never lived?"

"And without any further ado...." Odas's boisterous voice interrupted the tranquility of the moment. "You have some killin' to do, bud. We need to get ya in the air."

Jon nodded and said his farewells to Cay and the man inside the cage before telling Pneuma, "I'll see you when this is done."

"You will." Pneuma said with confidence he struggled to accept. "Alright Odas, take him back." As the words left his mouth Odas obliged and began backpedalling out of view from the others.

Upon reaching his designated mark, he leaned over and whispered to Jon, "It'd probably be best if ya tucked your legs for this first part." Jon did as suggested and so Odas continued, "Now take a deep breath...and...go get 'em!" After the large man heard Jon inhale a large amount of air, he let go of the seat.

It seemed as though all of the air surrounding Jon was envious of what resided in his lungs, because as soon as Odas released him from his grasp it all made a frantic effort to join the large gasp he had taken. He did not give in to its advances, nor could he if he even wanted to, for his mouth remained vacuum sealed from the force. Jon also had no problem staying firmly embedded in the seat as he quickly approached the place where the other three had been standing, awaiting the fast-paced arrival of the soon-to-be airborne member of their group.

"3...2...1..." Cay heard Pneuma whisper right before a flash of green shot past them. Jon could barely identify the colors of their armor as he flew slightly above them. He made his best effort to wave, but his hand was being firmly held in place.

"Well...there's no going back now," Jon nervously thought as he felt the seat release him into the air. Moments after that, the forest exhaled the soldier into the sky. This is where the trust he had in Pneuma and Odas would prove its worth. There was no longer anything to reach out and grab. There was no option of walking away. There definitely was not the option of somebody else doing what he was assigned to do. Full commitment was needed at this point. His nerves began to calm after he exhaled the breath that he had been holding in his lungs, but they returned the instant he cleared the forest far enough to look down. A slight sinking feeling filled his stomach as he looked over the expansive canyon below and the forest waving goodbye behind him. Anxiety suddenly rushed to his head, and a lump grew in his throat as he drifted away.

Jon searched the tree line for the opening he emerged from in hopes that he would see one of his traveling companions before he began his descent, and he was not disappointed. All three of them were waving enthusiastically at Jon, which brightened his spirit immensely. As he was now free to lift his arm, Jon joyfully waved back at them and took another deep breath. After he saw this somewhat small gesture an abundance of confidence seemed to overtake any apprehension he had. The nervousness he had was still present, as was to be expected, but it was not the paralyzing feeling he had just moments before. "I can do this," he reassured himself and turned his gaze back down toward the gaping canyon which awaited his arrival.

The image filled Jon's eyes with instantaneous beauty. The wide, glimmering river was staring back up at him as it continued its flow toward the southeast. On either side of the river Jon could see strips of land separating the water from the incredibly steep cliffs it had carved into over the years. Jon took in its features, which included the waterfall to his left that he had heard earlier, until he felt his momentum slowly diminish. He had begun his decline into the canyon and toward a curiously large, and moving, object below.

There was something moving lazily along the river bed, almost resembling a man in its appearance. It was the only thing in Jon's view other than the waterfall, a couple of deer, the river, and the majestic canyon surrounding it all. Jon squinted his eyes as he continued in his approach to see that it was a mixture of a malorum and a giant of a man. Its arms dangled helplessly from its blackened hunched-over torso. Its legs dragged along, stumbling occasionally under the immense weight they carried. Long, oily, jet black hair draped over its face, so Jon could not see its eyes or any of its other facial features. A broken tail slightly protruded out of the back of its shoddy loincloth and tattered wings stuck to its back, prohibiting it from any attempts of flight. Jon felt sorry for the creature until he saw it reach out and grab one of the deer drinking from the river. Without any hesitation, the malorum-like creature bit off its head and disrespectfully disposed of its body into the water. It tried to chase after the other deer, but they scattered off in time so their fate would not be the same as their companion's.

As Jon got closer he realized he would be landing directly on its back, completely unseen by the creature. "Remember, Jon, just

The Battle

hold out your sword and shield, and let them do the work," Jon said to himself as he remembered what Pneuma had said before. He could not bear to watch as he held them out, as Pneuma had demonstrated, and closed his eyes.

The next few instances all happened in a matter of seconds. Due to the sheer velocity of Jon's plummet he collided with the near-thirty-foot creature with enough force to knock it to the ground. Jon became detached from his sword as he was sent rolling forward from the momentum. He finally opened his eyes to see that his shield was still secured onto his forearm, but his sword was left protruding from the creature's back.

Jon got to his feet and lightly dusted himself off before he cautiously approached the enemy. Jon used a piece of driftwood that he found nearby to gently prod at its head. He yelled at it a few times, well-prepared to run if it decided to stand up, but there was no response. He circled around to get a better view of his sword and, against his better judgment, decided to climb on top of the fallen adversary to see where his weapon had pierced. After he clambered up its slippery torso, he found that his sword was handle-deep in the top middle of its back but slightly to the left of its spine. "Did I...did I kill it...?" Jon stuttered as he tried to get a better view of its face. To his utter amazement Jon found that the creature's eyes were lifelessly staring back up at him. The hideousness of its face left Jon speechless as he looked it over. Blackened blood trickled from its mouth and what slightly resembled a nose. Its face was violently scarred from previous battles. Its teeth were sharp and jagged, but also scarcely filled its mouth.

Jon still could not believe what had just happened, so he poked it with the driftwood. There was still no reaction. Jon had indeed killed this monster, and now there was the small task of somehow retrieving his sword from its now motionless heart.

He returned to where his sword resided after he let everything settle in his mind. He knew it was going to take some work after a couple of attempts, so he stood over it and grabbed what he could with both hands. After many attempts of wiggling and twisting the sword, he felt it give in to his efforts. It slowly but surely emerged with black blood and bits of flesh covering every inch that had been immersed. "A little rain would help." He pleaded for the sky to unleash its cleansing water; however it did not relinquish its contents. After many failed attempts at wiping it clean with the freshly slayed creature's remains, Jon had an epiphany. "I could use the waterfall!"

So the exhausted soldier ran over to where the large waterfall was and held his sword under its downpour. After it was completely cleaned and Jon returned it to the sheath behind his head the rain began to fall. Jon could appreciate the humor in the situation as he looked toward the now overcast sky and laughed. Once the rain ceased and his clothes were completely clean, the only way he found to get out of the canyon was to call for an eagle to rescue him. It worked out exceptionally well, since he also greatly desired to speak with the King. Once an eagle saw the familiar shine of his freshly cleaned shield, Jon was almost instantly lifted out of the canyon and was soon standing in his usual place before Iam and the King.

He began his usual armorless walk, mug of water in hand, with the King navigating along their usual pathways. As Jon walked with his King, he noticed a smile never faded from his weathered face. "Thank you for believing in me," the young soldier said to his superior.

The Battle

"Always," he gently responded. "Because of your bravery I am appointing a new task for you to do for me."

A mixture of overwhelming joy and nervousness grew inside Jon's chest at this announcement. "What...what do you mean? I didn't really do much."

"Young Jon Smith, you need to start to see things as I see them. You did the work I appointed for you to do. That is all I asked, correct?" The King grinned at Jon's innocence.

"What is this new task you want me to do?" He did not see much use in arguing, so he accepted the compliment.

"In three months I am going to station you west of where you just came from. I will have some work for you to do there," the King answered as he stopped and rested his mug on a nearby lamp post.

"What do you want me to do in the meantime?" Jon humbly asked.

After he picked a couple handfuls of fruit from a bush and gave some to Jon, he answered, "Get to know the people where I send you back to, learn as much as you can from them and Pneuma, and keep your eyes open for people you need to help." The two of them talked until Jon had his armor returned and eventually left the tranquility of the garden. He was dropped off in the forest by the canyon he had been propelled into.

Pneuma and Odas were already there awaiting his arrival. "So...how'd it go, bud?" A weighty hand met Jon's arm.

"It looked like everything went according to plan. We didn't have to scrape you off the side of the canyon, now did we?" Pneuma's voice was also heard over a gust of wind.

"No you didn't. I should have never doubted you," Jon answered as he basked in the forest's jubilation. "What's all this about?" The trees swayed, fallen leaves danced in the wind, and a few animals gathered around like Jon had never seen before.

"The forest wants to express its gratitude," Pneuma nonchalantly replied. "You see, that monster you killed was one of many that have been terrorizing this area for a while."

"You mean there are more of them?" Jon asked with his mouth agape.

"Nasty things, they are." Emet emerged through the trees to join the conversation.

"There ya are! It's about time ya showed up, old buddy!" Odas happily welcomed the gold- and silver-armored soldier.

"Ah yes...good to see you too, Odas," Emet responded in a less-cheerful manner. "So who is this, may I ask?"

"You may ask, but I'll go ahead and tell you. This here is someone close to Jon," Odas answered. "Pneuma has been using your rope to bring him here, Jon."

The large metal cage was, indeed, still attached to the rope Jon had tied to it before he left. Pneuma handed over the reins and said, "He watched when we flung you into the canyon, and he took kindly to Cay before she left."

Jon received the rope from Pneuma and stooped down to greet the man inside the cage's bondage. This time he looked up, just for a moment, and seemed to acknowledge Jon's attempt. "Thank you both for watching over him."

Odas motioned that it was no problem and asked, "So are we ready to get training? We heard that there's something else the King wants you to do in about three months."

"Of course you guys already know." Jon expressed his bewilderment as to how they already knew of his upcoming travels, but quickly suppressed his questions when his stomach started to announce its food deprivation. "Could we get something to eat first? I've only had some fruit from the garden."

"Follow me everyone. I've got a surprise for the young soldier," Pneuma answered, and the three of them, with the caged man being dragged close behind, followed after their guide to a small opening in the forest's dense undergrowth. The sight which came next made Jon's mouth water to the point of almost overflowing from his lips. There were four stumps around a campfire, with a plate full of food resting atop each one. Jon rushed over to see that each plate had a large steak, a steaming potato, and a medley of vegetables covering its surface.

"How do ya say it? Bone appetite, Jon," Odas cheerfully said as they each chose their seats.

"I'm not sure that's how you say it, Odas," Jon replied. "It looks like I need to kill things more often, huh?" he joked before he gave a thankful nod to Pneuma for preparing the feast.

The remainder of the day consisted of much eating, exploring the forest around them, and some training now and then. Jon noticed throughout the night that Emet grew increasingly excited the longer he spent time in the forest, and his bickering with Odas seemed to lighten up the more they traveled with each other. Pneuma enjoyed showing them the various ponds, bushes, and other features of their surroundings.

As they prepared for sleep, Jon shared the story of what happened in the canyon with Emet, since he was not there to see it. It provoked much laughter from the older soldier as Odas thought it to be a good idea to illustrate the story throughout its telling. After sharing in each other's good company, Pneuma retreated into the forest to do his usual surveillance, and the other three slept peacefully beneath the forest's moonlit canopy.

Chapter 12:
A New Land

    The prairie in which Jon woke up was similar to the areas in the forest that he had already been to. The forest surrounded the prairie, but the northern mountains were, remarkably, still in view toward the west. The campground and the battlefield became somewhat familiar to him as he spent much time exploring and helping those that he could. The only real change was the muggier weather he had to endure for the next couple of months until the winter weather arrived.

    Odas and Emet stayed with him during his time there to show him more of the forest, increase his skills in fighting, and provide him with familiar faces as he met many new soldiers. It was quite obvious from the start that Emet knew this area better, because he greeted all of his fellow gray-haired people with a smile and a firm handshake. Odas got along better with the soldiers closer to Jon's age, so it was easier for the young soldier to get comfortable around everyone.

    The older soldiers in this region seemed to enjoy being within the campground's walls, opposed to being outside and fighting. Jon found their attitudes to be a little strange, since there were many cages around their campground with their locks still intact. Jon wanted to ask why they did not get out more often, but he thought he was too young to question the more knowledgeable soldiers' decisions.

The three months Jon was there passed more quickly than he thought they would. The knowledge gained in using his sword proved to be beneficial to him as the weather got colder and it became more difficult to move his hands. He had received a specially made, dark green, long-sleeve shirt, which went on under his vest and t-shirt, from a recent visit with the King and Iam, so he was not too cold to perform his duties.

Most of his time was spent with soldiers his own age, but also with the two that had traveled with him. Walks with Pneuma, conversations with the King, and Cay's letters were also integral for Jon to keep his sanity in the midst of all the chaos of the new land. There were several instances Jon was overwhelmed by the chaos and lack of help, when Odas and Emet would be in another area, to the point of waking up on a bed in the darkened infirmary of the campground closest to the area he resided.

It only frustrated the young soldier when he awoke to know that the enemy had gotten the upper hand on him. Several times Jon was in such a hurry to get back onto the battlefield and retaliate that he paid little attention to the door he repeatedly sent off its hinges. The nurse that was there made many attempts to chase after Jon to have him repair what he had done, but it was to no avail. He had grown to dislike that door, because it prevented him from seeing if anyone else was inside and needed his help, so much so that he began to get ideas of how to remove it from its hinges in more creative ways. He did not act upon any of his impulses, of course. He thought the task of permanently removing the door from its position was the task of an older soldier, so he just did what he had been doing until one day things changed for the better.

It was a cold and breezy winter day, no snow was on the ground yet, and Jon had just descended the short hill which led up to the campground's outer walls. Usually after making this trip Jon would continue on and try to find either Odas or Emet to travel around with, but this day there was an eagle patiently waiting for him several feet from the bottom of the hill. As Jon cautiously approached the large bird, a castle messenger dismounted, silently gave Jon a sealed letter, and returned to the eagle. The messenger lingered a little while longer than he usually did when Jon received a letter from Cay, so the young soldier eagerly opened it to see what it read.

Joy instantly filled him as he finished reading its message. "I need to write a letter to Cay! Could you wait to leave so I could write it? It'll only take a minute." He asked, and the messenger consented to his request. Jon's hand shook excitedly as he wrote and handed over the paper. After the eagle left, Jon exclaimed, "I need to tell Pneuma!"

So he ran to the forest along the northeast side of the hill he was standing at the bottom of, and quickly found Pneuma sharpening his sword atop a mound of boulders. "I presume you have news to share with me?" Pneuma stopped what he was doing and turned to Jon.

"I got a letter from the King! I'll be leaving here soon!"

Jon read the letter repeatedly before Pneuma joyfully replied, "Excellent! It sounds as though you have a flight to make."

"Yes! I need to go thank him and find out what's next," Jon replied and left Pneuma to go to the castle.

After he got his mug of water, the King opened the conversation by asking, "I take it you received my letter?" Jon smiled, so the King continued, "Very good. Do you have any questions for me?"

"I do." Jon tried to corral his excitement and formulate everything he was thinking into a sentence. "What do you want me to do when I get there?"

"There is something else that I want you to kill. It is a little different than the previous enemy, but I do believe it is something you will have to see when you get there," the King replied as they stood atop one of the many bridges sewing the garden together. "There is something peculiar happening that I wish to inform you of."

"Is it bad? Did I do something wrong?" Jon eagerly searched his mind for what could have happened.

"It is quite the contrary, actually." The King looked peacefully at his soldier. "It appears as though the enemy is taking notice of you. You are causing quite a stir amongst them, and I feel as though it will only increase exponentially after you accomplish this next task for me."

"I...I don't know what to say. It doesn't feel like I did much of anything yet," Jon humbly stammered.

"My dear Jon, what have I told you before? Do you remember?"

"You told me that as long as I am doing what you ask of me, that's all you require. I'm sorry for forgetting."

"Very good." The King smiled as he leaned on the wooden rail. "I do have to inform you, the enemy is going to be more determined to kill you after you do this."

The Battle

Jon looked solemnly down at the river which ran under them. "Will I have your help out there after it's done?"

"You will."

"Then I will be ready when that time comes, I suppose." Jon gulped down the remainder of the water in his mug.

The King smiled at Jon's reflection in the water. "You will." The two of them stood back up and silently walked toward Iam patiently waiting under the tree's massive canopy. Without saying much else Jon hugged the both of them, thanked them again for everything they had done, and flew away with his armor glistening in the retreating sunlight.

He had plenty to think about that night after being delivered into the forest's welcoming arms. Soon after landing Jon prepared himself for sleep to ease his mind's worries. As he began his rest, many of the forest's nearby occupants gathered around the perimeter of his shield to help calm Jon's mind.

Jon spent the next week or so saying his goodbyes to all the soldiers he had grown close to during his time there. Some of the older men had even broken their traditions of only shaking hands to reach out and hug the younger soldier. Jon's peers wished him well and expressed their gratitude for him having their backs many times during battles with nearby malorum. Jon told them he would return when the King permitted, but he would remember their camaraderie in his travels. He held back many tears that night as he walked through the forest and spent much of his time with the caged man.

Before Jon drifted off to sleep, Pneuma came by and assured him that he would provide the travel accommodations necessary to take the man to where Jon was headed next. The young soldier knew it would have been a strenuous task to drag him the entire way, so he expressed his gratitude and raised his shield after Pneuma had left.

Jon awoke the next morning knowing it would be his final day in that land. Tears appeared in his eyes for a short time, but eventually subsided upon his acceptance of what needed to be done. After calling for an eagle and conversing with the King, Jon climbed atop the large bird to join the castle messenger already situated in place. Since there was a message needing to be delivered in the same area, the King made arrangements for Jon to ride along.

The flight was longer than usual, but Jon knew it would have been much longer if he had to walk the entire way. The soldier did not know what to say to the messenger, so he kept to himself and watched the landscape flow by underneath his feet. He watched the treetops sway under the eagle's wings and wondered how many soldiers were going on with their usual routines as he rode above them.

As the majestic bird began its descent toward an opening in the trees, Jon looked down and saw two recognizable soldiers facing each other. Odas and Emet had told him a couple of days previous that they would be returning to the land where he started his journey, but Jon did not expect to see them so soon. "Could you take me down there?" he asked of the messenger. He agreed and lowered Jon several feet away from his traveling companions before flying off.

"When are ya going to give it up, bud? I told ya before; I'll start using my sword when you start getting dirt under your fancy little fingernails!" Jon had walked up on Odas holding his right shoulder and yelling at Emet.

"What's going on here?" The peace of mind Jon had acquired over the past week had instantly been disrupted.

The Battle

"I don't know why he utterly refuses to use those magnificent swords of his, and now he got himself injured again." Emet sneered at the much larger and much stronger man.

"Well are you going to help him? He's bleeding!" Jon rushed over to see a trail of blood streaming down Odas's arm.

"It's like I said. He doesn't want to get his hands dirty. He'd much rather stay up in the campground with all the others, but then he won't be able to show off his old man moves."

"And who has slain more malorum, may I ask?" Emet pridefully retorted.

"If you aren't going to help, then please just leave, Emet." The older soldier was taken aback by the boldness of the eighteen-year-old and stormed off into the forest toward the campground. "What can I do to help, Odas? It looks like you're losing a lot of blood." Jon searched for anything that would stop the bleeding in one of his belt pouches, but he had nothing.

"I need to get to the infirmary."

"How do I get you up there?" Jon thought to himself as he climbed under Odas's massive wounded arm. Blood began to drip down Jon's face as he tried to keep his comrade upright. It was clear Odas was getting light-headed and they would not be able to make it up the campground's steep hill before he passed out.

Just before Jon's knees could give out, he heard a loud whistle pierce the air and felt his load lighten considerably. Pneuma had arrived and put Odas's other arm on his shoulders. "Quick! Tear off one of your sleeves and hand it to me." The gravelly voice leaped into Jon's ears. He did as he was told, and Pneuma pressed the green t-shirt sleeve firmly upon Odas's wound.

"What do I do now?"

"Just wait. There's some help coming. When he gets here I'll need you to take Odas to get fixed up," Pneuma answered as he poured water into Odas's mouth.

Before Jon could ask who was coming, he saw a powerfully large Clydesdale galloping toward them. Jon's mouth fell open, and he whispered, "I see."

"Hurry up and get on," Pneuma said, and Jon listened. "Now brace yourself the best you can, or else we'll have to peel you from the horse's neck when you get up there." Pneuma led the horse to a nearby boulder, hoisted Odas onto his shoulders, climbed atop the rock, and lowered Odas onto the massive back of the horse.

"You *are* stronger than you look." Jon sat stunned by how easy Pneuma made it look.

Pneuma smiled and said, "The horse knows the way. I'll meet you there." He firmly patted its side, and Jon was off toward his destination with Odas heavily leaning on him.

Several minutes passed as the two of them effortlessly wove through the trees and across the plain. When they arrived at the base of the campground's hill, the Clydesdale confidently marched up its face with relative ease. It picked up its gait once again as it saw the entrance door fling open with Pneuma standing there, motioning with his hand for the horse to come inside.

Once inside, the horse came to a sudden stop before the infirmary door. "You'd think by now that they'd take this down, or at least leave it open once in a while," Pneuma said in a rarely seen frustrated moment. He helped lower Odas from the horse and took him inside with Jon following close behind, his hand firmly pressed down on the cloth over the bearded man's wound.

The Battle

The nurse quickly patched it up and wrapped an actual bandage over the twenty or so stitches she had to give him. "They should fall out when your arm has healed, Odas," she quietly said to him. "You wouldn't have to come up here so much if you used your swords instead, you know."

Odas grumbled loudly and got to his feet. "I thank you for your help nurse, but I seem to have received that advice before." He nodded to Jon and Pneuma, waiting by the doorway, as he stormed out of the infirmary.

Pneuma thanked the nurse again for her assistance, and he, along with Jon, followed after Odas, who was furiously pacing back and forth in the courtyard. "Well...this could get interesting," he calmly foreshadowed the events to come.

"They want me to start using a weapon instead, do they? I have a grand idea." Odas stormed off toward the man-made wall surrounding the campground and ripped an entire tree trunk from its rank amongst it companions. He then marched over to a large, and somewhat rectangular, boulder—which had more than a few deep cracks carved into it—lodged into the ground, and hoisted the sharpened and decaying tree trunk above his head. He took a deep breath and drove it into the ground with all the strength he could summon. The large man repositioned his hands on the tree and raised it back into the air with the boulder firmly attached at its end, making a rather unique looking hammer. "How's this for a weapon?" He bellowed toward the infirmary and the elaborate mead hall.

Once he arrived at the door of the campground, his chest heaved at every heartbeat while he tightened his grip on the tree's trunk. He took one final deep breath and raised his makeshift hammer into the air as if it were a feather-weighted baseball bat. A powerful groan filled Jon and Pneuma's ears as he violently swung it into the large door. The door and tree trunk shattered upon impact, while the boulder split in half and fell to the ground. The noise it made caused the ground to quake underneath them. Soldiers flooded out of the mead hall to see what had interrupted their meal, and the nurse waddled out from her seclusion with her mouth wide open. Odas did not even consider looking at the speechless expressions on each of their faces before he abruptly retreated from view.

"I trust you can ride back on your new horse while I talk with our bearded comrade?" Pneuma leaned over and asked Jon.

"I can...wait...new horse?" Jon stammered as he answered him.

"Yup, take good care of it...oh and try blowing in its nose a little bit. I'll meet up with you soon to explain," Pneuma said in a nonchalant way. He turned to the nurse and the well-fed soldiers and continued, "It feels a little breezier in here. Do you feel it?" A departing nod was shared between him and Jon before Pneuma left to find Odas, making sure to tiptoe around the abundance of wooden and stone shrapnel which littered the ground in front of the vacant doorway.

Jon remained where he stood and could not summon any words to speak until his new horse began to affectionately nudge his shoulder. Jon turned around in time to feel a moist tongue lick between his eyes. "I guess I get to give you a name now, don't I?" He remembered Pneuma's parting words and reluctantly blew into its nostrils as he tried to think of a proper name to give it. "What about Clyde? It seems pretty simple." The horse sniffed Jon's face a little more, which Jon took as a sign of acceptance. "Are you ready to get out of here, too? Let's go." Jon struggled slightly to mount the impressive animal, but once he got his footing he became instantly comfortable.

Before galloping out of view, Jon looked back at the other soldiers and the nurse to see them all still standing in their same places. He tried to say his goodbyes, but it was as though he was invisible to everyone else. He shrugged his shoulders, patted Clyde's neck, and they too left through the vacant doorway.

Jon spent the remainder of the night trying to get accustomed to his new companion. They immediately headed into the forest once the sun fell completely below the horizon, which was almost a poor decision on many occasions due to rapidly-approaching tree branches, which routinely sprung out in front of his face. Clyde could sense his new owner was growing increasingly anxious, so he headed for the nearest moonlit clearing.

"That was fun!" Jon exclaimed as his feet touched the frostbitten ground where he had come to a stop.

"I'm glad you enjoyed it." Pneuma was sitting on log a few feet from where Jon stood.

"Whoa! It's like you're everywhere!" Jon was pleasantly surprised to see his guide so soon. "Where's Odas? Is he ok?"

"He has calmed down since you have last seen him. He's been assigned to a mission east of here. Do you both want some food?" Pneuma passed Jon a couple of apples to share with his horse.

After he had distributed the nourishment, Jon asked, "May I ask you a question, Pneuma?"

"Always, Jon."

"Who was right earlier, Odas or Emet?" Jon found a seat next to him.

"Ah! That is a very good question." Pneuma smiled toward the clear sky. "They both were."

Not expecting this answer, Jon sought clarification. "What do you mean?"

"It's simple. You need to use both your hands and your weapons to fight. That way you don't miss any opportunities when they present themselves." The gravelly-voiced man leaned back to lay on the ground and motioned for Jon to do the same before he continued. "You see, both Emet and Odas are very good at what they do, but they each have a knack of missing opportunities to do more."

"Do they know this? I mean that there's more they could do?"

"They do, but traditions and habits are very difficult things to get over. When you do something for so long, and it appears that it's working fine for you, you have a tendency not to try anything else…but you'll learn more about that much later in your travels, I venture to guess," Pneuma added.

Although he wanted to quench his curiosity at that moment, Jon trusted Pneuma's timing. After a few moments of silence, Clyde decided to find a place to lay down next to his new rider, which caused Jon to remember another question he had for his guide, "Pneuma?"

"Yes, Jon?"

"Why did you have me blow in his nose earlier?" Jon began to gently pat the animal's neck.

"Ah…another good question." Pneuma sat up to explain, "You see, horses are interesting creatures. They can tell much about a person from their breath, and by the looks of it this one is fond of you."

The Battle

"There you are! The King told me you came back." Cay had emerged from the forest behind them.

"Cay!" Jon sprung to his feet as soon as the moonlight touched her helmet. "I didn't expect to see you tonight!"

"I thought I'd just stop by to see if you were still alive," Cay retorted by slapping Jon on his helmet with her sword. For the remainder of the night the three of them talked and told stories of their travels. Cay was able to fill in any missing parts she had left out in her letters, while Jon did the same. He told her of what took place between Emet and Odas just a few hours earlier, which included the acquisition of his new Clydesdale. Cay saw it still lying on the ground and asked, "So what's its name?"

"His name is Clyde," Jon answered as he patted it on its neck again.

"Ah! I like the originality. The Clydesdale's name is Clyde..."

"I wanted to keep it simple." Jon caught the not-so-subtle sarcasm in her voice.

"And I assume the name 'Horse' was taken?" Pneuma laughed as Cay prodded her much taller comrade. "Are you going to ride him to our meeting tomorrow morning then?"

"We have a meeting tomorrow morning?" Jon immediately looked toward Pneuma.

"Actually, Cay, I have a use for Clyde this next month. I know, Jon...short notice." Pneuma answered, and then offered an explanation upon seeing Jon's surprised expression. "You'll have him back when you need him. Don't worry." Jon relaxed and they concluded their conversation. Pneuma and Cay went their separate ways, with Clyde following close behind the gravelly-voiced man, and Jon fell asleep shortly after.

The next morning Jon awoke to the sound of breathing in his ear. He opened his eyes to see Cay's Arabian war horse standing over him. Jon yelled and leapt to his feet, sending Cay into a fit of laughter. "You must've smelled interesting."

"Well good morning to you, too." Jon scrambled around to get his armor back on as Cay tried to lend a hand with his boots.

"Good morning! Are you ready to go?" She energetically asked as he rubbed his eyes. "Everybody is excited to see us back; you don't want to keep them waiting."

"I suppose not. Let me grab some fruit, and I'll be ready." Cay had mounted a unique saddle onto her horse, which had two places to sit. After Jon had gotten his food, he quickly climbed up and the two of them were off toward the campground and the people they had not seen for a few months.

"I guess they haven't gotten around to putting another door on here yet. I kind of like it better this way, actually." Cay inspected the vacant doorway as she walked through it.

"I guess not. They cleaned up the courtyard though." Jon did not see any of the stone or wooden debris on the ground.

After they were pleasantly greeted by their fellow soldiers, Jon and Cay found seats in the mead hall. The meeting was conducted in the same way as Jon remembered from before. They listened to the older members teach, they sang, and then they went up to the castle to have a meal with the King at the round tables. After they returned to the campground Jon and Cay went out into the courtyard and shared some of the stories of their travels with the other soldiers. Jon eagerly scanned the crowds for Odas, but he was nowhere to be seen.

The Battle

Jon searched for the bearded man endlessly until the familiar golden helmet of Emet approached. "What are you looking for, young Jon?"

"I'm looking for Odas. I can't find him anywhere. There are a couple of soldiers that look like him, but they aren't him." Jon finally looked down at his feet, defeated.

"Don't worry about it, my dear boy. He's probably out there destroying more doors and getting unnecessary wounds as we speak. He's probably the happiest he's ever been," Emet spoke with a smirk on his face.

"I do like it better without the door." Jon looked at the entrance.

"It makes the place a little drafty, I'm afraid. We're working on getting it fixed...as well as the wall over there. This kind of destruction should not be applauded. It's more of a distraction than anything."

"What do you mean?" Jon looked up with a confused look on his face.

"You see all these soldiers out here talking about it? They aren't getting anything done." Emet motioned to the crowd staring at the damage. "Let's go train."

Jon gave Cay and some of the other soldiers a farewell hug before he traveled into the forest with Emet. Jon relocated the cage he had been watching over for the past few months and dragged it to the area of the forest where they were training. He learned an abundance of knowledge from the gray-haired man until the sun began to set under the tree line. Emet certainly did not want to miss a soldier's meeting, so he promptly ended their session and sped off toward the campground. Jon knew he had a little more time before he had to traverse the flat land and cross the river, so he stayed in the forest and imitated the moves he had learned earlier.

    Cay had said she planned on giving him a ride through the arrival of another letter, so upon hearing her horse's approach he quickly grabbed some food and rode off with her. The meeting that night was similar to the other meeting he had been to before. The man standing in front of the mead hall did not say anything Jon had not already heard of the forest or ways of fighting, but he listened just so he made sure it was all firmly engrained in his mind for instinctive recollection.

    This same routine went on for a month. Jon's knowledge and skill with his sword improved, but he would have liked to train with Odas, who had not been seen since the night at the infirmary. Pneuma reminded the young soldier that Odas was needed elsewhere and he would return when the King wanted him to, but Jon could not help but feel he was missing a lot of useful knowledge. Other than his visits with the King, Iam, and Pneuma, the one constant that helped Jon maintain his sanity was the presence of Cay. They often fought alongside one another on the battlefield, and they always sat and stood next to each other during the soldier's meetings. Jon did not want to be separated from her again, so it was hard for him to hear where the King was ready to send him.

    It was a routine visit at the King's garden on a cold wintery Saturday afternoon. It was as though the garden was unaffected by the elements, because Jon was able to still walk around comfortably in his shirts and pants. He thought he remembered Pneuma saying there were hot springs in the ground atop the mountain, which gave it the year round warmth, but Jon could not entirely remember if this was the case.

The Battle

As the two of them walked along the river the King said to Jon, "I am ready to send you to your next mission."

"Will Cay be able to go with me?" Jon pleaded in hopes the King would be willing to make the accommodations.

"She will not. I have plans for her just an hour's ride south of where you will be."

"An hour's ride? How will I be able to fight?"

"How were you able to fight when you both were a day's ride away?" The King calmed his nerves. "And remember, Jon, you will have my help. Pneuma will be down there anytime you need him, and I will be up here whenever you need me. You have learned many useful skills since the moment you emerged from your cage. Do not forget this."

"I won't...I mean I'll try not to." Jon swirled the contents of his mug and watched it all settle down again within its secure sanctuary.

"I tend to enjoy hearing the former." The King smiled as they walked back toward Iam. "You will be leaving with Cay tomorrow. She will take you to where you need to be and then go on her way."

"Does she know this already?"

"I have already talked with her about this, yes." After they sealed the rest of the plans, Jon was hanging from the eagle's talons, returning to his much colder residence within the forest's confines.

Upon his return, Jon instantly began to write a letter for Cay to coordinate their travels the following day. A castle messenger flew down, without Jon needing to whistle or call, and delivered the letter. Cay replied immediately thanks to the messenger's willingness to help.

After the last reply was sent, Jon heard a rustling in the bushes nearby. Pneuma emerged, dragging the cage behind him. "I thought you might want to say your goodbyes before you leave tomorrow. I figured it'd be a little complicated to try and tow him around while you rode on the horse...unless you want to try it."

"I trust your transportation skills more than my ability to hold onto that rope. Thank you." Jon knelt down and peered through the bars, which appeared to be denser than they had ever been, to speak face to face with the man inside. While Jon talked, the man actually looked up from his hands and had a tear cascading down one of his cheeks. "I'll talk to you when I get back." Jon concluded, trying not to imitate the man's reaction, since he knew it had to be done.

After Jon picked off some of the shards of broken glass and metal barbs with his fingers, Pneuma looked back at Jon and said, "You should get some sleep. You have a long ride ahead of you." Not only did Pneuma want Jon to get a sufficient amount of rest, but he knew there were two eyes peering at Jon through the forest. The hooded malorum did not dare to come any closer, since it knew it would not fare well at the moment, so it kept its distance. Jon had no idea he was being watched, but he took Pneuma's advice and trailed off into a deep and refreshing rest.

Chapter 13:
Finding the Balance

The next morning Jon awoke to the sound of someone sharpening metal. After he quickly got his armor on the young soldier reached for his sword, only to find out it was missing. "Good morning, Jon! I got you some food for your trip." Pneuma's voice carried across the clearing as Jon frantically looked around for his weapon. "Is this what you're looking for?" Jon looked over to see Pneuma was holding the shining metal blades. "I thought I'd sharpen them for you before you headed out."

"There they are. I thought I'd lost them."

"Well hurry up and get over here before I eat your food." Pneuma motioned to the pile of fruit and coconut meat resting on a stump. "Cay will be here soon, and I'm almost done...eat up."

Jon hurried over and watched his sword's original owner sharpen both of the blades with amazing care. He ate the food which had been gathered for him, finishing just in time for Cay to arrive on her horse. "Hey, Pneuma! I never got to thank you for sharpening my swords before. I appreciate it a lot."

"You are plenty welcome. I just finished with Jon's, so he should be ready to leave." Pneuma concluded, returning the sword and waving at the two of them as they rode off toward the campground.

Their meeting was relatively similar to all the meetings they had been to before. They sang, listened to Collin teach for close to an hour, went up to the castle to have their meal within the King's simplified mead hall, and returned to close it all out. Everyone knew it was time for them to leave, so a large majority of them stood outside in the freezing cold to watch Jon and Cay approach the double wooden doors, which had been replaced, at the entrance of the courtyard. A couple of the older soldiers held them open as Jon and Cay waved goodbye to everyone and headed west.

Although there was much beauty to be seen along their way, Jon and Cay did run into a few obstacles which needed to be chased away with the glimmering of their swords. The scenery surrounding them was a mixture of large patches of trees and vast prairies. They climbed many hills and cascaded into deep valleys. They passed many campgrounds and hard-fighting soldiers, as well as many cages and malorum corpses along the way. There was much time for conversation and getting to know one another as they rode through the mountainous terrain. Jon was able to hear more of what the King had Cay doing while he was away. As he listened to the battles she had fought, he gained a deeper respect for his much shorter companion.

Several hours passed before they began to hear the sound of a large river off in the distance. "What is that?" Jon spoke over the powerful sound.

"There's a really wide river up here. It's pretty cool looking. Don't worry though...there are a few bridges we can use to get across it," Cay answered as she motioned toward the large steel bridge they were about to cross.

"Is there enough room for us?" Jon noticed there were many soldiers on horseback venturing across it, some dragging cages behind them.

"Are you doubting my riding skills?" Cay looked back with a raised eyebrow. "Just make sure you're holding on!" Jon did not say another word as his fearless companion effortlessly maneuvered her horse through the traffic. Once they had reached the other side of the river and were far enough away from its thunderous voice, Cay turned to Jon again, "Well...was there enough room for us?"

"I am sorry to have ever doubted you...or your horse...madam," Jon playfully retorted.

"Your apology is accepted; just try not to do it again," Cay winked.

They continued their journey, heading slightly northward, and could see nothing but prairie land ahead. "Wow," Jon whispered under his breath, but loud enough for Cay to hear.

"I've never been up this way," she said.

"You haven't?" Jon asked, still gazing everywhere around them.

"Nope. The King has me stationed south of here. All of this is new to me."

An odd sense of elation filled Jon and Cay as they rode together. The sun was setting and lingered in place until they approached the area where Jon was to be let off. It was a quiet patch of forest within walking distance of a large hill. "Is this it?" The joy Jon had acquired from the beauty of their travels quickly vanished once he realized his ride was over and Cay was about to leave again.

"I guess so." Somberness also grew inside Cay as she looked around at the vastness of the prairie they just traversed. Many hills could be seen in the distance, man-made walls snuggly rested atop the summits of at least three hills that Jon could see. Patches of darkness moved across the land, but did not get close enough to the forest's edge to instigate an impromptu battle. There were more dark areas across the plain which appeared to be shadows. However, they were not moving as the malorum were. In fact they were not moving at all. They just sat there unattended and neglected. There were what seemed to be thousands of these cages with their locks gleaming in the retreating sunlight. "It looks like there's a lot of work to do," Cay interrupted the deafening silence.

"I guess this is what the King wants me to do." Jon helplessly looked out over the land. "I need to get some rest first."

"I guess I need to get going so I can get some sleep too. Remember though," Cay continued after she noticed Jon's shoulders drop, "I will only be an hour away. You can write any time, and we'll be able to visit each other more often than when you were at the other place."

Jon's spirits seemed to lift slightly at this consolation. "You're right. I'm sure I'll be ok…I just wish you'd be able to stay and help."

Cay dismounted her horse and stood in front of the much taller soldier. "This is what the King wants, and he has promised to help, so cheer up." She took her sword from its sleeve and slapped the top of Jon's helmet with it just as she had done many times before.

"It'll be ok. You better start heading out. The sun is almost gone."

The Battle

"I'll send you a letter once I get there," Cay assured him after they said their goodbyes and she mounted her saddle.

"I will wait for it." After Jon answered, Cay sped off southward and out of sight.

Jon was alone once again in a new land, and a great task was in front of him. That was, until a familiar voice spoke behind him. "It's about time you got here! We've been waiting for you."

"Pneuma? How'd you get here so fast?" Jon turned around to the see the smiling barefooted man with the cage and Clyde in tow.

"Ah! My dear Jon, you wouldn't understand even if I tried to tell you. I've got a couple of things to keep you company while you're here...other than my presence of course." Pneuma stepped aside to show Jon the caged man and his new steed. "They've been excited to hear from you."

"They have?" Jon curiously looked through the metallic bars at the blue eyes staring back at him, "Both of them?"

"Yes, both of them. Well, aren't you going to say anything?"

Jon knelt down and greeted the man, who nodded his head and smiled back. Jon could have easily leapt to his feet in excitement, but he did not want to startle the man or his horse. After this he turned to Clyde and patted the horse's mane while it licked his face.

"Do you want me to show you around while you wait for Cay to let you know she's gotten to her destination?"

"How did you know that she was going to write to me?" Jon rubbed his patchy beard in confusion.

"Ha! I do have quite a bit of knowledge, remember?" Pneuma patted Jon on the shoulder. "So, are you ready to go?"

"Definitely! Wait...are they coming with us?"

"They are going to stay here and rest for a little while. Clydesdales don't have much stamina when it comes to long trips like this one. They'll be here when we get back though; don't worry." For the next hour or so, Pneuma led Jon throughout the forest to get him acquainted with all the new wildlife and greenery.

When they had arrived at the patch of forest from where they originated, a castle messenger was there waiting for Jon. Jon's eyes gravitated toward the familiar piece of paper he had received many times before. "It's from Cay!" he exclaimed and happily accepted the letter. It was just as he had thought. Cay had arrived safely and was settled into her surroundings. Jon also found out that, unlike himself, she had plenty of soldiers waiting for her to arrive. Jon thanked the messenger and the eagle departed.

"Well Jon, shall we continue these festivities in the morning? It looks like you need some sleep." Pneuma had noticed the reddening of his eyes and the heaviness of his eyelids.

"Sounds good." Jon yawned and the two of them said their goodbyes once more. The cage and Clyde were the only familiar things around Jon after Pneuma left. The rest of his company was composed of trees, bushes, forest animals, and a few other cages resting nearby. "You could go run around, bud. I'll call for you if I need you," Jon whispered to Clyde as he noticed the horse was having a difficult time standing still. The massive animal snorted and nudged his rider's shoulder before excitedly galloping away.

The man inside the cage was as good as gone as well. Sleep had overtaken him just as it was trying to overtake Jon. He felt alone, but he did not want to go to sleep yet. He kept his eyes transfixed on the relatively flat land before him and watched the battles happening in the distance. Young soldiers were gathering everywhere around

Jon, all within a few years of his age, but he remained motionless and silent. He missed Cay and Odas, and sometimes even Emet, and this longing seemed to immobilize him. So there he sat, until something sent a familiar chill down his spine.

The hooded malorum had been watching Jon for the past few hours, soaking in all of the young soldier's fear of his new surroundings. It did not attack that night, but instead it just waited. Once Jon felt the shiver down his back, he immediately reached for his shield and huddled beneath it.

When Jon awoke the next morning, the enemy was gone and the caged man was awake. After saying good morning to him, Jon decided to make a trip to the northern mountains. The trip consisted of many thank yous on Jon's part and much consolation on the King's part. Jon left with his spirits raised and his stomach full from the garden's food.

That day, much like most days during that spring season, consisted of Jon exploring the land and trying to fit his key inside as many locks as possible. He tried his hand at battling many times, and fared well at it, but he chose to spend the majority of the daylight within the forest's enclosure, often walking with Pneuma. Much time was also spent talking with the King, as Jon routinely became exhausted and lonely.

In times of real need the King arranged to have Cay visit, which helped a considerable amount, but she had to leave a couple days after arriving to get back to her mission. They fought together rather well during her time there and discovered many interesting things in the process of exploring the trees. The knowledge Jon obtained grew so much so that he was even able to show Cay a few things on special occasions. Impressed by his increase in intellect and skill, Cay often instigated spontaneous training sessions in an attempt to show Jon what she was learning. She got the upper hand on him many times, which encouraged Jon to spend more time learning better ways of defending himself.

One of the more saddening moments of Cay's visits was when she informed Jon that the King had plans to send her far south during the autumn season, which was about six months away. Jon knew this meant he would be even more alone than he had been, since the King already confirmed Jon would remain in this region. After sulking over the thought of being separated from Cay by such a long distance for such a long time, Jon accepted the fact he could not do anything to prevent the relocation and chose to embrace their time together while they had it.

During the first month of that spring, Jon visited a few of the campgrounds and campsites nearest to him in search of his much-missed bearded friend, but to his dismay none of the other soldiers had seen Odas for quite some time. Emet, however, made appearances at each of the soldiers' meetings and devoted much of his time to teaching and showing Jon around the area. Emet was frequently sent to this area by the King so he was familiar with the geography and the numerous older soldiers.

After receiving a couple of letters of encouragement from the soldiers back home, Jon decided to make the closest campground the one he would routinely go to. It was uniquely characterized by its abundance of peculiar plants by the front gate. Jon later found out from one of the older gentlemen that they were called heartleaf nettles and were harvested by the locals for the poison they contained.

The Battle

The locals chose to use bows and arrows, opposed to their swords, and they would dip the tips of their arrows in the poison to hurt the enemy. Luckily for the soldiers, who would accidentally get nicked by these weapons from time to time, the poison only had a numbing quality to it. Rarely was a malorum fatally injured during these attacks, but the older soldiers continued to haphazardly release their arrows into the sky. Jon attempted to learn how to use a bow from the minimally trained soldiers, but he did not like to be so far removed from the battlefield. He chose to stick with his original weapon of choice, and he was often wounded and dirtier than the others. As a result of his frequent trips to the region's infirmary to get fresh bandages, Jon learned how to effectively treat other soldiers' wounds by watching the nurse repair his own.

His first four months in the new region came and went rather quickly, which provided Jon with an abundance of beautiful scenery as he rode through the forest and plains. Trees and flowers transitioned effortlessly from white to green, fruit and vegetables were in abundance again, and the campground had more nettles growing along its walls. The sun's heat began to warm the ground underneath its protective custody, and Jon could feel his hands get warmer as the days went by. As his fourth month there concluded, Jon knew he would be returning to the wooded region once again, so he made arrangements with Cay to ride back with her.

Before they departed Cay and Jon conversed with the King, as was their usual custom before long trips, and made sure Cay's horse was well fed. Jon made one final attempt to locate Odas before he rode off, but his search yielded no further results. He did, however, begin to see a particularly large shadow looming overhead as he scanned the land for the bearded man. Since his attention was so heavily invested in locating Odas, Jon disregarded this new development and carried on as though it were not happening. He and Cay eventually headed eastward when Jon accepted his findings, and they rode off on the same trail as they did a few months earlier.

They arrived in the forest around dinner time and ate a meal with some familiar soldiers before Cay made her trip to where she would be staying. They were now only thirty minutes apart instead of having an hour's travel separating them as before, which allowed them to see each other quite frequently that summer. The two of them would travel around and see other soldiers in the area and take turns pulling around cages while they were together. They learned how to work increasingly well together, but it did not come without a few mistakes made along the way.

The malorum were annoyingly opportunistic in their attacks and would strike while Jon and Cay were distracted by each other. This was not a common occurrence, but it still was aggravating whenever it happened. They gradually became less distracted over the next few months and learned how to fight alongside one another, but it was a learning process. It also did not help matters that those few months were the hottest Jon had experienced since being out of his cage. He made every effort to stay hydrated and focused—and would often dive into rivers and streams to cool off—but it was only temporary relief from the humidity and heat.

As the summer season concluded Cay reminded Jon of a trip she needed to make, which forced him to think of the loneliness he was sure to experience in her absence. The King had asked her to go a few thousand miles south with another group of soldiers. It was a long and sorrow-filled goodbye when it was time for Cay to leave. A few other soldiers were present when she left underneath the wings

The Battle

of an eagle. Jon did not want to leave that place, in hopes it was some sort of elaborate joke on Cay's part. He was eventually peeled away by one of the other soldiers and reminded it was part of the King's plan and that he had his own work to do.

Jon sulked for the remaining days in that land, but came to his senses when Pneuma approached with a surprise to share. "Are you alive over there, Jon?"

"Yes." Jon stopped picking at his sword to notice Pneuma had two large objects behind him. "What are those?"

"These are going with you on your trip. They may look familiar to you." Pneuma stepped aside to reveal two large cages with a single rope strung through their bars to keep them together. The occupant of one was a male that looked somewhat similar to Jon but was a year or two older. The other cage's occupant was a woman, still resembling Jon somewhat in appearance but about twenty years older.

"I remember them!" Jon leapt to his feet as he remembered his time in his own cage. "My cage was next to theirs for as long as I could remember. You said they're coming with me? Where's the other cage...the one with the older man inside?"

"I'll make arrangements for both him and Clyde to be waiting for you again, so don't you worry your scruffy face about it." Pneuma patted Jon's shield with his own sword. "These two, on the other hand, will be riding with you."

"What do you mean, they will be riding with me? Why can't I use Clyde?"

"Clyde is best used for short distances...unless you want to carry him around with you, too." Jon shook his head at the thought of even attempting to move that large animal. "I didn't think so, but I wanted to double check."

"So what about the 'riding with me' part'? What will we be riding?"

"You're always asking questions, aren't you?" Pneuma handed Jon the rope protruding from the cages and said before walking away, "Let's use that new muscle of yours."

Jon had gained around twenty pounds in the last year, but could not imagine how he would be able to move the weight of both the cages. "Wait up!" He called after his guide as he situated the rope around his shoulders. Once it was secure, to the point of Jon believing he could start walking with the cages behind him, the young soldier tried taking his first step. To his amazement, the cages followed quite easily. He quickly caught up to Pneuma with a fast-paced walk, and the two of them were off in search of the object that will be used on his journey.

After about a mile of walking Pneuma smiled back at Jon and announced, "There it is. Your carriage awaits."

Jon marveled at what stood before him. Two white Percheron horses stood valiantly beneath the forest's canopy. "What is this?" Jon asked when he approached the moderately sized wooden cart fastened behind them.

"It is your means of transportation, obviously. Would you please grab a couple of apples from that nearby tree while I load these two on?" Pneuma motioned at the man and woman patiently watching the events unfold.

"Sure!" Jon excitedly plucked a couple of apples, and before he could turn around and ask if Pneuma needed any help he saw the two cages were already secured onto the cart. "How did you do that?"

The Battle

"With skill and knowledge, of course." Pneuma gave each horse an apple and asked Jon, "So are you ready to go?"

"Uh...already?"

"I'll help you up; hold out your arm." Pneuma took Jon by the arm and effortlessly hoisted him onto the cart to be in the company of the two new people. "I will see you when you get there. Have a fun trip." The horses rode off after Pneuma gave them each a pat on their necks, and Jon waved back at his guide.

The cart ride lasted for the next eight or nine hours, with the horses taking them along the same route as Jon traveled with Cay several months earlier. They crossed over the large metal bridge after traversing through the hills and Dead Woods, and Jon discovered his two travelling companions were a lot more receptive to conversation and looked around at their surroundings than the other caged man he had spent so much time with. He took advantage of this opportunity by showing them everything he could before the sun began to set. Jon's expectations of the trip were diminished when he watched Cay depart, but he was pleasantly surprised at how the King and Pneuma provided him with listening ears and eager eyes.

Upon arriving at his destination Jon saw Pneuma waiting for him with the older caged man and his horse, as he had promised. "So how was your trip?" The gravelly-voiced man asked as the Percherons came to a stop.

"It was great! Thank you for proving me with company." Jon answered as he looked to the caged people.

"Thank you for providing them with company," Pneuma retorted as he passed Jon a bucket of water. "Would you give the horses some water for me? They must be exhausted."

Jon smiled and nodded his head before he turned to care for the horses. Pneuma had removed both cages by the time Jon realized he had another opportunity to watch, which caused him to feel slightly frustrated. "I missed it again!"

"You'll be ok. These three are in your care now, Jon. You ok with that?" Pneuma motioned toward the caged people. Jon nodded his head as the overwhelming fact set in. "Good! Because that means you have four more eyes watching you. Sleep well." Pneuma smiled and grabbed the reigns of the Percheron horses before leading them off into the forest.

A faint "thank you" trailed through the air, toward Pneuma, as Jon realized the responsibility he had. "Well does everyone want a tour of the land before getting some sleep?" The newer members of the group nodded while the older man remained silent. Jon shrugged his shoulders and decided to just take the woman and younger man around to show off the sights while Clyde watched over the older man.

After a couple of hours passed, Jon and the two new people returned to see Clyde and the older man already asleep. They quickly joined the festivities after scavenging around for a meal and sharing in more conversation. They all got a good night's rest, and it was much needed for the adventures to come the following day.

As was his custom the previous time he was in this land, Clyde stayed within the forest's custody while Jon went out to fight. The massive horse grazed alongside his fellow equestrian brothers and sisters until he was summoned by his owner. It was plenty for Jon to keep track of during those next few months, but Clyde seemed to understand the situation.

The Battle

    Not only was Jon's attention divided amongst his newer companions, but it was also being consumed by the peculiar group of soldiers he had begun to spend much of his time with. Jon had met them shortly after arriving and was drawn to their ways of fighting. They reminded him of Odas with the constant usage of their hands and unbalanced approach to using their swords, but they got injured and overcome with wounds much more often than Odas had. Not only was their fighting technique a peculiar trait, but there was also the matter of those in cages constantly yelling out to distract the enemy. It was as though they were unaware of the bars which separated them from the battlefield.

    Jon devoted much time to their group in the autumn months, and regularly fought alongside the few who were out of their cages. He occasionally would get aggravated when people would yell from within their cages—acting as though they had their own armor on—to the point of being fine with the thought of letting his sword collide violently with their metallic bondage. He resisted following through with this action more often than not, but even those times of resisting often wound up distracting him from completing the task at hand. Even though there were many frustrations which arose from this eclectic group, they did keep Jon company during the times he awaited a letter from Cay, so he was grateful for their friendship.

    There was another matter taking place during this season, which took Jon a while to realize. The shadow, which loomed overhead, began drawing attention to itself. Jon could not help but to notice it after random areas of the battlefield started to catch fire. He had many things striving for his attention, more so than at any time before this, so it took him a couple of months to realize the giant shadow was in fact a dragon-like creature that was about sixty feet in length. He kept this realization to himself, hoping one of the older soldiers would take care of it, so he could focus solely on adjusting to his new responsibilities. He knew they had taken notice of it from the conversation he overheard in the mead hall, so he concluded that it must not have been a big deal due to their inaction.

Toward the end of the season the King made arrangements for Jon to travel back to the land he had come from to see Cay and the other soldiers. He was ecstatic to hear this news and counted down the days until his departure. He wanted to see Cay as soon as he could and fought on the battlefield as though it would help him see her earlier. Although the intensity was much appreciated, it did not affect the King's plans. Nonetheless, Pneuma helped Jon transport the three cages and their occupants but left Clyde to play with the other horses.

Jon arrived safely back to the wooded land and soon met up with his greatly missed comrade. For the next month they exchanged story after story of their travels and the battles they had fought. The flying monster quickly became a topic of discussion once Cay first heard of it, and she would not ignore it as easily as Jon would. She pressed the issue until Jon admitted it was probably a bigger deal than he originally thought.

After having repeated conversations in the forest, campground, and battlefield, Jon shared how the other soldiers have responded to it. "The older soldiers aren't doing anything about it. They almost seem glad for it being there because it occasionally kills a couple of malorum."

"Is that what they've said?" Cay asked as the two of them found a nearby log to sit upon.

The Battle

"More or less. I don't think any of them would say it out loud, but I can tell they're all thinking it...I wish I could see Odas; he would know what to do." Jon lowered his head at the thought of not seeing his fun-loving friend in quite some time.

"Have you spoken with Pneuma about it? He'll know what to do."

"No. I haven't thought of it, to be honest. It didn't seem like it was that big of a deal," Jon answered.

"Well if it's burning stuff down..." Cay began until Jon interrupted.

"I know. I know. It's bad...but I'll wait for a little while before doing anything about it. I mean...shouldn't the older soldiers be helping with this?" Jon groaned in his frustrations. "If Odas was there, that's what he would do. Emet just stays in the campground and tells stories. It seems like he got lazier since Odas left."

Cay sat in silence for a little while before she spoke, "Let me ask you this. What would Odas do if he was there?"

"I supposed he'd chase the monster down and rip its heart out."

"Why can't you do that?" Cay asked her taller counterpart.

"Have you seen Odas?" Jon laughed. "He's huge! I'm not as strong as him. I can't do what he does."

Cay paused again before suggesting, "So...get stronger."

"I don't think it's that simple, Cay."

She chuckled and stood up before answering, "Ok, I just don't want to hear anything else about it then. It looks like the sun is going down. We should get some sleep soon." Jon agreed, and the two of them went their separate ways for the night.

Her words stung in Jon's chest for the remainder of the winter months. They consumed Jon's mind until the day they made the trip back to the western prairies. Pneuma had taken care of the cages once again and waited in the forest for Jon to dismount Cay's horse and bid her farewell. He knew something was on the young soldier's mind, and so he asked, "Is there anything you wish to talk about, Jon?"

"Not yet, Pneuma…maybe later."

"You know where to find me." Pneuma politely handed Jon his rope and added, "There's a storm coming, Jon. You might want to prepare yourself for it. Do some training to stay warm."

Jon thanked him for the advice and followed through with it when the cold rain approached. He did not know it at the time, but Jon had begun his training to defeat the enemy he was sent to destroy. He avoided the discussion of the topic for the following months. Much of his routine was similar to the autumn season, but Cay was able to make frequent visits since she was stationed closer. Jon watched as the flying malorum terrorized the land, and he frequently woke up in the infirmary as a result of collateral damage from the battles fought near him.

The hooded malorum also made its presence known on multiple occasions, and since Jon's attention was constantly being pulled in many directions he often fell unconscious from its malicious attacks. The doors to the infirmary and the campground's entrance remained annoying to him, but they stayed on their hinges—much to the satisfaction of the nurse and overweight mead hall occupants. Jon suppressed his objections and dissatisfactions with how apathetic other soldiers were until he was either alone in the forest or writing a letter to Cay. Cay was supportive through all of

The Battle

it and listened to his complaints when it all would get to be too much for him, but she always made frequent attempts to focus his mind on the things of virtue by hushing his complacency.

The colder months passed slowly that year, which gave Jon plenty of opportunities for training and getting stronger. As April came to a close, something in Jon changed. He was alone in the forest one evening and had grown tired of the monotony of his routine. So he decided to leave the cages he had spent much time with by a newly blossoming group of trees and ventured toward the battlefield. "What am I doing here?" he muttered to himself. "I am here to do more than this." His own complaining and whining had begun to annoy him far worse than the malorum or oblivious caged people. He had allowed himself to be distracted and fade into the backdrop of the ongoing war taking place.

The sky was cloudless that night, and he could see the flying malorum clear as day. The fire which emitted from its mouth illuminated its darkened silhouette, and Jon knew he had to talk with the King. The eagle ride which ensued was one of the most refreshing he had experienced since he left the cage.

He arrived before the King moments later to receive his usual cup of water and leave his armor with Iam. Jon began their conversation by saying, "First off...I would like to apologize."

"For what, my dear Jon?" the King asked as he placed his hand on Jon's shoulder.

For the next several minutes Jon poured his heart out to the man he had sworn allegiance to. He apologized for not doing what he needed to do after being shown what the tasks were. He apologized for pushing blame on others when he stood by and did not do his part. He apologized for his constant visits to the infirmary, which he had already been forgiven for after they had occurred, instead of keeping his eyes opened and fighting. Half of Jon's cup was filled with tears after he finished what he had to say. He looked into it at the mixture of water and sorrow and saw his reddened eyes staring back at him.

The words that came from the King's mouth sent a wave of joy throughout the young man's body. "You are not dead yet, Jon Smith. Go do what you know you should."

These simple words reverberated through the entirety of Jon's chest, causing him to surround the King with his arms in gratitude. After Jon stepped back, he smiled and asked, "Where do I start?"

"That is simple. Pneuma will be waiting for you to return. Go talk with him." After the King said this Jon smiled and turned around to see Iam patiently standing there with all of his belongings.

"Thank you both." Jon wiped the tears from his eyes and wrapped himself with his green and white armor. The eagle hovered overhead in preparation of Jon lifting his shield. The moment it was raised he was carried out over the garden and toward the area where Pneuma stood waiting.

"Is there anything you wish to talk about, Jon?" Pneuma asked once the eagle had released the dark green shield.

"There is."

"I knew you would come around." Pneuma winked.

"So how do I kill it?" Jon refastened his shield and removed his sword from its resting place.

"I have a fun idea. The malorum won't see it coming, I can tell you that. Follow me." Pneuma smirked and led Jon to the other side of the forest. The outskirts of the tree line faced a valley in

The Battle

between three relatively large hills. Jon had visited this place many times before while he watched the enemy circle around overhead. "It usually comes through here to get its strength back and regroup with the other malorum. So this would be a perfect spot to kill it."

"What's your plan?" Jon asked as he began to see the area in a new light.

"This area is like a borough or campground for malorum like these, but the King only wants you to kill the largest of the flying ones. Leave the other dragon looking ones for the other soldiers." Pneuma motioned over the horseshoe-shaped land.

"Got it."

"Now the idea I have in mind should kill plenty of the malorum that are restricted to the ground, so there will be a nice story for you to tell later." Pneuma's eyes widened with excitement. "Oh...and you won't have to worry about cleanup either. That'll be taken care of."

"How's that?"

"By fire, of course!" Pneuma had a difficult time controlling his enthusiasm.

"Wait...you mean that fire?" Jon pointed toward the flames emitting from the flying malorum's mouth.

"Yeah! Doesn't it sound like fun?" Pneuma composed himself before he added, "The King wants you to do it when you return at the end of summer to give you time to prepare. It'll also give me time to prepare the field for the festivities."

"What about the people down there in the meantime? Will they be ok?" Jon asked as he noticed a few dark patches of cages which were huddled together.

"I'll watch over them. Don't worry." Pneuma nodded his head.

"Am I going to have to wait to see you until then?" Jon realized it would be another three to four months before he came back to the region.

"Nope, just leave it to me. You'll see me around." Pneuma smiled and patted Jon on the shoulder. "You should be getting some rest though. You'll be leaving tomorrow."

It was true that Jon would be leaving in the morning. He had stayed a couple weeks longer than Cay that season and was eager to see her once again. She had traveled east for the summer, and Jon stayed behind to do more training. He was beginning to grow tired of Emet's attitude and wanted to be around more supportive soldiers.

He slept peacefully that night and awoke to the sound of horses snorting in his ears. The Percherons had arrived, and the cages were already loaded onto the cart. Jon gathered a few items for his trip and climbed aboard to join his company. The sun relentlessly beat down upon him as he rode off, but his attention was rightly focused on the flatlands he would soon be returning to.

Chapter 14:
A General Imitation

Upon Jon's arrival to the frequently visited wooden region, Cay stood waiting for him to dismount the cart and join her in a meal. Pneuma was also there and gave Jon a smile to indicate he would unload the two cages. Jon hugged the gravelly-voiced man and sped off with Cay into the forest. As soon as the two younger soldiers had left, Pneuma heard a peculiar sound coming from within one of the cages. "Psst!" The older woman tried to get his attention. "Are there anymore locks left to be taken off?"

"There doesn't appear to be. Why do you ask?" Pneuma stooped down to get at eye level with her.

"I think I'm almost ready to come out. Could you ask Jon to take me to the next campground meeting? I'd like to come out then," the woman pleaded with the watery-eyed man.

"Of course I will. You could do it at any time, you know. The King prefers for it to be done as soon as possible."

"I know...but...that's when I would like to. I'm not ready quite yet."

"I will talk with Jon about it; don't worry." Pneuma wiped the tears from his eyes and finished unloading the cart. He grabbed the rope, which was still secured to both cages, and led them into the forest and out of harm's way.

A few days passed before the next campground meeting was scheduled, and Pneuma had fulfilled his promise of petitioning Jon to bring the cages up the steep hill with the single oak tree. Jon had gotten abundantly stronger during his training while he was away, and he dragged the two cages up without much trouble. The first meeting passed without a response from the woman inside, but it was during the nighttime meeting when things changed.

After the meeting had adjourned and people began to get up from their seats, there was a knock at the mead hall's large wooden door. Collin smiled and looked straight at the woman through the mangled steel bars as he made his way toward the entrance while everyone watched. "Psst! Jon...I'm ready." Jon looked down to see the woman smiling up at him with tears in her eyes.

"Ready for wha...oh! You're ready to come out?" Jon's voice cracked with excitement. "You're ready now?" He frantically looked around to see if anyone had heard what she had just said. "Um...what do I do?"

"You don't need to do anything right now, Jon. It's up to Marie to open the door." Collin was crouching down in front of the cage's large metal door showing her where to put her hand so she would not get cut.

Marie did what Collin demonstrated. As the door to the cage swung open, the mead hall's wooden doors followed suit. The large building was instantly filled with the sound of rain, which was steadily pouring down outside. "I am here for a young lady by the name of Marie," a familiar and gentle voice said over the ambient sound.

"It is always good to see you, Iam. She is right over here," Collin said. Jon's head whipped around to see Iam walking toward the woman.

"It's really happening," Jon thought as everything seemed to be going in slow motion. "She's really coming out."

"It's going to be a little wet outside, Marie. Are you sure you are ready?" Iam had arrived at her cage and stooped down, just as Pneuma had earlier, to ask her.

"Hopefully it'll be able to wash all this dirt off before I get to the castle," Marie nervously laughed.

"It will. Jon, over here, could attest to that." Iam looked over at Jon as he recalled his journey two years previous.

Jon sat motionless as he watched the woman emerge from the cage's unforgiving bondage. With the Iam's help, she got to her feet and looked around at the soldiers who chose to stay and watch her leave the structure's bondage. She stood almost as tall as Iam and had long, dark hair. She wore a simple white dress, but it had been dirtied from her many years spent in the cage's confines. Her eyes, which looked exactly like Jon's, were filled to the brim with tears. Iam reached out and gave her the most genuine hug she had ever received, and it was with that gesture that the water flowed down her cheeks and splashed onto the stone floor below. Just about every inch of her was covered and stained with dirt except for where the tears had traveled.

"You can all go up to the castle. We'll be there soon," Iam spoke to the crowd. All at once the soldiers reequipped themselves with armor and followed Iam and Marie out into the rain. Jon gave her one final hug before leaving, and he thought of Cay, who the King had stationed west of there just a few days previous.

R.W. Allen

    This time he was on the other side of things and knew what Marie was about to go through. He watched as each soldier raised their shield into the sky and a stream of colors sped off toward the northern mountains. Jon followed closely behind as he watched Iam and Marie ride toward the forest on a large Percheron. In a matter of minutes Jon found himself entering the banquet hall, which had been elaborately decorated for the festivities about to take place. The King sat upon his throne at the head of the room and thousands of castle messengers filled the benches in anticipation of Marie emerging from the dark tunnel.

    After several minutes passed and a few songs were sung, the crowd grew silent. A faint whisper of Iam's voice was heard coming from the steps at the back of the room as well as two pairs of footsteps. The silence quickly subsided once their faces came into view. Marie's eyes squinted as the light met her face. The sounds of cheering and clapping filled her ears as she, with Iam's guidance, made her way between the rows of benches to meet the King. After her induction, Marie quickly found Jon and a few other recognizable soldiers to enjoy the feast which had been supplied.

    Once everyone had their fill Iam gently placed his hand on Marie's shoulder to indicate it was time to get her custom made armor. Everyone finished their meal as Iam led Marie down the same hallway Jon had gone down earlier. Jon did not see Marie again until later that night.

    After the feast had concluded the banquet hall emptied and Jon returned to the forest's guardianship under the familiar shine of his shield. He knew Pneuma would be around the area making the sword the new soldier would be using, so once he landed he listened for the familiar sound of clanging metal. The tune which met his

The Battle

eardrums was not that of metal but of another familiar noise. The ground rhythmically vibrated as though a horse were approaching. Jon assumed it must have been Clyde making his way through the brush, but he was mistaken. He stooped down to get a better vantage point and saw a breed of horse which was unfamiliar to him.

The horse was all white, except for the few patches of brown on its face and hind legs. "Do you like him?" Marie's familiar voice came down to meet Jon's ears. "I think he likes me already."

Jon stepped to one side as the animal came to a stop in front of him. "Um...yes, he's very nice." Jon tried to find where the voice was coming from as he surveyed the horse. "What breed is he?"

Marie answered, "He's a Paint." After she patted the horse's neck, Marie dismounted and stood before Jon to show off her newly acquired armor. She now had a reddish-brown helmet covering her long dark hair. He could barely see her belt, boots, and shirt in the moonlight since they were black. Her vest was a dark red to match the handles of her two basic swords. Lastly, her shield was revealed to be covered with the same shade of black as her boots, but it had a thick burgundy trim.

"Your armor looks nice on you," Jon said as Marie smiled.

"I guess I'm ready to start fighting now. It looks like I've got everything I need."

"Have you had any training yet?" Jon tried to slow down the new soldier.

"Well...no...but I've watched for a while." Marie confidently remounted her painted horse. "I'll get some training in the morning."

"You might need some rest first. You've had a long day," Jon hurriedly said before Marie rode off. "Has Pneuma showed you how to use your shield yet?"

"That's a good idea. He has; I'm sure I'll remember." Marie wasted no time saying goodnight before she sped off into the moonlit forest.

Jon, who was feeling drowsy from the day's events, searched out his own patch of moss to rest his head. He did not go to sleep immediately, but instead just lay silently underneath the stars. The only movement that night came not from a malorum or a passing soldier, but from the wind-blown leaves traveling around the swaying tree trunks. The peaceful joy he felt kept him awake for hours until his eyelids could no longer win their battle with gravity.

When he finally awoke from his rest, Jon had a humbling reminder that there was a war still to be fought. He opened his eyes to see Emet standing above him, yelling for him to grab his shield. "What's happening?" Jon frantically searched for his armor as he stumbled to his feet. There was a large group of malorum approaching, and the older soldier was the only one around to fend them off.

"Hurry up! Get to your feet!" Emet yelled as he clasped his sword's dual handle.

"I'm up! I'm up!" Jon rushed to his feet as he finished adjusting his helmet. Jon had barely enough time to fasten his shield and grasp a sword in each hand before malorum began flowing out of the forest at every turn. No time was wasted initiating the fight. Emet struck the first blow, and Jon followed his lead. Back and forth they went. When Emet would slay one, Jon would closely mimic his actions. He was not trying to outdo the older man, but that was how Emet appeared to be taking it. Everything became so easy for Jon in those few moments of fighting. It was as though he could predict the malorum's movements before they even thought of making one. As

The Battle

Jon carried on with his dodging and heart piercing, Emet became increasingly irritated.

Once the battle ended and all the malorum were slain, the ceremonial rain flooded the scene below. The blood and dirt on Jon's armor were carried off as he stood silently in the rush of self-confidence he had recently acquired. Emet did not seem to share the same sentiments about the events which took place as he looked over at Jon and said in his best condescending tone, "You feel good about yourself now? Do you? You could have cut my head off with all that nonsense."

It was as though Jon was smacked in the face with something extremely heavy. "Um...what do you mean? I was just fighting."

"What do I mean?" Emet stormed over to get uncomfortably close to Jon's face to scold him some more. "You could have taken my head off with your blatant irresponsibleness."

"I heard what you said. Did you get cut at all?" Jon put his sword away as Emet's eyes opened as wide as they could.

"Just watch where you swing your sword next time, boy. I'm not out here to risk my head for someone who doesn't know what they're doing."

"They are all dead, aren't they?" Jon concluded Emet's silence was an affirmative. "So...I guess I did know what I was doing." Emet apparently could not think of a tactful response, so he instead chose to storm off, as was his usual custom. "You are welcome for helping...by the way!" Jon hollered after him.

"He'll be alright," Pneuma's familiar voice chimed in Jon's ear.

"Pneuma?" Jon turned around to see Pneuma's green eyes watching Emet's silhouette disappear into the forest. "Where do you think he's going?"

"Probably up to the campground. Somebody will surely listen to him there." Pneuma turned his attention onto the soldier standing in front of him. "Nicely fought battle, by the way. You are definitely getting better at this."

"Thank you." Jon's self-confidence returned just as the rain ceased to fall. "You don't think I almost cut his head off?"

"You didn't even come close. A knock on the head could've done him some good though," Pneuma assured him. "So are you ready to do some more training?"

"Definitely!" Jon's eyes immediately lit up at the thought of training with Pneuma. "What will we be doing?"

"Well, since you have gotten stronger from your last training session, it looks like you're ready to learn how to use your rope in battle." Pneuma noticed the weight Jon had gained while he was training.

"Using my rope to fight? What do you mean?" Jon asked.

Pneuma returned the rope, which had been previously tied to Marie's cage, to Jon and answered, "It'll require some practice, but I'm going to teach you how to use it as a lasso for bringing down large beasts and such."

Jon instantly recalled the flying malorum that awaited his return to the flatlands. "Ooh! I like this idea."

"I thought you would; follow me." Pneuma motioned toward the area of the forest he came from a few minutes ago.

During the remainder of the summer, Jon learned everything he could from the training sessions with Pneuma. The humid weather did not assist his efforts in any way, but it made him appreciate the rainfall even more whenever it would unleash its refreshing water. If it were not for the frequent castle visits, spontaneous battles, training sessions with fellow soldiers—including the newly inducted Marie—campground visits, and random letters from Cay, Jon would have easily had to fight to maintain his sanity from the constant barrage of Emet's complaints.

The two of them only grew further apart during those months. Jon was beginning to hold his own on the battlefield, and, much to the older man's dismay, he relied less on Emet's supervision. Emet started to spend more time within the campground's man-made walls and would only see Jon when the infirmary's door was *accidentally* sent to the ground and whenever the soldier's gathered for a group meeting.

The lack of constant company was short lived due to the arrival of a familiar face. Cay returned during Jon's final week in the woods and was greatly excited to see Marie out of her cage. They exchanged stories of what the King had them do in each other's absence and trained together in the forest. Cay was greatly impressed with Jon's new abilities, as was Jon with Cay's.

During their final week, before leaving for the flatland, Cay asked Jon after a period of intense training, "Jon, do you remember that younger boy you met a while back? He was about my height and wore a gray helmet?"

Jon remembered meeting the boy, Konnor, of whom Cay spoke. "I do. What about him?"

"He's going to be down this way today and will be traveling around with us until we leave. He should be here soon, if I read the letter correctly," Cay said as she looked around the forest surrounding them. Nothing stirred in the trees until she reached in one of her belt pouches to reexamine the letter Konnor had sent earlier.

"Would it be alright if I joined you both?" A young, proper voice said. A rather short and scrawny young man approached the area where Jon and Cay were resting. "The journey to reach you wasn't as complicated as I anticipated."

"It's good to see you again, Konnor. We were just wondering where you were." Cay stood up to hug the younger soldier, whose armor appeared to be a size or two larger than his frame required. "You remember Jon, don't you?"

"I do. It is quite good to see you both again. I was hoping I would catch you before you ventured off."

"We just got done training for the afternoon." Jon received a surprisingly firm handshake from him.

"Well…I'm ready to go if you'd like another round." Konnor reached for his large dark-red handled sword. The sheath was not in its usual position, behind the handler's head, but it was attached to his waist.

"Isn't your armor a little too big to move around in?" Jon commented on his gray helmet, thickly padded vest, and baggy pants. The young man's green and gold shield seemed to be larger and bulkier than a normal custom fitted shield was supposed to be.

"It's no matter. Are you afraid to fight?" Konnor retorted with a raised eyebrow under his drooping helmet.

"Not at all. It was just curiosity." Jon checked the leather straps on his forearm and gripped a sword in each hand.

As the two of them circled around each other, Cay found a log to sit on to watch the events about to unfold. "This should be amusing." She laughed as she plucked a few berries off a nearby raspberry bush.

Once they had established the boundaries of their impromptu battle, Konnor wasted no time in striking first. He led with his shield, only to be tripped up by Jon's lingering foot as he side-stepped the eager soldier. Konnor fell to the ground, which prompted Cay to announce a point had been awarded in favor of Jon. Instead of arguing the call, Konnor regained his footing and lunged at Jon once again. Jon side-stepped him once again and gave Konnor a pat on the head with his green- and white-handled sword. "Point for Jon!" Cay announced again.

"What would you like to go to? Three points?" Jon asked.

"You want to end it that soon, do you?" Konnor teased as he re-secured his shield's straps. "The next three shall be mine then."

"We'll see." Jon smiled at Cay, who was proclaiming the score by holding her fingers in the air. "Next time we should just give me a head start then, yes?"

As Jon smiled at Cay, Konnor found a stump nearby, climbed onto it, and jumped off. His large shield collided violently with the side of Jon's face and sent the larger man to the ground. "Shall I warn you not to let your guard down? Or shall I do that again?"

"You're a scrappy little guy, aren't you?" Jon said as he returned to his feet.

"Point for Konnor!" Cay announced as she held a lone finger into the sky and wagged it for Jon to see.

"Shall I use my sword to finish you off? I think so," Konnor answered himself as he rushed toward Jon.

"I don't think so," Jon said as he stuck his swords into the ground, loosened his shield from his forearm, grabbed it with both of his hands, and swung it at the eagerly approaching training partner. The dark green exterior of the shield struck the front side of Konnor's helmet with enough force to send him immediately to the ground. "And that should do it." Jon held the position as he looked down at his fallen comrade.

He returned his shield to its rightful position and helped Konnor up as Cay announced with three fingers wagging in the air, "Jon wins! Are you alright Konnor?"

"I didn't see that one coming. I'm quite alright though," he answered as he readjusted his helmet. "Well placed swing, Jon."

"Thank you." Jon helped dust Konnor off. "Now let's get something to drink. There should be a palm tree around here somewhere."

"Would you like me to get a few down for us, Jon?" Cay chuckled as she told Konnor of how Jon took the difficult route of retrieving them in the first few days of being a soldier.

"Very funny, Cay. I actually want to try something out that Pneuma has been showing me," Jon answered as he grabbed the rope he had tied around his chest.

The three of them navigated through the forest's dense underbrush in search of a palm tree nearby with enough coconuts to share. Once they found one Jon began to swing his rope above his head and released it toward the batch they had picked out. On his first try Jon managed to wrap the loop around three of them and pull them from the tree's unshakeable grasp.

"That was actually pretty cool," Cay said as the nourishment fell to the ground.

"What are you three up to?" Pneuma joined the festivities, drinking from his own coconut. The three soldiers motioned toward

The Battle

the husk-covered prizes. "Would you mind if I helped crack them open?" They all stood in awe of how easy Pneuma made the task look. He wielded a sword with one hand as he used his other to hold his drink. "Nice work pulling those down, Jon. You have learned well."

"Thank you," Jon answered in a joyous tone.

Pneuma sat with them as they drank, told stories, and learned more of Konnor's travels. He left when the sun began to lower beneath the tree line, taking everyone's empty coconut shells with him.

"Well, it looks like Konnor and I need to get going as well. We'll most likely see you tomorrow though, Jon," Cay announced as she stood up and dusted the dirt and debris from her legs.

"It was great to get to know you more, Konnor," Jon said as he shook the soldier's hand. "I do hope to see you later, Cay. I'm glad you're back from your trip," Jon added as he hugged her. They all said their farewells, and Jon was left in the peaceful serenity of the forest's isolation. After basking in the summer breeze for a few moments, he soon decided a trip to the castle garden was in order. He joyfully held his shield in the air and was carried off toward the northern mountains. Most of his time there was spent thanking the King for everything he provided and allowed to happen that day. The remaining time was spent asking for the tools which were necessary to complete the task set before him in the flatlands.

This was much of his routine during that final week. He sporadically mixed fighting on the battlefield and searching out cages to unlock into his regimen, which resulted in many unfortunate trips to the infirmary when he momentarily forgot his training. The hooded malorum contributed to more than half of these trips and easily became the biggest nuisance Jon had to deal with during his everyday travels. During moments of supreme confidence Jon would try to lure the malorum out of hiding, but it was to no avail. It seemed to take pleasure in catching him during his weakest moments.

The day Jon and Cay were scheduled to leave was the day before the region's soldiers were going to have a meeting. The two of them were saddened by the thought of not seeing the other soldiers one last time, but they knew they had to make the deadline set before them. Konnor and Marie were two of the last people to see them leave before they climbed atop Cay's horse.

Pnuema followed beside them as rode, and as soon as they were out of earshot from the others he told Jon, "This trip is going to be a little different, Jon. I'll deliver your horse to the area, but the caged man will be staying here."

"What? Did I do something wrong?" Jon tried apologizing for the times he had accidentally cut the man or made an enormous amount of racket in his attempts at breaking the cage's welds.

"It's none of that." Pneuma stopped him. "It's not anything you did wrong. The King just wants him to stay here. It could give the other soldiers a chance to burn off some of their stored energy."

"Alright...just let me know how it goes," Jon pleaded, and Pneuma agreed to do so. With a final farewell, Pneuma fell back to make the necessary arrangements for Clyde's travels, and the two young soldiers went on.

They went a different route during this trip. It was much more scenic and mountainous than their usual way until they reached the familiar sound of the large river. It instantly became flat and swampy. The new route led them across a different bridge, but they could see the much larger one they took last time off in the distance. Upon seeing the familiarity of his surroundings, Jon remembered what he was about to do. He had told Cay of the monster, but he had not yet revealed to her the plans to defeat it. When they stopped to have something to eat, she could tell something was on his mind even though he was doing his best to forget about it all.

"Your mood changed, Jon. What's wrong?"

"You remember me telling you about that malorum that breathes fire? The one I'd see sporadically circling around the area?" Jon pulled handfuls of wheat from the ground to feed the horse.

"Yes. What about it?"

"Well...the King wants me to kill it," Jon said, not wanting to make eye contact with the wide-eyed girl.

"So...you are sure that he wants you to do this and not another soldier?" Cay sat still with unfinished food in her hands.

"Yes. Pneuma has been working on something and wants me to do it when I get back." Jon looked at her with worry in his eyes.

She sat there silently for a while before saying, "Well...we must be getting a move on then. You have a monster to bring down."

"But what if I die?" The reality of the situation grew in his mind as he visualized the malorum burning everything down.

"You said that about the last one, right?" Cay asked, and Jon nodded. "Well...you didn't die then."

"This one is different though. You know...with the fire and its ability to fly."

"The King must trust you a lot; so I know you can do it." Cay patted his helmet. "We'll assess the damages after it's done. Just do what you have to do."

"I just don't understand why he trusts me. I haven't done anything like this before."

"You haven't done anything like this yet, you mean." Cay smiled as she stood up and held out her hand to assist Jon.

He grabbed it, stood up, and smiled. Worry lingered in his mind, but for the moment it was suppressed enough to get back on the horse and ride toward the malorum's borough. Cay kept his mind off the task by singing songs and talking to him about various things. It took them a couple of hours before they saw Pneuma waving at them in the sun's retreating glow.

Once the horse came to a stop, the two of them hopped off Esvia and greeted their gravelly-voiced guide. After several minutes of talking and walking around Pneuma asked Jon, "Are you ready to see what I've set up for you?" Jon nodded his head with forced confidence.

Let me thank Cay again before she leaves. He turned to his close friend and pledged, "I will write to you to let you know how it goes...if I survive."

"Don't make me wait too long, Jon Smith. I'll be expecting it soon. I'll let you know when I get to my destination, also," Cay said.

The two of them shared a hug after Jon thanked her again for her help, and she rode off toward the south. As Jon watched her fade away, a familiar snorting echoed in his ear. Clyde had made it safely and was eagerly waiting for his rider's return. "Let's go ahead and ride over there," Pneuma said as he sat upon his own speckled Percheron.

"How did you..." Jon began only to be interrupted.

"You honestly didn't think I walked everywhere did you? Hurry it up. Clyde is ready to run." Pneuma smirked as he circled the

The Battle

area. Jon obliged and the two of them rode off. As they descended into the valley, Jon could see something peculiar up ahead. Pneuma shared that, while Jon was away, he had concocted an extremely flammable tar-like substance to spread on the ground. It was laid out in a circular pattern, and the middle of it was where Jon was designated to stand as he grounded the large beast. Pneuma warned the young soldier of the intense heat he would be sure to experience and offered him one last chance to back out.ABOUT Jon declined the offer and sat solemnly atop Clyde as they rode back to the comfort of the forest. Pneuma left shortly after their arrival, and Jon fell asleep that night with Cay's letter firmly clenched in his hand.

The next morning Jon went to the soldier's meeting at the campground with the nettle bushes outside its walls. Pneuma told him the work would start the following day, giving Jon a day of writing any letters he needed to write. He took his guide's advice and decided to write to Collin—the soldier who commonly taught in the wooded area—and Cay each a letter. Collin immediately replied and gave Jon some much needed advice. Cay was overjoyed to read of the encouragement and wisdom Collin provided, in regards to Jon carrying out the King's orders, and she added her own support before she raised her shield into the air.

When Jon waited for sleep to come upon him he felt a familiar chill run down his spine. "Not tonight! Stay away!" He hollered into the darkened forest where he chose to sleep. The malorum never approached that night, but chose to watch from afar. Soon after he said this, Jon's eyes closed and his shield surrounded him, keeping the enemies at bay.

"Today is the day we put some more facial hair on that chin of yours!" Jon awoke to Pneuma standing over him. "I got you some breakfast," Jon quickly sat up at the thought of food, "but I ate it, since you took too long to get up. I'm sure we could find you something else though...like this pinecone."

Jon politely declined the gesture and put his armor back on. After they found actual food and something to drink, Jon went up to have a conversation with the King while Pneuma sharpened his sword. Jon returned and spent the morning and noontime hour with Pneuma in preparation for the upcoming battle. The sky was cloudless that afternoon, which made the sun's unrelenting heat even hotter. Pneuma had kept his mind focused up until the moment they stood in view of the horseshoe-shaped hills which housed the flying beast.

Every muscle in Jon's body tensed up at the sight of fire streaming from his foe's mouth. "Are you sure this will work?" Jon muttered to Pneuma.

"I'm sure." Pneuma words carried weight as they entered Jon's ears and sank in his mind, acting as an anchor to prevent his body from fleeing. "Just do everything I told you, and I won't be needing to scrape your ashes from the ground down there." Pneuma motioned to the valley which rested in the middle of the horseshoe.

"And the malorum on the ground...those will die too, right?"

"Trust me; that tar is quite flammable. Just make sure you get out of there as fast as you can." Pneuma was referring to the black, sticky substance he had spread around the area where Jon would be standing.

"So what do I do next?" Jon asked, following a series of deep breaths.

"Go see the King. He's waiting for you," Pneuma calmly answered. "I will be seeing you soon, Jon." Jon took a few more deep

The Battle

breaths and waited for the familiar grasp of an eagle's talons. He closed his eyes as his feet lifted off the ground. The plan was the only thing he could think about. He did not want to mess this up. He constantly needed to adjust his grip on the shield's straps, since his hands became sweaty at the thought of every mistake he did not want to make.

He opened his eyes to see if it would help calm his nerves, only to see that the eagle was hovering a couple inches over the ground in front of the King and Iam. "You can release him now," the King ordered. The eagle obliged, and did something out of the ordinary. Instead of flying off to its perch at the front of the castle, it landed right beside Jon.

"How long was I hanging there?" Jon embarrassingly asked.

"Only momentarily. You are here now though, so relax. You can keep your armor on," he continued as Jon was stooping down to untie his boot laces. "You have an enemy to kill. Climb up."

Jon noticed the large bird staring at him. "Climb on this?"

"Go ahead," the King answered as Iam walked over to help Jon up. "Remember your training." Jon felt for the rope wrapped around his chest and smiled. "I will see you after the work is done."

A surge of self-confidence grew inside Jon's chest as the King spoke his words of encouragement. "And I will see you both after my sword is cleaned." Jon and the eagle both bowed their heads in gratitude before the bird rose off the ground and flew away. This was the first time Jon actually thought it was possible to bring down the malorum that had been causing so much trouble.

The next series of events happened so fast they bypassed Jon's tendency of overthinking. When the eagle had gotten within the range Pneuma had designated—above the malorum's consistently travelled flight path and out of its line of sight—Jon released his grip on the eagle's feathers and carefully got to his feet atop the bird's back. Once he got his balance he tucked his shield behind his head, securing the leather straps to his sword's handle, and began swinging the knotted rope over his head like a lasso. He calmed his breathing as he waited for the malorum to pass below. As soon as it began to fly past, Jon heaved the looped end of his rope toward the beast and desperately held on to the other end with Odas-like strength. He looked on through the cloudless sky as the rope found its mark.

The loop wrapped itself around one of its wings and jolted the massive enemy from its routinely travelled path. Jon looked the eagle in the eyes as a thank you for its help and jumped. He yelled in excitement as he fell toward the ground below. Any lingering fears had were now gone as he tightened his grip. Soon the slack on the rope would tense up and Jon would know whether Pneuma's plan would work, but in the meantime Jon watched as the ground-restricted malorum began to take notice of the soldier falling toward them.

The inevitable happened when Jon was just a hundred feet from becoming an indention in the valley; the rope tightened, but it did not budge from his grasp. Instead, Jon found himself heading toward the ground at a much slower pace, as if a parachute had been deployed. The momentum he generated from jumping off the eagle was enough force to disrupt the malorum's position in the sky and bring it downward.

The terrifying screech it let out pierced the air. The wing that had the rope tied around it was still attached to its body, but its joint became dislocated during Jon's descent. The other wing, which

The Battle

helplessly flapped in the air, could not generate enough thrust to combat the two-hundred-twenty pounds Jon added to the equation.

Jon's boots lightly touched the ground moments later, and when they did the flying malorum expressed his displeasure with a fiery exhalation, which Pneuma predicted would happen. Jon knew what he had to do next. Although his hands were calloused from the physical training he had done the previous year, he knew the ground malorum were making their way toward him, so he summoned all the strength he could muster and began slowly turning in place. The tar-like substance was instantly ignited as the malorum lit the surrounding land ablaze. The only patch of land which was left untouched by the fire was where Jon took his stand.

The lightweight boots adorning his feet dug firmly into the ground as he brought the beast down to his level. All the malorum marching toward him turned to ash as they were engulfed in fire. The wounds on Jon's hands burned as his sweat tried to escape and find its own refuge.

He was in a furnace. Not one made of metal—like the one his sword was forged in—but one made from the fears and doubts he had about himself. Each malorum that could not escape represented a part of him that doubted he could become anything greater. Each malorum wanted to either see him dead or back in his cage, so he could not carry out the orders the King had given him. Jon watched them all through the fire. He watched them try to run away, and many ran into those already engulfed in flames. They did not care for each other. They pushed one another down so they could survive. The only thing Jon could see in their eyes was emptiness. It was the same thing Jon saw in the malorum residing at the end of his rope. Jon knew what separated him from them. He had something to fight for and fellow soldiers who would fight for him. It was in that instant Jon knew he would not die that day.

He stood in the middle of the fire and smiled as the winged beast violently collided with the ground. Soot shot into the sky, darkening everything around. Jon squinted through the murkiness in the direction his loosened rope was positioned. He let his end spill from his hands as he marched toward the fallen enemy. The next step was simple, as Pneuma explained it. Jon just needed to pierce its heart. Fortunately for him, the malorum was completely unconscious from its fall and lay motionless.

The silence was deafening as Jon reached for his shield and sword. He slipped his shield on before grabbing the sword with both of his mangled hands. The adrenaline shooting through his body made his pain endurable for the time being. Soot rained down upon the scene as Jon located the malorum's collarbone. Pneuma had informed him this would be the easiest way of getting to its heart, by slipping his sword underneath the collarbone and into its chest. Jon exhaled into the silence and forced his blade against the skin. With one final breath Jon lunged with what remained of his strength and drove the dual-sword straight into the malorum's heart.

The large beast, which was about the size of twenty normal sized malorum, twitched slightly and issued its final breath. It was dead. Jon withdrew his blood-drenched sword from its chest and basked in the silence. "I... I did it," he muttered in disbelief.

"And THIS is for good measure!" a familiar voice called through the murky air. Jon watched as a massive metal-headed hammer came down upon the malorum's head. Its skull was instantly shattered into thousands of pieces. "Did ya miss me?" the man asked Jon.

The Battle

He could barely see the large silhouette of a man with an exceptionally large beard. "Odas? Is that you?"

"The one an' only!" Odas set down the blood-drenched hammer and hoisted Jon into the air for a customary hug. "You've gotten bigger since I've last seen you. Been training, have ya?" he asked after returning Jon to his feet.

"I have. I needed a bit more weight on me to bring this thing down." Jon smiled and motioned toward the now headless enemy. "I could've used your help a little sooner though."

"It looks like I was well represented." Odas reached down to grab the hammer. "Do ya like my new weapon?"

"Your new weapon?" Jon stared at the enormous object.

"Well..." Odas paused to reach behind his head. "I actually have two." A few pieces of ash flew inside Jon's mouth as it hung open in astonishment. "Iam re-stitched my vest so they would stay on." Odas held the large hammers out so Jon could inspect the craftsmanship. Each block of metal had what appeared to be a small tree trunk lodged inside of it to serve as the handle. Each handle was elaborately decorated with green and white cloth, much like the handles on Jon's swords. "These won't shatter like that one did up at the campground, I assure you of that." Odas pointed out the fastenings Pneuma had made to secure the wood into the metal head.

"Where did your swords go?" Jon noticed they were nowhere to be found.

"Pneuma used the metal for these. Pretty cool, huh?" Odas answered as he held them out to appreciate their beauty. "Pneuma's up there waiting for us whenever you're done admirin' this lump of death." Jon was eager to return to Pneuma, so he untied his rope from the malorum's wing and motioned for Odas to lead the way.

The soot-filled air was slowly overcome by the presence of an incoming storm front. The mixture of the wind and rain that followed washed their armor and weapons as they made their trek toward the forest. The remaining fires were extinguished, and the horseshoe-shaped land was quickly flooded. Jon looked back at the destruction and could not believe he had caused it all. He also could not believe Odas had returned—and now delighted in using weapons no less. The adrenaline had worn off, which reminded Jon of the cuts left open on his hands. Odas heartily laughed at the irony and helped him bandage the wounds properly.

Meanwhile within the castle's walls, the King looked at Iam with a joyful expression on his face after watching Jon's battle take place and said, "He reminds me of someone."

"I agree. I also think he is going to be needing a new drink soon." Iam smiled as he watched Jon and Odas walk toward Pneuma.

"We'll make two of these when he's ready." The King held up his mug in recognition of Jon's efforts.

Chapter 15:
A Warrior Returns

"I told you you wouldn't die!" Pneuma said over the rainfall. Jon and Odas arrived to the top of the hill to see him sitting on a couple of large rocks.

"You were right," Jon acknowledged his guide's accurate prediction. "How much of it did you see?"

"All of it, and I wasn't the only one." Pneuma motioned toward the northern mountain range, which was not visible to either Jon or Odas.

"What do you mean?"

"You were the entertainment for the afternoon for everyone in the castle. I think I might have heard applause, now that I think about it." Pneuma nonchalantly shrugged his shoulders as if Jon was supposed to know of this happening.

"Wait...everyone in the castle? What...who..." Jon struggled to wrap his mind around the thought of the castle's occupants watching his battle.

"It was a good thing ya didn't know that beforehand, bud," Odas laughed.

"Good thing you didn't die in front of them all. That would've been bad." Pneuma got to his feet and dusted off his robe. "While you go talk with the King, Odas and I will prepare a meal for when you return."

"You do need to kill things more often." Odas recalled what Jon had said during their steak and potato meal two years ago after he drove his sword through the back of the canyon beast.

"Yeah...I guess I need to get used to having an audience," Jon said as he raised his arms in the air. As he went up to visit the King and Iam, Pneuma and Odas ventured off into the forest in search of nourishment.

"That was a sensational showing down there, Jon." Iam was the first to greet Jon upon his arrival. "Do not be cautious in taking a souvenir for your troubles...you know...for next time." Iam winked before taking his armor to the base of the immense tree.

"The next time?" Jon thought to himself, contemplating how many other giant creatures the King had plans of him slaying.

"I would have to agree with Iam, Jon. That was very well fought," the King's thunderous voice boomed. "Shall we walk?"

After Jon received his usual cup of water, the two of them walked along a new path he had never been on before. Different trees surrounded them, each with an abundant amount of fruit growing from its lively branches, and different variations of flowers sprouted up between the ornate stone bricks. "I've never been this way before."

"This place is fairly large, Jon. It would take you a while to see and appreciate it all, I would say." The King plucked a couple of pieces of fruit from a nearby tree. "Do you remember what I said before I gave you this assignment?"

"I think so. Was it about the enemy taking more notice of me?" Jon asked.

"Yes it was. Well I can say for certain that it has come true."

"They have?" Jon's voice cracked in excitement.

"Your circumstances are going to get much more difficult; I must warn you of this. The enemy does not favor an individual of the opposing party who does well in the face of adversity."

"Do you think I'm ready to handle it?" Jon asked.

"By yourself? I do not," the King calmly answered. "I like to think it is a good thing you are not by yourself, though. You have a tremendous cast of soldiers, and one particularly imaginative man, down there who have no reservation in giving you all they have. Treasure the loyal ones and be an example to the disloyal ones. Agreed?"

"Agreed," Jon responded. "He is pretty creative isn't he?" he asked, referring to Pneuma's unusual methods of killing monstrous creatures.

"He is." The two of them continued conversing as they traversed the landscape. "It appears to be the case that he has finished setting up the meal. Although, you might want to write to Cay before sitting down for it." Somehow the King knew Pneuma and Odas had finished setting up the meal in the forest, so the two of them made their way to Iam. Jon bid them both a grateful farewell and safely landed within the tree's boundaries.

"A good talk, was it?" Odas asked upon Jon's return.

"It was. Let me write to Cay before I join you guys," Jon requested. He excitably composed a letter explaining all the events that had taken place to his trusted comrade and sealed it with a stamp of dried berries. A castle messenger had arrived by the time he completed it and whisked it away toward the south. "Thank you for waiting," Jon said as he walked into the clearing where Pneuma and Odas waited.

As was promised, three plates filled with steak, potatoes, and a medley of vegetables sat atop waist-high stumps. "Time to eat!" Odas excitedly announced. Jon took his seat on a rock between his two friends and bowed his head in appreciation.

Just as they began to indulge, a familiar voice arrived. "Where is my plate, may I ask?"

"You may ask; however, there is not one here for you…it seems." Pneuma lightly searched the ground for a spare plate.

"There ya are, Emet! Long time no see," Odas mumbled as he stuffed his mouth with the remaining bits of his vegetables.

"What is this all for?" Emet was oblivious to the battle which had occurred.

"Jon over here just fought a flying malorum. It breathed fire and everything!" Odas firmly patted Jon on the back, which forced him to swallow an unchewed bite of steak.

"You just missed it! It was really exciting!" Jon spoke after he stopped coughing.

"You mean to tell me," Emet rubbed his neatly trimmed beard, "that Jon killed one of those things?"

"Yeah, and I even made sure of it with this." Odas held up one of his new hammers.

"Now you are trying to tell me Odas actually used a weapon?" Emet lifted his head in laughter. "Very funny, guys. I'm just a little saddened I was not included in the feast."

"Well, Emet, we would've been overjoyed to fix you a plate if you had helped." Pneuma spoke.

The Battle

"If Jon actually did kill one of those things, then I would have known about it."

"Well...this is you 'knowing about it'. Have a splendid evening then, Emet. There might be a plate for you in the mead hall. Go check there." Pneuma motioned in the direction of one of the surrounding hills.

"Thanks for coming!" Jon politely called after the older soldier as he marched off.

"Let's finish eating!" Odas smiled as he cut off a large portion of his steak.

The three of them joyously finished their meal and spent the remainder of the night in each other's company. During their time under the stars, Pneuma informed Jon he would be spending the autumn months training with Odas and learning everything he could from the bearded warrior before taking his seasonal trip to the wooded land. Jon was overjoyed with this news, since he had not seen Odas in quite some time.

That night, when the others had left for sleep, Jon sat alone in the wilderness, rejoicing in his accomplishments and filled stomach. A familiar chill pierced the hot air, and Jon jumped to his feet with his sword drawn. He tried something new that night. He did not attempt to taunt the malorum or scare him away. He just simply waited for it to get closer. He closed his eyes to listen better and trusted the instincts that had gotten him this far.

Just a few feet separated the two of them, and the hooded malorum thought it had gone undetected. It raised its metal club over its head and prepared to put an end to the soldier's night. Just when the club had reached its pinnacle, Jon turned around and thrust his sword into the base of the enemy's neck. The malorum's club instantly fell to the ground as Jon silently stared into its eyes. "Not tonight," Jon whispered as he turned the blade. He withdrew the sword to take another shot at its blackened heart, but as he did the malorum fled, leaving his own weapon behind. "You dropped something!" Jon shouted in hopes of the creature returning so he could finish what he had started, but it was to no avail. The hooded malorum failed to come back that night and did not visit Jon again until more than a month later.

The metal club lay still on the mossy ground. It was the weapon that had sent him to the infirmary for the first time, the one that got the better of him during his initial days after joining the King's cause. Jon knew it was his chance to destroy it. He sat there staring at it for nearly an hour, contemplating how to make sure it would not do him, or any other soldier, further harm. He had an idea after recalling how easily Odas had crushed the flying malorum's head. "I'll get Odas's help tomorrow." He thought out loud and covered the weapon with leaves and branches.

He slept peacefully that night, and awoke to the voice he was hoping to hear. "What is this?" Odas kicked at the black object.

"Good morning, Odas," Jon yawned. "I need your help to smash it...like you did with the malorum's head yesterday."

"Alright then. Stand back!" Without any hesitation or preparation Odas lifted his hammer overhead and made short work of the club. The pieces went in every direction, which gave Jon much relief. "That wasn't too hard. Good way to start off a day of training!"

"I agree!" Jon sprung up at how easy the large man made it look.

"So are ya ready to get started?"

The Battle

"Let's go." Jon followed after Odas in search of some nourishment before exerting further energy.

Jon trained with the massive soldier for the next three months, learning how to use his body and sword together. While Odas was away, Pneuma had been working with the bearded man to teach him how to be effective with his fighting but take less damage so he could fight for longer stretches of time. Jon quickly learned how fortunate he was to have Odas on his side through the many battles they fought together. Jon also learned from his comrade how lonely it was doing things in an unconventional way.

After one of their intensely fought battles Jon nonchalantly asked the large man while he wiped sweat from his brow, "Where did you learn to fight like that?"

"From the stories I've heard of how Iam fought, to tell you the truth." Odas slumped down beside a riverbed to wash his hands.

"What do you mean?"

"I'm sure you've heard the story of him fighting the dragon, yes?" Odas answered. "I think I've actually told you that story a couple of times...anyway, the moment I heard it while I was inside my cage," he made a fist in the air, "I was hooked. I was absolutely hooked."

"I forgot you must've started out in a cage, too." Jon realized his naïve mentality. "I guess I've always thought...you know..."

"That I was always like this?" he finished Jon's sentence.

"Well, yeah."

"Nope, I actually...come to think of it...was a bit heavier set than I am now. No muscle whatsoever though, if ya could imagine that."

"So what happened after you heard of Iam?" Jon asked.

"I wanted to be like him. I realized who the enemy was, and I was doing the world no favors by just sitting down and watching it all happen." Odas began to rewrap the cloth around his hands. "I also wanted to be able to rip their arms off, so...I started to train inside my cage, much like you did."

"I remember you yelling at me between the bars." Jon and Odas shared a laugh as the younger of the two reminisced of his previous life.

"You were a skinny kid, but you had something about ya."

"So what then? I mean what happened when you started training in your cage?" Jon continued asking questions he realized he should have asked sooner.

"Same thing that happened with you, I realized the cage was too small, and the world was much more accommodating for my size. I wanted to get out. I needed to get out." Odas said with a grimace as he thought back to metal shards digging into his skin.

"What helped you the most...to get out?"

"The soldiers who paid attention to me really knew what they were talking about. I've tested it all. Now here I am, beard and all." Odas stroked the mangled hair on his chin.

"When was the last time you shaved it?" Jon asked as he felt his own whiskers sprouting up.

"Let me think..." He paused. "I can't really remember. I've never really been able to grow one, so when I finally could I just never looked back. A lot of the older men have tried telling me to trim it to look more *presentable*, but I just don't see much use in that. I'm not tryin' to look pretty out here."

Jon paused for a while before he asked his next question. "Could I ask you something about your fighting?"

"Go for it," Odas laughed.

"Why didn't you like to use your swords?"

"Ah!" Odas began washing the malorum's blood from his hammers. "There were a few reasons, but all of them were poor excuses, to tell ya the truth. It went back to when I was in my cage. I won't name any names, but a few of the older soldiers didn't know how to use theirs the right way, so they left a bad impression on me as I was trying to get out. I always preferred to train with my hands anyway, ya know? So that also kept me from training with a sword. I was never really good at it. I tended to hurt people a lot more during training, so I just stopped trying. There are soldiers that frustrate me, but I would never want to do them harm."

"So why do you like the hammers?" Jon motioned toward the freshly cleaned metal.

"I'm a fan of blunt-force trauma. It's fun," Odas laughed. "To tell ya the truth Pneuma helped me a lot with it. When I was gone for that length of time, I was trainin' with him. He's a far better fighter than I am, so I wasn't worried I would hurt him. Plus, he knew I would do better with these, so he made them for me." Odas smiled at the ground for a while before breaking the silence. "So now Emet can't get on my case for *just using my hands*. That's always a bonus."

"Very true. He also doesn't take too kindly to those doors being knocked down," Jon added.

"No he does not. Not many soldiers do, I've realized."

"Yeah! I've noticed that too. I try to tell them it's an accident, but it doesn't seem to matter much to them." Jon wiped his hand along the grassy floor.

"They like their privacy, don't they?" Odas asked and Jon agreed. "I don't care too much for all that nonsense. I mean we're supposed to be helping each other, right?"

"Right."

"So how are we supposed to know who needs help if we can't see them?" Odas lamented. "I just don't get it."

"They were all pretty upset when you shattered that entrance door," Jon chuckled.

"I could imagine. Did they try to tell you it was a *distraction* or something like that?" Odas raised an eyebrow in disagreement.

"Yeah, Emet said it distracted everyone from discussing more important matters."

"HA! Like what, the weather?" Odas let out a boisterous laugh, indirectly taunting any nearby malorum. "That's what they usually talk about up there. They usually complain that there's too much rain. I mean...really? Complaining about the rain as if you can do anything to change it?" It was as though Odas could explain the frustrations Jon held inside whenever these matters were brought up. "I tell you this, bud. The older soldiers like to complain that 'they don't make them like they used to' when they reference you younger guys? Well I am glad of that fact. Maybe things will start getting done around here."

"What do you mean? Aren't things getting done?"

"Hardly," Odas instantly responded. "Don't you find it a little bit odd there are so many cages just outside the campground?"

"Well that could just be because the people inside them don't want to come out yet," Jon presented the idea.

"Most of the cages still have all their locks on them...untouched no less," Odas answered. Jon was speechless, so the large man continued. "Also, don't you find it strange the soldiers don't spend more time with each other? I don't get why everyone wants to fight by themselves."

"True...I mean...we *are* in a war, aren't we?" Jon remembered the King's recent words of encouragement. "So we, kind of, need each other."

"Kind of," Odas sarcastically replied. "You're right though, bud. They don't remember what they got themselves into."

"I guess not," Jon agreed.

They sat there for a minute before Odas decided to ask Jon a question. "I was wondering where that guy is? The one inside the cage you drag around everywhere."

"The King wanted him to stay back in the wooded land. I haven't talked to him in a while," Jon somberly answered.

"How much did he talk since you've been out?"

"Never. There were a couple of times I thought he was about to say something, but I probably messed it up." Jon remembered all the instances where he would try to get some sort of dialogue established between them.

"How often did ya talk back then?" Odas found a place to sit away from the water's consistent voice.

"We talked fairly often. We had more in common when I wasn't seen as the "enemy". Jon remembered the pleasant conversations they used to have. "I am still trying to learn how to communicate with him, but it's so hard to get through that metal. I wind up doing more damage to him now than I ever have."

"You just want him out," Odas summarized the frustrations Jon felt about himself.

"I do. Sure it's bad out here at times, but I just wish I could show him it's all worth it." Tears began to trickle out of Jon's flooded eyes. "He'd like you a lot, though. I know he would." He wiped some of the tears from his cheek. "I know you can't be everywhere at once...I know that...but I just wish there were more people like you..."

"I know, bud." Jon felt Odas's massive hand lightly pat his back. "There's soldiers out here that know what they are doin', so hopefully they're able to get over to him. I will do what I can to help."

"Thank you." Jon took a few deep breaths to calm his nerves.

They continued talking for the next hour before they eventually returned to seeking out more locks their keys would open. Jon gathered plenty of insight from the bald man during that season. After each talk, Jon would instantly write a letter to Cay, when she was not visiting, and explain to her the best he could the revelations he was having. Most importantly, during all of this, Jon would converse with the King about what he was hearing. The King refined a couple of the points to make sure Jon was not interpreting the truthful statements in a wrongful way, but he ultimately shared the same frustrations as Odas.

During the final week of Jon's seasonal stay in the flatland, he made a routine visit to the garden and had a refreshing walk with the King. After he left, Iam turned to the King and inquired, "How long do you suppose it will be?"

"Another season of letting everything take root. Prepare in the winter for the grass to grow in the spring."

"Should we tell him of the next one?" Iam asked as he drank from his own mug.

"Not quite yet. He will get overwhelmed," the King answered. "Send word to Pneuma of what Jon will need to fight it though."

"I will," Iam calmly replied as he finished the remainder of his drink.

Meanwhile, in the land below, Jon had met back up with Odas and Pneuma for more training. During the few days Jon had before he left for the wooded land for the beginning of the winter months, he devoted his time to learning everything he could. He also would often write letters to Cay, asking her how everything was where she was stationed, and he visited the archers at the campground, who he would meet with three times a week.

During mid-December Cay had ridden up to where Jon was, so they could ride back together. Unbeknownst to them, the next time they would return to the flatlands there would be much harder challenges for them to overcome.

They had arrived safely in the wooded territory just before the sun had completely disappeared beneath the horizon. Jon was dropped off in the same section of forest he departed from just a few months previous. Cay had orders from the King to carry out, so she rode off after they exchanged heartfelt goodbyes. As Jon looked around at his familiar surroundings, he saw the familiar glimmer of a rust-colored helmet quickly approaching.

"You're back!" Marie hollered before dismounting her uniquely colored horse. "I have some food for you. Are you hungry?"

"I am. Thank you." Jon held out his hands to receive an assortment of fruit and a coconut full of milk. "Have you eaten?" he asked, making sure he was not consuming some of her food as well.

"Yes. It's all yours," Marie assured him. "I have some exciting news to share with you, but first tell me of your travels." The two of them spent the remainder of the night navigating the forest, telling stories of what had happened to them in the previous months. Jon mainly told her of his training with Odas, although he also briefly summarized his battle with the flying malorum. Marie told Jon of her travels and of her time spent with the younger caged man he had devoted some time to as well. The moonless night briskly approached, and the chill of the winter wind soon joined. Marie decided she needed to rest, so she informed him the exciting news would have to wait. Jon reluctantly agreed to the postponement, and so they went their separate ways for the night.

During the following week many events took place. Jon had committed much of his time to training with Pneuma, Odas, and Cay, as well as travelling around with Marie when she would be near. On one particular afternoon Jon was greeted by a castle messenger after concluding another one of his much needed talks with the King. The messenger held out a peculiar-looking envelope for Jon to read. His eyes widened and his jaw hung open upon seeing who signed it. It was a request from the older man inside the cage for a meeting later on that day. Jon hastily composed a reply, and the messenger sped off to deliver it.

Jon had told Odas and Cay about this development, which was returned with joyous excitement. The young man visited the King once more to calm his nerves before an eagle delivered him to where the caged man resided. Jon did not know how he would react upon seeing the man. He stood frozen where the bird had released him. A part of him wanted to run out to the lone cage sitting in the middle of the clearing, but another part of him wanted to remain still so he would not do further harm to the man. There he stood for what seemed like several minutes before he remembered the King's words. "You can't undo what I have done." The King trusted Jon with this moment, and the young soldier, in return, needed to trust what the

The Battle

King has been doing while he was away. So Jon, struggling against the resistance of his legs, began walking forward. The man inside the cage instantly smiled at his arrival, which erased any sense of nervousness from Jon's mind.

The two men, who still looked eerily similar in appearance, spent the next couple of hours enjoying each other's company and navigating around the forest's landscape with the older man's cage secured to Jon's rope. The caged man did not talk much, but he still spoke more than he ever had while Jon was around. While Jon was in his company he picked a couple loose shards of metal from the heavy structure, for which the man was grateful.

"Small talk" never felt more important to Jon, as he embraced every moment of listening to the older man talk. Their travels eventually led them back to the clearing from which they began. An eagle was patiently waiting there to take Jon up to the castle, which he felt bittersweet about. The two men shared a long, heartfelt goodbye, and Jon was whisked away toward the northern mountains. He watched as the forest clearing slowly faded from view. An overwhelming sense of peace flooded his body, drowning out what remained of the fears and nervousness he had felt just a couple hours previous.

"Thank you." This was the only phrase Jon could mutter to his King as he lunged out for a hug. The King stayed silent, allowing the events to settle inside the soldier's mind. After he had released his grasp the King motioned toward the edge of the river for the two of them to have a seat. They sat gazing down upon their reflections until Jon broke the peaceful silence, "Do you think he'll ever want to come out?"

"I hope so, but that is a decision he must make," the King answered as they watched the flowing water.

"Can't you just...maybe...start him out with a fresh cage...to make it easier?" A faint tone of desperation was heard in his voice.

"That would not be for the best," the King calmly answered, knowing the words would sting the young man. Jon sat in silence for several more minutes—tears welling up in his eyes—before the King helped him to his feet. "Just keep doing what I have asked, and let the outcome be what it may. I assure you, I want him out more than you do."

It was Saturday night when Jon had returned from the castle's garden, and Marie was sitting on a stump with a rope slung over her shoulder. "I remembered what I was going to tell you!" she exclaimed as Jon approached.

It took him a few moments to remember the conversation they had earlier that week, but his face lit up when he did. "Really? What is it?"

"It'll have to wait until tomorrow," Marie answered as she readjusted her grip on the rope in her hands. "It'll be worth it though, I promise."

It was as though he had just experienced a sugar crash of monumental proportions. "Great!" Jon thought to himself. "Now I'll be up all night wondering what it is."

"Goodnight!" Marie shouted as she walked away, hauling a fairly large and recognizable cage behind her.

"Goodnight!" Jon, unsure whether she heard his reply, hollered after her. Shortly after he had settled his mind—which only took a couple of hours—Jon found a patch of comfortable moss on the ground and drifted off to sleep.

The Battle

As was his usual custom, Jon woke the following morning with a breath of warm air filling his nostrils. Remembering it was winter time, Jon sprung up to see Marie's horse standing over the spot where he laid.

"Don't startle him!" The woman, twenty years his elder, dropped the food in her hands to tend to the unaffected animal.

"I don't think he's startled." Jon raised an eyebrow.

"You don't know that." Marie patted its large neck. "Hurry up and get ready. We need to go." Jon quickly placed his shield on his arm and sword in its place before gathering some of the fruit which had spilled onto the forest floor. They both mounted the painted horse and rode off toward the campground a short distance away.

The morning meeting came and went with no major news or surprises. Marie explained to Jon the "excitement" would most likely take place that night, so Jon calmed his nerves once again by spending his afternoon training inside the forest with Clyde. That is where they both stayed until the sun began to set, signaling the start of the nighttime gathering. He hurriedly mounted his large horse and made his way back to where Marie was waiting.

They soon met up with Cay, who was patiently standing by the mead hall's massive doors. They excitedly greeted each other and entered the hall. After they had their usual meeting, Marie excitedly looked over at Jon and whispered, "You remember that exciting news I wanted to tell you?"

Jon excitedly nodded his head. Marie smiled, and just a couple of seconds later they heard a loud clanging noise. The door to the young man's cage fell open and collided with the stone floor. The sound echoed through the large building, getting the attention of the soldiers who were still present. The tall wooden doors at the entrance opened, and Iam stood triumphantly in the dimming sunlight, which was making its best effort to see around the clean-robed man. "I am here for a young man by the name of Eugene," he announced. Before walking forward to retrieve the man, Iam turned to face the sunset and slightly tilted his head toward the cloudless sky, "Some rain would be nice." Almost instantaneously storm clouds rushed into view and began to bathe the ground.

"How did he...?" Jon began to ask Cay, who giggled at the curiosity in his voice, but instead chose to focus his attention on the young man—a year or two older than he—being assisted to his feet.

Iam had traversed the mead hall's floor and arrived in time to grab hold of Eugene's hand. Jon heard Iam mutter something to the man, but he could not make out what was said. Moments later Iam was leading the narrow-framed man through the crowd. Eugene was within a couple of inches of Jon's height and had similar hair and eyes. Short, dark hair inhabited his head and a full goatee rested upon his chin. "We will get you cleaned up; do not worry," Jon could hear Iam say as Eugene tried to wipe the dirt from his hands. Eugene kept his head bowed as Iam spoke to the crowd, "You can all go up to the castle. We will be there shortly."

"This is so exciting!" Cay gleefully said as she hugged Marie. They watched as the crowd of people march into the steady downpour occurring outside.

"Surprise!" Marie announced as she hugged Jon. "Now wasn't it worth the wait?"

"Yes." Jon smiled as he watched the stream of colors, disappear from sight. "Well, let's get up there!" He reached for the shield he had rested against one of the nearest benches and led the way out of the partially vacated building.

The Battle

Before long, the three of them were taking their place amongst the horde of soldiers and castle occupants in the banquet hall. The boisterous noise quickly subsided as everyone's eyes gravitated toward the stairway at the back of the room. Eugene was still nervously staring toward the ground as Iam confidently led him across the room. The induction went as smoothly as anyone could have hoped for. The heartwarming smile on the King's face was an accurate reflection of everyone's thoughts in the room. Eugene's cage was littered with a variety of different harmful objects and was, by the young man's own admission, extraordinarily comfortable to sleep inside of, but he chose freedom instead of that comfort. Eugene did not have to voice a single word to his new King. He knew it would be difficult, but he knew the cause would be worth the reward.

Eugene quickly sought out Marie, Jon, and Cay after Iam gave him a nod and motioned toward their table. The feast was had and Iam returned to take the newest soldier off toward the armor room. "The colors I have chosen for you are very vibrant." Jon heard Iam's calm announcement before they turned the corner to walk up the tall staircase.

The banquet hall slowly emptied as the castle occupants ushered out the soldiers so they could clean the tables and dispose of the remaining food. As Jon, Cay, and Marie returned to the forest, they were instantly greeted by Odas's deep voice. "Well, that went well."

"Odas!" Cay excitedly shouted. "Where did you sit?"

"Front and center, madam ." He smiled. "I always like to hear the King's reaction when the new soldier gets up there."

They stood there and talked for a moment until a slight rustling was heard near them. "I believe they are just through these bushes." Jon could hear the faint sound of a gravelly-voiced man. Seconds later Pneuma appeared with a soldier adorned with electric blue and lime green armor. It looked to be in a camouflage pattern, but there was not a place this soldier could go unseen. "Here he is!" Pneuma proclaimed as he stepped to one side and allowed everyone to get an adequate look at the young man. Odas filled the air with applause as Marie's eyes filled with tears. Jon and Cay were speechless, as they were engulfed in the moment.

"Can we go kill some malorum now?" Eugene asked Pneuma as he removed two slender blades from behind his head and began to scan the moonlit forest for the enemy. "I want to get back at them for what they've done."

"That's the spirit!" Odas hollered as he reached for his own weapons. "I'm with ya on that one!"

"Let's go train first." Pneuma calmed the crowd from being too overambitious. "He needs to know how to use his swords. Marie, would you like to come as well?" Marie agreed and followed after Odas, Pneuma, and Eugene after they all waved goodbye to Jon and Cay.

The two young soldiers talked for a few moments after but soon went their separate ways for the night. Two people he had spent much time with while he was inside his cage chose to leave their own behind and rescue others from their bondage. Jon knew Marie and Eugene were capable of doing great things but was unhappy he would not be able to watch them fight due to his seasonal travels westward. The times he would be able to train with them or see them would be during the winter and summer months. He decided to focus on those opportunities instead, which eased his mind as he prepared himself for rest.

The Battle

He eventually drifted off to sleep while he watched a pack of large white wolves play in the distance. If it were not for the multicolored markings sparsely arranged on their fur, Jon would have easily mistaken them for sheep and overlooked their presence. He counted thirteen wolves in all as they wrestled and jumped over various objects. They disappeared into the forest as he faded away into unconsciousness.

R.W. Allen

Chapter 16:
Time Apart

    Jon and Cay remained in the wooded land for the following month, training with their rapidly growing group of soldiers. It was relatively easy for them to forget they were scheduled to return to the flatlands soon, and the recent battle with the dragon-like malorum became an afterthought. Jon was eager to discuss what happened that day with those he had not shared the story with yet, but, sadly, not many of the soldiers cared to listen. The lack of interest from the others caused Jon to wonder how they could not be more curious, but he chose to not let it develop into contempt and instead let it go.

    Cay provided him with an abundant source of encouragement during that time. She would lean off the edge of her stump to listen to Jon's story as if it was the first time she had heard it. She would also devote much of her energy to training with him, even if she had become tired. Their friendship grew tremendously when Jon needed it most, but they were tragically unaware of what was to come in the following six months.

    After saying their goodbyes to everyone in the wooded land Jon and Cay climbed atop Esvia and ventured toward the large river. They arrived in the land of nettle bushes after the sun had set. Cay excitedly expressed that she wanted to see the horseshoe valley where the flying malorum was slain, so they went in search of it.

They stood at the top of the valley, in the same area Pneuma stood as he watched the enemy fall. As they peered into the darkness Cay noticed a large motionless mass lying in the middle of the land. The snow lightly blanketed the fallen malorum, which had been slowly decaying. A small breeze would start up now and then, revealing its non-existent head. The cold air which surrounded Jon was a stark contrast to the fiery oven he had to endure as he brought the enemy down.

It was as though the clouds mocked the beast. It was no longer able to defend itself by scorching the earth it once had dominion over, so the overcast sky took full advantage of adding insult to injury. Sure there were other malorum which would fly around and send fire below, but there was now one less occupying the sky and disrupting the clouds' well-planned choreography.

Not a word was said between the two of them as the white confetti descended upon their spotless armor. They hugged each other a final time before Cay reluctantly rode off toward the southern flatlands. After she left Jon lingered for a few moments longer before going up to see the King.

During the visit, Jon was reminded of the impending challenges he would experience during the latter half of the winter months, as well as the entirety of the spring. The soldier graciously accepted the responsibility and thanked both the King and Iam for the trust they had in him to accomplish such a task. Jon, drinking his mug of water, walked around with the King for a while before returning to the forest where Pneuma patiently stood.

"It doesn't look like the malorum around here are too happy with you right now, Jon."

"Yeah…" An uneasy feeling washed over Jon as he pictured an innumerable amount of malorum charging over the prairieland, "that's what the King told me."

"You'll be ready for them though…with a little more training." Pneuma walked over and placed a comforting hand on Jon's shoulder. "Let's get you some food before you rest." They ventured deep into the forest in search of nourishment, passing by bushes, flowers, and trees with a light coating of snow sprinkled on them. Jon did not know how to find much food during the snowy months, so he was fortunate Pneuma was guiding him. The barefooted man knew exactly where to look.

"I was wondering something, Pneuma," Jon spoke as they sat down to eat.

"What is it?"

"I was wondering how that malorum got so big in the first place." Jon knew the road ahead would be harder because he had to defeat the large creature, but he first wanted to understand how it got there to begin with.

"Another good question, Jon." Pneuma smiled. "Do you remember the story of the dragon Iam fought?"

"I do. He took its arm as a souvenir." Jon then realized what Iam meant earlier in the garden when he suggested Jon to do the same after defeating a larger-than-average enemy.

"Very good. Do you remember how it got so big?"

Jon thought for a moment before answering, "Wasn't it because it was left alone?"

The Battle

"Right again!" Pneuma hollered into the cold air. "The same thing happened to this one here. Nobody wanted to fight it, so it kept growing. It was neglected."

"I noticed it didn't really have any cuts on it." Jon recalled the times he was able to get a closer look at it. "So you mean to tell me that all of those other flying...things will continue to grow until someone kills them?"

"That's right," Pneuma answered.

"So why don't I just kill some more of them?" Jon reached for the rope he had tied across his chest, after it had been washed by the rain and river.

"Slow down there, dragon slayer." Pneuma smirked. "They aren't for you to kill."

The determined expression on Jon's face quickly turned into confusion. "What do you mean?"

"The one you killed was for you, and the rest of them are for other soldiers when they are ready," Pneuma explained.

"Why was that one just for me? I don't understand."

"That malorum," Pneuma motioned toward the horseshoe valley, "started growing when you were born."

"Like when I came out of my cage?"

"Not quite," Pneuma began to explain but saw it would be best to finish at a later date. "I'll explain later; don't worry."

"I'm trying to follow, but I guess I'm too tired." Jon desired to know what his guide wanted to share, but was not able to focus too well.

"I know; all in due time. Get some rest, and I will see you in the morning." Pneuma reassured the soldier he was willing to finish his explanation before he walked into the forest.

Jon woke up the next morning, as he did most mornings, with Clyde's warm breath engulfing his face and Pneuma offering him some breakfast. "Time for some morning training!" he exclaimed as Jon struggled to open his eyes.

"Already?" Faint grumblings slowly crept from Jon's mouth as Clyde began to nudge his side. "Don't I already know how to kill the malorum?"

"Not the ones that'll be coming for you next." Pneuma began to eat the food he had prepared for the sleepy warrior.

"What's so different about them?" Jon finally sat up to see his breakfast being consumed.

"Well, you know how the previous waves weren't able to fly or use their tails?" Pneuma asked.

"Um...I guess so." Jon racked his brain trying to remember.

"Think of it this way. If the enemy thinks it could kill you with its...reserves...then it is able to use its stronger forces to defeat the soldiers that give them more problems." Pneuma tried to lessen the blow to Jon's confidence.

"You mean those were the runts that I was fighting before?" His confidence level plummeted.

"Well...yes. I do realize I'm the bearer of bad news here." Pneuma shrugged.

"They almost killed me...multiple times actually!" Jon hurriedly got to his feet and reequipped himself. "Does this mean the malorum coming for me now can fly?"

"Correct." Pneuma broke to news to the unsettled looking soldier. "And they have stingers at the end of their tails which could easily paralyze you for hours."

"Well...training sounds like a reasonable thing to do."

"After we get you some food." Pneuma showed him his empty palms, at which Jon's shoulders slumped. They traveled into the forest, with Clyde following closely behind, in search of morning nourishment Jon could have.

The training Jon had for the next couple of days focused on how to defeat airborne objects without the use of an eagle to fly above them. Pneuma would throw an assortment of frozen pinecones and branches into the air which Jon was meant to bring down with his rope. Jon, understandably, found it plenty more difficult to lasso these smaller objects than the tree-sized enemy he previously used his rope on. Day and night he practiced, only being interrupted by previously wounded malorum, which were all relatively easy for him to defeat.

His stretch of training concluded one slightly warmer afternoon when Pneuma abruptly turned to Jon and said, "One of them is close by. Follow me." He sped off through the undergrowth toward a large rock formation by a small creek bed. He motioned for Jon to jump behind the natural wall and not to make a sound. A curious look on the soldier's face prompted the forest guide to explain, "There's one of those malorum just over this hill. It looks like it's ready to attack that herd of deer."

"Can I see?" Jon whispered. He peered around the rock wall after Pneuma gave him clearance to see the enemy less than a hundred yards away from a family of deer. Jon could see its dark body contrast the snow as it crawled along the forest bed. It looked slightly larger than the malorum Jon would routinely fight, and plenty stronger. Its wings were unharmed, as was its tail—which resembled a scorpion's.

"I'm thinking it wanted a snack before it came to attack you." Pneuma watched in anger as the malorum pressed on.

"Can I kill it?" Jon eagerly asked as he saw Pneuma reach for his sword.

"I was hoping you'd ask." Pneuma smiled. Jon's chest inflated at the thought of pleasing his teacher, and he quickly unraveled his rope. "Now is your chance to strike them first. Trust your training." Jon nodded and took a few deep breaths before crawling halfway down the hill they were stationed on. "Wait for it to jump in the air before catching it," Pneuma loudly whispered before Jon was out of earshot.

Once Jon was less than twenty yards away from the malorum it began to stand as if it was about to jump. Jon took another deep breath and began to swing the knotted rope above his head, as he did in his training. Moments later the enemy sprang into the air. Jon kept his wits about him and let the looped end of his rope fly from his hand. No other thought crossed his mind but to trust what Pneuma had taught him.

On the first attempt the rope found its mark and wrapped itself around the malorum's tail. Once Jon realized this he guided the rope—with the enemy attached—over the herd of deer and into the side of another small hill. The sound it made echoed through the forest and shook the snow off the surrounding foliage. Instead of finishing the task at hand Jon decided to turn his attention to his teacher for approval. He had turned his back on the fallen enemy, which gave it time to recover and make its way toward the oblivious soldier.

"Watch your head!" A familiar voice shook the trees.

The Battle

Jon quickly ducked and spun around to see the malorum smack against the same hill it just left. Jon looked up to see Odas holding one of his hammers as if he just swung a baseball bat. "Now go make sure it doesn't get back up!" Odas hollered, and Jon immediately ran over to the malorum and thrust his sword in its caved-in chestplate.

"I was just checking on the..." Jon began to explain.

"You almost got a stinger in your neck." Odas wiped the remnants of the malorum from his hammer with the sole of his boot.

"Thank you for coming, Odas." Pneuma had climbed down the hill and joined them.

"I'm glad I got here in time." Odas smiled at Jon. "I saw a small group of these things coming this way, so we better keep our eyes open."

"This should be fun." Pneuma started rubbing his hands together in excitement. "I'll take the high ground so I can call down their positions to you." Pneuma climbed a nearby tree with ease and sat perched like a large bird.

"You ready for this, Jon?" Odas reached for his other hammer after checking his shield to make sure it was secure

"I think so," the younger man stammered as he imitated his comrade's preparations.

"Hey." Odas noticed some uneasiness in Jon's eyes. "What's done is done. All is well."

"Here they come!" Pneuma's excited voice rained down from the tree's canopy. "They are all going to be in front of you! About six in all!"

Both Odas and Jon stood prepared, a weapon in each of their hands, as a small group of malorum came into view. A confident smirk was visible through the opening in Odas's helmet, which consequently diminished any nervousness Jon still had up to this point. "Time to give 'em a good show." The bearded man glanced toward the northern mountains. Jon had forgotten the castle occupants, including the King and Iam, must be watching the battle which was about to take place.

Worry and anxiety could have easily returned to Jon upon this realization, but what happened instead was a total immersion of confidence. He remembered the words of encouragement he received from them all, and a smile slowly appeared on his face, which must have been visible to Pneuma, who let out a hearty chuckle.

As the cheerful noise filled the air, Odas raised a hammer toward the man in the tree, "That's the spirit!" he shouted and braced himself for the fight.

It was a relatively short battle. The enemy was never able to mount much of an offense, especially with Pneuma calling out their movements and positions. The only real threat of injury came from the soldiers themselves. The blades of Jon's swords barely missed cutting Odas on multiple occasions, and if it was not for Odas knowing how to wield his hammers they would have connected with the side of Jon's helmet while he was energetically jumping around.

After the final malorum fell, an abundance of rain gave in to the earth's gravitational pull. Pneuma left his post, dusted off his hands, and joined the victors in the ceremonial downpour. "That worked quite well," he stated as he looked around at all the carnage.

"We didn't even get too sweaty." Odas had a look of disappointment on his face.

"We can do some more training after I clean this mess up." Pneuma picked up a dismembered arm and threw it to the side.

The Battle

"Let me go talk to the King first. Then I'll be up for some training after I get back." Jon's request was gladly received, so he sped off to the castle garden.

Once he arrived he went through his usual custom of handing Iam his armor in exchange for a mug of water. The King motioned toward one of the lavender-adorned pathways and drank his own mug of nourishment. "There is something I wish to discuss with you, Jon. Come with me." Without any hesitation, Jon hurriedly joined his King.

"What is it?" he asked.

"There is a short trip I would like for you and Odas to make for me. I will inform him of this when I see him next."

The King was noticeably saddened by something, so Jon asked, "Is there something wrong?"

"There was an equally important trip that I would have liked for you to make, but a few of the other soldiers decided to be apathetic with their preparations." He took a long drink from his mug before continuing, "I will handle it, but you must make sure you are fit to do this for me."

"When will it be?"

The King gave a subtle smile underneath the rim of his mug and said, "It will be during the first week of spring."

Jon, who was oblivious to the smile, asked, "So where is it you want us to go?"

"To the ocean," the King nonchalantly answered.

Jon blankly stared at the path ahead of them. "There's...an ocean?"

"Oh yes...many of them, in fact," he answered.

"Which one do you have in mind?" Jon began to realize the world was much bigger than he had pictured before.

"There is one much farther west of where I have you stationed right now. It will take you a few days to reach it, but there are many things I want you to do along the way."

Jon wrestled with the overwhelming feeling. He knew the King trusted him to carry out his orders, but he still could not help but to feel unworthy to do so much of what was asked. "Are you sure you want me to do it? I mean…I'm so young," he stammered as he thought of so many other soldiers that could easily take his place.

As he began to rattle off names of older soldiers from the various campground meetings he had been to, he felt a comforting hand on his shoulder. "I would not ask you if I did not believe you were able," the King gently spoke. "You must stop believing you are too young to do what I ask of you."

"I'm just afraid some…" Jon began.

"Do not be afraid." The King stopped him. "I will be with you, and I will rescue you."

"Ok." Jon nodded. "I'll go."

"Very good." The King smiled and patted the young man's back before they turned to walk toward the enormous tree in the middle of the garden. They conversed for the next several moments before an eagle carried Jon away and released him in the forest Pneuma and Odas were waiting.

"Have a good talk, did ya?" Odas asked as Jon cheerfully walked toward the two of them.

"I did," he answered. "He wants to talk to you about something when you get up there."

The Battle

"What is it?" Odas asked as Pneuma quietly sharpened Jon's swords.

"A trip he wants us to take."

"Oh really?" the large man excitedly asked.

"Yup! Me and you." Jon was pleased to see the positive reaction from his future traveling companion.

"Well that should be exciting!" Odas reached for his hammers and continued, "We better get training some more then."

"Let me finish sharpening these first, big guy." Pneuma looked down at the swords Jon had given him. "Jon, it might be wise to go write a letter to a certain young lady." He winked at the soldier.

"Oh yeah!" Jon got another surge of excitement, "I do need to tell Cay about what the King said."

"I guess I'll go up and talk with him now." Odas realized there was no better time than the present to speak with the King, so he instantly reached for his shield and was carried off toward the castle.

Jon found a blank piece of paper in one of his belt's pouches and began to write the best summary of his upcoming travel plans and handed it over to a castle messenger who had appeared just as Jon completed it. A reply from the female soldier arrived before Odas had returned from the garden, and Jon was overjoyed at what it read. "Pneuma! She says that she'll be coming to visit soon!" Jon hollered to Pneuma as a rush of excitement filled the air. The warnings that the King gave him about there being more difficult struggles ahead were suppressed in the young soldier's mind as thoughts of spending time with Cay filled its vacancies.

Once Jon composed a reply to Cay's letter, Odas's presence was felt by the sudden gust of wind the eagle generated upon their arrival. The ground slightly vibrated when the large man was released, just as Pneuma finished sharpening Jon's swords. "So, are we ready to train yet?" Odas cheerfully asked. Pneuma nodded his head, and the three of them began their training.

Over the following two months, Odas and Jon grew accustomed to working together. Fighting, training, and helping people in their cages filled most of Jon's time, so much so that he found that he started to forget how to work with the other soldiers. It was not the intention of the training, but moreso a negative side-effect Jon had experienced due to concentrating too hard on the week-long travel he was about to experience. It became more apparent to him that something was wrong when Cay visited and they would frequently wound each other while they fought off the enemy. They tried to correct the miscommunication while they trained with each other, but their time together was often short lived due to them having to return to their respective areas before many of the issues had been resolved.

The King had been watching what was happening below, and so during one of Jon's visits, in the latter part of the winter season, he addressed the issue. "Jon, I wish to speak with you about something occurring between you and Cay."

"I wanted to talk to you about that." Jon spoke with his eyes staring at the ground.

"Why have you not spoken with me much about it sooner?" the King inquired.

"I've just been so focused on this trip you wanted me to go on…and the caged people…and all those malorum. They are a lot harder to fight now…and I know there are a lot of people in those cages who are watching me." Jon had indeed spent more time with the caged men and women during this time than he had in previous seasons, and he had become more mindful of the audience around him.

The King could tell that Jon was becoming exhausted with everything he was asked to do, so he simply reached out his hand and placed it on the young man's shoulder. "Your energy is well spent, but you must remember how to fight alongside the soldiers I place around you."

"I know. It's just hard." Jon began to rub his forehead.

"How so?" The King knew the seed he planted in Jon's mind was beginning to take root and fight against the soil it was bound to emerge from.

"There aren't many people down there that are doing much of anything...honestly. I listen to the caged people's stories, and they all sound...neglected." Jon's tone changed from exhaustion to mild frustration. "I know Odas fights...I see it...but as for a majority of the soldiers in the area I'm in, there's hardly anyone fighting. I don't mean to put Cay in that group, but it's hard when I only get to see her in short bursts of time. I know she fights; and I know she does amazingly well...but it's like a habit I'm forming while she's away and it gets taken out on her when she visits."

The King patiently listened before asking, "What habit is that?"

"I guess it's a habit of being extremely skeptical of everyone. The majority of soldiers just seem to want to wait for meetings and meals. They are smart, but they aren't teaching, fighting, or unlocking cages." Jon's frustration grew the more he thought of the apathetic soldiers. "I just...I just want to yell."

The King let out an unexpected chuckle before patting Jon's shoulder. "I understand what you mean, Jon."

"You do?" A confused look splashed across his face as he looked at the King.

"I do. I notice it as well." The King somberly took a drink from his mug. "But you must remember that there are people you can trust, like Cay. Your trip is coming up this next week. When you return I need for you to resolve the miscommunication and the bad habits. I cannot have my people hurt each other. The enemy is already trying to do that. Is this clear?"

"It is." Jon nodded as he looked down into his mug.

"Good." The King smiled. "Now let us return you to Pneuma."

Jon was readily returned to the forest's confines, where Pneuma and Odas stood patiently waiting. "Ready to do some final trainin' before we head out?" Odas asked.

Their departure time was scheduled for early in the morning, so they needed plenty of sleep. "Yes. I do want to get to sleep soon though."

"We'll see about that." Odas reached for one of his hammers lying on the ground.

"I'll go make preparations for the both of you. Try not to kill each other; you both need to be alive for this trip to happen," Pneuma joked before he followed a nearby path into the forest. The two soldiers ended their training session an hour later, when Pneuma had returned, and soon found places to rest their heads for the night.

As was the usual morning custom, Jon awoke to the warm breath of a horse beating down upon him. It was an extremely large draft horse, much like Clyde, and it had a double saddle already

The Battle

strapped to its back. Jon knew it belonged to Odas from their countless days of training and fighting alongside one another, but he was still taken aback by it.

"Good! You're up!" Odas's deep voice pounded on Jon's eardrums. "Pneuma is getting us some breakfast before we head out. He'll be back soon, so you might want to get your armor on, bud."

Jon stumbled around, getting his armor on just in time to see Pneuma emerge with a couple plates of food. "Dig in! You are going to need this for what's ahead of you."

They had no problem doing what Pneuma suggested, and they made sure the plates were spotless of any traces of food which were once on them. "You don't have any more of those eggs do ya, Pneuma? They hit the spot!"

"You don't want to eat too much, Odas. Carit won't be very happy with you." Pneuma referred to Odas's horse that appeared to be mindful of his owner's desire for a second helping.

"Calm down, Carit. I won't eat anymore." Odas set down his plate and asked Jon if he was ready.

"Aren't you coming, Pneuma?" Jon realized Pneuma's horse was not anywhere in sight.

"I'll be around; don't you worry." He smiled.

"We better get a move on then." Odas climbed onto the saddle and helped Jon get situated behind him. "We'll be seeing you soon, Pneuma!"

"You must keep your eyes open out there." He smiled. "I don't want to see your helmet rolling around in the dirt later. Just remember that the purpose of you doing this is to find the locks your keys fit into and to learn from your fellow soldiers along the way.

Understood?" Jon and Odas both nodded their heads in agreement and soon departed after making sure they secured their belongings.

  For the entire week the two of them traveled many miles and experienced many things Jon had never done or seen before. They encountered many caged people along the way and put their keys in the locks designated for them. The soldiers they met up with provided an abundance of teaching, as well as much needed food for their outspoken stomachs. Every region of land they came to—whether it was the plains, desert, or hilly regions—they instantly stood out among the locals due to their unique statures and camaraderie with each other.

  Once they reached the ocean the King had told Jon about, they came upon a caged man who went by the name of Gary. The older man enjoyed talking with them, so Odas and Jon cheerfully tied their ropes to his cage for the next three days before leaving him, at the King's request, by the coastline. From there the King instructed them, via letter, to head back to the flatlands by way of a desert and up into a snow-covered mountain range.

  After staying with some generous people Odas knew, it was another day's journey to the flatland they started in. "I can't believe we're actually back." Jon looked around at the familiar moonlit landscape.

  "I'm sure Carit's glad she can finally rest." Odas patted the large neck of his horse as he yawned. "That's not such a bad idea, actually. I'll see ya in the morning, bud." Odas walked Carit into the forest, which was no more than twenty yards away, and found a patch of grass to rest his head.

  "I need to tell Cay that I'm back!" Jon excitedly thought as he wondered what he should do with the remainder of his energy. He

The Battle

found a large rock to sit upon as he composed a letter to his fellow soldier. A messenger from the castle must've exchanged a dozen letters that night between the two of them before they decided to get some sleep.

Throughout the remainder of the month, Cay and Jon visited one another on a couple of occasions. Even though they tried to reconcile their miscommunication they still had trouble with wounding one another in battle. Many attempts were made to rectify that; however, their efforts were to no avail. Many trips to their respective infirmaries were made and countless bloodied bandages were discarded from the injuries sustained. Their frustrations grew as they struggled to mend the discord between them.

Toward the end of the month a castle messenger flew down from the mountains and delivered a letter to the both of them on behalf of the King. It was a request for a meeting to be had in the garden as soon as they could raise their shields. Jon and Cay tearfully flew toward the north and hung their heads before the King. He reiterated the statement of not wanting his people to injure one another, so he ordered them to spend time apart to sort out the growing pains they were experiencing in the land below.

The two soldiers flew back separately, and Cay rode off on her horse after exchanging a tearful goodbye with Jon. There he sat, alone in the forest. Cay was gone. He sobbed uncontrollably as the weight of the situation was relentlessly pressing down upon him. He gasped for air as his lungs pressed against the inside of his ribcage. He began to claw at his vest in an attempt to release the constriction he felt. What was happening inside his mind at the time was far more crippling than even the cold air traveling down the back of his neck. He sat alone.

The hooded malorum was close, and Jon could feel it. However, something out of the ordinary happened that night. The enemy kept its distance. It neither smiled nor laughed maniacally as it usually did. Instead, it had a look of fear in its eyes as it stared at the soldier sitting alone in the dirt and gravel. The malorum, which stood no more than fifty yards away, chose to keep its distance while Jon obliviously cried himself to sleep. The malorum knew it would not fare well against the soldier that night with the weapon it had brought to fight with, so it backed away into the shadows.

Meanwhile in the garden, the King and Iam both looked on. Once Jon had fallen asleep under the protective custody of his shield, the King held up his mug and said to Iam, "He is going to need a stronger drink. Prepare two of these when he arrives in the morning." Iam nodded his head gently and walked into the garden.

Chapter 17:
The King's Drink

The following morning Jon awoke to complete and utter silence. There was no horse breathing down upon him. Odas was nowhere in sight. The only scenery Jon could see through the fogginess of his widening eyes was the forest and someone sitting afar off inside of its confines. Loneliness was not something Jon desired at this time, so he quickly sprang to his feet, put on his armor, and sped off toward a solitary figure in the distance.

To Jon's great pleasure, he recognized the silhouette almost immediately. Pneuma sat upon a tree stump as he ate an apple and stared off into the distance. Although the young soldier tread softly, the rustling of leaves under Jon's boots was still heard by the forest guardian. "I'm glad to see you're awake," he said, still staring off. "There's something on your mind." Jon nodded, although Pneuma was not looking at him. "Well, what is it?"

Jon cleared his throat, and without any hesitation he firmly said, "Make me better."

Pneuma looked down at his finished apple, flung it into the forest, and smiled. "What do you mean?"

"You told me when this all started that you would help me if I wanted it, right?"

"Right." Pneuma calmly looked over at Jon, who stood a few paces away from him, and smiled.

"Well...make me better. I need to be better." The look on Jon's face was a mixture of determination and desperation.

"Why do you need to be better?" Pneuma got to his feet and faced the young man.

"I can't keep hurting other soldiers. I want to help them get better, not send them to the infirmary every time I'm around."

"Are you talking about Cay?" Pneuma inquired.

"Not just Cay...but everyone else out there. I know I can do better," Jon pleaded.

"What if you can't handle what I have in mind?"

"Will it make me better?" Jon asked.

"It will."

"Then I trust you." Jon walked over to Pneuma and looked him in the eyes as he pleaded, "Make me into what I'm supposed to be, and I'll keep getting up if I fall."

Pneuma got to his feet and stood in silence for a long while as he looked deep into the blue and yellow eyes in front of him. "There aren't many people like you, Jon Smith. You are quite strange." Pneuma took out a strip of beef jerky from a pouch draped across his chest and held it out for Jon to take. "Don't you think it's strange how salt keeps food from spoiling? I think it's pretty strange, myself. Nobody wants to eat spoiled food...well...unless you're a malorum, I suppose. It isn't *that* beneficial for the body. It makes you feel nauseous and queasy. It makes you want to throw up, right?"

The Battle

"Right." Jon wondered why Pneuma was giving him a lesson on the saltiness of beef jerky.

Pneuma smiled and stood in silence for a long while, again, before saying, "You're ready, but first you must eat your food and speak with the King." Jon did just as Pneuma said and raised his shield for an eagle to carry him away.

He soared toward the castle walls and was softly lowered in front of the two cheerful looking men. "I have been expecting you." The King's thunderous voice navigated its way to Jon's ears. "Give Iam your armor, and come with me." Jon was pleasantly surprised that the King was so happy to see him. He did as the King said and received a mug from Iam, as was the usual custom, but this time he could tell it smelled peculiar.

"This doesn't smell like water." Jon sniffed the contents of his mug.

"You have a keen sense of smell," the King responded.

"What's in it?" Jon asked as he swirled around the murky liquid.

"It is the same thing I have in my mug, but mine is a little stronger." The King held up his own mug and took a drink. "You should try some. It is ginger tea."

"Why do I have this instead of water?" Jon hesitated.

"You have been feeling slightly nauseated lately, have you not?" he asked as they walked along a trail which led between two fields of lavender.

The King was correct in his assessment. Jon's insides had been bothering him as of late, but he had been doing an adequate job at suppressing any food from rising to the surface. "And this should help?"

The King nodded and said, "It will. I've been drinking it for quite some time now, and it has done exceptionally well."

"Why have you been drinking it?" Jon asked.

"There are things in my body which are not agreeing with me that well," the King answered as they walked.

"Why don't you throw them up or spit them out?" Jon wondered aloud.

"I will, all in due time. However, for now I will drink this."

"These smell really nice." Jon stopped to smell the purple flowers on either side of the trail.

"The aroma compliments the tea well, I must say. Make sure to drink up before it gets cold," the King insisted as he drank more from his own mug. "I believe you are going to need it more as the summer progresses."

Jon took a sip and made a questionable face. "Is there a way to make it taste better?"

"There is. Would you like some honey?" the King calmly asked.

"Do you have anything sweeter?" Jon answered. The King smiled and turned down a nearby trail, which had a small patch of simple-looking plants sprouting up from the soil.

The King reached down and plucked one of the leaves, ground it up in his fingers, and sprinkled it into Jon's mug. "Try that."

Jon drank again, and to his amazement the tea tasted much better than before. "Thank you." The King nodded, and the two of them continued traversing the garden. "I have another question," Jon said as the large tree came into view.

"What is it?"

The Battle

"Why have I been feeling this way? Was it something I ate?" Jon asked as he drank more of his tea.

"Not quite," the King began. "It is more of a mood change which is causing it. It is completely natural."

"Is it going to get worse?" Jon thought of how it would affect him in battle and training with other soldiers.

"I do hope so." The King confused Jon with the curious answer but added shortly after, "Just continue to come up to see me, and Iam will make you more tea any time you desire. Jon thanked his King, and the two of them talked for a while before an eagle took Jon away and delivered him to train with Pneuma.

"Now that you're back, let's get started." Pneuma tossed Jon a wooden replica of his sword.

"What's this?" Jon examined the carved object. "This looks like my sword...well one of them. It's a little heavier, too." The weight of the sword was roughly ten times the weight of Jon's swords combined, so it was considerably more difficult for him to wield.

"If you can swing this around without knocking yourself out, then I'd say that's an improvement."

"Is anyone else coming to train with me?" Jon looked around for another soldier to join the festivities.

"It's just going to be me and you," Pneuma answered.

"What if I hit you with it?" Jon nervously asked his guide.

After laughing for several minutes, Pneuma composed himself and answered, "My dear Jon, I would like to see you try."

For the following week Jon trained exclusively with Pneuma, learning how to maneuver the much heavier weapon and developing a better sense of awareness. Not once did Jon strike Pneuma during their sessions, although he did become more accustomed to the wooden sword's weight. Jon wanted to be better, and Pneuma helped tremendously. Jon began to see the world more clearly during his time in the forest. In a week's time he quickly found the ginger tea to be of great benefit, because his stomach had begun to give him more issues than it ever had before. It was on an evening trip to the garden, when the moon was already well above the horizon, that Jon received news that brightened his mood considerably.

After Iam took his armor and laid it down at the base of the majestic tree, the King called Jon to the nearest bridge which crossed over the peaceful river. "Jon, I have some news you will be quite pleased to hear." The King motioned for Jon to rest on the bridge's wooden structure with him.

"What is it?" Jon could not help but to yell in excitement.

"You are scheduled to return to the wooded region shortly, are you not?" The King reminded Jon of the journey he would soon be making for the summer season.

"I am."

"When you arrive, Pneuma has something to present you with." The King gave a gentle smirk.

"What is it?" Jon racked his brain trying to figure out what he would be receiving from his mentor.

"It will be a torch he crafted himself." As the King answered Jon stood in disbelief. "You will have the responsibility of carrying a torch to lead other soldiers around the forest."

"Isn't that something for the older soldiers to do? I mean…I'm…"

"Too young?" The King finished his sentence. "You must remove that phrase from your vocabulary, Jon. If I thought you were too young, then I would not be entrusting it to you."

The Battle

"Will I be leading the older soldiers around, too?" Jon began to rub his head as he envisioned the wrinkled faces glaring at him.

"I do not see why that matters," the King spoke solemnly.

Jon could not move his lips the way his brain was telling them to move. "I...I don't know what to say. Why me?" Jon thoughts about how just a week previous the King was ordering him to cease his training with Cay.

"Why not you?" the King answered.

"Well, Cay and I still can't train alongside each other, so I don't understand how I'm going to teach others."

"That is another bit of news I wish to discuss with you." The King stopped him. "I trust you to train with each other once again. Not to fight, but to train."

Jon stood frozen in disbelief. "What?"

"You will be returning to the wooded lands with each other in a week's time. Continue your training, and we will discuss what will happen afterward."

Jon felt as though every one of his internal organs was leaping in celebration. "I'm able to spend time with her again?" He excitedly thought to himself.

"Yes, you are," the King said with a gentle smile, as though he heard Jon's thoughts. "Now you had better fly back to Pneuma. He is awaiting your arrival." Jon jumped over to hug his King, gathered his armor, and flew toward the forest's swaying canopy.

When he landed, Pneuma was there to greet him, holding the unlit torch the King had promised him. It was no longer than the length of Jon's forearm and was customized to fit perfectly in his hand. "I believe this is for you." Pneuma held out the wooden object, and Jon took it.

"Thank you," he said quietly, still unsure of what he did to deserve the honor.

"You have a place on your belt to secure it." Pneuma pointed toward a loop Jon had never noticed before. "You alright?"

"Oh...thanks again. I'm alright...sort of," Jon answered as he secured his new gift.

"What's on your mind?"

"I just remember how much I hurt Cay before, and I don't want to do it again. And on top of that, I don't see how I deserve this." Jon motioned to the torch secured in his belt loop.

"Oh Jon..." Pneuma stood with his arms folded. "Listen here. Even though you've gotten knocked to the dirt and sent to the infirmary on more than a few occasions, you never stay there. You get back up and go back out as though nothing happened. The King notices this."

"But I fall down so much, and I've seen the inside of too many infirmaries."

"Yes," Pneuma stopped him, "but you keep fighting. This is very important. There are many soldiers out there who have stopped fighting and just sit around. I haven't seen many of them in the forest for quite some time, and some of the ones I have seen out here tend to go look at the same trees they've looked at for ages."

"They still know more of the forest and more fighting tactics than I do."

"Tell me this, Jon; would you drink from a stagnant stream of water?" Pneuma led Jon to a deep stream which flowed peacefully around the landscape.

"No."

The Battle

"What if the stream had as much water as a lake? Would you drink from it then?" Pneuma asked.

"No."

"Why is that?" Pneuma stooped down and ran his fingers over the top of the water.

"Because it could make me sick. It could have a bunch of stuff in it." Jon answered as he watched Pneuma.

"Ah! Very true." Pneuma cupped his hand in the water and held it to his mouth to drink.

"So you're saying it'd be better to drink from a moving stream than a lake? What about a shallow one?" Jon was beginning to see the comparison Pneuma was making with his situation.

"If the stream is too shallow, then all you get in your mouth is sediment, right? Not very nourishing if you ask me." Pneuma dipped his hand in for another drink.

"So the balance is drinking from a flowing one which is also deep enough." Jon stooped down next to his teacher and took a handful of water to drink, feeling rather impressed with himself for figuring out what Pneuma was saying.

"Correct. Now, I want you to understand this. This is the way we see you." Pneuma motioned to the water they were drinking from. "Notice that it runs into dirt now and then?" Jon nodded as he watched it flow downstream. "And what does it do when it comes to it?"

Jon answered softly, "It keeps going."

"Just as you do, it keeps going. You see yourself differently than how the King, Iam, or I see you. This must change. If we trust you, then you must trust yourself. Understand?" Pneuma stood up and wiped his wet hands on his robe.

"I understand." Jon took another drink from the stream and joined Pneuma.

"Good. Now let's go add even more water to that stream of yours." Pneuma slapped Jon on the shoulder and led him through the forest. That is where they remained for the next few days until Jon was scheduled to join Cay for their trip back to the wooded region.

Jon did his morning routine of getting dressed, eating, speaking with the King, and traveling around the forest until a familiar horse made its presence known. Atop the horse was the brunette soldier he had longed to see. "Hey!" Jon's voice excitedly cracked. "Long time no see."

"It is good to see you, too." Cay smiled as she dismounted the horse. "Before we leave I need to find some food for the trip." She greeted Jon with a handshake and went in search of fruit to gather. They were both slightly apprehensive around each other, which made for an awkwardly silent ride at first, but they eventually decided to make small talk—seeing as how they would be together for the next several hours. After a couple of hours passed they filled each other in on what had happened while they were apart. Jon showed her the torch Pneuma had made for him and told her how nervous he was to use it. Cay reacted encouragingly, which raised his spirits tremendously. "So what will you be showing them in the forest?" Cay inquired.

"I'm not entirely sure right now. I kind of want to wait to see what areas of the forest they haven't explored yet, you know?" Jon answered.

"Gotcha. It wouldn't make much sense to show them what they've already seen before."

The Battle

"Exactly." Jon explained some of the vague ideas he had during the trip, and Cay would occasionally ask a question or two while she steered the Arabian horse beneath them. As the sun set and the storm clouds rumbled, the two soldiers came within sight of the hilly, wooden region. Jon was dropped off in the area of the forest where he would regularly spend his days, and Cay rode off to her own designated location.

Jon sat alone in the forest for quite some time until two recognizable figures ventured toward him. He recognized Marie's black-and-red armor, and knew the vibrant green and blue colors belonged to Eugene. "I'm so glad you're back!" Marie ran over and gave Jon a motherly embrace.

"It's good to see you again." Eugene smiled as he gave a warm hug as well.

"It's good to be back and see the both of you." Jon smiled as he welcomed the family-like reception.

"So tell us about your time away," Marie said as she and Eugene sat on a log across from where Jon stood. He gave them a brief summary of the training he received and of the adventure he went on with Odas, which was greeted by much cheerfulness. He also told them of the time apart from Cay the King instructed him to take, which did not bring a pleasant reaction. After showing them the torch Pneuma had given him, Jon began to ask them questions of what has happened in the region while he was away, as well as what has happened to each of them. The three of them conversed for the remainder of the night and spent much time together the following day.

When he had time to himself, Jon remembered the task which had been entrusted to him. Soon he would be leading other soldiers through the forest and teaching them whatever the King desired for them to learn. Many trips were made to the garden during his occasional moments of self-doubt, but he always came away refreshed and ready to begin anew.

      During his times of observing the routine happenings of the wooded region, Jon also developed a need for a stronger concentration of the King's drink. He began to see more clearly what the King had warned him of. The amount of cages lying in the dirt far exceeded the number of soldiers roaming around with their keys at the ready. Jon spent many unproductive hours just sitting, hopelessly watching so many of them being passed by.

      He would also see many soldiers getting blindsided by the enemy when he took occasional breaks from training with Odas. They would regularly train with each other, while Pneuma encouragingly watched close by, and at times Cay would even join in. Many issues were settled during those three months, but it was not until after Jon's last opportunity to speak in front of everyone that the King looked at Iam with a confident smile as they watched on from the castle's garden.

      Jon had plenty of opportunities to teach that summer, many of which included personal trips throughout the forest with individual soldiers, pulling along caged men or women, leading small groups through training sessions, or even standing in front of the entire gathering of soldiers during their meetings, but it was his departing message which made the most impact with those residing in the northern mountains.

      It was a usual Sunday morning. The sun was climbing up the sky, and the humidity was rolling over the landscape like a blanket ready to smother everything in sight. The summer breeze, which Jon

The Battle

had not yet been felt during his stay in the area, was unknowingly building within the forest's confines as Jon rode atop Clyde to the campground on the hill. He rode with determination and controlled frustration as the large draft horse swiftly galloped beneath him. After entering through the large wooden doors of the camp, Jon dismounted and tied Clyde to a post inside the large courtyard and made his way inside the second set of wooden doors, which led him inside the lavishly decorated mead hall. He nodded and greeted many of the soldiers as he silently made his way to the closest bench to the front of the room. He sat there in silence and waited until he was called upon to speak.

    Jon slowly marched to the podium, made eye contact with all the soldiers and caged visitors, cleared his throat, took a deep breath, and removed every piece of armor which adorned his tall frame, leaving him with just his shirt and pants. He stood barefoot and confident before them all, and then he spoke. "To all the King's soldiers...good morning. To all those who have been brought here by one of them, good morning to you as well." The culmination of his experiences thus far had led up to this moment. Every instance of cages being passed by and soldiers being overwhelmed by the enemy in battle, as well as every image of wounded comrades leaving the campground unassisted flashed through his mind at once.

    Jon paused and took a sip from the mug he had brought with him before he continued. "I have noticed many things over these years of being a soldier. I've seen skilled fighting tactics unfold brilliantly before my eyes, and I've seen men and women emerge from the confines of their cages. I've seen camaraderie between old and young soldiers, and I've seen many wounds treated. I wish it was all like this. I wish every experience that I've either taken part in or observed inspired equal boldness and bravery within me, but I am here today to tell you all that it hasn't. Over the past few months and years, I have watched as many of you have forgotten how to fight. I have watched as many of you have forgotten about those still inside of their cages. I have watched as these meetings have become the reasons for being a soldier. I have watched as skillful soldiers have been prematurely peeled away from the battlefield, mid-fight, to tend to the decaying garden outside the mead hall. I have watched as soldiers have been more concerned with replacing the doors of this camp than removing those on cages. I have watched as wounds have been neglected and wounded soldiers have walked down that hill untended to. The surface of these man-made walls is routinely cared for, but has no one noticed the rusted nails and the rotten smell coming from within? We are called to be soldiers, to be warriors, but we can't swing our swords while our overfed stomachs get in the way.

"When I joined this cause," Jon paused and looked down at the swirling contents of his mug as the forest's tall trees swayed outside, "...when I joined this cause I was promised a close-knit relationship with all of the King's soldiers, as I'm sure you all were promised when you emerged from your confines years ago. Well where has that promise gone? I have seen numerous soldiers overwhelmed in battle while some of you sit up here and discuss the weather over an undeserved meal. You see, this doesn't work if we aren't helping each other. We don't stay alive if we don't join together. Have we forgotten why Iam came in the first place?"

Those who are still in their cages are learning what they could expect if they leave their false comfort behind, and as of right now I do not blame them for staying inside. Let me remind you all that there is a war going on." Jon's voice, bubbling with passion,

The Battle

navigated itself around every stone pillar which supported the lofty roof, while outside the walls the summer breeze gathered at the imaginary line between the battlefield and the forest, ready to flood the entire land. "This is not a time of peace, although many of you act as though it is. You have become afraid of arrows as though you have no shields. You have avoided the dirt and run scared to the hilltop as though there is no rain. You have run and hid as though you have no King. You have stayed within these walls as though you never left your cages. You have stayed far from the forest as though you have no guide." As a newfound confidence in him emerged, Jon remembered what he saw as he walked through the valley with Iam on the day he, himself, left his cage behind. In that moment he realized what he must do. His frustration calmed and his voice lowered before speaking again.

"When I first came out of my cage, Iam led me past something that I had no business crossing. He told me something about it that I'm sure he's told all of you before. You see...there's a bridge hanging over the valley. It's hanging there almost entirely out of view. He told me that no one has even attempted to cross it in quite some time. On the other side of this bridge is another part of the forest, almost completely unexplored. Those trees were planted there in the same season as the ones you regularly visit. I was told that the King put that bridge there. Why has no one dared to cross it? There is a danger of falling, but there's also the same danger if we choose not to trust our King, our general, and our guide. As I leave you today, I leave you all with the reminder of the call we all signed up for. If we put on this armor, then we better be willing to do what the King wants us to do, fight as the general fought, and learn what our guide wants us to learn. If we do not, then have we really left our cages?"

      Jon silently left the podium after grabbing all of his armor, and he walked to the back of the room to take a seat nearest to the door. There he sat, stunned as to where the words he just spoke came from. The moment the meeting was over he was greeted by a few of the soldiers who desired to offer him encouragement and new bandages they got from the infirmary. After bandaging other soldiers, Jon searched for Clyde in the courtyard and rode off toward the western mountains. That was where the tall, swaying, wooden bridge resided. As he entered the mountain range's forest, the summer breeze was released from its containment and easily took over the humidity to meet the landscape with the gentle embrace it longed for.

Chapter 18:
Tremors

Pneuma stood just within the tree line, waiting for Jon to arrive. The smile on his face was wider than any Jon had seen before. He could tell the gravelly-voiced man was pleased. "Did you listen to that?" Jon asked after he dismounted Clyde.

"Every word...and I wasn't the only one." Pneuma glanced toward the castle.

"If you're smiling then they must be." Jon gave a nervous chuckle.

"They are. Don't worry." Pneuma comforted Jon with a pat on the shoulder and motioned toward the swaying trees. "Shall we?" Jon nodded, and the two of them ventured farther into the forest. They were in there for the entire afternoon as the King and Iam joyfully looked on.

When they came to the bridge, Jon was finally able to see what it looked like in the daylight. It was not as daunting as he remembered. He knew that if he chose not to cross it, then he had no business calling others to do it, so he took a deep breath, looked at the smiling face of Pneuma, and placed his foot on the first plank. A cool breeze came down from the mountains, which caused the rope bridge to gently sway over the valley. Jon froze for a moment, until the wind had subsided, and took another deep breath.

"It's just a bridge, Jon. You'll be fine...well...if you don't fall off that is." Pneuma tried to lighten the mood as he watched on.

"Yeah, it just so happens to be seventy-five feet above a fast-moving current. No worries," Jon retorted as he hesitantly placed his other foot on the next plank.

"Exactly! I see that I'm growing on you." Pneuma smiled.

Jon looked back at his guide one final time before deciding he should just get the task over with. His first two steps quickly became ten, then twenty. When he arrived at the midpoint of his trek he decided to appreciate how far he had gone, so he stopped, grabbed the ropes on either side of the bridge, and looked around. He could easily see the expansive river running beneath him, but he decided to marvel at its beauty instead of fearing its power. It looked like moving glass as it flowed by, and he could vaguely see the bridge's reflection as it went on undisturbed.

"It really is peaceful, isn't it?" Jon heard Pneuma's gravelly voice behind him. The barefooted man stood a couple of feet from Jon with his hands clasped behind his back.

"How long have you been behind me?" Jon instantly became aware he was not crossing the bridge alone.

"I've been here the whole time."

Jon, who was partially startled and partially relieved, smiled and continued his walk. "It's surprisingly peaceful, and that breeze feels really nice." Occasionally there would be a rush of wind which caused the bridge to sway, but Jon chose to appreciate the refreshment rather than complain about the slight movement the ropes made. After several more minutes of walking and absorbing the sights and sounds of the forest, Jon finally stepped foot on land. Joy overcame him as he looked at the chasm he just crossed, which oddly appeared to be a shorter distance than he remembered traveling. "Does the bridge seem shorter to you than it did before?" Jon scratched his head and asked Pneuma.

"That's a very good question, Jon." Pneuma gave an approving glance before heading into the forest. "Let's keep walking. I have much to show you." The first peculiar-looking object they came to was a welcoming group of trees each in the shape of a "Y". A calm breeze navigated its way around them to greet Jon in the same manner as the forest had after he received his sword from Pneuma.

"You can tell this area doesn't get many visitors." Pneuma laughed as leaves rained down upon the soil, as if a carpet was being unrolled before Jon.

"Yeah, there aren't many paths to walk on. The trees and wind seem happy though." Jon trailed behind Pneuma the entire afternoon as they observed many of the forest's qualities, which included a pack of white wolves playing nearby. "What are those?" Jon curiously asked.

"The wolves?"

"Well...yes...but more so the markings on them," Jon referred to the unique colors on their fur, which varied with each of them. "I've seen those wolves around the forest before."

"Ah! Another good question. I am going to have to tell you the answer at a later date. It looks like the sun is setting, and you are needed back at the soldier's meeting." Pneuma placed a hand on Jon's on the shoulder and continued, "You can always come back here though, remember." Jon reluctantly agreed and Pneuma led him back to the bridge they had crossed hours before. Clyde was patiently waiting on the other side to deliver Jon to where he needed to go. Jon crossed the bridge with relative ease and mounted his large horse before waving back at his guide. Jon gestured in the direction of the campground, and Clyde did the rest.

As they arrived to the bottom of the campground's hill, Jon realized he still had several minutes before the meeting began. With the time remaining he decided it would be a good opportunity to speak with the King about something that had been on his mind. He hopped off of Clyde, patted the large horse's neck, and quickly raised his shield into the air.

The King congratulated Jon for speaking boldly and addressing the issues he was asked to discuss. The soldier was filled with joy at the thought of pleasing the King, which gave him courage to ask something of the man he had agreed to serve. The request was taken with a cheerful smile and response, "I will think about it, and I will let you know of my decision soon. Agreed?" Jon agreed and went on his way to the meeting before the sun had disappeared under the horizon.

The meeting went along as it usually did. Many of the soldiers were unattended to and many of the visitor's cages went seemingly unnoticed, which slightly confused Jon about whether the crowd of soldiers understood the urgency of what needed to change. After the meeting concluded, and while Jon was bandaging another comrade's forearm in the courtyard, Cay, Odas, and Mel—who was dressed in yellow and white camouflage armor—cheerfully approached him.

"Do you want to train with us?" Cay's refreshing voice spoke. Jon kept his composure quite well as he joyfully nodded his head at their request. The four of them rode off through the doorless entry to

The Battle

the campground, which was a result of Odas's hammer usage, and immediately headed toward the closest area of forest. They trained throughout the forest, off and on, for the following week until The King sent word to Jon of his answer to the soldier's recent request. Upon receiving the letter from a castle messenger, Jon instantly called for an eagle to retrieve him.

"That was rather swift." The King smiled at Jon's arrival.

"I've been excited to hear what your answer is." Jon spoke as Iam passed along the customary mug of ginger tea.

They ventured off toward the river, and the King began to speak. "I have been watching you, which I am sure you are well aware of, and I have decided to grant you your request...only if she agrees."

"What? Really?" Jon's eyes widened and his jaw hovered just above the garden floor.

"Yes. I am rather pleased with how your training has progressed with Pneuma and the other soldiers," the King spoke. "We are also pleased with your growth aside from the training and battling."

"I...I don't know what to say..."Jon scrambled to find words which expressed the emotions surging through his tall frame.

"I will tell you this. Tonight I would like for you to return here with Cay, and we shall discuss things further."

"Thank you, again." Jon wrapped his arms around his King and returned to the forest shortly after.

Later that night, after Jon had finished training with Cay and Eugene, Jon asked Cay if they could spend a little more time together in the forest. She happily agreed, and they both ventured off into the wilderness. They came to a nearby pond, sat at the edge of it, and talked for a while before Jon asked Cay if they could go up to the castle together. Cay agreed once more, and the two of them were whisked away by two separate eagles.

Upon their arrival Iam gave each of them a mug after they gave him their armor. The King asked them to walk with him through an orchard, so they smiled and followed after him. "Jon has asked something of me, Cay, that I wish to discuss with you," he announced as they traversed the wide pathways between the grapevines. "He has asked me if I would allow the two of you to fight alongside each other once again."

Cay's eyes darted toward Jon's as she nervously stammered, "He did? What did you say?"

"I am willing to grant him his request, but I would like to hear from you on the matter." The King smiled at the young soldiers, who were standing frozen in their places.

"I...I don't know what to say." Cay smiled nervously toward the ground. She thought back to all their recent training sessions and time talking in the forest, but she also remembered how often they would hurt each other in battle the last time they were allowed to spend so much time with each other.

"Jon, would you return to Iam as Cay and I talk? He will inform you when Cay and I have concluded," the King asked, to which Jon quickly obliged and returned to the large tree at the center of the garden where Iam was carving into a large block of wood.

After several minutes had passed, Iam nodded toward the grape orchard Cay and the King were walking throughout. Jon calmed his nerves and walked toward the area Iam was motioning toward. "We have reached a decision," the King's booming voice spoke. "Cay has agreed, so the two of you are welcomed to fight together once again." Jon immediately reached out and hugged Cay, who was beaming at the announcement. "With that being said, I will have another announcement for you both in a week's time, so continue to train with each other and carry out my orders until then." Jon and Cay expressed their gratitude for the decision with hugs and an abundance of "thank yous" before returning to the forest below.

They devoted much of their time the following week to slaying many malorum together as they tried to make up for lost time. They fought as though there was never an issue of miscommunication. They listened and learned how one another saw the world around them, and their developing trust showed in how effortlessly they fought together. The King was immensely pleased and congratulated them whenever they arrived in the garden for a visit.

At the start of the following week, Jon and Cay visited the garden to hear the announcement the King had promised them. Without much pause, he began, "I am pleased to inform you both that I will be stationing you, Jon, an hour south of where you have been going for your seasonal travels."

"Isn't that where she'll be going back to?" Jon pointed to the short brunette at his side.

"It is."

"We'll be in the same area?" Cay's raspy voice cracked with excitement.

"Correct," he calmly answered. "You will be leaving shortly, so I hope you can get everything together within the next few days, Jon."

"Most definitely!" Jon excitedly answered as he thought about all the soldiers he desired to inform.

Their remaining time in the woods passed by more hurriedly than they would have liked. Jon and Cay made their rounds to see everyone they could before departing. The morning of their travels Mel joined Cay to meet Jon where he'd fallen asleep the night before. After they each gathered some food, they saddled up and rode off on their horses, Jon and Cay on one and Mel on another. Pneuma had made arrangements with Jon to take Clyde separately, because the horse could not travel long distances easily. For the next nine hours, Jon could not contain his enthusiasm. He knew of the land where he would be stationed, since he had visited Cay on a number of occasions, but it still felt as though it was all brand new to him.

Once the sun had set, Jon could see the lush grass where he would be stationed for at least the next three or four months. Although only an hour's ride separated the two regions in the prairieland, the new landscape looked vastly different than the one Jon knew. Tall, swaying trees emerged from large riverbeds that cascaded effortlessly through the land. Patches of forests were spread out for miles, and clovers blanketed the entire ground. Red squirrels were visible in the moonlight as they scurried around tree roots and chattered from the high branches, seemingly unaffected by the soldiers' presence. As Jon and Cay got closer, they saw several hills with clay walls atop them through the dense tree limbs. A gentle summer breeze cooled the area as the two of them joined Mel at a nearby pond, which was surrounded by trees.

"It feels really nice here." Jon dismounted Cay's Arabian horse and absorbed as much scenery he could. "I could get used to this." The two of them spent the remainder of the night in the oasis, surrounded by chirping birds and squirrel chatter, as the moon valiantly rose overhead. They decided to thank the King for all he had

The Battle

done and get some rest for the morning to come—after they talked about their activities for the following day.

The clover-laden land where Jon was staying was lit with extravagantly carved wooden torches, which had been secured to moderately sized trees. The ground was covered with a generous coating of moss, so each soldier would have a comfortable place to lay their head at night. The area was also designated by the older soldiers for only men to retreat to when exhaustion set in from the daily training and fighting.

Jon awoke the following morning at the sound of singing coming from afar off. He knew there must have been three other soldiers who had settled in near to him for the night, because there were a few indentions in the moss that had not been there before Jon rested, but they had awoken earlier and already left the site. Jon quickly recovered his armor and ventured off toward the pleasant sounds which echoed in his eardrums. The scene he walked up on was truly a sight to behold. There was a large clearing in the forest, and this was the origin of the music. Thousands of soldiers sat in the clearing with their armor at their sides, most of them singing songs he had not heard of before.

"Are you ready to join in?" Cay asked as her long brunette hair came into Jon's peripheral vision. Jon nodded his head and smiled. "It looks like your cuts are already healing nicely." Cay motioned toward a few of the wounds on his forearms and hands as they walked up to the large group of soldiers, who were all facing a solitary young man making motions with his hand.

To Jon's astonishment, the wounds did appear to be healing for a reason yet unknown to him. "Where should we sit?" Jon asked, too enthralled by the music to pay any more attention to his arms.

Cay motioned to a couple of empty places, and they added their voices to the pleasant sound.

  After the singing stopped, another man stood in front of the crowd and taught the group something about the forest's ecosystem Jon had never heard before. He had been to these meetings a few times previous when he would visit Cay, but this time was different. He felt as though he was a part of the group. He was so peaceful in the moment that he was completely oblivious to the disappearance of the cuts and scratches on his arms and hands.

  Once the half hour passed and everyone began to reequip their armor, Jon saw many of the soldiers search out a wounded member to bandage up. He was in awe of the camaraderie on display as Cay just watched the smile grow on his face. "Do you want to get something to eat before we have to go?" Her calm voice broke the silence. They had talked about what his time in the land would consist of, so Jon knew of the regular meetings he would soon be attending. In this area many of the older soldiers led groups of young men and women through large patches of forests to teach them how to fight more efficiently and of the deeper inner workings of the forest's ecosystems.

  "That would be nice," Jon answered as he reluctantly peeled his eyes away from the numerous soldiers still helping one another. The two young friends sped off in search of food before they would go their separate ways. Cay would be following different soldiers than Jon, so they made plans to meet back together and eat again when there was a break from training and learning.

  That became their new daily routine. Every morning they would meet up with each other for the soldiers' morning gathering, get something to eat shortly after, and then speed off to join their respective groups until they could spend more time together later in the day. These activities stretched throughout the entirety of the autumn season and met the winter months with a warm embrace. The two soldiers would make occasional visits to the wooden land during that time, but they would always return to the clover-filled land to resume their training, rescuing, and bandaging.

One of their visits to the King's castle was to take part in an elaborate ceremony within the castle walls, which involved Eugene and a female soldier going to a different part of the castle Jon had never been to before. Another instance was to visit a couple of soldiers who went by the names of Rogsten and Annora and were dearly familiar to the both of them. They also took time to travel around with Odas, Marie, and Konnor, who was now only a couple of inches shorter than Jon due to a favorable growth spurt, whenever they were able.

Aside from taking part in all of these activities and travels, Jon and Cay encountered many malorum in the land where they were stationed together. Although they would easily fend off the enemy whenever it would sneak up, there would be occasional moments the malorum would get the best of them. During these times Jon and Cay would, unfortunately, wake up inside the infirmary—which sat atop a nearby hillside—and grow increasingly frustrated upon their realization that they had been defeated. The difference between this infirmary and those Jon had previously visited was that there was no door here to keep the other soldiers from seeing inside. In fact, Jon was pleasantly surprised there was not even a door at the entrance of the campground itself. There was more of a feeling of openness and transparency in the land that Jon was not used to.

Many of the other soldiers would often peek inside the infirmary's clay structure on their way back to the battlefield to see if their help was needed. This openness was something the older soldiers had routinely frowned upon whenever Jon was stationed in another land, but here it was different. Some of the first eyes Jon would see when he woke up would be surrounded by wrinkles and belong to weathered voices asking if everything was alright. Not only was this behavior consistent amongst the older soldiers, but it was also prevalent amongst several of the younger ones.

One late autumn evening, a horde of winged malorum surrounded Jon and Cay in the forest as they were in search of nourishment. They did their best to fight them off, but the enemy was exceptionally persistent that moonless night and flooded the land in numbers they had not experienced before. The malorum tried to separate the two to gain the advantage, but the young soldiers caught on to their plans from the start. They had been training the entire day with Pneuma, and had barely found enough time to replenish their bodies before the first arrow was shot by a malorum several yards away.

As another wave descended into the valley, Jon and Cay determined they would not be spending another night inside the infirmary's walls. They wiped the blackened blood from their swords with the soles of their boots and readjusted their helmets in preparation for the wearisome night ahead. Just as the last of their number crested over the hillside Jon heard a voice bellow from the darkness behind where he and Cay were standing. "Watch your heads!" The jolly male voice barely made its way to their ears in time for them to react to the sharp blades coming at them.

The Battle

Jon and Cay turned back toward the hillside to watch numerous silhouettes helplessly roll to a stop. "What's happening?" Cay whispered as more blades found their intended targets.

"I think I see...maybe...two people over there?" Jon pointed toward the region they heard the voice originate from. One soldier looked around six-feet tall and had an average build. The other was slightly shorter and seemed to be dressed in non-reflective, black armor, so Jon could not see much of the soldier's appearance.

Jon and Cay watched as every malorum from that group fell before getting to them, and they also saw another group come to a sudden halt atop the hillside. The malorum, whose knees were shaking visibly, looked down upon their fallen comrades and opted to keep their own blood from being smeared on the grass below. They spread their wings and promptly flew away—preserving themselves for another night—as the jolly-voiced soldier taunted them from afar.

Jon lit his torch, which he had removed from his belt loop, to get an adequate look at the helpful soldiers. The soldier dancing around in circles was light-skinned and looked a few years older than Jon. The dark purple on his helmet matched the color of his shield, vest, and the handle of his sword, which protruded from behind his head. After a cheerful introduction, Jon and Cay learned his name was Jay, and he continued to dance around the large tree trunks in the area.

The second soldier was a quiet man dressed in all black. The surface of his armor had a matte finish. Once the man had lifted his head from his hands—a result of being embarrassed by his traveling partner's antics—Jon could see only two narrow eyes and a light-skinned complexion. A torn-off, black, sleeve covered the lower half of his face, and Jon only learned his name, Hiro, when Jay called for him.

"Thank you, both, for helping us," Jon said after the introductions were made.

"How'd you know we needed help?" Cay asked as Jay finished taunting the enemy.

"Well I saw Hiro runnin' through the woods, jus' before he pulled those knives from his vest, while I was...uh...fertilizin' the ground," Jay nonchalantly explained. "I jus' had time to cover the hole before I ran after him to see what was the matter."

"Well...that's nice," Cay responded to the abundance of information she was not expecting.

"You gotta do what you gotta do. No need to hide it, right?" Jay confirmed the sense of transparency which was felt in the land. Just as they were about to conclude their night with a round of goodbyes, Jay looked off into the distance and smiled, "It looks like we got ourselves a straggler. Hiro, would you do the honors?"

Without needing to be asked a second time, Hiro looked in the direction Jay was pointing and reached for another one of his throwing knives. The silver blade was only visible for less than a second as the silent soldier effortlessly flung it toward a lone enemy descending the hillside. Hiro did not have to reach for another blade, as the enemy joined the rest of its company at the base of the hill.

"I have to admit, that's pretty cool." Jon chuckled as he dusted his sleeves and hands.

"Thank you, again, for your help. Will we be seeing you around here more often?" Cay asked as she, too, wiped the remaining remnants of malorum from her armor.

The Battle

"We'll definitely be around. Hiro you might not hear so much, but you'd be remiss not to notice me. We tend to be around each other quite often though," Jay answered as Hiro gestured his agreement.

The remainder of Jon and Cay's night went undisturbed as they left the company of their new comrades and ventured toward where Cay would be resting her head for the night. They had grown accustomed to spending a great deal of time around each other during those brisk months and enjoyed sharing all the knowledge they gained with each other while drinking hot cocoa and wandering through the forest.

Jon also became greatly acquainted with the forest across the bridge during this time, so much so that he offered to lead Cay across it when they had returned to the wooded land for the first month of winter. Cay excitedly agreed to the excursion. So, with the guidance of Pneuma, the two of them began to spend much of their time across the valley and within the forest's grateful embrace. Cay had a much easier time navigating the rope bridge, embracing the forest's welcoming breeze with open arms, and journeyed through the land with an eager mind and wide-open eyes.

It was a time of great peace for the young soldiers. The fruits of their labor were fully ripened and were being enjoyed in each other's company. They fought peaceably alongside one another, as well as alongside many of the other soldiers in the area. They made the most of their training together as well as times apart, when they would learn from the older soldiers. They were experiencing the communication and cooperation they had longed for. However, there was a conversation taking place within the castle's garden which they were unaware of.

After Jon and Cay had made a visit to the warm confines of the torch-lit garden and learned they would be returning to the clover-laden land for another span of four months, Iam gently approached the King with a warm drink in his hands. They solemnly watched the two soldiers as they sailed off underneath the same eagle's wings. "When will we tell them what they need to do?" Iam lowered his mug and softly asked.

"They will feel it coming," the King clasped his hands behind his back and answered. "Then we will tell them."

"They are going to need each other to kill it," Iam spoke again. "They will not fare well by themselves."

"I know. I have faith in these two." The King smiled before turning to Iam. "You will need to decorate for the ceremony for when it is done."

"I have some colors in mind," Iam cheerfully responded. The two garden occupants watched as Jon and Cay were delivered to their respective locations on the field below and, after a series of letters were exchanged between the two, each trailed off to sleep.

The winter months were exceptionally cold and icy that year. After they spent the remainder of their visitation in the wooded land, they eventually had to return to the region across the river. Jay, Hiro, and many of the other soldiers were excited for the two of them to return. Jon and Cay were greeted with warm embraces and warm meals as they adjusted to the snow blanketing the ground. They trained. They fought. They bandaged. They taught. They devoted much time to the people who were imprisoned within the black cages, which sparsely littered the area around them.

After the sun had adequately melted the ice around them, the King informed them they would even be making a trip westward,

The Battle

near to where Jon and Odas had traveled the previous year. Upon their return Jon and Cay excitedly told stories of their trek to anyone that was interested, as it further renewed their bond with one another. The news only got better after they made an impromptu visit to the wooded land, as Jon and Cay witnessed yet another cage opening. The new soldier's name was Graham and he was approximately the same age and build as Jon, when he chose to leave his own "comfort" behind.

The peacefulness continued throughout the springtime, that is until Jon and Cay returned to the land where they were stationed. Upon their arrival, Jon could tell the atmosphere felt drastically different than it had felt before. He tried to ignore the new presence of the dense fog-which occasionally rolled in, and the unusually strong winds that caused each tree in the region to sway violently, but he could not ignore the subtle rumblings in the earth as he went along with his daily work.

They started off as small, rhythmic vibrations under his feet, spaced out by only a few seconds, and they echoed through his bones with each step he took. As time went on, Jon could feel them getting louder as if something large was coming closer to where he stood. Eventually he felt the urge to take the matter to the King during a routine visit.

After he received his drink, he said, "May I ask you what's happening down there?"

"You mean with the fog and the winds?" The King clasped his hands and led Jon throughout the garden.

"Yes...but more so...the tremors that are happening. It doesn't seem like anyone else is noticing them...well, except for Cay," Jon answered.

"Ah! I am pleased you asked. You see, Jon, there is something rather large that I wish for you to defeat," the King nonchalantly answered.

Jon paused for a while before asking, "Is it anything like the other malorum you had me kill?"

"Even though it will die in the same manner, it will be considerably more difficult for you to fight this one." The King stopped and glanced over to see Jon's face flushed and concerned. "Remember, you won't be alone in this, although it may feel that way at times."

"Does Cay already know?" Jon asked.

"We are leaving that for you to inform her." The King looked toward the man resting in the hammock at the base of the large tree.

Jon took a long pause, drank the remainder of his tea, took a deep breath, and asked, "Will I be able to ask Pneuma for help?"

"I count on you doing so."

"And I can come up here whenever I need to?"

"We will have a drink ready for you whenever you decide to raise your shield." The King turned to face Jon before continuing. "I will tell you this: It will be a long battle, and you will be tested more than you have ever been before. It will not be easy."

Jon paused again, swallowed the swelling lump in his throat, and looked his king in the eyes. "It wouldn't be worth it if it was easy."

A strong breeze swirled throughout the garden as the King winked and spoke a final time before Jon departed. "That's the spirit."

Once Jon had gathered his armor, he raised his shield and was carried back down to the land below. When his feet touched the

The Battle

moss-covered earth he ran in search of his shorter, feminine counterpart. They had a lunch scheduled that day in the forest, and that was where he informed her of the news the King had shared with him. The reaction on her face was one that Jon did not foresee happening. He fully expected her to be nervous, scared, or even slightly worried, but the smile which grew between her ears was an image Jon took much delight in seeing. He knew the task ahead would be difficult, but it would also be rewarding, for reasons he was not yet aware of.

    It would be a battle which would exhaust every resource and bit of sanity Jon withheld and leave him with a scarce supply of strength after it was completed. He was not promised "easy" when he emerged from his cage four years ago—rather he chose the opposite. He chose to contribute instead of sitting off to the side as an observer of everyone else's stories while they valiantly unfolded before his eyes. He chose to fight, and that is what he was being called to do.

    Jon wandered the battlefield alone that evening. He had just trained with Pneuma and Cay and was traversing the grounds back to his place of slumber. The fog had rolled in, as usual, and rain began to descend from the clouds with a roar he had not experienced since the first night out of his cage. The ground had been shaking more violently than ever, since the King informed Jon of the plans he had for him. The tremors shook the trees and reverberated off the hillsides. Small groups of malorum separated Jon from the mossy patch of land he usually slept on, but he easily disposed of them all and continued on his way as the relentless rainfall cleansed his armor of dirt and the enemy's blood.

    As piles of their arms, legs, and tails laid around him, Jon felt the tremors stop. He lifted his head from watching the dirt wash from his boots and looked straight ahead of him. Through the dense fog and thunderstorm, Jon could vaguely see a silhouette approximately a hundred yards from where he stood. It was nearly a hundred feet tall and wider than most of the patches of forest in the area. It was not facing him at the moment, so Jon crept closer to it to get a better view. The large beast was covered in dark hair, patches of black scales, and was powerfully built. Jon could see the weapon it was holding in its right hand. An extraordinarily large, black, metallic club was what it chose to fight off any soldier who desired to give it problems.

As Jon got within fifty feet of this massive creature, he felt as miniscule as ants probably do next to humans. He knew this was what the King wanted him to kill, so, without any further ado, the young soldier refastened his shield and re-gripped his sword. The rain fell down his helmet and vest, doing its best to imitate the waterfall he had ascended as he went to meet the King for the first time. His six-foot-three-inch frame was forty pounds heavier than it was back then, and the rain no longer flowed down a smooth-shaven face. He was finally able to grow a bit of facial hair to cover the scar he had gotten the first time he had been sent to the infirmary.

He was more skilled and more confident than he was on that day, and the overwhelmingly large beast would soon test everything Jon had experienced since then. As the rain fell Jon took a moment to separate his uniquely designed sword and grasp both hilts with his hands. As he did so the blades touched and made a noise louder than the thunder booming around the scene. The monstrous beast looked down to see where the noise came from to see Jon confidently standing there. It bellowed loudly into the air, hoping to send the soldier fleeing toward the nearest refuge, but Jon did not move.

The Battle

A second time the beast tried, but it led to the same result. Jon simply grinned and yelled as loud as he could while steam blew out of the beast's ox-like nose. "I am going to kill you! I just thought you'd like to know!" The battle had begun, and Jon Smith was more prepared than he had ever been.

To the reader,
Thank you for making the decision to read my story. I cannot express my immense appreciation of you doing this. If you wish to learn more about me or see what other projects I am working on please visit my website.

www.theAllenHub.com